Fractured Souls
Colliding

B. N. Kruse

Copyright © 2026 by B.N. Kruse

All rights reserved.

No portion of this book may be reproduced in any form without written permission from the publisher or author, except for the use of brief quotations in a book review.

Cover Design by Alana Glover

To the one in four and one in six...
For those who have had their light dimmed by another's darkness...
Fuck them.
GLOW.

Author's Note

Fractured Souls Colliding **does contain sexually explicit material/language** and is recommended for 18+. Certain scenes and/or themes in this book could be upsetting; reader discretion is advised. Such themes include mentions of **SA w/one fade-to-black scene, drug use, child neglect, brief mentions of suicidal ideation,** and **physical assault**. You can also visit bnkruseauthor.com for a more detailed list.

One

Tillie

April 28th, 2024

Panic burns through my chest and sears my throat as his short nails dig into my skin, strangling my bicep. He doesn't want the gesture to look threatening to the guests he's invited, especially the one I'm currently trying to get as far away from as possible, but we both know it is.

"If you leave this house, you will never be allowed back. Do you understand me?" he murmurs in my ear with an eerie calmness.

How did we get to this point? I've asked myself that a hundred times, despite it being inevitable. My truth can never be known, and the only thing my dad sees when he looks at me is failed potential, dysfunction, and a waste of space.

"I'd rather sleep on the side of the road curled up with a fucking cactus than spend one more second in this house with you." My voice cracks on the last word as I rip my arm from his grasp.

The withering glare on his face almost has me running back upstairs to my room. Almost. But I hold back the tears that are threatening to fall. Once upon a time, tears rarely ever fell from my eyes, as my emotions were scarce, thanks to the crutch I heavily leaned on. Escaping with a bottle of pills, a fifth of Jack, or a loaded needle isn't an option anymore. I have to face everything with a clear mind, and that...

That is my hell.

"Expect your account to be emptied and your phone to be turned off."

"Wouldn't expect anything less, Dad." With my duffel bag on my shoulder, I hold my head high and walk out, slamming the door.

Goosebumps rise on my arms, and my head feels lighter but weighed down at the same time. Taking a deep breath of the crisp night air, I focus on the slight sting in my lungs. For once, I have no idea where I'll end up, although I'm lucky I'd already been taking money out of my account little by little.

Before my dad can have my phone deactivated, I call Presley. We've known each other for a long time, but cultivating lasting friendships hasn't been a priority over the last few years. Thankfully, she still gives a damn about me, though, she may be the last person on earth who still does.

The phone rings a few times, and guilt curdles in my stomach over the late hour. "Hello?"

"Hey, Presley. It's Tillie. I, uh...I left my dad's house for good. I..."

There's only one person I've ever felt comfortable enough to ask for help: my best friend from high school. But Rhett's drawn his line in the sand. "Never mind. I'll figure—"

"Go to the shop, and I'll meet you there. It's closer than the house."

I'm not telling her I don't have a car because it would be one more thing I need help with.

How is this my life?

Emotion bubbles up my throat, and I clear it away before I respond. "Thanks. I'll meet you there."

Twenty or so minutes later, headlights catch me in their blinding beams. For a second, I panic, ready to throw myself into a side ditch. Except the panic-inducing brights would be shining from behind me.

The car slows, as do my steps, until I realize it's Presley. Relief melts away the tension in every muscle when she pulls up beside me and rolls the window down.

"Figured you didn't have a car when I beat you there," she says sheepishly.

Glancing into the back seat, I cringe. Emmy, her daughter, is sound asleep in her car seat. Her long eyelashes rest against her flushed chubby cheeks, and a beanie covers her dark hair. The innocence of this beautiful baby girl hits me right in the organ I'd love to rip out of my body.

I offer a small smile and mumble a thank-you once I'm in the car. Her husband, Dane, is good friends with Rhett. To say I'm nervous about how he'll react when he sees me is an understatement. Slightly terrified is more like it. I don't believe he'll be an outright asshole, thanks to Presley, but the worry about what he thinks of me is there nonetheless.

Group therapy, which I was forced to partake in, taught me how the filth of our pasts or mistakes can taint our self-image. When another person looks at us, we expect them to see that version of us. As if the darkest, ugliest parts are always on display.

"Are you sure it's okay for me to stay with you guys?" My wariness stems from knowing how close they've become with Rhett since my father accused him of being my dealer last year. One serious misunderstanding after my overdose, and our town turned its back on him. He wasn't—my dealer, that is. In fact, he'd been clean for a while, but my dad wouldn't listen.

She glances over at me with a look of sympathy, and I hate it.

"You have nothing to do with what your father did." She sighs. "As for you and Rhett...Whatever happened is between the two of you. It's not Dane's business or mine. But if you ever want an ear, I'll always be here to listen."

Nodding, I stare out the window. Everything starts to feel heavy. My eyes. My limbs. My heart. The stress of being twenty-five years old and having no prospects for a career. Knowing my phone and account are about to be turned off and emptied...It all weighs me down, drowning me.

If I'm being honest, I've never felt more like a junkie than I do right now, completely sober.

The therapist at the rehab facility told me life after addiction might seem unbearable. I'd need to take it *one day at a time*. That phrase used to annoy the hell out of me. Now I finally understand it. The weight of everything happening and the uncertainty of my life could temporarily lift if I went out and found a fix. That euphoric, warm feeling rushing through my veins and wrapping my demons in a blanket, tucking them away.

But no, I have to get through tonight completely sober. And the next day and the day after that. It has to be a choice every day. I can't lull my demons to bed with a liquid lullaby. I have to face them head-on and hope that one day we can coexist peacefully.

A porch light shines through the dark as we roll to a stop in her driveway. A beacon guiding her to the front door and into a safe place with the family she created.

That sickly, emotional feeling rises, clawing at my throat and causing an ache.

Their house is an older brick ranch-style, but I know Rhett did a lot of work on their small porch and wooden shutters. He's a master carpenter. I've never seen him build something that wasn't perfect. Two windows on the front of the house put out a soft glow of light. Their door is painted matte black, which would make it hard to see at this time of night, if not for the fact it's more frosted glass than wood.

As we walk up the short cement sidewalk, I keep my eyes locked on Emmy, who's sleeping soundly on Presley's shoulder. Once we step inside, though, I'm slammed with nerves. I wasn't always like this. Maybe I was never extremely outgoing, but I was comfortable enough around people. I didn't want to crawl out of my skin as soon as I walked into new surroundings.

Presley takes her shoes off by the door, so I do the same.

"You can go ahead into the kitchen. I'm going to lay her down really quick," she whispers, nodding to the room where the light is coming from.

The hardwood floor creaks with every step I take through the living room before I enter another room to the right. My steps pause when I spot Dane at the table, drawing sketches for his tattoo appointments.

Clearing my throat, I walk to the small round table and pull out a chair. He looks up, and our eyes lock for a few seconds. His face is blank other than his occasional blinking.

"How's sobriety been?" he asks.

"Hell," I respond, because why lie? It has been.

He nods to himself and straightens up his papers, putting his pencils away. "Do you want anything to drink? We have juice, milk, water, coffee..."

"I'm good. Thanks."

It would be easy to judge him based on his outer appearance. Such a contradiction to Presley, who's an absolute ray of sunshine, with mousy long brown hair and vivid round hazel eyes. Short and petite. Whereas he's covered in tattoos from his neck down. His bright blond hair is always cut in a high fade, with the top slicked back. His facial features are sharp, but his crystal-blue eyes soften his natural expression.

Soft creaks caused by Presley's footsteps draw closer from the hallway, and I let out a little sigh of relief.

She huffs a laugh. "Didn't wake up once."

"I'm sorry again that you had to bring her out. I didn't think about it when I called."

She reaches for my hand that's resting on the table and gives it a little squeeze before pulling away. "Don't worry about it. She needed a bit of help getting to sleep tonight. A car ride usually does the trick."

"So, what happens now?" Dane asks. There's no malice in his tone, unraveling the knot of anxiety in my stomach.

"I…" My face crumples, and I press the heels of my palms against my eyes.

I have no fucking idea. Once, I might've had somewhere to go, but it's not an option anymore. The need to escape this town has my restless body feeling as if there's a bomb inside me. Tick. Tick. Ticking away. But I've fallen so far down into the trenches with no way to climb back out.

"I don't know," I croak out.

While my thoughts are spiraling out of control, they murmur back and forth to each other.

"What about the houseboat?" Presley mumbles.

"You guys don't have to worry about me." I wipe beneath my lower lashes with my sleeve. "I'll figure it out."

"You won't," Dane says, so abrupt and certain, tears spring to my eyes again. "I take it your controlling, dick of a father didn't like the idea of you getting a job when you got out of rehab."

"Dane," she hisses.

He didn't. He said I needed to focus on staying well, but I'm not naive; he didn't want me back out in town. Not because he cared about my sobriety, but because keeping me locked away assured no more embarrassment could tarnish his name. Without my own money or a steady place to stay, there were no options.

Shrugging, I tell them the truth. "He didn't want to worry about the possibility of me embarrassing him again."

"How much cash did you manage to save?" He raises a brow.

"I have around six hundred in cash. There's no point in looking at my online account. I know he's already emptied it."

"That was a smart move." Presley smiles at me, and I inwardly glow from the compliment.

Dane catches my eye, his stare contemplative. He absentmindedly runs his thumb and fingers across his jaw a few times like he's formulating a plan, and all I can do is sit and wait.

"We have a houseboat on a lake a few hours out of town. Ever been to Lake Nova?"

I shake my head. "I've heard of it, but I've never been."

"It's insulated and ready to go. I'll give you a couple of space heaters to take with you, and that should keep the inside pretty warm since the temperature has been falling at night. It has a small TV and kitchenette with a tiny-ass bathroom and bedroom, but I won't charge you anything to stay while you get yourself set."

When I open my mouth to protest, he cuts me off. "We'll also put you on our phone plan tomorrow before you head out, but you'll need to keep in contact with Presley."

Suffering a sense of foolish pride that one with nothing to her name should have no business feeling, I shake my head. "I can't. It's too much."

"You deserve a fresh start, Tillie," Presley argues, though she keeps her tone soft.

"I don't," I choke out. "I really don't."

"You *do*," she insists as she tips her head to catch my eye. "You think I don't know that something happened? I remember how full of life and laughter you were, and I remember when those things dimmed."

Her observation causes me to wince, but she continues, "You're not a bad person, Tillie. You only need help getting away from here and whatever memories this town holds for you."

Bile rises in my throat because I feel like she can see it. The metaphorical filth that clings to my body no matter how hard I try to cleanse myself of it.

"There are a few places around the lake where you can apply. Once you find a job, we can discuss rent or whatever, but you can stay there for as long as you need. My only conditions are you stay in contact with Presley at least once a week, and you stay sober," Dane explains.

Speaking won't be possible right now without breaking down, so the only thing I can do is nod. We've never been close, yet they're willing to do this much for me. A part of my psyche refuses to believe this is real; nothing good has happened in my life for a very long time. I give them both a watery smile, hoping that in this moment, they can sense my thanks.

"All right." He knocks on the table once with his tattooed knuckles. "Tomorrow, we'll get everything sorted, but for tonight, you can take the couch."

After Presley gets blankets, I lie alone in the darkness, and the tiniest bit of weight lifts from my shoulders as excitement mixed with fear of the unknown settles in.

Two

Tillie

Some mornings, waking up is enough to ruin my entire day. The second my eyes open, memories of yesterday come rushing back, and the only thing I want to do is forget. An ache forms low in my gut. It's a beckoning call to a familiar darkness, disguising itself as light to blind me from my inner turmoil.

As soon as I open my eyes, a different life will begin. A life away from this shithole of a town. Away from my father. Away from *him*. We all need a purpose or reason to keep going. This morning, disappearing is mine.

With a less bitter attitude, I sit up on the couch. The house is quiet, right up until a car door shuts outside. Dane walks in the front door, wiping his boots off on the rug and shrugging out of his jacket.

"I picked up my old car from my parents' house. It should run good enough for the next few months without needing a tune-up."

What the hell?

"You're giving me a car?"

"No one uses it. It's on its last leg, so you'll need to save for another one. But it should be enough for now, as long as you're not taking any long road trips after settling in Novaridge."

Prideful words begin to crawl up my throat before I swallow them down.

"Thank you," I croak.

His gaze catches mine for a few seconds. "We'll go ahead and get your phone once you're ready to go. Knowing your old man, he's probably already got people out looking for wherever you ended up."

His accusation jump-starts my system, and I rush from the couch to get ready. Trouble doesn't need to find its way to their doorstep. After all, my father isn't the person I'm worried about finding me.

The faster I'm away from here, the better.

·····•·••··

"We could've just done the pay-as-you-go. I appreciate this, but ya'll didn't need to go all out." Fire licks at my cheeks from the worthless feeling churning in my gut.

He sighs. "Presley wants to be able to track your location in case something goes wrong or you need help."

I'm slightly pissed and bothered, but also oddly comforted she cares enough about me to do so.

"One day, people won't have to treat me like a child," I murmur, my temple resting against the cool glass of the passenger window.

"She's not treating you like a child," he snaps, and I sit up, immediately on high alert at his tone. "She's treating you like a friend, and she cares about you. Do you know how many of her friends share their location so someone knows where they are?"

I wring my hands together in my lap. Confrontation has always been a trigger for me. The only thing I can do is stay silent. If you stay silent, what more can someone say? Eventually, the noise stops.

Suddenly, his hand touches my shoulder, and I jump, plastering myself to the passenger door.

"Jesus," he mumbles as he pulls off the road and puts the car in park.

"Tillie, you're okay. I'm sorry I snapped."

My nod is jerky due to the tremors racing through my limbs.

"What happened to you?"

"Nothing." I hate that question with every fiber of my being. I'm too much of a coward to answer it.

"You never told him anything either, did you?" he whispers.

No, I never did. Burdening Rhett wasn't an option. He would've shouldered it. He would've done it without complaint because he is the strongest and most caring man I know. And that's why I couldn't. He would've smothered me with his demands to help myself. And when I refused, he would've told someone himself.

"There was nothing for him to know. Besides, he made his choice about me, and it was about time."

"I think you'd already made the choice for him," he mutters as he pulls back onto the road.

We're silent the rest of the drive back to the house.

My heart races once we've parked; I know this is it. The beginning of a journey with so many unknowns. *I'm leaving this town and my dad behind.* That single thought simultaneously calms and cracks my heart.

After my bag, the heaters, and the other small items are loaded in the trunk, I stand there awkwardly. I've always hated goodbyes, even though I know we'll be in consistent contact. This moment feels monumental. A barrier I'm breaking through, and it wouldn't be possible without them.

Presley pounces on me with Emmy in her arms, and my body naturally recoils, but I force myself to remain still, my hands dangling at my side.

"Take care of yourself and have some fun," she whispers as she squeezes me.

Dane walks up behind her and grips her shoulders, gently pulling her back. "You're suffocating her."

I could say so much at this moment, but my mouth can't communicate the words trying to fight their way out. So I give them a small wave and watery smile before getting in the car and backing out of the driveway.

Before I leave town, there's one person I want to try to see, and as soon as I pull onto his street, he comes into view,sitting on his front porch waiting. I'm guessing Dane had something to do with this, because Rhett told me he didn't want to see me again; so did his mom when I showed up at his house before dawn the day after leaving rehab. Not my finest moment, but the desperation I felt to see him, talk to him, make him understand my side, overrode my judgment.

I park on the street in front of his house and sit here, taking him in. His dark hair looks a little shorter than the last time I saw him, and his body is more muscular. His fingers are interlaced, forearms resting on his thighs. Inhaling a deep breath to calm myself, I climb out of the car and wait, giving him the chance to tell me to get the hell out of here. But he doesn't. Instead, he tips his chin back, beckoning me over.

"I guess Dane called you?" I ask, walking up the path to his front porch.

"He said you might stop by on the way out of town." His words come out in a rough voice I'm not used to hearing, and when I really study him, he looks exhausted. Melancholy.

I take a seat in the black cast-iron chair next to his. "How are you?"

Scoffing, he shakes his head. "It only took you how many years to care enough to ask that question?"

"That's not fair, Rhett, and you know it."

His head tilts so he's facing me. "Isn't it, though? My dad died, Tillie. You were the most important person to me, and you were nowhere to be found. I tried so many times to get you help because I knew your addiction was my fault, but you just—" He shakes his head, rubbing his palms together.

"The first day we got high together wasn't the first day I'd done drugs. It was only my first time using them with *you*. My addiction had nothing to do with you."

Shock, and maybe a little betrayal, radiates from his narrowed eyes as he sits up straight. I had no idea he felt like that, but now...

"Is that why you put up with me for so long? Out of misplaced guilt and obligation?" I blink rapidly, looking away from him.

"I don't know," he murmurs. "You were my best friend, but in all of our memories together, I can't remember a time when you trusted me with anything other than superficial bullshit. Then I thought I was falling in love with you, and I swear a part of me did love you, but when I got sober and you refused...I had more perspective with us, and I felt so fucking guilty."

Rolling my lips, I swallow the emotions threatening to surface. I'm not exactly sure why it feels like I'm being knifed in my damn chest. Maybe because I'd always depended on him being there. Maybe a part of me believed it was because of an unconditional love he felt for me when I'd never had that before, and now he's spoken his truth. It was never unconditional; it was a result of his guilt. I could be angry right now, but I choose to sit with his confession for a few minutes.

He doesn't know he's the only person I've ever *chosen* to be intimate with, even if it could only happen while I was high.

He doesn't know I felt safest when I was with him, but when he started pushing me to get better, to *be* better, he only pushed me away.

He doesn't know I used to depend on our drives to the creek he had found in the woods because it gave me a secret place to hide away.

He doesn't know any of these things because I never told him.

A part of me wants to spill it all out right now, if only to see if it would make a difference, but first...

"So, when you told me off months ago, you said you had someone in your life now. What's she like?"

A soft laugh slips from his lips, but there's no humor in it. "It's complicated. Seems to be a common theme with the women in my life." He cringes as he finishes the sentence.

"What happened?"

A tense silence stretches between us. He was right when he implied I never cared enough to ask him about his life. I always let him confide in me, but I can't remember asking because I *wanted* to know. The sudden pinch in my chest makes my breath hitch because, right now, on a beautiful April afternoon, with the sun beaming down, I begin to see myself through his eyes.

After a steady inhale to contain the disappointment slithering through my veins, I do my best to keep my voice even. "We both know this is probably the last time we'll ever speak again."

The absolute truth of that statement turns that pinch to a full-on ache.

It must hit him hard too, because he blows out a breath. "She's been through a lot, and my accident freaked her out. I think it was too much for her to deal with."

I'd heard a little about his accident, but I won't ask more questions because a sheen appears in his eyes. He loves this woman, but he doesn't understand that sometimes our trauma can make us do things we don't want to, like walking away from someone. He's always been an open book about his emotions and his life.

"She'll come around," I say with conviction.

He only shrugs, and I take the gesture as my cue to get back on the road. But first, I need to say what I came here for.

"I'm truly sorry for hurting you. I never intentionally meant to because you're an amazing guy, Rhett. And this woman—"

"Lucy," he interrupts.

"Lucy," I repeat. "Lucy *will* come around. I'd bet my life on it."

Both of the dimples in his cheeks become visible as he grins. "Your life, huh? You're so sure?"

Shrugging, I quirk my lips. "Yes, because I came around too. Only a little too late." A car speeds down the road, reminding me I have a place waiting beyond this town. "But I think it's time for me to go."

When I stand, he does too, and shock sparks down my limbs as he pulls me into his chest for a hug. The last time I'll ever feel the warmth of his arms wrapped around me. The only person whose touch doesn't cause my body to enter fight or flight.

"Be safe. I hope you find everything you're looking for," he says gruffly.

I take a few more seconds to soak up his warmth before pulling back and walking toward my car.

"Tillie," he calls out.

Pulling the door open, I look back at him.

"Tell me one real thing. Just one."

He stands there, looking defeated because he expects me to get in my car and drive away without a word. It opens my eyes to the dynamics of the relationship we had.

"You won't understand why, but you saved my life, Rhett, and not only the day I overdosed. You've saved my life every day since we were sixteen."

Without looking back at him, I press my foot on the gas and drive toward the new life waiting for me.

∙∙∙●●∙●●∙∙∙

Holy fucking haven. I didn't know what to expect pulling into the marina, but boats resembling tiny box houses line the docks, and decorations hang on the bows. Flags, flowers, lights. It's almost like a little neighborhood on water, some areas more crowded than others. The lake stretches far and wide.

Each dock has a black number on a white metal sign attached to a thick wooden post, and I drive until spotting sixty-three. My jaw drops in awe. Black siding covers the outside, interrupted by reflective windows. The boat's bow is a small enclosed sitting area with cable railings and a sliding glass door.

The anticipation of getting inside builds the longer I sit here gawking. After my one bag from the passenger seat is in hand, I get out, taking in the distant sound of people chattering, the ripples of water caused by the ducks swimming around, and the musky, metallic scent filling the air. Not the most pleasant smell, but I'll get used to it.

Stepping onto the boat, I walk around the left side until I'm standing in front of the door Presley gave me a key to. My steps falter once I enter.

The interior is beautiful. This entrance leads me into the small kitchenette with all the appliances, minus an oven, but a four-burner stove top sits next to a full sink. The cabinets are painted black, with white marble countertops. A small two-seat dining area with a wooden table is set up on the opposite wall.

When I look to the right, I spot what I'd consider a living room if this were an apartment. A single grey couch sits against one wall, with a floor lamp resting beside it and a TV mounted opposite of it. To the left are two doors, and I know that's where I'll find the bathroom and bedroom. What really stands out are the tongue-and-groove wood ceilings, left in a natural golden color, with the floors to match. White wood paneling covers the walls.

This is more extravagant than I was expecting. Not that I knew what to expect, but it certainly wasn't this. Staying here rent-free feels more like a crime than a blessing.

I drop the duffel and call Presley, who answers before the second ring.

"Why didn't you tell me this was so nice?" The panic in my voice is obvious.

"Because you wouldn't have agreed."

I scoff, but then my reality sinks in the way it often does. Twenty-five. No career. No family. Six hundred dollars—less now after the cost of gas and food—to my name.

"I don't have any words to..." I choke out, unable to finish.

"We did some remodeling last summer, but feel free to make it your own with decorations while you're there. *Enjoy* it, Tillie."

As if she's taken the phone away from her ear or covered the speaker, her voice is muffled before coming through clearly. "Dane wants to talk to you."

His voice sounds over the line. "We haven't been there to de-winterize yet, so I let Ron know you're there. He'll be over in about ten minutes or so."

Blood rushes to my head, drowning out the rest of his words, as panic from being alone with a strange man I've never met before floods my body.

"Tillie?"

"Yeah," I squeak.

"I've known him for years. He's a good man, but we can stay on the phone with you while he's over."

"Yes. Please."

All three of us are quiet as the minutes drag on, and I startle upon hearing a knock on the side door. When I open it, a man in his sixties, I'd guess, and in surprisingly good shape, stands outside. His silver hair is pushed back, and he's wearing a light blue T-shirt with a boating logo in the left corner and khaki shorts. He looks harmless enough, but I know all too well that *looking* harmless doesn't equate to *being* harmless.

"You must be Tillie. I'm Ronnie or Ron." He extends his hand to shake, and I hesitate to accept. Understanding dawns, and he drops it, placing both hands in his pockets.

After releasing a shaky breath, I find my voice. "I'm new to the boating scene. I'm sorry you had to walk over," I explain, stepping aside to let him in while I continue to hold my phone in a viselike grip, remaining by the door.

"It's no problem at all, darlin'. I've lived here for the last fifteen years, and in that time, I've helped a lot of folks out. Dane says you'll be staying here for a little bit while you're getting settled into town, so if you ever need anything, I'm in slip ninety."

I manage a small smile. "Thank you. I'm sure I'll be fine."

He steps toward me, and I wince. His eyebrows draw in slightly before he stops and nods to the door. "I'm going to head outside and get the engine taken care of and check the battery. I'll knock when I'm done."

His gentle, reassuring tone makes me feel both thankful and irritated.

"Thanks," I murmur, moving out of his way.

Once he's outside, I bring the phone back to my ear. "I've got it from here, guys. I'll text you later, Presley," I blurt out before hanging up.

After locking the side door, I walk through the space again, this time making a mental list of what I'll need. It seems as if food is the must-have at the moment. Plenty of linens and towels are stocked, along with bedding. I go ahead and put away my bag of clothes in the small built-in dresser in the bedroom.

A knock sounds at the entrance, and I take a steadying breath and grab my phone before opening the door.

"Everything is all set. On the side wall here"—he points to the buttons on the wall next to the door—"you'll find your switches for the water heater and lights. On the wall by the sliding glass door, you should find a thermostat. All of the plugs should work fine now that I've got your battery on, but if you have a problem at all…slip ninety."

"I appreciate you doing this. I would've been lost."

"Anytime, darlin'," he says with a one-handed salute before he starts to walk away, only to stop and turn around, looking back at me. "The marina has been emptier than usual this year. The slips next to yours probably won't be filled. Oh, and Dane said you were going to be looking for a job. There's a bar hiring. It's a pretty clean and safe establishment. The new management makes sure of it. It's called Clovers."

Little does he know, bartending is ironically the one thing I *do* have training in.

"I appreciate the tip. I'll check it out. Thanks again, Ron," I call out before closing the door.

A beautiful houseboat. *Check.*

A potential job. *Check.*

I'm feeling even more invigorated about this whole move. Before getting too lost in my opposing thoughts, I make a list of things to keep me busy today, with a plan to stop by the bar tomorrow.

Fingers crossed.

Three

Jansen

Mason knocks once and enters before I can respond. "Boss, there's a woman here asking if we're hiring."

Respect of privacy in this place is nonexistent.

"How about *waiting* until I *tell* you to come in?" I drawl while shuffling some papers around on my desk.

The slow grin and waggle of his brows can only mean he's about to say something ridiculous or immature, or both. "Wouldn't want to interrupt all the scandalous shit you get up to back here."

Going with both this time.

I glare at him, shaking my head. "The interview yesterday didn't pan out, so you can send her back."

Mason was the first bartender I hired when taking over Clovers months ago. He's also the first person I'd consider a friend while doing this job. It's hard getting attached to people with the kind of business I'm in. Stepping in to save businesses to sell for profit can cause certain tensions. I replaced the entire crew at Clovers, which pissed my grandfather off, but he wants to bring life back into this place and sell it so he can retire. Needless to say, his crew wasn't cutting it.

The amount of work I needed to put in couldn't have been achieved without the team I've hired now. This bar was defunct until I came in. Now we're packed on the weekends, and we have a pretty good crowd from four to midnight most weeknights.

Novaridge is a small town sitting thirty minutes between two larger cities, so I knew foot traffic wouldn't be entirely dependable. I had to think outside the box—themed nights, sports section, vintage pub appeal to build upon the name Clovers.

A soft knock filters through my thoughts.

"Come in."

A woman walks through the door, and my brain lags. Raven hair rests on her collarbones. She's wearing a navy-blue T-shirt with a rounded neckline, paired with flared dark blue jeans showcasing her perfect curves. A look of skepticism takes over her features, with a small twist of her full pink lips and sculpted brows, which are currently furrowed.

My throat could be labeled as a desert. I swallow while I stand from the seat behind my desk and extend my hand. "I'm Jansen Quinn."

She leaves the door wide open and walks the rest of the way to my desk. "Tillie Porter. Nice to meet you."

Her hand is soft and small in mine, but her grip is firm as she shakes it once before quickly pulling back and sitting. A sweet but citrusy scent followed her in, and I find myself inhaling more deeply, trying to catch it again as we sit here, sizing each other up. Long enough for me to notice her eyes are a vibrant shade of green with a brown freckle in her left one.

I busy my hands, tidying up my desk further to end our little stare off. "Do you have any experience with bartending?"

The tension in her shoulders relaxes as she sits back further in the chair. "I took a course when I was twenty-one."

That voice. Her tone is more than compatible with her appearance. A low and rich, husky sound.

"Do you have any references from previous establishments?"

A look of defeat blankets her face, but she quickly corrects it, setting a mask of confidence in its place. "I never got the chance, but I remember a lot, and what I don't know, I'll be quick to learn."

Bartending is the main gig here, but...

"Any waitressing experience?"

My gaze falls to her slender throat as she swallows. "Uhm, no, but like I said, I'll be—"

"Quick to learn." I cut her off with a raised brow.

Her lip twitches. "Exactly."

Rubbing a hand over my jaw absentmindedly, I try to come up with a way to turn her down. Usually, I don't have a problem with this. Turning people away. It comes with the territory, and I've been in a number of awkward and heated situations.

"Please," she pleads, but her tone is direct. "I'm not married. I don't have any kids. I'll work whatever hours you throw my way, and I can get the drink list and steps memorized in no time."

My relief in hearing her imply she's single should be enough for me to send her on her way, but she seems desperate, and desperation can be a great motivator.

I should know.

"I'll give you a week. You start tomorrow. If you can keep up with our pace, then I'll officially hire you."

The smile lighting up her face is enough to knock the breath out of any man. She extends her hand again, and my eyes trace a path to it. That's when I notice, and my stomach bottoms out.

"You're an addict?" I sneer, unable to keep the judgment out of my tone.

"Recovering," she clips, her full lips pressing together.

"How long?"

How long has it been since you've injected poison into your veins?

"Almost sixteen months."

I remain silent as her eyes bounce back and forth between mine until she speaks again.

"I've never been arrested, so I don't have a record."

"You start tomorrow at four. We'll see how the week goes," I deadpan. "You can see Mason at the bar for a list of drinks we serve and a form to fill out to bring with you tomorrow."

She stands, wiping her palms down her thighs before she thanks me again and leaves my office. I'll give her the week because I've already agreed to it, and the last thing I need is for someone to blast that Clovers is discriminatory, but after the week is up, she's gone.

I won't let another woman with an addiction ruin my life.

············

Unfortunately, she's an amazing bartender. It's been two days, and Tillie already has most of the drink list memorized. It took Mason a couple of *weeks* to get the hang of the Irish cocktail list.

For two days, I've stayed out of her way, and she avoids me like the plague, going to Mason and Ivy with any questions.

While those two are my full-time bartender and waitress, I have a total of ten employees now, including her.

Marlee and Claire are part-time waitresses. Bailee and Remi are part-time bartenders. And Jones and Riley are the cooks. We only offer the food menu after three, and it's kept light. Mostly appetizers with burgers and wings. My ninth hire was supposed to be for a person who could do waitressing and bartending, but Tillie hasn't had the chance to waitress yet. I'm hoping she'll be absolutely horrible at it, and tomorrow is Friday. One of our busiest nights. The perfect opportunity to overwhelm her, even though I have a feeling she'll excel.

I'd never encourage women to use their bodies or overcharm patrons for tips, but most do. They know a little cleavage and coy smiles can go a long way. Stroke a man's ego, and cash flows abundantly.

Tillie doesn't dally or slip sly smiles for tips, but her efficiency affords her them anyway. The sound of her raspy laugh is always quiet, never boisterous, but hypnotic all the same. A dress code isn't required here, but she stays in jeans and a plain black T-shirt with a flannel.

Why do you notice so much about her if you're doing your best to avoid her?

I've been asking myself that since laying eyes on her. The choices she's made in life are abhorrent, but they're also contradictory to what I've witnessed about her so far. She's a magnet, drawing my every sense to her whenever she's near. It's why I try to stay away.

I'm going through inventory and payroll, sitting at a table with a burger, while the closing clean-up takes place. Her voice fills the space, soft but sure.

"I'll get the cleaning done tonight if you want to head out," Tillie offers Mason.

I internally groan at the prospect of being left here alone with her, but Mason deserves a break if she's offering. So, even though she puts me on edge and I hope he'll tell her no, I remain silent.

"Are you sure?"

Fuck.

"Absolutely. I have nowhere to be. Enjoy an early night out of here."

Mason thanks her and clocks out after being reassured with one of her soft smiles.

"Later, Bossman," he calls out to me.

Waving him off, I keep my head down. He doesn't know I plan on letting her go, so he has no idea his leaving is traitorous.

Once she's done wiping the tables, restocking the bar, and shelving the clean glasses, she walks to the back hallway to grab her things. I see her from the corner of my eye as she heads toward me but then shakes her head, stalking straight for the door.

"Tomorrow night, you'll work the floor. Need to see how you'll do before I decide if you're staying on," I call out in a clipped tone.

The steady rhythm of soft steps pauses, and the door remains closed. Lifting my eyes beneath my brows, I find her facing me with a look of incredulity.

"If you're going to fire me after the week is up, then get to it already so I can move on." I don't miss the small flinch after she finishes speaking or the tremble in her hands as she straightens her spine, standing tall.

A sliver of respect for her forces its way into me, unwanted. I lean back in the chair, crossing my arms over my chest. I could go ahead, fire her now and be done with it, but I have no justifiable reason...*yet*.

Do I need one? Technically, no, though I do have morals.

Firing employees when I take over businesses is one thing, but firing someone out of prejudice is another.

The latter makes me a scumbag.

If I'd seen the marks on her arm before saying yes, then I wouldn't be in this predicament. Taking a deep breath, I try to calm the anger brewing beneath my skin, then release it while pushing my hair back. After a week, I'll tell her she doesn't fit, and that's if she doesn't bomb tomorrow.

"I'll see you tomorrow unless you happen to be a no-show." I wouldn't call her smart, considering the choices she's made, but I know she can read between the lines.

Her throat works as she swallows and nods, keeping her gaze fixed on mine for a few seconds before she turns to the door. "I'll be here."

With those parting words, she walks out.

Fan-fucking-tastic.

Four

Tillie

My boss is a judgmental dick. I'm not sure what possessed me to call him out tonight, other than the rush of anger I felt when he made the implication of letting me go after the week is up. And it *was* an implication. I could tell by his tone and the way he's treated me for two days. He acts like I'm a walking disease, always steering clear of me.

I should've quit.

I shouldn't go in tomorrow, but the asshole doesn't deserve the satisfaction of believing his judgment of me is accurate. Wearing a short-sleeved shirt for the interview was a mistake. The scars on my arm are faint, but he proved they're noticeable. I've stuck to long-sleeved flannels at work since then, not wanting to disgust Mr. High and Mighty any further.

Despite his piss-poor attitude and blatant disregard for my feelings, working at his establishment has been enjoyable so far. Mason is welcoming and somehow manages to make me laugh. And Riley has let me help in the kitchen if the bar isn't busy. I haven't had as many chances to talk to Ivy, but she seems sweet.

The interior of Clovers is stunning. Dark cherry wood makes up the center bar, wainscoting, and the floor. The paneled ceiling matches the pine-green walls, and brass light fixtures hang over the circular wooden tables scattered around the remaining space. Televisions are mounted on every wall, with different sports or music videos playing throughout the day.

My greatest shame is that this is the first real job I've had apart from my dad's finance company, and the job was bullshit. I pushed papers around a couple days a week, but when my addiction amped up, I stopped going in. At the time, I knew my dad wouldn't cut me off as long as I was still living under his roof while keeping myself presentable.

But that's what makes me love this job. I got it on my own. I've proved I can do it well. The ninety-five dollars in tips in my wallet tonight—on a slower night, I might add—further proves it.

So if Mr. Quinn thinks he's going to let me go on work performance alone, he's about to be extremely disappointed.

With groceries in the fridge, throw blankets on the couch, and the boho bedding I picked out for my room, the boat is feeling more and more like my sanctuary. The only thing worth complaining about is the shower. I'm not a tall girl. Five foot six is pretty average, but in this shower, I feel like a Goliath. So after making quick work of it and locking up, the bed calls my name.

The exhaustion weighing me down at night is incredible. Mentally, from interacting with people all day, and physically, from being on my feet.

Exhaustion makes it easier to fall asleep.

Except for tonight. Tonight, a certain six-foot-something asshole with a swimmer's build, cropped sandy-brown hair, and judgmental amber eyes stays at the forefront of my mind. It's disgusting how attractive he is, yet I still fall asleep to the mental image of him firing me and me kicking him straight in the balls.

Fridays are karaoke night, which means everyone needs a bit of liquid courage and carbs to absorb it. Since getting sober, I've learned that staying busy is crucial. Having a task or something to work on keeps me from getting restless and my thoughts from spiraling, so tonight, I'm killing it.

The glare on my boss's face, which he saves only for me, proves it.

Ha.

"Can I get you all anything else?" I ask the group of three young guys who've already ordered two rounds of beers and don't look to be closing out their tab anytime soon.

"How about your number?" Guy No. 1 asks.

"Thanks, but I'm not dating at the moment." Before I can excuse myself or say anything else, he's quick to let me know what his intentions are.

"We don't have to *date*." He smirks.

Guy No. 2 snickers, while Guy No. 3 shakes his head, looking down at the table. I'm feeling more partial to No. 3.

I'm not fond of male attention, and avoidance is how I handle it, but something about this guy gets under my skin. Being away from my normal surroundings has altered a part of my brain. Or maybe it's because we're in public, surrounded by people. Before I can stop myself, I look directly at Guy No. 3, hoping his answer is what I think it'll be.

"Do *you* want my number?"

His brows almost meet his hairline. "Uh, well...I actually have a girlfriend," he stammers.

Thank God.

Guy No. 2 laughs out loud, clearly the instigator of the group, and claps Guy No. 1, Mr. Maybe Too Confident, on the back, who's currently glaring at Guy No. 3.

"She's a lucky girl." My lips tip with a small, genuine smile, causing a pink hue to grace his cheeks before he ducks his head.

"If I can get you anything else, let me know."

"We'll take the check," Mr. Maybe Too Confident grumbles.

Without another word, I walk away to close their tab, rolling my eyes.

The rest of the night goes smoothly, without patrons making a complete ass of themselves. Tonight's crowd is full of women and men in their early twenties, and the karaoke machine hasn't gotten a break since six o'clock. The energy is upbeat and has me wishing I were another girl, in another bar, able to sing and dance without a care in the world.

After I've done my rounds with the tables I'm working, I lean on the end of the bar, listening to a woman belt the lyrics of "Unwritten." A permanent smile takes over my face as I watch her giggle at missed lyrics and point to the crowd when she belts the chorus. I whoop and cheer for her along with everyone else after the song ends.

Before I can move, a solid mass leans onto my shoulder, and my body stiffens.

"From now on, offer guys your number on your own time," Bossman sneers in a deep voice.

An involuntary shiver rolls down my spine from the warmth of his chest, heating my skin through the long sleeve.

He ignores me and treats me like a walking plague, but somehow, he didn't miss that.

What a dick.

Scoffing, I turn to the side, craning my neck to look at him. "From now on, get all the facts before you throw around accusations."

His dark brows draw together, blazing with accusation. When I open my mouth to ask him why the hell he even cares, I remember he only needs one reason to fire me. I'm sure yelling at him in the middle of his bar would be the perfect excuse.

Shaking my head, I step away, but his hand wraps around my forearm. Though his grip is light, it still causes every muscle in my body to tighten as it enters flight mode. The force I use to rip my arm from his hand causes me to stagger backward.

"Do *not* touch me. *Ever*." My voice shakes, and I hate that he's seeing me so vulnerable.

Black spots edge my vision as I stumble toward the bathroom, not daring to look back. The door slams behind me, and I turn and lock it before heading to the sink, splashing cool water on my face. My entire body trembles as I grip the corners of the sink with both hands and stare at my reflection in the mirror.

"You're fucking weak. Why can't you just let it go? Let it fucking *go*." My voice cracks on the last word, but I refuse to cry.

I wait until the trembling in my limbs fades before opening the door. Jansen is leaning against the wall across from me, but I'm done dealing with him, so I keep walking.

"*Tillie*." The commanding tone stops me.

Sighing internally, I turn around to face him, keeping distance between us.

He prowls closer with slow, measured steps like I'm a wounded animal, and it pisses me off.

"I shouldn't have touched you. I'm sorry," he says in a gruff voice.

"I don't date, and I don't have casual sex. You don't have to worry about me causing problems with patrons. Apology accepted." I cross my arms. "Can I go?"

Something indiscernible crosses his face before he schools his features, nodding, and I walk back to the bar. I don't bother volunteering to stay and close. As soon as my tables are wiped down, I practically run out and speed home.

Before I can get the key in the houseboat's door, I notice a note taped to it.

I'd like to invite you kayaking tomorrow morning. I'll be going out on the water at 9 a.m. If you're free, meet me at my dock.

-Ron

The next morning, I'm sitting on the boat's balcony with my coffee, contemplating Ron's offer. After last night's shift, I'm not in the best frame of mind to sit by myself all day. And Ron seems like a good guy. Mind made up, I head inside to get ready and walk over to his dock.

Five

Jansen

AFTER TAKING GRANDDAD'S CALL this morning, I decided to drive his way. I've been so busy I've barely had time to see him. Two days ago, I called him to complain about the new hire and my plan to let her go when the week was up. Technically, Clovers is still his business until we sell, so I try to keep him in the loop, not that he cares one way or another. Granddad knows I'm good at what I do, but for some reason, he gave me shit over firing Tillie. He doesn't even know the woman, yet he was defending her, which pissed me off because he knows why I feel this way.

I park my Jeep, and as I'm walking up the ramp, a familiar head of raven hair catches my eye. Her back is to me, but she's kneeling, tying the kayaks to the dock. My steps slow when I hear her voice.

"I love the job. The only thing that would make it better is having a new boss."

"Having problems with the current one?" he asks her.

The second I heard her asking a patron if he wanted her number, an irrational bout of jealousy burned through me. After shutting myself in my office for a bit to pull myself together, I thought I'd be fine. But as soon as she came into sight, smiling while leaning against the bar, I couldn't stop myself from confronting her.

I shouldn't have grabbed her, but I knew my accusation pissed her off. Even though it was my intention, after her comment about getting the full story, I wanted to make sure those guys didn't act inappropriately.

Halting my steps, I listen to what she has to say about her *boss*.

"I'm used to being looked down on. The choices I've made so far guarantee it."

"You don't deserve to be looked down on, darlin'. Your character shouldn't be judged based solely on what you've been through or the mistakes you've made, but on how you fight to overcome them."

His words piss me off and make me feel like an ass at the same time. Addiction is a choice, and regardless of her being clean now, my experience with addicts tells me she'll use again.

She nods a few times. "It'd be nice if you were my boss."

He chuckles, meeting my gaze over her shoulder.

"Are we kayaking today?" I ask.

Her shoulders tense as her head falls forward, shaking back and forth. She stands, turning around slowly.

"Hey," she breathes out. "What are you doing here?"

I cock a brow. "Visiting my granddad. What are *you* doing here?"

She looks between me and Ron as her mouth opens and closes, struggling to find words.

No wonder Granddad defended her. He *knows* her. Now that I'm thinking about it, I guarantee he's the reason she knew we were hiring. I hadn't advertised it anywhere, going through the resumes we already had first.

"Technically, he *is* your boss," I say to break the tension.

Her brows furrow.

"He owns Clovers. I'm here to do a business flip of sorts so he can sell it." I haven't a damn clue why I'm explaining this.

"That's...nice." She looks back at Granddad. "I'll come back another time, Ron."

Unwanted disappointment settles in my gut, but I remain silent as Granddad glares at me while she walks past.

For fuck's sake.

"You should stay, Tillie. I promise I won't be...an ass."

"It's fine. I don't want to intrude on family time," she calls over her shoulder as she continues walking.

When I look back at Granddad, his hands are on his hips while he shakes his head.

"You set this up," I spit out.

"I did. When you get to be my age, it's easy to spot a bullshitter, and she's not. She's been through something and deserves a fair chance."

"So tell me you know her over the damn phone. Don't throw us together, against our will, outside of work," I bite out.

He scoffs. "Because you would've listened. Her slip is number sixty-three. Go convince her to come out with us."

He's already walking back into the houseboat before I can respond because he knows I'll do it. I don't fight Granddad on a lot of things. I'm not sure if it's misplaced guilt over my mom's actions or that when Mom cut him out of her life, he lost me too. At thirty-one, it's still hard to tell him no—not that he's ever asked for anything, other than my time, outside of help with the bar.

I stroll toward her dock, trying to figure out what in the hell I'm going to say. It's clear she doesn't want to be in my proximity, in or outside of work, and I don't blame her. I don't particularly care to spend time with her either.

Coming up on number sixty-three, I spot a pair of legs stretched out on the railing, with their ankles crossed. And as soon as all of her comes into view, my steps halt while I take her in.

Her head is tipped back on the chair, eyelids closed, and she's not wearing any makeup today. It's the first time I notice the smattering of light-colored freckles on her cheeks and nose.

"What do you want?" she asks without peeking.

I step onto the deck and sit in the chair beside hers. "How'd you know it was me?"

"I'll ask again." She opens one eye, squinting at me. "What do you want?"

"You're a cranky little thing in the morning," I muse.

Both of her eyes open as she sits up fully, pulling her legs down from the rail.

"I'm not cranky. I deal with you at work but refuse to deal with you outside of it."

"Your week's almost up." I smirk. "Then you won't have to worry about dealing with me at all."

"You're not firing me." She purses those full lips that I hate to admit thinking about on more than one occasion.

My jaw drops as I choke out a laugh. "Excuse me?"

Her spine straightens, and she dares to look down her nose at me. "I'm good at my job. I'm sober, and if you hadn't seen the scars on my arm, we wouldn't be having this conversation at all."

"Well, I did see them," I grit out.

"You don't know me. You have no fucking idea what I've been through in my life, so who are you to judge me?" she spits out with the quick rise and fall of her chest.

"Why did you start using?" It's none of my business, but I need to know. There's something about Tillie that draws me in. It's hard to stay pissed off in her presence when I feel things against my will.

I don't want to find her attractive.

I don't want to give any fucks if she hands her number out.

I don't want to care if I hurt her feelings.

She crosses her arms, rolling those emeralds she has for eyes. "My past is none of your business, not to mention it's extremely unprofessional for you to ask."

I sit back, spread my knees, and rest my hands on them, shrugging.

"Then don't come in tomorrow, Freckles."

Now her jaw drops. "So now you're blackmailing me? Tell you, or I'm fired?"

When she says it like that...

Sitting up a little straighter, feeling properly chastised, I run my hand through my hair. "I only want...*need* to understand."

Her eyes bounce back and forth between mine before she reclines in her chair and deflates a little. "It started with alcohol so I could get through it. When the alcohol stopped working, I tried smoking, but it made it worse. So I tried pills, and they helped...a lot. As most users do, I moved on to something cheaper."

"Get through what?" My brows draw together.

She shrugs and crosses her arms. "There are a multitude of reasons people turn to drugs. Genetics, traumas, doctors shoving pills down their throats. Unless you've experienced it—"

"I have a pretty good understanding of what drugs can—"

"*Unless* you have experienced it *personally*, you could never understand what it's like to be at war with your own mind and body. You know one day it'll be too much to turn back from, but your brain is convinced you need it to survive. When you try to get clean, your body revolts against you. And the conscious part of yourself that knows it's wrong, how you're hurting the people around you, or how it could even kill you...gets buried deeper and deeper until it doesn't exist at all."

She leans forward, with her arms resting on her knees. "So don't tell me you have an understanding, Bossman, because you don't. If you're planning on firing me, get it over with now so I can start job hunting."

I *should* fire her right now. Be done with it. But the thought of never seeing her again has my guts twisting. It's hard to separate her from the woman who half-assed raised me, but she's already done what my mother couldn't.

"I can randomly drug test you if I feel it's necessary. If you're okay with that, you can keep your job."

She dips her chin. "Deal."

We sit there for a minute, holding each other's gaze until I speak up again. "Do you want to head back to Granddad's?"

"Sure." She stands, and I follow, stepping onto the dock, but she stops and turns toward me. "Can I borrow your phone to call mine? I can't find it anywhere."

A bit skeptical, I pull my phone from my pocket, unlock it, and hand it to her, which I find out is a big mistake when she smirks.

Way to trust your gut.

She reaches for my phone, and as soon as she's got hold of it, her other hand darts out, shoving me with the kind of force I wouldn't expect from her.

I try to find my footing as my arms flail but fail as my body falls sideways into the water.

Surfacing and spluttering, I shout, "Are you fucking *crazy*?"

A sexy, wicked smile takes over her face. "Don't ever blackmail me again, Jansen."

It's the first time she's said my name. Fuck if I don't love the way it sounds passing through her lips.

She places my phone on the dock and walks away as I growl, lifting myself out of the water. Before I can stand, she's already inside.

When I get back to Granddad's, he tries to cover up his laugh with a cough, but he can't hide the amused glint in his eye.

I can't get out of this fucking town fast enough.

Six

Tillie

I walk over to Ron's later in the day—once I'm sure Jansen is gone—to apologize and take him up on his offer another time, but he insists on going out. After he instructs me on how to move the kayak paddle to turn, go straight, and go backward, we paddle out on the lake.

"He's honestly not a bad guy," Ron says, keeping pace with me while I figure it out.

"I think you may be a little biased," I retort, unable to help my chuckle at the memory of him falling into the water.

His gruff laugh melts away a little more of my irritation caused by his grandspawn. "I may be. He's been through a lot. Doesn't let people in easily, and he's always on guard, but he has a good heart."

I shouldn't be fishing for information, but after the shit Jansen just pulled, my give-a-damn about it being wrong doesn't exist. "What happened?"

Ron contemplates for a few seconds but relents. "He had a rough childhood. My daughter, his mother, couldn't stay on the right path. She fell into a bad crowd. I thought his dad had her set straight, but when he passed away, she lost sight of what mattered, and he suffered for it."

"I'm sorry about your daughter. Is she better now?"

His throat works, and he clears the emotion from it. "No. She passed when he was seventeen. My oldest daughter took him in after that."

Shit. Now I sympathize with him.

"I'm so sorry. My mom left when I was two," I murmur. "It's not the same, and it's hard to miss someone you never knew, but sometimes I miss the idea of her."

"So it was just you and your dad?"

"It has been for a while, but..." My words drift off.

It's hard to stomach the idea of ever living with him again, let alone looking at him. Once upon a time, my dad and I were close. He was my favorite person until I found out his moral compass didn't exist, and I ended up paying the price for it.

"You don't have to explain anything to me, Tillie."

I nod and tilt my head back, letting my face soak up the sunrays. We paddle and make small talk, but it's not uncomfortable at all. He shares a little about his late wife, Clover. They'd been with each other since the age of fourteen. She encouraged him to open the bar because of how much he loved bringing people together, but when she passed, so did his passion for it.

On the paddle back, I ponder the pieces of me that used to radiate joy, but at much simpler things. A good grade on a test I studied all night for. Silly text threads with my friends—when I had them. A boy I thought was cute, who'd smile at me in the hallway. Knowing my dad was having a tough week and baking him brownies to watch a little of his stress melt away as he'd pull me in for a tight hug. A part of me wants to shed those memories the way a snake sheds its skin, if only to spare myself the pain from memories of a girl I'll never be again.

Once we've eased the kayaks up to the dock, I secure the rope around the T-shaped hook and help him pull them from the water.

"We should make this a regular thing," he offers.

"I'd love that. It's a good workout," I agree while stretching my arms out, knowing I'll feel the effects tomorrow while having to serve. "Do you have any advice on how to break through your grandson's stone-wall exterior?"

He cants his head, squinting at me from where he's crouched on the dock. "I think you'll do just fine figuring it out."

·········

The next couple of weeks prove my failure at figuring it out. Luckily, he did *not* end up firing me after I shoved him into the lake. Instead, he keeps his distance. If we have to speak to each other, it's short and curt. I should be grateful, but for reasons I can't explain, I'm not. I thought we could move past the "I hate you" stage and into a friendlier one. It's tough to watch him get along with all of his employees so well while acting like I'm invisible.

"Hey, girlie pop. How's it going?" a familiar voice says from behind me, and I groan under my breath.

Bailee is nice enough, but the kind of nice she presents is an illusion. If you walked out of line with her, she'd come out claws swiping.

"It's been a pretty slow day. I don't see it getting busier with the storms coming in," I respond while shelving the clean glasses.

"Perfect. Slow days give me more chances to move in on Jansen."

"Mmm," I hum.

This could be another reason I'm not as friendly with her. Watching her apply lip gloss and shake her hair out like she's going to walk back into his office and have her way with him bothers me. It shouldn't; he's been nothing short of a giant dick to me. But it does. Mainly because I've heard him shut her down in the three shifts we've worked together, and she doesn't seem to take no for an answer.

Before I can stop myself, I say, "He's told you it isn't going to happen. Don't you think it'd be better to move on?"

A familiar throat clears behind us, and she answers me with a withering glare instead of a response. It's almost scary how quickly she replaces her usual mask before turning to face Jansen.

"Hey," she beams. "What can I do for you?"

I cringe at the insinuation in her tone and go back to checking the stock behind the bar without looking at him.

"We might close up early tonight. The storm could cause outages, and I want to have everyone home before it gets too bad."

"That's so nice of you," she fawns. "A nice bubble bath while listening to the rain sounds like a perfect night."

My jaw drops as my head whips toward her.

The audacity.

"Hope you enjoy your night," he clips, glancing at me before heading back to his office.

Once he's out of sight, she turns to me. "I don't need your advice or input when it comes to him."

My face heats from the anger raging through my veins. "Got it."

The rest of the shift drags. Jansen ends up sending Bailee home earlier than intended, much to her dismay, and I'm absentmindedly cleaning when a customer walks through the door. Before he can look my way, I'm on the floor, crouching behind the bar with a hand over my mouth to stop my cry from escaping.

Riley walks out of the kitchen and sees me. I shake my head vehemently, and he quickly diverts his eyes to the customer before walking back to Jansen's office. Curling up in a ball, I make myself as small as possible.

His fake-velvety voice fills the space, and I hold my breath.

"Hello," he calls out, knocking the bar top.

Jansen strolls out of the office and down the hallway, not sparing a glance at me on the floor as he walks as close to me as possible.

"We're closing up early," he says calmly, but the hint of anger he's trying to tame bleeds through his tone.

"No worries. I'm passing through, hoping to see if anyone has seen this girl?" He rustles around before showing Jansen what I assume is my picture. I grip his pant leg and squeeze my eyelids shut.

Please no. Please. Please. Please.

I silently beg him to say—

"No. I've never seen her before," he deadpans.

"Can I leave my card in case you happen to? She's my sister, and I haven't been able to locate her. I've been searching every weekend, going through different towns. I don't know if she's safe or alive," he chokes out. Bile rises in my throat at his implication that I have any relation to him.

"No problem," Jansen responds.

He knocks on the bar top again. "Thank you. It's much appreciated."

The door closes behind him before Jansen looks down at me, and I cry out, trying to stand, but my legs have no strength. The pure terror still running through my veins has me paralyzed. He stands there for a few minutes, staring out the window, while my panicked cries fill the space. Then he bends and scoops me into his arms. There's no reaction from him putting his hands on me. Instead, I cling to him, wrapping my arms around his neck so tightly it could be considered choking.

He walks us to the very back of the bar, passing his office, until we come to a staircase around the corner, which he climbs with care. Once we're through the door, I note it's a small apartment. The space screams bachelor. It's sterile, big enough for a bed, kitchen setup, and couch. I'm assuming the door leads to a bathroom. The aroma of spice and leather fills the space, and it's oddly comforting.

He sets me down on the couch gently and walks over to the kitchen, filling a glass with water. The lightheadedness from crying has me accepting the glass he offers, and he watches my trembling hand as I bring it to my lips.

A bit of water sloshes over the rim, and I groan, spurring him to take the glass and hold it to my lips. Our gazes lock, and unexpected feelings I've never felt, not even with Rhett, flood my system. He could've told him. He's wanted me gone since I walked out of the interview, but he kept silent. He could've patted me on the back and sent me on my way, but he didn't.

I take a few sips before pulling back.

"He's not my brother," I choke out as tears stream down my face again.

"I need to know what's going on, Freckles," he says with a softness he's never used with me before, and my insides melt a little from his use of the nickname again.

It's exhausting keeping secrets. I never told Rhett what was going on because he'd try to fix it. He wouldn't have been able to let it go. And other than him, I've never even thought of telling another soul. Not even my therapist in rehab. Maybe trusting Jansen is a mistake, but I'm so fucking tired. *Too* tired. Finding a spot on the wall, I verbally and mentally release my most shameful secret.

"He raped me when I was sixteen."

His intake of breath is sharp, but he's silent for a few seconds. "The alcohol. You said you needed alcohol to get through it..." His gravelly voice drifts off.

"It was storming, and my dad got stuck at his office..."

"I'll be home later, Sweets. The damn storm took the power out, and I need to make sure the system didn't crash when the generator kicks on. Holden is stopping by to drop off dinner."

Ugh. *"He doesn't need to, Dad. I can make something."*

"He's already on the way, but I'll call as soon as I'm headed out. Love you."

"Love you too."

After we hung up, I ran upstairs to change out of my shorts into sweats and a hoodie. Something about Holden always made me uncomfortable. My dad took him on as a partner last year. He bragged about how he may have been twenty-seven, but he'd shown more promise in the past two years than most of his employees. Apparently, his drive and knowledge had helped to grow their portfolios.

Fifteen minutes later, a loud knock echoed through the entryway.

"Thanks for the food," I said after opening the door, hoping he'd leave as quickly as he came.

"No thanks needed. Do you mind if I come in to use the restroom?"

I bit my lip, wanting to say "not a chance," but also not wanting to be rude.

"Sure." I opened the door wider.

My stomach growled when the aroma of teriyaki and stir-fry filled my nostrils. I was pulling the Styrofoam containers from the paper bag while he sauntered down the hall to the kitchen.

"You've really filled out this year," he remarked.

My cheeks blazed from the uncomfortable comment, but he must have taken it as something else.

"Don't be embarrassed. You've turned into a beautiful woman."

"Thanks." I tried to grin, feeling even more uneasy.

"How old are you now?"

"I turned sixteen three days ago."

"Wow...Sixteen, and you look no younger than twenty with a face and body like yours."

Despite my changing into sweatpants and a baggy hoodie, he somehow managed to make me feel like I was wearing nothing.

"I need to get some homework done for school," I said, trying to hint that his time at my house was up.

"Hmm." His eyes continued to take me in, and that earlier discomfort turned into nauseating panic. "I found some things out recently about your dad."

"Oh?"

"He's been embezzling money. Do you know what that means?"

My breath caught. "He wouldn't do something illegal."

"Oh, but he has, and I have proof." An evil smirk stretched across his lips. Dread filled my gut as a warning buzzed in my head.

"I think you should leave," I said firmly as I struggled to stand on legs that were trembling, along with the rest of my body.

"I don't think I should. In fact, I think there's something you should do for me. You wouldn't want that information to get out, would you? Your dad is a respected man in this town. Once it gets out..." He whistled mockingly. *"He'd be done. His share of the business would be liquidated. Your house would eventually get foreclosed on because no one hires a thief. You'd be run out of town. Your college fund, gone."*

Every breath leaving my lungs was shallow, my body seeming to understand the insinuation before my brain did. "What do you want, Holden?"

"You."

As soon as his response registered, I took off to the living room, where I'd stupidly left my phone, but arms wrapped around me from behind, pulling my body against him.

"You do this willingly, or I'll leak to every finance company in a one-hundred-mile radius, after the police, that your dear old fucking dad is as crooked as they come," he growled in my ear as he pushed my sweatpants down my hips.

"Please, Holden. Please don't do this," *I begged while squeezing my thighs together.*

His hand paused. "You've never been fucked, have you?"

Every muscle in my body tightened as he chuckled, his breath causing an unwanted quiver to run down my spine as I whimpered.

"Even better," *he whispered as he lifted me and tossed me on the couch.*

Seven

Jansen

"I HATE STORMS NOW," Tillie says in the same monotone voice she used to tell the story of how she was assaulted, and I know without asking this is the first time she's ever told anyone.

My body is still trembling with rage as she continues to speak. "I started using because I hated feeling the shame, and the drugs made it…I never wanted it, but my body…it didn't—"

"Stop." I cut her off, not wanting to hear what she was trying to put into words.

"I'm disgusting. The things I let him do. I've only been with…one…person completely…willingly, and I couldn't…even be intimate with him…sober." Her breathing is choppy as she cries and fights to say everything she's kept bottled up, and I can't fucking stop her because she needs this. She needs to get the words out.

Tremors rack through her as she folds in on herself. "He was my best friend…and…I couldn't. I loved him, but…I was a used-up…junky. I'm broken."

Something in me snaps.

"Look at me," I growl.

Her folded form snaps ramrod straight as her lips part. I palm her cheeks, forcing my anger down, as I stare deep into pools of emeralds.

"You are not disgusting. You are beautiful, smart, and strong. I'm so fucking sorry I made you feel less than any of those things, Tillie. You did what you needed to do to survive the assault. Your body did what it needed to do to protect you, and if that piece of shit ever appears in front of me again, I *will* kill him," I say with every bit of conviction I feel.

Her eyes drift to my mouth, and I know this isn't the time, yet I gravitate toward her anyway, our faces an inch apart. Every breath she releases brushes against my lips, but then a loud crack of thunder sounds off, and she whimpers in fear.

In my thirty-one years, I've never felt the kind of pain for another person I do in this moment. Not even my mother.

"You're staying here tonight. I have a T-shirt and joggers you can change into. I'll sleep on the couch."

She quickly wipes her face and stands. "No, it's fine. I'll go home. I'll be fine." She rushes to the door, but before she can fully open it, I'm behind her, careful to keep my body off hers as I push it closed with my palm.

"Please, Freckles," I whisper.

The rise and fall of her chest quickens, and her throat works as she inches around to face me. She looks confused, as if she can't believe I'd want to be in her presence after what she's told me.

The things I want to do to Holden right now would make the devil weep.

"Can I shower?" she asks meekly.

I back away enough to give her space but stay close enough in case she tries to bolt. I don't want her out of my sight right now when I have no idea where the fucker is.

"The towels are under the sink, and I have a pack of toothbrushes in the top drawer on the left."

Her eyes shine as they look back and forth between mine, but she nods. A small smile graces her face before I gather the clothes and she walks into the bathroom. While she's showering, I grab a pillow and blanket from the bed to lie on the couch.

It's an hour before the soft click of the door sounds, and she appears. Every inch of her visible skin, minus her face, is red and irritated.

She scrubbed herself raw.

The thought causes a sharp pain to spear through my chest. Our gazes clash, and I note that the white around her irises is bloodshot. So many emotions pass between us, but I remain silent. In this instance, there are no adequate words to say.

She makes her way over to my bed and climbs up.

"Night, Jansen," she whispers.

"Goodnight, Freckles," I whisper back.

······•••······

The next morning, I wake up feeling groggy and sore. This couch is a bitch to sleep on. When I look over at the bed, it's empty. My limbs are moving in a panic-induced state before my brain can catch up. But as soon as my feet hit the rug, I spot her wrapped in a blanket, sleeping soundly on the floor beside me. Her hair covers the side of her face, and I don't think before leaning down to brush it back, causing her lids to flutter open.

"Why are you on the floor?"

"The storm got bad last night," she rasps, her voice huskier than usual. Everything about this woman is arousing, but she's traumatized and my employee, so I will my dick to behave as she continues talking. "I'm surprised you slept through it. The entire building was shaking."

"I'm a dead sleeper. You should've woken me up."

She shrugs, bringing the blanket up to her nose.

After rising and stretching, I bend down to scoop her up and lay her on the couch. "I'm going to grab some food. Any requests?"

She starts to sit up. "You don't need to—"

I sigh heavily, cutting her off. "Let me take care of you, Tillie, even if it's only for this morning. Please?"

Her lips twitch before twisting. "I'm not a picky eater."

"Perfect." I grin. "I'll be right back."

I stop by Nelly's Dine or Dash, the only diner in town that makes the best French toast I've ever eaten. While I'm waiting for our food, I call the one man whose friendship has lasted over several moves and years. He's also a talented hacker. I've had to use his services when two business deals went awry, and Gabe found the information I needed as leverage to get us back on track.

"How's it going out in the middle of nowhereville?" Gabe asks as soon as he answers.

"It's going, but this call is for your services."

"Interesting. What do you need?"

I reach into my wallet and pull out the business card the lying bastard gave me last night.

"Anything you have on a man named Holden Warren. He currently works at Porter-Warren Capital in Arkansas," I explain.

"Do I want to know what this is about?"

"I'll share the details soon. See if you can find anything on him."

"Will do. It'll take some time, but I'll send word when I'm wrapping up." He hangs up, and I grab our order.

Having to spend months in this fuck all state that holds the most painful memories for me doesn't touch—not even the tip—the anger and disappointment simmering in my gut when I notice her car is gone from the Clovers lot. I can't believe she left. She doesn't even know if he's still in town, and she risked her safety, for what? As I'm about to drive to the marina, my aunt's contact fills the screen.

"Hey, Aunt Lin," I answer, pulling out of the parking lot.

"I need your help, Jansie."

"Nix?" I ask, knowing my cousin has been the main source of her recent stress, from what Granddad has told me.

"Could he stay with you while you're in Arkansas? I need to get him away from these delinquents he's attached himself to. Maybe he'll end up staying close to Granddad. He's always looked up to you."

"He's a grown man now, Aunt Lin. I doubt he's going to listen to me anymore."

"Please." Her voice cracks, filled with the desperation of a mother who loves her son. If only her sister could've loved me the same way.

"I'm on my way. I'll see you soon."

After hanging up, I call the woman who's consumed most of my thoughts since walking into my office.

Tillie answers on the second ring. "Hello."

"I have some family business to deal with, but when I get back, we're going to talk about why you ran out on me and risked your safety." I hang up before she can respond, hoping my dipshit cousin isn't as bad off as my aunt's making it seem.

Unfortunately, he is. He's lost weight, looks like he forgot what sleep is, and his attitude toward Aunt Lin is about to get his head knocked.

"I'm twenty-three years old, Mom. You don't decide where I go."

"Watch it," I snap.

He has the sense to close his mouth, but he shoots a glare my way.

"It's only for a few weeks, Phoenix. Give yourself a chance to get away from here. Maybe you'll even love Novaridge."

"I have nothing there. It's been two years since I've seen Granddad. And we all know as soon as he's done flipping the bar"—he nods my way—"he'll be gone in the wind. I don't see the fucking point. If you want me to leave the house, I'll leave, but I'm not leaving Sayersville."

All right. Enough of this shit.

"Listen, I drove three hours to get here. So you're getting in my damn Jeep. I'll drive you back if you want to come home next week. Think of it as a vacation. Granddad lives full-time at the marina now, so we can go kayaking, hang out on the water, whatever you want to do."

His eyes narrow. "You're not going to be too busy?"

"Kid, I run the show. I can leave whenever I want."

"I'll go if you stop calling me a damn kid," he murmurs.

"Then step up and act like a grown man," I retort.

Uncle Tony snickers as he walks past us. Nix's eyes track him, and he glowers at his back until he disappears outside through the door in the kitchen.

"I'll go pack my shit."

Once he's out of sight, I turn to Aunt Lin. "I won't force him to stay with me, but I'll do what I can until I leave."

She nods as she cranes her neck to look out the window into the backyard.

"What's up with Uncle Tony? He didn't have anything to say."

Her cheeks turn crimson. "Those two are constantly at each other's throats. I don't know what to do anymore, Jansen. It's like he's given up on him and expects me to do the same, but I'm his mother. He's the only child I have."

Pain spears my chest from the anxiety blending with her words. An emotion, I'm sure, my mother never had the brain capacity or heart to feel for me. Being back in Arkansas brings with it the most pitiful feelings. I shake the self-indignant thoughts away as I pull Aunt Lin into my chest, hoping to calm some of her worry. "It'll all work out. He's being young and dumb. You two are great parents."

She sniffs. "I thought so too, but you've seen him. He looks terrible, he's not taking care of himself, and he won't talk to me about anything anymore."

After saying our goodbyes, we're back on the road. Nix is acting agitated, and I turn on the radio to fill the awkward silence after my small talk with him failed. Despite the eight-year age difference, we used to be close when he was a kid, and I always looked at him like a little brother. I'm aware I haven't been around much in the past few years, but I've been busy. He always used to talk to me, though, so I don't understand how shit got this bad and nobody thought to tell me.

Normally, I would keep pushing him, but my mind can't focus on him right now. The only person I'm focused on is three hours away, and I'm counting down every minute until I'm in front of her again.

Eight

Tillie

"Hey, Presley," I greet as I answer our weekly call.

"How's it going with the boss?"

Skipping over the small talk, I see.

We've talked every week, and she's quickly become what I once would've considered a best friend.

"Well, it's a lot better than it was. I think he's come around."

"Good, I'd hate to sic Dane on him."

I laugh out loud. "Dane's a puppy dog."

She scoffs. "Don't let how he acts with us fool you. The man can be a bulldog when he cares. It's pretty sexy."

My nose wrinkles, and I chuckle. "I'll take your word for it."

"Seriously, though…You're doing well?"

I sigh softly. One day, people won't question my sobriety, and I'll celebrate loudly. "Dryer than a desert in July on all fronts."

"Maybe…" She pauses.

"You always say whatever you're thinking, Pres. Don't stop now."

"Maybe you could get back in the dating scene."

My heart clenches because she doesn't understand I've never been *in* the dating scene. I've never dated at all. Rhett was casual sex with a friend, but we never *dated*.

"We'll see," I breathe out. "I'll text you later. I'm about to run into work."

We hang up, and my stomach does this thing it hasn't before as I walk up to the doors of Clovers. It feels like my guts are twisting, but a fluttering sensation takes over. I'm not sure if I'm nervous, excited, or scared to see Jansen again. Maybe leaving yesterday was a bad idea, but after everything I shared, it was hard to face him fully, eating breakfast like he hadn't listened to me share my most kept secret the night before.

Steeling my spine, I walk through the door, and thankfully, he's nowhere in sight. To delay a run-in, I set my things behind the bar instead of the break room close to his office and clock in.

"It's going to be a busy night," Mason says, coming up behind me.

"I'm counting on it. I love the days we barely have time to stop."

He snorts. "Yeah, well, you're the bar queen. We peasants can have a hard time keeping up."

Before I can respond, his face takes on a serious expression as he places both hands on my shoulders, making my skin crawl, and I force a small smile while shrugging him off.

His brows crease, but he drops his hands. "I talked to Riley when I came in and heard about what happened last night. If you ever see that asshole again, tell me. I'll take care of it."

Shrugging it off, I grin like it was no big deal.

He doesn't let me. "I'm serious, Tillie."

Having people genuinely care about my well-being causes my throat to ache. I nod, swallowing around the lump of emotion. "I will. Promise. Thank you, Mase."

From the corner of my eye, I see someone approaching from the hallway, and my heart beats a little faster in anticipation.

Definitely new.

Except, when I turn my head to look, a guy who appears similar to Jansen but...isn't...takes slow steps our way, and Mason follows my line of sight.

"That's Jansen's cousin. He looks like shit. I think he has the flu or something," he says as he sets to turning on the taps behind the bar.

He's a few inches shorter than Jansen and skinnier, but he looks far from healthy. I can see the bags under his eyes despite the distance between us as he staggers around. Pausing in the hallway, he leans his forehead against the wall and pounds his fist against it.

Shit.

"I'll be right back, Mase," I call over my shoulder.

I approach him slowly, and when he glances up, his eyes—with pupils almost covering the entirety of his iris—widen while his lips part.

It's not in my nature to take care of people, but a need to comfort him, to make sure he's all right, overrides my usual judgment, making it impossible for me to walk away.

"Let's get you back upstairs."

"It's fucking suffocating up there. I can't fucking breathe," he groans.

An acquired understanding has my chest aching for him because I know what he's going through.

Stepping a little closer to him, I ask, "How long has it been since you used?"

His expression reminds me of a child being caught doing something they know they shouldn't have. "No, I...It's not...I haven't," he stammers.

"It's okay. I'm not judging you. What if I go up with you for a little bit?"

"You'll stay?" he croaks out.

"For as long as I can."

He nods, and I step to his side. "Put your arm around my shoulder and lean into me if you need to."

He only nods again.

Once we're upstairs and through the door, I ask him if he'd rather lie on the bed or the couch, and he chooses the latter. The cushions dip as I sit him down and then start to walk away, only to stop when he grabs my wrist lightly.

"You promised you'd stay," he chokes out.

"I'm going to see if Jansen has any Tylenol or—"

"It doesn't work. Nothing works anymore," he whimpers, and if my heart could physically crack, it would.

"Okay. I'll get a cool washcloth. I'm not leaving. I'm Tillie, by the way," I tell him.

"Nix," he murmurs.

Cool water drips from the washcloth, down my wrist, but I ignore it as I sit beside him, grab the pillow next to me, and place it in my lap. He looks at me for a few seconds in confusion before lying his head on the pillow. After placing the rag around his neck, I massage his temples.

Memories of my time in detox play out in my mind. It was excruciating. The headaches, the body aches, the nausea. The nurses at my facility were nice enough. They did their job and tried to keep me comfortable, but I would've given anything to have someone sit with me through it. To have the comfort of another human being.

He groans and turns so his body is facing me, resting his face as close as possible to my stomach, while leaving me enough room to keep the massage going. His body tremors start to relax, and his breathing turns slow and even. I don't stop massaging him until his body stills, but when I go to stand, he buries his face in my stomach and wraps an arm around my waist. I only catch parts of what he says next since he's mumbling.

"No...my angel...didn't listen..."

He falls asleep at the same time the door opens, and a familiar deep voice calls out, "What the fuck is going on?"

Turning toward Jansen, I glare and shush him. "He just fell asleep."

His stance widens as he crosses his arms over his chest. "I don't give a fuck. Mason said you helped Nix upstairs, and I walk up here to find him lying in your lap, clinging to you like a damn monkey."

"Yes, and I'm staying, so you should call someone in to take over my shift."

His jaw drops. "*Excuse* me?"

"He's going through withdrawal, and you left him up here, *alone*."

"No, he's—"

"*He is detoxing*," I speak over him. "You have no idea how painful it can be, and you left him alone."

"Nix wouldn't do drugs. He saw..." He pauses, then shakes his head. "He wouldn't. You're wrong."

I scoff. "I'm an addict, Jansen. I know what withdrawal looks like. His pupils are huge."

Jansen's hard gaze locks on his cousin, and he balls his fists at his sides. "Well, now I know. I've got it from here."

Laughing wryly, I throw my head back against the couch. "If you think I'm leaving him here alone with you after how you acted toward me, you're delusional. I can stay here, or he can come back to mine."

"Freckles, my patience is paper-thin right now," he grits out.

A rush of heat unfurls in my core, causing my eyes to widen, but he mistakes my reaction for fear. His posture immediately relaxes, and his face softens. He runs both hands through his hair, mumbling under his breath, but the only word I catch is "Sayersville."

"What did you say?" I ask.

Jansen looks at me in confusion. "I said the town of fucking Sayersville is cursed. It's the town he lives in."

Looking back down at Nix, I study his face. "How old is he?"

"He's twenty-three. Why?"

As I take in all of his features, the few words he mumbled earlier rush back to me, as well as his expression when he first saw me. *I remember.*

"What's wrong, Tillie?"

"I know him. Well, I don't know him, but I talked to him once. I'm from Sayersville."

Jansen walks closer to me with crossed arms and a guarded expression, waiting for me to say more.

"It was a few days before I went to rehab. He looked so out of place and uncomfortable. The guy he was with came all the time, but I'd never seen Nix before. He walked to the kitchen, where every type of alcohol in existence was laid out on the table, but he went for soda. I approached him and asked what he was doing there."

The memory of him and the night we met becomes clearer. More vivid.

"I could tell he was shy. He said he'd just started hanging out with Blaine, the guy he was with. I'm not sure why. I was so out of it, but I told him he didn't belong there. Because going for the soda in a house full of drugs and alcohol told me he was a smart guy, and he should stay that way." I blink away the moisture the memory causes, but a small smile takes over my face.

"He looked at me for a few seconds and said I didn't belong there either. It was the first time I felt like someone saw the person I wanted to be instead of the person I was—the used, dirty version of myself. I felt this...pull...to stay close to him all night. People kept pressuring him to take this or that, and I'd snap at anyone who did. When we were about to leave, Blaine handed him a little packet. But I walked over to him and snatched it away."

I've never been so grateful I snatched that baggie out of his hand. And as I peek up at Jansen, I see him looking between me and Nix with a look of caution.

"I overdosed on whatever was in the baggie two days later. I was with Rhett when it happened."

"The guy who had sex with you while you were high out of your mind? Yeah, I haven't forgotten him," Jansen sneers, and maybe it was wrong, but it's also not that simple.

I glare at him, feeling defensive of the boy who used to be my safe space. "Don't. You have no idea what you're talking about. He never touched me again after he got sober. He refused unless I got sober too. He lo—"

I don't finish the sentence because it's still painful to know his love for me wasn't as true as I thought but rather guilt for believing my addiction started with him. "He saved my life, did CPR until the ambulance got there."

As if he needed me to say it, I explain, "Your cousin would probably be dead if I hadn't taken the baggie from him. I was with someone who helped me. Not everyone is so fortunate. Blaine died the night after the party and wasn't even found right away because he didn't." I sniff.

I wiggle free from Nix's grip and carefully place his head and pillow on the couch cushion. This sudden feeling of responsibility to make sure he stays sober hits me square in the gut, stealing my breath.

Is this what Rhett felt with me?

Passing Jansen without a second glance, I head to the bathroom, but his steps sound behind me as he follows me in, closing the door behind him.

I'm unable to utter a single word before his hands are on my waist. I'm lifted onto the bathroom counter, and his lips—expertly, might I add—part mine before he brushes my tongue with his.

My lips stall all movement as my brain lags because...I'm not panicked. I'm not disgusted or scared. Rather, I feel so much desire right now; it's pooling between my legs. He takes my stone lips as rejection and starts to pull away, but I grab the back of his neck, holding him in place.

I've never kissed anyone sober. Never. My grades were my main priority in school before...

He rarely ever attempted to kiss me. There were no affectionate moments. My first kiss was with Rhett, but I've never had the desire to be intimate with a person while clear-headed.

My body quivers from anticipation and nerves with how badly I want this. I *choose* this. So I brush my lips against his lightly, giving him the green light. The kiss is slow, and he lets me take it at my own pace. His tongue grazes my bottom lip, and they part fully. All the built-up desire in my body from every stroke of his tongue against mine feels like a tsunami of pleasure I'd gladly drown in.

My body moves with some primal, sexual prowess I didn't know existed as I wrap my legs around his waist and rock my hips, feeling his hard length. A masculine groan slips past his lips, and I can't help the moan that escapes mine, forgetting about the other person in this apartment.

Gasping, I pull back and frantically apologize. "I'm sorry. I'm your employee. Your cousin is right outside."

"And if you don't bring your lips back to mine, I'll fire you right now."

Nine

Jansen

Her soft chuckle fills the small space as she places her palms on my chest, gently pushing me back. "You wouldn't."

"Jansie," Nix calls out in a hoarse voice.

"Fuck me." I hang my head.

"Jansie?" she asks with a raised brow, flushed cheeks, and swollen lips. Wisps of raven hair that have escaped her ponytail rest against her cheeks.

"He started using the name as soon as he could talk. It stuck, and he's the only person, aside from my aunt, who I allow to call me that." I fix her with a pointed look.

Her full lips twist to the side as she cocks her head. "Hmm. I don't know. It suits you."

"I'm rethinking the firing comment," I tell her as I adjust myself in my jeans, which draws her eye to my crotch, and her cheeks redden.

I want to make a joke about it, but right now, my mind is on my cousin in the next room, who watched me go through hell and still walked down the wrong path. I have little faith in addicts staying sober, but I refuse to lose Nix. If I have to tie the little fucker up and hold him hostage, I will.

Swallowing my emotions, I look to Tillie and find her watching me with a softness I haven't seen before.

"I can go while you talk to him, or I can stay. It's up to you," she offers.

"Stay. I think he'd want you to stay."

I need you to stay.

She nods, and we leave the bathroom to find Nix sitting up with his head in his hands. When he looks up to see her, he scans her up and down as his throat works. I'm not too fond of that reaction. She works for me. She's my employee. And I've always had a system of ethics. No sex with employees. However, I just got a taste of her, and I'm already consumed by the need to devour more of her.

Tillie hangs back, leaning against the post by the kitchen.

I try to keep my voice calm as I sit on the table in front of the couch. "How long, and *what*, have you been using?"

Nix's eyes meet mine, and there's a vulnerable sheen in them, reminding me of the little boy I grew up with.

"Off and on for the last year. Mainly pills. Uppers."

"Mainly?" I ask, gritting my teeth.

He has the sense to look ashamed. "I've used coke a few times."

"What the fuck, Nix?" I stand and pace the short distance in this tiny-ass apartment.

"I took on extra courses to graduate faster, and it was harder than I expected to keep up with the course load. A guy suggested Adderall, and it took off from there. I'm not some fucking junkie."

"Do your parents know?" Tillie murmurs, but I catch the small wince his words caused.

He looks between us, to the bathroom door, and back, narrowing his eyes. "I'm not a child."

I scoff, which agitates him more. "Fuck this. Take me back home, Jansen."

"I'll take you home when you're clean and I believe you can stay that way."

"Then I'll find my own way." He walks toward the door, only stopping and straightening once Tillie steps in his path with her hands on his shoulders.

"Have you thought about rehab?" she asks.

His sigh is heavy. "I'm not going to rehab. I don't need it."

"The fuck you—"

Her hard glare cuts me off.

"How about we make a deal?" she implores him.

He doesn't say anything, so she continues, "What if you stay with me?"

"Not happening," I announce, walking close enough to see the smirk on Nix's face.

"Your boyfriend seems to have a problem with that."

"He's not my boyfriend, and it's not his decision. It's yours."

A frown mars his face. "Judging by the noises coming from the bathroom a few minutes ago, I'd say different."

Tillie's cheeks turn red as she crosses her arms. I'm about to rip this fucker a new one for embarrassing her when she steps toe to toe with him, fixing him with a steely glare I've been on the other end of before. Nix's posture deflates like a scolded child.

"What your cousin and I do, or don't do, isn't your business. You can stay with me at the marina. Me, Jansen, or your granddad will be with you at all times. If that doesn't work for you, then sure. Go back home. But you know as well as I do you'll end up using again. It'll get worse, and you'll end up dying in that town if you don't get ahead of it. And you *can*, Nix."

I'm about to say fuck no, he isn't staying with her, but I can't think of a reason that doesn't make me sound like a jealous or possessive asshole. Still, my mind works overtime for an excuse.

Two addicts living together.

One is withdrawing.

It's a recipe for disaster.

Then his throat works, though, and the words die on my tongue.

"Do you really think I can?" he rasps as his shoulders deflate.

"I *know* you can."

Nix nods slowly, rubbing the back of his neck. "Okay."

She smiles, and both Nix and I are affected by it. "Be ready to leave at nine. I'm going to finish my shift." She looks at me before continuing, "And then we'll go."

When she leaves the apartment to get back to the bar, I only wait long enough for her to be out of earshot before I can't hold back anymore. "She's not for you, Nix."

He hangs his head before looking at me and straightening his spine. "And how long are you sticking around this time, Jansen?"

I search his eyes, feeling a distance between us I've never noticed before. After all, we're eight years apart. I never would've thought a woman would come between us.

"I'm hoping to sell by the end of July," I say, crossing my arms.

"Sounds like she isn't for you either."

He closes himself in the bathroom before I can respond, but a dark thought crosses my mind. This situation could get fucking messy.

·····・・····

The night Tillie took Nix with her, I almost begged her not to. It was pathetic. Nix was right about how she's not for me either. However, he's practically living with her now, and I feel sick every night thinking about it.

The past few weeks have been pretty uneventful. He spends Tillie's workdays with Granddad, who has loved having both his grandsons in the same town. They kayak, fish, and watch the old western shows they both love. We filled him in on what was happening and why Nix needed to be with someone at all times. The one time I went over there, the tension between Nix and me was palpable. Granddad could sense it too, because he called me later the same night. He assumed my tension came from knowing Nix was an addict, and I let him believe it.

The long, heated glances when Tillie and I see each other at work and our cordial conversations aren't enough, but the now constant knot of tension in my stomach keeps me from seeking her out for more.

Now I'm sitting in my office on a Friday when I could be off because I don't want to have to make a random excuse for ditching them today.

A knock sounds on the door, and I lift my head to see Tillie.

"Can I come in?"

"What can I do for you?" I ask in a professional tone.

"It's about Nix." She closes the door and takes a seat in the chair in front of my desk. She's wearing her usual black tee and flannel, even though the weather has been warmer. "Did you know he has an IT degree?"

I lean back in my chair, gritting my teeth. "No. I wasn't aware he'd graduated."

How the hell did I distance myself that much from my family? Yes, I've been busy, but damn. I didn't even get an invite to the graduation.

"It was recent. He said he didn't want to do the ceremony or make a big deal of it, but he's had a hard time finding a job..."

I quirk a brow, knowing exactly where this is going. "I'd imagine. It can be a hard field to get started in."

"Well." She bites her lower lip, looking suddenly nervous, and my eyes are drawn to her mouth. "You're a successful businessman, and I'm sure you've made connections over the years. Do you think...Is there any way you'd be able to help in his job search?"

What the hell. Might as well put myself out of my misery. "How's it been going?" I clear my throat. "You two living together?"

Her small smile has a scowl taking over my face. "It's been good. We mainly binge-watch shows, sit outside, or try to get creative with the food we're limited to cooking in the houseboat. He spends a lot of time kayaking. He's starting to look a little healthier than he was."

I shuffle some paperwork on my desk, nodding, but guilt gnaws at my insides.

All of those things are great. Truly. I love that my cousin seems to be thriving, but I also want to punch him in the throat because he gets to spend all of his time with her, experiencing the mundane moments with her, and now it's all I'm picturing. The bond they've formed and continue to form will be strong.

"Jansen," she says on a sigh.

"Mmm," I hum. "I'll make some calls to see about any available job openings. Thank you for letting me know, Tillie." I smile tightly, dismissing her.

Her shoulders drop a little. "What happened the other day—"

"We don't need to discuss that." My tone is hard, businesslike.

She narrows her eyes, tipping her chin, and a glimpse of the firecracker who pushed me into the lake comes out to play. "I believe we do, *Boss*."

It's cute how she believes calling me *Boss* will have me backing down. Normally, it would, but I've never been in this position before. What I feel about her isn't my norm.

I steeple my hands on my desk and smirk. "Okay, *employee*. Would you like to discuss my tongue in your mouth or the way you wrapped your legs around my waist, grinding your pussy against my cock?"

Her breath hitches, and her pupils dilate, darkening her usual emerald. My cocky expression drops. I'm an idiot bastard. Of course, I could never forget anything about what she told me. And I probably shouldn't be so brash with a woman like Tillie; she's a survivor. I'm about to beg forgiveness when she stands and walks around my desk. I turn the chair to face her, and my gaze fixes on the heavy rise and fall of her chest until she's standing between my legs, a look of annoyance on her face.

She wraps one hand around my jaw—a little fucking forcefully—and tips my face up to hers. "I didn't tell you about my past so you could pity me. I don't want you pretending you're anything you're not because you think I'm weak."

I start to say something, but she slides her pointer finger over my lips. "You've been actively avoiding me if it doesn't have to do with work. Yes, your cousin is living with me, but nothing has happened between us. I'm *helping* him because he needs it. If you're regretting the kiss, I can handle that, but if you're only avoiding me because of Nix, please don't. You are the first person I've ever *wanted* to share anything with. To know *me*."

Her words incite a reaction. Holding back the other day and letting her take control took effort. I'm used to being in control. I need it. But the second she gripped my jaw...

My cock probably has an imprint of my zipper.

I nip her finger still resting on my lips and palm her waist, pulling her down on my lap. Her emeralds flare, and a gasp slips past her lips. She's wearing a full face of makeup today, and even though she looks as enticing as always, I miss being able to see the freckles hidden underneath.

With my hands still on her waist, I rock her hips back and forth over my lap, bringing my lips to her ear. "Does it *feel* like I have any regrets?"

She struggles to sit back, but I hold her in place.

"Don't stop moving your hips," I demand, and her breath catches, but she continues the motion on her own.

"I don't fucking pity you." The raspy whimper she releases as I nip her earlobe has my hold on her waist tightening while I try to contain the groan building in my chest. "And I don't believe for a second you're weak."

Her hips move faster, and I groan against her neck, placing an open-mouthed kiss on the spot behind her ear, sucking gently.

I'm about to clear my desk and lay her out to feast when a knock sounds on my door, causing her to jump to her feet in less than a second.

Before I can say anything, the door opens, and Bailee appears.

Fuck me.

She looks between me and Tillie, aware that something has happened from Tillie's appearance alone. When her eyes narrow, a surge of anger rises.

"Do *not* enter my office until I tell you to," I bark. Bailee stumbles back a step as her cheeks turn three shades darker, and she nods.

Tillie walks past my desk, and I'm about to tell her to stay when she turns around. "We're having dinner tonight at six. Come."

She slips past an annoyed-looking Bailee.

"What do you need?" I bite out.

"I…" Words escape her because she probably didn't have an excuse at all. I'm half tempted to fire her right now, but I need someone else lined up.

With a wave of my hand, I dismiss her. "Get back to work."

Ten

Tillie

I'M IN THE MIDDLE of making two Irish coffees when Bailee returns behind the bar.

"I cannot believe you had the audacity to judge me when you're screwing our boss in his office," she says with a haughty tone.

"I haven't slept with our boss, and if he wanted to sleep with you, it would be your business, but I've heard him shut you down."

She slams the glass she grabbed down on the bar, noticeably pissed about my observation. "At least now I know he doesn't have a problem fucking employees."

"What part of 'I didn't fuck our boss' did you not understand?" I ask calmly.

"Oh, I understand a few things now." She smirks, and it goes right through me, causing my chest to burn with white-hot anger.

Before I can get a word in, the useless hole on her face gapes open again.

"I'll have my time with him before he leaves. He'll have his fill of you soon enough. I wouldn't have thought he'd be attracted to..." She makes a show of taking me in from head to toe before she goes back to making her drinks.

This feeling of possession has never risen in me before. I've always found it extremely disgusting, but right now...I'm possessive enough to claw this bitch's eyes out. It's no secret to the people who have known me for years that I've put on some weight. Healthy weight. As in, I regularly eat now, so fuck her.

"You know, Bailee," Ivy says, appearing out of nowhere. "I haven't said anything because it's not my business, but I've had enough of your bitchiness."

"Ivy, I—"

"No," Ivy scoffs, cutting her off. "What you're doing concerning Jansen is called sexual harassment. He's made it clear. You are his employee, and he wants nothing more. Whatever happens between Jansen and Tillie is between them, two consenting adults. Did you catch that part? *Two*."

Bailee's face turns splotchy from anger or embarrassment—I can't be sure, but I hope it's both. Ivy is typically quiet. She comes in, does her job, and goes home. The only person she talks to a lot is Mason. We've been friendly with each other since she showed me the ropes with waitressing, but I never expected her to defend me.

And it seems as if she's not done.

"So stop coming in on Tillie's days off and talking shit. Stop finding excuses to get close to a man who has repeatedly told you no, and stop talking about her looks like a jealous bitch, because we both know she's hot." Ivy smirks.

Bailee's hands noticeably tremble as she takes the tray and heads toward a table. I stand there dumbfounded but grateful.

"You didn't have to step in. I don't want anyone else caught up in whatever goes on in her head." I smile at Ivy. "But thank you."

She smiles, and honestly, she's one of the most stunning women I've seen—a natural tan, thick curls, and full lips.

It's a wonder Jansen hasn't made any moves on her.

Scolding myself internally, I shake the jealous thought from my mind.

"You don't need to thank me. She's undoubtedly not a girl's girl, and it's sickening how she acts around him."

"How long have you worked here?"

"I was one of the first to get hired. Mason and I." Her cheeks turn a shade darker, and the earlier jealousy disappears.

"So, you two…?"

She laughs nervously. "No. We're only friends. I just turned twenty, and he's twenty-eight. He's made it clear that he sees me as nothing more than a friend." She wrinkles her nose.

I'm usually not one to initiate physical contact, but the look on her face has me reaching out to put my hand over hers. "His loss will be someone else's lucky gain. Or maybe he'll come around."

A small smile stretches across her lips. "Maybe. I guess we'd better get back to work."

"Could you take these coffees to table three?" I ask before she walks away.

"Sure thing."

············

At four sharp, I'm clocking out and racing out the door like a bat out of hell. Away from Bailee's bitchy attitude and hateful glares. Even the busy aisles of the grocery store where I pick up a few necessities, along with the rotisserie chicken for tonight's dip, can't sour my mood. Though, I'm sure when I'm attempting to cook in my miniature-sized kitchen, I'll crack a little. Having a place of my own is amazing, but damn, do I miss a full-sized…everything.

Once I'm home and the dip is made, I focus on tidying up the place a little. Nix isn't a slob, but he could work on putting things back where they belong or folding a blanket up when he's done using it. Right now, he's kayaking with Ron, which they do almost every day. I join them once a week, sticking to the agreement we made before Nix arrived in town.

He's opened up a lot about how he got into his situation. The pressure he felt was put on him, mostly by his dad, to succeed in everything he couldn't. He took on extra classes to graduate and find a job sooner so he could put distance between himself and his parents. He's told me stories about his childhood with Jansen—or "Jansie," as he calls him. Nix looks at him more like a brother than a cousin, but I can tell he's hurt by the amount of time Jansen spends away.

I invited Jansen to dinner so he could see we can all coexist peacefully, and he'll stop putting even more distance between them. At first, I thought maybe it was because of the drug revelation. After our chat in his office earlier, I'm sure it's because of me, and I don't want to come between family.

Nix does his signature "one, one-two-three" knock before opening the side door.

"If my arms aren't jacked by the time I leave here, I might have to start protests worldwide about the absolute fuckery of kayaking as exercise."

He's filled out a tiny bit, making him look even more like his cousin than usual, but there are noticeable differences. Where Jansen has amber-brown eyes, Nix has hazel—both almond shaped. Jansen has super-light brown hair; Nix's is dark brown. They do have the same sharp jawline, though.

"Mmm. I want to say kayaking equals lean muscle, and weights would equal jacked muscle, but I'll do my best to support your 'kayaking is fuckery' protest." I laugh.

He nudges my cheek with his knuckle and grins. "Smartass."

"I invited Jansen to come over tonight," I say while wiping down the countertops and table.

"And is he gracing us with his presence?"

I turn to see Nix leaning against the door. "Don't be an ass. You said you wished you could see him more, so I invited him."

"Yeah, I'm sure that's why," he mutters.

I'd be lying if I said there was no attraction to Nix when I'm obviously attracted to Jansen. But Jansen makes me feel things I never have. There's a liquid fire that races through my veins when he's near me, and Nix...I feel safe with him. He's a good friend. He's been polite and playful. He's great to look at, but I wasn't lying to Jansen when I said nothing has happened between us. Nothing has even come close to happening.

"If you have something to say, then say it. Don't whisper under your breath." I fix him with a pointed look, crossing my arms.

"Fine. Did you invite him here for me or you? Because I don't feel like third-wheeling tonight."

"If you'd like, I can hole myself up in my room while you two hang out. I invited him here so you two could spend time together, Nix. If you'd like me to leave, I will."

His face softens as he pulls me in for a hug. He's a big hugger, but since the first day I met him, there was an unnatural ease between us. I didn't hesitate once when it came to being alone with him or touching him. It could've been because of my being able to relate to the state he was in, or that he's related to Jansen, but the ease stuck around.

"I'm sorry. That was shitty. You and Jansie aren't my business." He sighs, resting his chin on my head. "Thank you for inviting him over."

I pull away to look at him, and his hands are still around my waist when a knock sounds on the sliding glass door. We both look over to find Jansen standing there.

I'm not sure what Nix sees, but I don't miss the way his fists are balled at his sides. He's currently staring at his cousin's hands, still touching my back, and I can't help but think maybe this wasn't the best idea when Nix steps away and toward the door.

"Hey, man," Nix greets him, wrapping his arms around him.

"You look even better than the last time I saw you," Jansen says, clapping him on the back while staring at me.

My body heats, thinking about the last time I saw him.

"Yeah, she's been taking care of me." He laughs and steps aside so Jansen can make his way in.

Jansen hums. "I'll bet."

Turning, I go to my room, grab a cardigan, and take a couple minutes to rid off the nervous energy that began fluttering in my stomach when he walked through the door. Once I've done that, I find them sitting on the couch, but I don't miss the somewhat dirty look from Nix.

"You'll have to send him your resume, but the position is yours if you want it. I brought my spare laptop, which you can use while you're here. But don't fuck it up."

The hope of this night bringing them together is swirling down a never-ending drain. Jansen is tense because of seeing Nix's hands on me. And Nix is tense because I went behind his back and talked to Jansen about his employment.

For fuck's sake, it's no wonder I opted to keep people at bay for so long.

"Okay, boys," I announce, walking in front of them before clasping my hands together. "Nix, I did talk to him about seeing if there were any job opportunities he was aware of because you've been looking. It's a hard field to break into, and there's nothing wrong with accepting help."

He goes to say something, but I stare him down, and he lifts his hands in surrender, grinning.

I look at Jansen, who runs a hand through his hair nervously. "Nix and I are friends. We hug, we goof off, and we live together. If we didn't have a good friendship, it would be awkward as hell, but I won't stand in the way of you two. I'll go to Ron's if it makes you both more comfortable."

"*No*," they shout in unison, side-eyeing each other.

I smile sweetly, bringing my palms together. "Good. Then, let's eat."

After we've got our plates loaded down with dip and a bowl of chips set out, we argue about what to watch.

"I say we go *Marvel*," Nix suggests.

"I'd rather watch the fucking *Notebook*," Jansen counters. "How about a thriller?"

"What do you want to watch, Tills?" Nix leans forward to look around Jansen because he planted his ass right smack dab in the middle of us.

"Yeah, *Tills*." He's got a hint of a *tone* as he looks at me with a raised brow, and his face gravitates closer to mine. "What do you want to watch?"

"How about horror?" I breathe out, clearly affected by our proximity. I'm a sucker for romance, but it seems like a counterproductive suggestion right now.

Nix rests his chin on Jansen's shoulder, facing me. "I say we go old school." He waggles his brows. "*Silence of the Lambs.*"

Jansen rolls his eyes at his cousin's antics, shrugging Nix off his shoulder, and I laugh.

"I've never seen it."

They both snap their heads to look at me like I've sprouted a dick from my forehead.

Jansen nods at him. "Turn it on."

Eleven

Jansen

"He wanted to protect her," Tillie argues.

Nix turns to her with comically wide eyes. "He eats people. Did you catch that? The mask they had him in because he *eats* people."

"I didn't say he wasn't a psycho. I'm saying, when it came to her—"

"Freckles, the movie was in no way, shape, or form a romance."

Why do women have to see romance in everything?

She huffs out her frustration. "I'm not saying it was, but if he was a true psychopath, then why show any emotion? He shed a tear. That was clear emotion."

I laugh. "Probably because he lost his chance at having a taste."

She narrows her eyes at my choice of words while discreetly pressing her thighs together.

"I read once about how spam could be used to wean cannibals off human flesh," Nix shares.

My face screws up—spam forever ruined—and I turn to look at him. "Where the fuck did you read that? CannibalsAnonymous.com?"

He shrugs. "I can't remember. I don't think it was true, but I haven't eaten spam since then."

Tillie crinkles her nose, and I shake my head in equal disgust.

"Do you need help cleaning up?" I ask, but don't get a response before they're leaning over me, facing each other.

"Nose its," they say in perfect unison, touching their noses with a pointer finger.

But it doesn't stop there.

"*Rock, paper, scissors, shoot.*"

Both of their hands form a fist.

"*Rock, paper, scissors, shoot.*"

Tillie's hand forms a scissor, and Nix lays his palm flat.

"Every time," he growls.

She smiles cheekily. "You're the one who made the rule. It's not my fault you lose more times than not."

They would make quite the pair; if I hadn't already staked my claim, maybe I'd be happy he found someone like her, but I have, and I'm not. They've formed a friendship while I've been keeping my distance, and the jealousy sparking through my chest and gut tells me enough about this situation to know I need to step up. I shouldn't. Nix is right about me leaving soon, but while I'm here, I want more of her time.

Nudging Tillie's shoulder with mine, I ask, "How about tonight, you and I get it cleaned up together?"

"Take notes, Nix." She smirks at him.

He rolls his eyes and looks at me pointedly. "I'm going to take some of this dip to Granddad. I'll be back in a few."

She gets a serving wrapped up for him, and once he's out the door, I walk up behind her at the sink, my chest to her back, soaking in her heat, before I slide sideways to stand beside her. I don't want her to think I'm only interested in her body. She may have told me her biggest secret, but I want to know what makes her, her.

"Your place is nice," I say sincerely, taking in the updates that have modernized it.

"Thank you." She blushes. "It's not mine. Friends from Sayersville are letting me stay here until I can get an apartment or something."

"So you're planning to stick around here?" I start cleaning up the counters and putting stuff away while she does the dishes.

"I honestly don't know. The only thing I do know is I'm never going back to Sayersville. Wherever I end up permanently, it'll be far away from there."

I nod along, but before another question can form, she's asking me one.

"Where are you heading next?"

"I'll start looking into businesses in a few weeks and go wherever the job takes me."

She glances at me over her shoulder while I wipe down the dinette table. "You've never wanted to settle down somewhere for good?"

"I've never had a reason to. After college, I wanted to travel and get the hell out of Arkansas. I started with this small grocery store in Kentucky. The owners were ready to file for bankruptcy. I got a small loan and put in the work. Business was more than breaking even after three months. The owners sold the store, and I got a cut of the profit. After paying off the loan I'd gotten, I used the remaining cash to continue on that path. The busier I am, the more in control I feel. I'm sure that doesn't make sense."

She rests her palm on my back, and my skin beneath it heats. "It does. That's why I love the busy days at Clovers. It helps me to put all my focus into the job instead of myself and the past."

Stepping back from her to stop myself from doing something stupid, like picking her up and locking us in her bedroom, I reach for the towel on the counter and start drying the dishes.

With a white-knuckle grip on the plastic cup I'm holding and grit in my throat, I ask, "Do you have any siblings or cousins you're close to?"

She surprises me by stepping between me and the sink, facing me. Tilting her head back, she bites her bottom lip, her gaze bouncing back and forth between mine. In some kind of trance, I slowly reach up, rubbing my thumb along her bottom lip to release it.

Her slender neck jumps as she swallows, and her voice is breathless as she answers, "I'm an only child. My cousins on my dad's side are all older than me. My mother left when I was little. I don't remember her."

Imagining Tillie being abandoned as a little girl tightens my chest.

"She didn't deserve you." My lips graze her forehead, and I inhale a trace of her citrusy scent. A sudden, almost violent need for my lips to map out every inch of her smooth skin slams into me.

"No, she didn't. My dad made up for it at one time. It was always the two of us."

Mention of her dad causes my shoulders to tense and the fog of lust to clear a little. Gabe texted me yesterday and said to expect a phone call in the next couple of days. Soon, we'll know everything about her dad's alleged crimes, and hopefully, have something on Holden.

"You and your dad were close at some point?"

How could he not know what kind of soulless monster was working for him?

"I don't understand why you're still asking me questions when we're alone, outside of work, and I'm standing in front of you."

Her statement is the green light that has me palming her hips, incapable of keeping my hands off her any longer. "Because I don't want you to think the only thing I care about is...physical. Normally, it would be, but...seeing you with Nix..."

Her eyes bounce back and forth between mine as she tilts her head. "What?"

"I don't want him to know you better than I do. I want to know every fucking part of you by memory." I let out a heavy sigh, staring into her emeralds. "I'm thirty-one years old, and I'm jealous of my twenty-three-year-old cousin because he gets to experience every day with you, and it's path—"

Her lips cut me off. The first nip of her teeth on my bottom lip has the tether to my already fraying control snapping as I claim every inch of her mouth with my tongue. And her needy whimpers cause my cock to swell even more. The side door opens suddenly, and Nix walks in, forcing us to break apart like he caught us doing something we shouldn't have.

Her face is flushed, pupils dilated as she stares at me with parted lips.

I'd love nothing more than to drag her to her bedroom, Nix present or not, and give her every ounce of pleasure I'm sure she's been denied, but he's important to me. Our relationship is important to me.

So I adjust myself discreetly through my joggers and bend to kiss her cheek before hugging my cousin goodbye.

Once I'm back at my place, my head spins. I undeniably want her, and I *will* have her, but a talk with Nix needs to happen first. We made plans to go kayaking in a couple of days, which feels like the perfect opportunity.

Heat travels through my body after I settle in for the night. Rapid images play out in my mind of Tillie on her knees, on her back with her creamy thighs wrapped around my neck while she moans and whimpers. Writhing against my tongue, demanding more. Her taste. *God*, her taste. The silk sheets cling to my damp skin as my heart works overtime to pump blood to more essential places.

I haven't had sex since being back here. Steering clear of this state has always been a goal of mine unless it had to do with family, but even then, I'd wrap up the visit as quickly as possible. Starting a relationship of any kind with a woman from Arkansas has always been a strict no. Until Tillie. Now she's all I can think about—her curves, her full breasts, the way she moves her hips, how dominating she can be.

That was the hottest kiss of my life earlier because she fought to claim me as much as I did her. Every glide of her tongue against mine felt like a duel. My hand squeezes my cock as I let the fantasy of what could've happened, had I not wasted time with her, play out in my mind. I won't take long to finish. Hell, it took every ounce of my self-control not to pull my dick out in the Jeep.

My breaths come out faster as my hand picks up speed, squeezing with the right amount of pressure. By the time my imagination conjures up images of my face between her thighs, ropes of cum line my stomach.

After cleaning myself up, I lie back down with one thought in mind. *This woman will be the end of life as I knew it.*

· · · • • · • • · ·

The next day, Tillie is off work, which is for the best because I would've had a hard time keeping my hands off her after last night. Saturdays tend to be pretty busy, but I called Remi to see if he'd be able to cover more of Bailee's shifts. He seemed enthusiastic about picking up more hours, so I'm reworking the schedule. Unfortunately, she is here today, so I've made myself scarce while I go through resumes.

My phone rings, Gabe's name flashing on the screen.

"What do you have?"

His loud sigh comes over the line, and I know whatever he's found, it isn't good. "I need more details. Not later, now."

My shoulders go rigid, and I fail to hide the strain in my voice. "What the fuck did you find out, Gabe?"

"Your macho bullshit isn't going to work with me. I'm across the world from you right now. So give me more details, and I should be able to make this clusterfuck make sense."

He won't let this go, and I don't blame him. However he gets his information, it isn't always legal.

Leaving my office, I don't speak again until I'm in my apartment. "I'm not giving you full details, but I'll give you enough."

"Fine," he clips.

"Holden works with Tillie's father. He assaulted her, and she never told anyone because he threatened her. He told her he had found out about Mr. Porter embezzling funds, and he'd leak the evidence. She was sixteen." My hand tightens around the phone, thinking about how fucking scared she must have been. How helpless she must have felt.

"Mr. Porter was never a part of any embezzlement schemes."

Rage I've never felt has my entire frame trembling, my vision tinting. "It was him," I grit out. "Holden."

"Do you know how long he…Do you know at what age it stopped?"

As my heart races, burning in my chest, my vision tunnels, and I think back on every word she has said. It was a lot to process, and knowing the details of the first time it happened further darkened a piece of my already grey soul. I've never pictured murdering someone with my bare hands before.

"No," I rasp. "I don't know when it stopped."

He's quiet for a few seconds. "How well do you know this woman?"

"Jesus Christ, Gabe. Spit it the fuck out."

"It took me a few days, once I found his home IP, to hack into his personal computer. I needed him to click a link to give me access. Luckily, his malware is shit, and he clicks on anything involving escorts. When I got in, I gained access to everything. The ballsy fucker took pictures of her. The last photo was taken a few days before Mr. Daniel Porter spent a substantial amount on inpatient rehab for Tillie Porter."

She said she had been clean for sixteen months. I quickly do the math in my head.

"Nine years," I breathe out.

"I don't know who she is to you, but you need to tell her everything. Holden purchased two one-way tickets to Cuba and applied for a marriage license two months ago. She needs to go to the police. This man is dangerous, and he won't stop…Nine years, Quinn."

"Did you wipe his computer of the pictures?"

"If I wiped everything *Tillie Porter* from his computer, he could become aware someone is looking into him. We don't want that. It's also evidence if Tillie ever wants to come forward. I do want to send Mr. Porter evidence of Holden's embezzlement, though. He'll be able to do his own in-house investigation from there."

My mind races, and my stomach burns like I've swallowed acid. "Do what you need to do, but keep me updated."

As soon as the call ends, my fury pours out of me. A red haze clouds my vision as I tear through my apartment with my thoughts firing through my brain at rapid speed.

Nine fucking years.

He stole her innocence and then proceeded to take nine fucking years of her life away from her.

His lies and manipulation of a child turned into an addiction she couldn't find her way out of because of his continuous abuse.

By the time the red haze lifts, I'm panting, sweating, and crying. My apartment is trashed, and I have never felt so ashamed to have judged someone in my entire life.

Twelve

Tillie

BEFORE MOVING TO NOVARIDGE, the male species wasn't even on my radar, and now I have *two*— cousin's, no less—invading every thought. The bell above Nelly's door chimes out, where Nix and I agreed to celebrate his new job. He officially starts tomorrow, and even though he was upset with me for talking to Jansen behind his back, he seems optimistic. Plus, it's remote, so he'll be able to work from anywhere.

The farther we step into the room, the more my mouth waters and my stomach growls from the aroma of food and coffee. If there's one thing I'm glad to have back after recovery, it's my appetite.

We pick out a table by the window. He pulls my chair out for me, as he does every time we come here, which is once a week since he started staying with me.

"Are you excited about tomorrow?" I ask him, scooting my chair forward.

"I don't know," he says as he takes a seat and releases a sigh. "I *am* grateful he put in a good word for me, but I don't feel like I've earned it. It feels like I only got the job because Jansen knew someone and called in a favor." He shrugs.

I rest my hand atop his on the table. "*You* went to college. *You* got the degree, and while battling addiction toward the end. Everyone has to start somewhere. Maybe Jansen played a role in getting you the job, but plenty of people accept help in their careers to start."

He looks out the window, avoiding eye contact. "Don't feel like I deserve it, I guess."

Removing my hand from his, I sit back and take him in. Why do we believe the mistakes we've made determine the kind of life we get to live? We do the work, make amends, and *still*, we don't believe we're worth more than every bad decision we've ever made. Getting sober was excruciating—physically and emotionally. Accepting help from Dane and Presley had me choosing humility over pride. But forgiveness of oneself…I believe that can be the hardest decision a person can follow through with.

"Do you think I deserve good things, Nix?" I murmur.

His eyes, similar to his cousin's, snap to mine and narrow. "What?"

"I'm asking if I deserve a good life, or have the mistakes I've made determined how much good I'm allowed to accept?"

The two-seat tables in this diner are small, giving him enough room to lean forward and brush his lips against my cheek, causing my heart to kick up speed.

"You deserve every good thing in life, Tills," he whispers next to my ear. And the warmth of his breath brushing against my neck sends a quiver down my spine before he pulls back.

Intimacy had been an issue for me until I met Jansen. My head *and* my body align perfectly whenever he's near, but with Nix, my head sounds a firm no, while my body reacts heatedly.

The confusion must be written on my face because he smirks. My cheeks heat even more, and luckily, the waitress interrupts.

"What can I get you to drink?"

"I'll take an orange juice," I answer.

"I'll have a coffee. Black, please." Nix smiles politely.

"Do you all need a few minutes to order?" Her sight lingers on him, and I wait for the jealousy to arise that usually does whenever Bailee blatantly comes on to Jansen. It does not.

"I think we need a few more minutes. Thanks."

"No problem. I'll get your drinks out." She smiles at him, forgetting I exist, before walking away.

I waggle my brows when he looks my way again. He chuckles and folds his hands on the table.

"Anyway, how are you doing? I've heard you up at night."

He runs a hand through his hair. "I've been having trouble sleeping. I am so damn tired, Tills. I miss being able to crash."

"Maybe wearing your body out before bed would help."

His eyes flare, and mine widen when I realize what I've said and how it could be interpreted.

"Kayaking," I blurt out. "Or exercise. Plain exercise."

The waitress comes back with our drinks, saving me from further embarrassment, and we order our food while I mentally kick myself for my word vomit. This is a good time to go ahead and set a firm boundary between us.

We eat in comfortable silence while I stew over what to say.

Be honest. You're friends, and you want to remain friends.

"Nix, there's something I think we need to talk about."

"Don't."

"I only want to make sure we're on the same page."

He reaches for my hand on the table, squeezing. "Tillie, please. Don't. Don't count me out yet."

"I don't want you to wait for..." I pause, trying to think of a way to phrase it without sounding harsh.

"You're worth waiting for." The sincerity in his voice burrows into my chest.

Before I can speak again, he does. "He *will leave*, Tills. He always leaves. Jansen will not settle, and if that's the life you want, I'll accept it. But I won't go anywhere. I already know what you're about to say. I'm only asking you to think about it, and don't put me in a box, tucking me away."

"I'll always want you in my life. You've become my best friend."

His sigh is heavy and his smile small. "You've already done it, haven't you?"

Yes, and I know I don't need to say it out loud. Maybe I shouldn't have, though, because he's right. The thought alone of Jansen leaving for his next business venture causes my stomach to lurch. He'll obliterate the few fragments of my heart I have left.

On the other hand, Nix and I together could be a disaster. If one of us relapses, the chance of the other following suit is higher. Living with that perpetual fear in the back of my mind is daunting. As his friend, I can compartmentalize. Anything more intimate, and I wouldn't be able to.

Giving him false hope is wrong, but I also don't want to crush him with the finality of an answer when he already knows.

Instead, I smile and lean forward, giving his cheek a quick peck. "I'll get the bill."

I don't miss the way his throat works or his downcast gaze before making my way to the front of the diner.

Luckily, things between Nix and me aren't awkward after our chat. Ron invited all of us to his dock for a little cookout before we head out on the water.

"Can I help with anything?" I ask him while he mans the grill, flipping the steaks he's cooking.

"My grandsons can get some plates and drinks ready." He points the tongs he's holding at Jansen and Nix. "You're our guest, so you can continue to sit and relax."

The boys head inside right as my phone rings. "Hey, Presley," I answer.

"Something creepy just happened, and Dane said I needed to call and let you know."

I sit up a little taller at the slight tremble in her voice.

"What happened?"

"A man stopped by today looking for you. He said he was here on behalf of your dad, but he gave me the creeps. I told him we had no idea where you were, and if you wanted contact with your dad, you'd get in contact with him when you were ready. He got extremely pissed off, Tillie."

"I'm so sorry, Pres. What happened?"

"Dane was here when he started shouting and came to the door. He stood toe to toe with him and told him your whereabouts weren't any of his business, but if he came back to our house, he'd wish he hadn't."

Tense silence stretches between us as the freedom I'm fighting for turns into nothing but an illusion, and every breath slipping through my lips is labored.

"Tillie?" she asks over the line when I haven't responded.

What am I supposed to say? If something happens to them because of me, I will never forgive myself.

"I shouldn't have accepted your help. I'm sorry for putting your family in this situation," I rasp.

I've always kept my private life close to my chest, or tried to. I'd hoped he'd give up his search, but it's clear now he has no intention of doing that. He must be going around town, asking questions, pretending to be my dad's doting and concerned business partner. *He's always played the role of doting well enough.* The thought brings some clarity. My dad. My dad would've known about Presley.

The boys have walked out, but the adrenaline rushing through my body is taking over my senses. Jansen walks toward me, but I shake my head, walking to the parking lot.

I should have known getting away from Holden wouldn't be as easy as escaping my town and evading him when he wandered into Novaridge. He's a fucking incubus, but I'm wide awake now. I can never go back. If that means running forever, then I *will* run.

"If you want me to leave, I will, and I won't hold any resentment toward you at all."

Presley scoffs. "You're not going anywhere. If he comes back to my house, I'll call the police. We were going to come down and see you next week, but I think it would be best to wait another week or so."

The small voice in my head that's pleading with me to beg her not to call the police has me on the verge of tears. That would most certainly end up getting my dad in trouble, revealing my secrets, but she needs to protect her family. I'm twenty-five now. *I* will never do anything to put my dad at risk, but I can't ask the same from her. I refuse.

"Do whatever will keep your family safe. It would probably be best to wait," I choke out, emotional about the damage done.

"Tillie...Dane and I are not upset with you. If or when you're ready to tell us about what you've been through, we will be here. We're more worried about you, and Dane will deal with him if he comes back around."

"Thank you, Pres. I'm going to Cash App you some money again this Friday for the phone bill."

"Sounds good. I'll call you in a few days. Stay safe."

She knows not to refuse anymore. I've sent them money every time I've gotten paid since I started working. After pocketing my phone, I pace, picking the skin around my nails.

I don't have enough saved up yet to make it anywhere new. The car more than likely wouldn't make it much farther. Where would I even go? I could go farther south to Louisiana or Florida. Then again, going farther west would assure my safety even longer. California is pretty far.

"What's going on, Freckles?" Jansen's deep voice interrupts my thoughts. He's standing in front of me with his arms crossed.

When did he get there?

"He went to Presley's house. I'm thinking California," I ramble while resuming my pacing. "California would give me years without him finding me. I need to save enough for a new car and enough for a place to live once I get there."

He stalks toward me and pulls me into his arms, squeezing me and effectively ending my spiral.

Only when I am fully pliant in his arms does he speak again. "Are your friends okay?"

His voice is gruff, as if he's containing his emotions, and it's comforting how much he cares. Loosening his grip, he rests his chin atop my head, and I nod against his chest, not trusting my voice.

"Let's go out and have a good time, then we can talk everything through, yeah?" He pulls back, waiting for my answer.

"Okay," I whisper.

A black folding table and chairs are set up on Ron's upper deck. My chest warms at seeing all three of them together, sitting around the table. The steaks and baked potatoes look delicious, and I waste no time in plating food and taking my first bite.

"Have you let your parents know about your new employment?" Ron asks Nix.

His hand pauses in cutting his steak, but he shakes it off and answers, "Called Mom yesterday."

"Still haven't talked to your dad?"

Nix looks up at his Granddad with a blank face. "I don't think I will for a while."

"What happened there?" Jansen asks.

"His expectations," Nix answers, forking a piece of meat.

"So he cares and wants what's best for you." Jansen circles his fork in the air. "That's a bad thing?"

"You wouldn't understand, so drop it," Nix says with a set jaw and a hint of venom laced in his tone.

Sensing the tension, Ron speaks up. "Jansen, leave it be."

"Why wouldn't I understand, Nix?"

Ron only shakes his head and sighs, while Nix's jaw hardens. He is definitely baiting him right now, and I don't like it. Maybe this is what they need, though. To lay all of their discrepancies out on the table and move on.

"Because your dad died when you were young. You have no idea what it's like to live with a man who sees you as the version of himself he couldn't be. I have never been allowed to be *me*. He hated that I didn't want to play sports in school, even though I played them my whole childhood. He hated that I didn't want to work as much as possible while I was still in high school. That made me lazy. I went to college for computers instead of getting into a trade. That made me entitled. No, you have no fucking idea, Jansie. You've gotten to live without the burden of expectations."

Jansens sits back with a steely look on his face; the anger radiating from him is nearly suffocating. "Boo-fucking-hoo, Nix. Your daddy wanted you to be like him."

"Here we go," Ron mutters, resting his forehead in his palm.

"Fuck you, Jan—"

"No, fuck you, Nix. You had everything. You grew up with both of your parents and wanted for nothing. You had a mom who came home every night and gave a shit about where you were. You had a dad who made sure you had all of the tools to succeed in whatever you wanted to do. Remember when you got all into robotics and he stayed up all night with you before your school science fair? But he was a bastard, wasn't he?" Jansen snorts, shaking his head.

Nix looks ready to leap over the table. Red colors his entire face, and trembles rack through his body.

"He sat up with me that night because my mom made him, and he bitched the entire time. *'I have to get up for work in six hours, and I'm sitting here helping you with something that should be easy enough for you to figure out,'*" Nix finishes in a mocking voice.

Jansen's eyes narrow on his cousin.

"You only saw the bare minimum effort he put in because you always fucking disappeared. That robotics project was years ahead of what a ten-year-old kid should have been capable of. I did the entire project by myself, with his bitching voice as a companion. Not once did he say he was proud. He didn't even take off work early to see the science fair. You know nothing," he spits out before standing up.

The day has already gone to shit. Great. I look to Jansen, whose stare is fixed on Nix as he steps away. "I'm sorry, Nix. You're right. I obviously did not know everything."

Every muscle in Nix's back stiffens, like Jansen's words have physically shocked him. His shoulders tremble as he drops his head. When he turns around, we all see why. He does his best to blink the sheen away, but his chest continues to heave.

"I know you had it rough, Jansen. He never let me forget it. The boy without anyone, who pulled himself out of hell and made something of himself, while the boy with everything took it for granted. I've heard it more times than I can count." His voice cracks as his throat works to swallow the emotion trying to erupt.

He brings his fist to his chest, rubbing the spot, and looks at me, panicked. He doesn't want anyone to see him break down, least of all the man whom he looks up to the most.

"Nix?" Jansen stands.

I hold my hand out to keep him from moving. "We're going to get ready, and we'll both be back if he's still up for it."

Jansen goes to walk forward, but Ron wraps a hand around his bicep. "She's got him, son."

He looks back and forth between us before giving me a small nod.

The second we cross the houseboat's threshold, Nix breaks down. One guttural sob escapes his chest before he runs his palms up and down his face, pacing.

"What the fuck is happening?" he whisper-shouts as he knocks his fist into his head.

I walk over to him, wrapping my hand around his wrist to stop his self-assault. "Please stop," I plead. "It's okay. It was a tough situation to talk about, and your emotions are probably more heightened right now."

He pulls me into him, wrapping his arms around me like a vise. "This is a safe space to feel how you want. Let it out, Nix," I murmur into his chest.

When I pull back, his hand palms the side of my face, and he tilts his head down. I turn at the last second, causing his lips to graze my cheek.

"Please, Tills," he whispers next to my ear.

"Nix," I breathe out, trying to back away from him, but his hold tightens.

"Tillie, please. I don't want to feel like this anymore," he chokes out, causing my chest to tighten.

His gaze roams a path between my eyes and lips. When I don't move, he dips his head down again before his mouth covers mine.

I stand frozen.

Am I sure I want this to happen?

I knew he was going to kiss me.

I never feel this hesitation or trepidation with Jansen.

My lips start to move with his.

An almost nauseous feeling in the pit of my stomach screams that this isn't right, but the warmth spreading through my core tells me it's not wrong at all. With our mouths still fused, he pushes me backward until my ass bumps into the small dinette table. His hands palm my waist, setting me on top of it as he fits his body between my legs. He runs his hands down my thighs, wrapping them around his waist.

Why didn't I do that?

He grinds his hips into my pelvis and groans, and a shock of pleasure pulses through my core, but instead of feeling like I don't want to stop, I feel sick. The confusion about my feelings has me backing away from him.

His eyes are heavy-lidded, full of lust, and I stay perfectly still as he brings his lips to my forehead. I push him back lightly with both palms on his chest and somehow manage to smile through the nausea building in my throat. "Let's get back."

Thirteen

Jansen

The sound of our paddles slicing through the water fills the silence, and it's obvious something is off with these two. Nix keeps side-eyeing her like he's scared she'll disappear, and Tillie is trying her best to ignore it, acting like everything is normal.

I'm positive nothing major—like fucking my cousin—has happened, and I try my best to tamp down this illogical jealousy raging through me because something *did* happen. Something that has her feeling noticeably uncomfortable. *Nix isn't Holden*, I remind myself. He was emotional when they left, so they probably had words. They're friends, so I'm sure it'll blow over, but I'll be asking her later.

"We're going to pull the kayaks out over there," I call out, pointing east toward a narrow cove.

Once we've paddled in as far as we can onto the bank, I jump out and hold my hand out for her to grab so she doesn't trip. When the kayak wobbles, she starts to fall sideways, and I grab her waist, lifting her out. Nix already has his kayak pulled onto the bank.

"Did Granddad ever bring you out here?" I ask him.

"A couple of times, yeah. There's a path to a rock ledge for cliff jumping, right?"

Tillie's eyes widen. "That's dangerous, isn't it?"

We both chuckle.

"We've never gotten hurt. The water is about twenty-five feet deep," I assure her. "For now, we can swim around if you want, or I brought some towels to lie out on."

I scan the cream linen long-sleeve shirt she has on with the sleeves rolled up to right below her elbow, paired with frayed blue jean shorts that hug her hips and thighs.

"Are you wearing anything you can swim in under your clothes?"

Nix speaks up. "I don't know why you wore a long-sleeved shirt, as hot as it is today."

Her cheeks turn red, and she narrows her gaze at him. "I wore my bathing suit."

A sheepish expression contorts his face before he looks away and lifts his shirt over his head.

She slides her jean shorts down her legs to reveal the one-piece black bathing suit with the sides cut out. Her cleavage is on full display, and I can't help but stare at her in awe.

"Earth to Jansen." She chuckles, laying out the blue striped towel I brought and sitting down.

A splash sounds, and I look over my shoulder to see Nix in the water.

"Is he good?" I ask her, nodding to him.

She brings her knees to her chest, wrapping her arms around them. "He got emotionally overwhelmed, but he's fine."

Pulling out another towel, I lay it beside hers. "How has he been with staying sober?"

After straightening her legs out, she leans back on her hands. "He's having trouble sleeping. I can tell he tries to hide his irritability, but it's there nonetheless. Hopefully, this new job will keep his mind busy."

"I'm sure it will. Security consulting is rigorous work, and the guy he'll be working for stays busy. He'll learn the engineering aspect of it too."

"Do you know the guy he'll be working for?"

I strip my shirt over my head and lean back on my forearms. "Gabe is one of the longest friendships I've had. We met in college."

I glance at her, catching her staring down the length of my body, and she blushes. I'm not heavily muscular, but I do stay in shape. Right now, her gaze is caught on the burn scar on my left side. As I got older and grew, it shrank, but it still takes up space. She surprises me when she doesn't ask about it.

"Because you move around a lot?" she asks, lying back completely and fixing her stare on the sky.

"That, and people tend to disappoint you the longer you give them."

She hums her acknowledgment or agreement. "Have you ever been in a relationship?"

"Nothing serious. It'd be unfair to ask someone to wait for me while I'm gone. This life isn't for everyone."

She turns her head my way, squinting at me. "You've never thought of a woman traveling *with you* as a possibility?"

"I've never cared enough about someone to consider the possibility." *Until you*, but I don't say the thought aloud. "Besides. Women my age want stability. A permanent structure to come home to. Kids to take to soccer practice. Christmases with matching pajamas."

"And you don't want any of those things?"

I'm starting to feel like I'm being interrogated or interviewed. I know it isn't her intention, but I like to keep my life private.

Shrugging my shoulders, I clear my throat. "I've never felt a desire for it."

She faces the sky again and closes her lids; meanwhile, I take my time looking at every inch of her. From her creamy legs and thighs down to her bare feet with toenails painted baby blue. A yellow, white, and green braided bracelet is tied around her ankle.

She opens her mouth to say something else when Nix's voice echoes from above.

"You're next, Jansie," he shouts from the top of the cliff across the bank on the other side. He backs up and takes off running toward the edge, leaping from it.

"*Wooooo*." His shout echoes.

Tillie gasps as she sits up completely. Nix's body hits the water feet-first with a splash, and we wait for him to break the surface. When he does, both of us relax our shoulders. The difference between my early twenties and my thirties is that I'm more consciously aware my time on this earth is limited. It makes risky moments like these less enjoyable, if I'm honest.

"I am *not* doing that," she exclaims, looking at me with wide eyes.

I chuckle, noticing the sweat beading on her forehead.

"Why don't you take the shirt off?" I suggest. "You've got to be burning up."

She looks away, clearing her throat and adjusting her rolled-up sleeves. "I'm fine. It's not too hot."

"The weatherman and sweat on your body say otherwise," I counter.

"Drop it, Jansen." She stands, stalking over to the kayak. "I'm going to do a quick lap."

"Alone?" I'm already up and walking toward her.

"I'm *twenty*-five, not five. I'll be quick." She pulls the kayak to the edge of the bank.

"I'll at least help you get in," I offer.

"Your help isn't needed. I—" Her body tips, unbalanced, and I make it just in time to pull her toward me, our bodies flush.

"You were saying," I breathe out.

She scowls, both hands still wrapped around my biceps. "Will you help me get in?"

"Wasn't so hard, was it?" For dramatic effect, I bop her nose with my pointer finger, grinning cheekily.

She bats my hand away and scoffs, using my arm for balance as she gets settled.

"I'd rather do things myself so I don't end up disappointing you with any kind of dependency," she responds while pushing away from the bank with the paddle.

Her takeaway wasn't even in the ballpark of my meaning when I said that earlier, but it seems to have struck a nerve in her.

Before she gets too far, I call out, "Your dependency on me would never be a disappointment."

I *want* her to feel like she can depend on me. She's going to need someone to lean on when she finds out the truth about her dad, and maybe it shouldn't be, because I'm leaving once I have a new job lined up, but I'm set on making sure that person is me.

"Where's she headed to?" Nix asks, shaking his hair out and catching his breath from the swim back.

"No idea. Probably to catch a breeze since she won't take her damn shirt off." Placing my hands on my hips, I watch her paddle around the corner.

"You haven't figured it out?" he asks haughtily, shaking his head. "She only wears long sleeves around you. When you're not around, she has no problems with short-sleeve shirts or tank tops."

"Did she say anything to you about it?" I don't believe I'm the only person she wears long sleeves around. She wears flannels to work, but...I'm there. Now that I think about it, I haven't seen her in a shirt with short sleeves since the night I gave her a T-shirt, but she came out of the bathroom and went straight to bed. And the interview.

The interview where I saw the scars on the inside of her elbow and called her out. *Fuck.* How will she ever be able to depend on me for anything if she doesn't even feel comfortable enough to show her damn arms?

Nix towels off his hair before laying it out and lying back to dry. "She didn't need to say anything. Anytime you're around, she grabs a cardigan or something to hide the needle marks I'm sure you called her out on at some point."

Fair and annoyingly fucking accurate observation there, little cousin.

"Yeah, well...that shit ends today." I take a seat on the bank and wait for her to paddle back.

Fourteen

Tillie

I THOUGHT ABOUT PADDLING back to Ron's but knew both of them would be worried if I didn't come back. Jansen confirmed everything Nix told me at the diner. He'll leave—he always does. And I've already formed some sort of emotional attachment to him. He's the only person who knows about Holden. He's the only person my mind and body simultaneously haven't hesitated with when he touches me, but he *is* right.

I'll only end up disappointing him.

Then there's Nix, and I've never been more confused about him. We've grown close, binge-watching shows together, talking about his life, eating ice cream on the dock every night I'm home since we both have a sweet tooth, and hanging out with Ron. I can relate to him. A small piece of us reflects the other. It's a dark piece, but a piece nonetheless.

Those thoughts spiraled into me thinking about Rhett. I hope Lucy can heal from whatever she's been through so she can see Rhett for the gift he is. I'll admit it doesn't hurt as badly as it should, and I know that's because, while I was his confidant, I never allowed him a chance to be mine.

How bad would it hurt right now if I had?

How bad will it hurt when Jansen leaves?

When the bank comes back into view, the man who consumes most of my thoughts stands with his hands on his hips, waiting. The yellow trunks he has on complement his tan skin. I've never appreciated the male form, but my eyes eat him up. Even from this distance, I can see the bulge of his biceps, defined abs, and a toned chest. I didn't ask about the scar on his side, but now I'm even more curious about it.

Nix catches my attention as he lifts onto his forearms. From this distance, they resemble each other even more, except for the difference in hair color and build. He looks from me to Jansen, then back to me, before lying back down and covering his face with his arm.

The closer I get to the bank, the more obvious Jansen's agitation becomes. I'm about to begin paddling backward when he lifts his chin with a steely gaze and waves me in. It's disgustingly attractive, and I find myself continuing toward him.

As soon as the front of the kayak touches land, he pulls it up enough to loop an arm under both of mine, before I can even attempt to stand, and pulls me out.

Once I'm on my feet, he takes a light hold of my wrist. "We're going to take a walk."

I scoff at the demand in his tone. "And if I don't want to?"

He looks back at me. "Then I'll throw you over my shoulder and carry you. Either way works."

I dig my heels into the ground hard enough that he jerks to a stop.

"Ask me nicely." I smile sweetly at him, batting my lashes.

Nix snickers from where he's lying, and Jansen's nostrils flare as we stare at each other.

"Please," he grits out. I can tell he's agitated, but my fight or flight doesn't exist around him, and maybe I'm testing his patience to prove something to myself. To prove that I can push him, and he'd never hurt me.

"Please, what?" I ask in a sickly-sweet tone.

Nix belts out a laugh. "He's going to have an aneurysm, Tills."

My smile widens when Jansen glares, but then he smirks with a devilish glint in his eye.

Before I can move, he's got his hands around my waist, and I'm hauled over his shoulder like a sack of potatoes as he takes off into the woods.

"*Okay. Okay*," I call out, trying to wriggle down. "I'll walk."

A second and a quick snap of his wrist later, a slight sting has heat building behind my hips.

"Too late."

My jaw practically unhinges. "Did you just *spank* me?"

"Been wanting to do that for a while now," he gruffs.

The shock of the sting and the fact I liked it haven't quite ebbed yet, but the longer he walks, the more self-conscious I feel.

Wriggling again, I attempt to lift my upper body. "Jansen, I'm heavy and you're going to hurt yourself."

Another snap of his wrist, and I gasp. His palm covers the area he slapped and kneads, causing a throbbing ache to form between my legs.

"Your body is perfection, and to suggest I couldn't carry you another mile is honestly insulting." He stops and slides me down his body.

I'm speechless, looking up at him.

"Take your shirt off," he demands, keeping eye contact.

I look away as my cheeks heat, but he slides a finger under my chin, tilting it to face him again.

"Take. Your. Shirt. Off," he demands again, and a shaky breath passes through my lips.

"No," I rasp.

"You do it, or I will, and I don't want to have to do that."

I back away from him, and he lets me, placing his hands in the pockets of his trunks, I'm assuming to restrain them.

"Please stop. Okay?"

His mouth opens, but I continue, cutting him off.

"I've told you the most vulnerable thing about myself and how disgusting it makes me feel."

His spine straightens, and a muscle twitches in his jaw. "And I assured you that night I couldn't and will never be disgusted by you."

"You did. You never once looked at me in disgust when I told you, but when you saw my arm. The look on your face—that was disgust."

My voice cracks as the memory of his face—lip curled and stony expression—replays in my mind. "I don't care about anyone else's opinion of my past choices, but I do care about yours. Because you know things nobody else does, and if you looked at me with disgust again, I think it would break me."

Without a word, he's in front of me, lifting me by the waist. My legs wrap around his automatically. He sways me side to side with his face buried in my neck and my arms strangling his. I breathe in his familiar scent of spice and leather mixed with his natural musk from the heat. In this moment, I realize I've never felt this level of intimacy with another person. It's lifting an invisible weight of fear that's sat heavily on my chest from the belief that I'd never truly be capable of it.

"I know I've been an ass, but I need you to trust me like you did that night." He pulls his face back to look at me, putting space between us. "Take your shirt off."

I sigh, releasing my legs from his waist. When my feet are back on the ground, I back up a couple of steps, pulling each arm out of the linen sleeves and letting the shirt fall. Looking away out of fear would be too easy, so I force myself to stare him in the eye.

His hand reaches for my wrist, lifting my arm, and he places a soft kiss on the inside of my elbow atop the tiny scars. My chest heaves with the sob working its way up my throat.

Releasing my arm, he pulls me into him, cradling my head against his warm, solid chest. Every thud of his heartbeat fills my ear. "I don't want you to hide any part of yourself from me, Freckles. I want it all."

A throat clears feet away from us, and I turn to find Nix standing there with a forlorn expression. "Ready to head back?"

"We're coming," I say with a small smile.

My body may be confused about Nix, but my mind isn't, and he has to know that what happened earlier can't happen again.

After making it to the dock and tying up the kayaks, we all three sit side by side to catch our breath after the paddle back.

"Granddad said you two were going fishing a little later?" Jansen asks Nix.

He nods. "Yeah. I'm trying to limit downtime."

"Do you want to come back to the bar with me?" Jansen's gaze clashes with mine.

The smile on my face and giddy feeling in my stomach have me feeling like a teenager with a crush. "I need to change, and I'll meet you back over here."

I throw on denim shorts and a black tank top with a flannel tied around my waist. When I come out of my room, Nix is sitting on the couch with his forearms resting on his thighs.

"He's going to break your heart, Tills," he says roughly, staring at the ground.

I take the seat beside him, resting my temple against his shoulder. "You're probably right."

He turns sideways, forcing me to look at him. The hurt on his face is evident, and the incredulity in his voice has my gaze falling to my hands in my lap when he asks, "Then, why? Why put yourself through it if you already know how it'll end?"

"Has anyone ever broken your heart? The kind of broken that has you lying in bed for days and wondering how you'll survive the remainder of your life without them. The kind of broken that has you choosing silence over music or solitude over company because being around other people laughing and living while your world is tinged in grey seems unbearable."

His throat works. "My first serious girlfriend senior year. We'd been together since the summer before, talked about what our future would look like, and right before graduation, she decided long distance wouldn't work for her. It was hell."

"I've never experienced that, and maybe all of us should at least once in our lives."

"Why would you want to?" he muses.

"I've had bits and pieces of my soul stolen from me, but never my heart. I'm not sure if I'll ever be able to fully share it with another person. But I want to find out, Nix." Emotion clogs my throat. "I care about you more than I probably express, and for some reason, I feel things for your asshat cousin I can't explain but want to figure out."

Questions swirl behind those hazel eyes, but instead of asking, he sighs heavily. "I can't be your second choice when he fucks up."

"No. You deserve to be someone's first choice," I say sincerely.

He swipes his palms up his face, pushing his hair back. "I won't lie to you and say this doesn't majorly suck, but I also care too much about you to push you away because of it. You're my angel. I want you in my life in whatever way I can have you."

A small smile tilts my lips while I nod. I drew the line and set the boundary. This has the potential to get messy, but if we can be honest with each other, I don't see why our relationship has to change. Maybe it's wishful thinking, maybe I'm being selfish, maybe I'll get my heart broken times two, and both of these men will own their pieces of it forever.

"Hey, Tills?" he calls out before I can make it out the door.

"Yeah?"

"How'd you know to explain heartbreak if you've never felt it?"

"Romance movies and a few romance books." Forcing a small grin, I shrug.

My dad taught me the most about heartbreak. When he'd start to miss the wife who abandoned him, he'd throw himself into work. Long hours and late nights. It'd last a few weeks before he'd snap himself out of it and make up for our lost time together. I once asked him why he didn't date, and his answer was simple but heartbreaking. He had nothing left to give.

"Right." Nix rests his back on the couch with his mouth tipping at the corners. "Speaking of which, I'll wait for you to watch the next episode of *Emily in Paris*."

"As if you'd even know about that show without me. I'll see you tonight," I tell him as I walk out the door, back to the man who could help heal or obliterate my heart, and the unknown about which feels more exhilarating than terrifying.

Fifteen

Jansen

TALL TREES LINE THE road on either side, and a random song from my playlist fills the cab. I've traveled to many places over the last decade, but nothing compares to driving down an open road, no traffic, only surrounded by nature.

The silence, however, becomes uncomfortable the longer I wait to ask the question I've been wondering. "What happened with Nix?"

"I already told you. He got emotional." Her answer is quick, automatic.

I glance over at her to find her gaze locked on the windshield in front of her. Something definitely happened, and now I'm even more curious.

"I asked if he was good earlier. Now I'm asking what happened between the two of you before we went kayaking?"

From the corner of my eye, I see her shift uncomfortably, and when I glance over again, she refuses to look at me. Reaching over, I place my palm on her exposed upper thigh, giving it a light squeeze. "You can tell me, Freckles."

I send a silent plea into the universe that he hasn't touched a single part of her in a way I haven't.

"Don't do that," she says, and when I look over, she's glaring at my hand.

Feeling like an ass and an idiot for not considering how she'd feel being touched, I start to pull my hand back, but she holds it in place, interlacing her fingers with mine.

"Don't use affection to manipulate me into telling you something. If you truly want to know, I'll tell you."

"I didn't touch you to convince you to tell me anything. I touched you because keeping my hands off you is damn near physically impossible."

She threw her hair into a clip before meeting me at the Jeep. And I love how the soft strands left out frame her face, which is bare, the freckles I love standing out. She's easily the most stunning woman I've ever seen, and she doesn't even try. She has no idea of the effect she has on the men around her. The men in the bar stare longingly. My cousin looks at her like he's a puppy dog waiting to be leashed. Me…

"Sorry. This is all new to me. I wasn't trying to accuse you of anything."

"I need you to," I plead, lightly squeezing her thigh again as I pull into Clovers' full lot. "You have to tell me if I do something you don't like. You have to communicate with me because I will hate myself if I do something you aren't okay with after everything you've been through."

Killing the engine, I turn all of my attention on her and find her staring at me with emeralds revealing every bit of lust she feels. Even the shape of her eyes adds to her natural sultriness. A cat-eye is what I'd use to describe them, and when she wears her usual eye makeup, it only enhances the look.

"You'll never touch me in a way I won't want, Jansen." She bites her full bottom lip and sighs, resting her temple on the seat. "He kissed me."

An unfamiliar sense of possession rises within me like a tide. By the look on her face, I'm not hiding it very well.

"Did you kiss him back?" I grit out.

"I…didn't stop it right away, but I ended up backing away. Before leaving to come with you, I made sure he knew how I felt."

"And how's that?" The *thought* of him touching her made me feel sick, and now I *know* he has. This whole ordeal is a little fucked, yet I still can't convince myself to drive her home and keep her at arm's length.

The way her throat works and the vulnerability she's failing to hide as her gaze wanders tell me she's not used to expressing her feelings. So I wait.

Her eyes come back to mine with a sheen filling them, but she speaks evenly. "I care about him, and you can be angry, but you can't let your relationship with him fall apart because of me. He needs you."

I don't respond because right now, I'm disgustingly furious that he knows how she tastes, but I also love him. He's the closest thing I have to a brother, and I don't want to lose him. She also used that as a deflection. That's not what she wanted to say; it was the easiest thing to admit because it had nothing to do with her feelings toward me.

After another minute or two of silence, I run my palm down her thigh, giving it one more squeeze, before opening my door and heading to her side to open hers. Through the passenger window, I notice her shaking her head while mumbling something.

As soon as I open the door, she immediately turns toward me and lets her thoughts spew through her lips. "If anyone is going to truly break my heart for the first time, I want it to be you. It *has* to be you. When this job is done, you'll leave, and I accept that because, when the time comes, I'll be leaving too. In another direction, on another adventure."

Her words are branded onto a bullet that's just lodged itself into the organ in my chest that's already taken one too many beatings.

I'm stunned silent as she steps out from the passenger seat and shuts the door. Leaning against it, she waits for me to have some type of reaction to her words. I'm a thirty-one-year-old bachelor who travels for a living. Flings are what have sustained me, and I've broken a few hearts along the way.

Talia, who called me for months. It was rough, but eventually, I changed my number, and I'm hoping she moved on happily.

Sammi, who swore she knew the score, ended up begging to come with me to my next job. She acted like I'd led her on. Like I was a heartless monster, and maybe I was because only a small part of me felt any kind of guilt in response to her pain.

"How are you going to let me go if you're already sure I'm going to break your heart? I won't ask you to give up your life for the kind I live."

Her deadpan expression doesn't change. "The same way I let Rhett go. I hugged him, told him thanks, and drove away."

"Did you love him?"

She twists her lips to the side thoughtfully. "Not in the way I should have, but he was the only constant in my life for years. He was the only person I could call if I was in trouble. Losing him was like losing a safety net. It wasn't fair to him, but it still hurt regardless."

"Have you talked to him since?" I fail to hide the slight edge in my voice. She may defend him, but I don't like the idea of her with anyone from that fucked-up town.

She steps toe to toe with me, tilting her head back to catch my eye, and smirks. "No, I've been pretty wrapped up in other...things."

Placing my palm on the small of her back, I push her body flush with mine and drop my forehead to hers.

"What if I can't stand the thought of hurting you?" I murmur.

Her response is quiet but sure. "Then take me home, and the next time you see me, I'll only be your employee. Or..." She pauses, tilting her chin back to look me in the eye. "Let me make this one decision for myself, and believe me when I tell you I'll let you walk away without making a scene."

The lampposts outside the bar have turned on now that the sun is setting, casting a glow over her dark hair and fair skin, making her look ethereal.

My lips move against hers as I say, "I should. I should drive you home right now, but I can't. Control has been my oxygen since I turned eighteen, but for you, I'd gladly fall to my knees and suffocate."

She brings her palms to the back of my neck, squeezing. "Careful, Jansen. You wouldn't want me to believe you've already fallen."

Chuckling, I take her full bottom lip between my teeth and tug, then slide my tongue along it to soothe the sting. But when her lips try to meet mine, I pull back with valiant effort.

Her face doesn't show confusion or hurt, only her agitation. So I raise a brow, smirking. "Can't have you believing I've fallen, Freckles."

In response to my antics, I'm blessed with her sexy, husky laugh. "Is it karaoke night?"

"It is." I wait, seeing if we've moved on from the conversation beforehand.

"Let's go inside. I've never been here as a patron." She winks, strutting ahead of me.

The full parking lot was an indicator of how busy we are tonight, but I still love walking in here and seeing the restored life in this place. It's why I do what I do.

"Tillie," a familiar voice calls out. Ivy walks up, wrapping her arms around her, and I spot her slight recoil before she relaxes. A surge of protectiveness rises within me, even though Ivy meant no harm. She's tipsy, and tipsy Ivy equals affectionate Ivy.

"You look like you're having the best time." Tillie giggles, raising a brow. "I thought you just turned twenty?"

Ivy rolls her eyes dramatically, scoffing. "I pregamed before coming in." She looks at me. "Don't worry, Boss."

I chuckle at her antics, and a quick glance at the bar makes it obvious Mason is slammed with drink orders. "Mason's bartending, so I know I have nothing to worry about."

Her features pinch, and Tillie reaches for her hand, giving it a light squeeze.

What am I missing?

"Oh my God, you have to come meet my friends. They're down to earth. Total girl's girls." She hits Tillie with pleading eyes, and I nudge her shoulder with mine.

"Go ahead. I'm going to help Mason with this rush, and I'll find you when it calms down a bit."

A girlish excitement radiates from the woman who never got to have these experiences. Her lips twitch as she turns her head to stare up at me. "You sure?"

"Absolutely. Go have fun. I'll be behind the bar." I go to kiss her cheek and pause. We haven't talked about PDA or whether showing affection in her place of employment, where I'm her boss, would make her uncomfortable.

Without missing a beat, she captures my lips for a quick kiss and then moves to walk away with Ivy, but something inside me has awakened. She's about to walk off in shorts that make her ass look even more perfect and a fitted black tank top, showcasing a hint of her cleavage and hourglass figure.

Every guy in this place would need to be half blind not to notice her, so I grab her hand, pull her back to me, and make sure anyone watching knows exactly who she's here with tonight.

A sigh mixed with a whimper passes through her lips as my tongue massages hers. And when I pull back, her face is flushed, lips swollen, and my cock is about to bust. She nuzzles her nose against mine before lowering back onto the heels of her feet.

Ivy chokes out a laugh. "Hottest thing I've ever seen in my life."

Tillie rolls her eyes playfully, grabbing Ivy by the hand and dragging her off as I chuckle, making my way behind the bar.

"So...you and Tillie, huh? When did that happen?" Mason asks while mixing a whiskey sour.

"It's new. You and Ivy?" I ask with a raised brow, crossing my arms.

He scoffs but keeps working, avoiding eye contact. "She's twenty years old, man. I'm twenty-eight. I'm ready to settle down, and she's just started her life. Can you pour the drafts?"

I scrub a hand over my jaw before getting to work.

"Have you asked her what she wants?" I ask him a few minutes later, once we've caught up on orders. The younger crowd typically orders whatever's on tap, but we've got quite a few middle-aged patrons tonight, and they tend to enjoy the cocktails and whiskey.

Looking out over the bar, I find Tillie with Ivy and the two other girls she's come in with before. Tillie adamantly shakes her head, but Ivy sticks her lip out, steepling her hands under her chin. The moment she drops her head, shaking it, I chuckle at how easily she caved to whatever Ivy is up to.

"I'm pretty sure she's too young to even know what she wants." He sighs, peeking across the room at her.

Who the hell am I to argue, having not the slightest clue about Ivy outside of this place.

We both stand a little straighter when the two women fucking with our heads walk to the front and stand in front of the microphones. The music starts playing, and Mason groans while I cough to cover up my laughter because Ivy is making a bold statement with her song choice. The beginning of "My Happy Ending" by Avril Lavigne fills the space, and the crowd goes wild. This is one of those early-2000s pop songs that'll stick around.

"Can I get a Guinness on tap?" a young guy asks.

"Got your ID?" Rule one of managing a bar. *Everyone* gets carded if they look younger than forty. If you can't tell, card them.

As he's pulling his license from his pocket, Tillie's voice filters through the room, causing me and the patron to pause what we're doing to look toward her.

Her voice is raspy and so fucking beautiful. She's a siren, and we're all entranced.

"Hey, what do you think she'd like to drink?" He nods toward Freckles, and my blood pressure spikes.

"She doesn't drink," I deadpan.

"You sure?"

This fucking guy.

"She's mine. I'm sure," I say, setting his drink down in front of him forcefully enough liquid sloshes over the rim.

He smirks. "And the other one?"

Smarmy little bastard.

"She's his." I nod to Mason, who's not doing a good job of hiding his feelings surrounding her, noting he doesn't disagree in front of *smarmy little bastard*. He puts a hand up in surrender, walking back to wherever he came from.

It's nearing the end of the song, and they both harmonize their voices. Ivy's is higher, while Tillie's is lower and richer. They both sound incredible together, but my girl is almost hypnotic.

Mason huffs, leaning on the bar. "We're so fucked."

I catch Tillie's eye, winking at her, and the smile she gives me is one I haven't seen before. It's pure glee.

Yes. We are.

Sixteen

Tillie

I haven't done anything so nerve-racking since I was a kid. Since *before*. "Thank you. That was kind of terrifying but fun."

"If I'd known your voice was so good, I would've convinced one of these bitches." She laughs.

Brynn scoffs, flipping her hair over her shoulder. She's twenty-two, was on the high school dance team with Ivy, and is home from college. Her long, thick, wavy dark hair falls down her back. Her cheekbones are prominent, with ocean-blue eyes and thick lashes. She's gorgeous.

Harley snorts. "She was like this with dance too. Very competitive." She's nineteen and Brynn's younger sister. Her hair isn't wavy or dark. It's a medium blond that she has in a slicked-back ponytail, but her eyes are a similar color, and she, too, is blessed with the cheekbones of a goddess.

Both girls have been extremely welcoming and eager for all the "tea" on my and Jansen's relationship. I can't blame them. The man is a walking wet dream, but the tea over here isn't piping hot...yet.

I've never cared much about what I looked like. After Holden, I did everything to appear as plain as possible. It never mattered, but damn did I try. Baggy clothes, messy buns, no makeup. Once the drug habit kicked off, I had even more reason, or none, to give a shit.

These girls are between three and six years younger than I am, but I feel a decade older. Maybe I even look a decade older. It's hard to think about what I've put my body through these past nine years. It's hard for my mind to conjure up an accurate depiction of what I look like because when I'm out and about, the grit of my trauma covers me from head to toe, distorting my mind's view, and I only find relief in a mirror until I have to walk around again without the visual reassurance.

Ivy sticks her tongue out and mocks Harley. Then both girls straighten up a little, and Brynn's cheeks turn a soft pink shade.

A solid mass presses against my shoulder, and when I turn, Jansen is there looking down at me. "You ready to go?"

"She hasn't gotten to have a drink with us yet." Ivy pouts.

"I don't drink."

"She doesn't drink," we say in tandem.

I look up at him in confusion because *what the hell?* Why bring me here if he was going to take me home thirty minutes after walking in?

"We haven't even been here an hour yet," I say incredulously.

He smirks, raising a brow. "I'm not taking you home, Freckles. We're going up to my apartment."

My mouth forms an O while my cheeks heat and butterflies swarm my stomach. It's such a foreign feeling; it's hard to hide my gasp of excitement, but I manage it. Barely.

Ivy and the girls snicker. "We'll do this again soon, girl. Go have fun."

Jansen holds his hand out, and I accept it as he leads me through the tables of people. When we pass the bar, I spot a familiar pinched face with the most hateful look plastered on it. If looks could kill, I'd be incinerated to ash.

"Shit," I mumble, breaking eye contact with Bailee and letting go of Jansen's hand.

He pauses his steps and looks down at his hand as if I severed a piece of it. With a furrowed brow, he looks around, and I notice the moment he spots her. Keeping eye contact with her, he palms my waist, pulling me toward him, and his other hand entwines in my hair as his lips meet mine.

This little stunt of his will cost me my sanity the next time I work with her, but he's the boss, so he'll ultimately have to deal with her crazy. PDA isn't something I've ever been into, but I love the way he claimed me earlier in front of everyone and the way he's claiming me now. The world falls away, and the noise in the bar dims over my heartbeat thudding in my ears. When he pulls back, he kisses a trail from the corner of my mouth to my ear.

"You really are a siren," he whispers, causing a shiver to race down my spine.

"And I've lured an Adonis. Lucky me," I breathe out.

With Bailee forgotten, he takes my hand, leading me down the hallway and up the stairs to his apartment.

Nerves slam into me full force.

Because yes, I want to experience everything possible with Jansen while I can, but there's a very real possibility I'll disappoint him.

What if I'm not good?

What if I panic?

What if I'm self-conscious the whole time and ruin it?

My mouth dries, and my breathing turns shallow as he guides us through the door. He turns and pauses, taking in my face.

"Hey, what's wrong?" he asks, wrapping a palm around the nape of my neck and rubbing his thumb over my pulse, which matches the pace of a hummingbird's wings.

I focus my sight on the couch behind him. "I don't want to disappoint you."

Still staring at the furniture, I don't see his face but hear the confusion in his voice. "How in the hell could you disappoint me?"

My aggravation settles in because being vulnerable about my feelings or thoughts is new, and I wish he could understand without me having to explain it.

A frustrated sigh passes through my lips before I can stop it. "Because...Because I've never done this...like this, and I don't want you to hate it or be disappointed with...me."

"Look at me."

"No." I hate this feeling. Vulnerability feels a lot like weakness.

"Look. At. Me." The demand in his tone has my eyes snapping to his.

"We only ever have to go as far as you're comfortable with—"

"And there you go again." I cut him off, walking past him to create some distance between us before turning to face him again.

He places his hands on his hips, letting out an exasperated sigh, and tilts his head toward the ceiling. "Where have I gone?"

"Victimizing me. You see me as some traumatized woman. Scared to touch me or do what you're dying to because you're afraid I'll cower or freak out."

His eyes harden, and the muscles in his jaw twitch. "You *are* a victim."

I go to cut him off, but he raises a hand. "No," he grits out while walking toward me. "You're *also* a survivor and a beautiful woman. I don't pause because of either of those things. I don't pull back out of fear you'll cower. I pull back because we're getting to know each other, and your consent is the most important thing to me. Until I know you like the back of my fucking hand, I *will* pause. I *will ask* for reassurance that whatever I'm doing is what you want."

Wrapping my arms protectively around my middle, I drop my chin, ashamed for lashing out. "If I were normal, you wouldn't need reassurance."

He places a finger under my chin, tilting it up. A soft, gentle expression rests on his handsome face. "Reassurance is consent, and consent *is* normal, Freckles."

His words have my throat closing from the effort it's taking to hold in my emotions. "I'm ruining this," I choke out.

Pulling me into him, he cradles my head against his chest. "You've ruined nothing. I'm more than happy just being near you. Plus, I didn't bring you here for sex. I..." His words drift off, and his heart rate picks up, beating rapidly in my ear.

Every beat of my heart quickens to match his rhythm, and I place my hands on his waist as I lean back to catch his eye. "What is it?"

You know the feeling—plain intuition—you get when your world is about to be turned upside down?

Do you run away?

Do you cover your ears, blocking the noise?

But your nosy-ass subconscious has already decided for you. His face takes on an eerily blank expression. It's almost like his mind is at war with itself right now, and it's freaking me the hell out.

"Jansen. What is it?" I ask more firmly.

He blinks and slides his palms down my arms before grabbing my hand and tugging me toward the couch to sit.

"Do you remember the friend I told you about, Gabe?"

"Yeaaaah." I drag the word out, confused.

"He's a hacker. When you told me about Holden, I asked him to gather as much information as he could on him."

My pulse skyrockets. "Why? Why would you do that?"

It means he likely knows...everything.

A storm gathers in his eyes, darkening them while a violent energy radiates from him. "Because I don't want that vile fucking asshole anywhere near you ever again, and I wanted to get as much dirt as possible on him."

A flicker of hope warms my chest. "Did you find anything?"

With one look from him, the flicker is gone, leaving a cold chasm.

His shoulders rise as he takes a deep inhale. The words that finally escape past his lips are claws digging their way through my psyche. "Your father has never embezzled money from his company, Tillie."

I snatch my hand out of his, cradling it to my chest.

My voice trembles as I say, "Y-yes he did. He...he did."

His next words are clear and direct. "No. He didn't. Holden was embezzling money. Your father doesn't know."

Something inside me shifts and builds as I jump from the couch, shaking out my hands, needing the movement because I'm terrified that if I still, I'll detonate.

"*No.*" My voice cracks. "No, because...and I never said anything...Oh my God, it was for nothing. *It was all for nothing,*" I cry out, falling to my knees and dry heaving.

For years, I thought I was protecting my dad, the only family I had, while also villainizing him.

All those years spent destroying my body with poison to get through it.

All those years of losing pieces of my sanity, my soul, and my future.

Jansen crouches behind me, gathering my hair and holding it back. The *something* inside me that was building catches like a flame to gasoline, burning its way through me. Jerking away from him, I rip my hair from his hand and crawl as far away from him as possible. When nothing is left of me but ash, I take a deep, stuttering breath, wipe my cheeks, and turn. My legs shake as I stand, stumbling.

"You had no right to pry into my life any further." My voice sounds foreign, even to me.

His gaze heats my skin, like flames licking at me from head to toe.

"I had every right," he says calmly, pulsing his fists at his side.

I sniff, trying to build up the mental fortress drugs helped me to escape behind, trying to ignore the way my body responds to him, but it isn't working.

It isn't fucking working.

The smoke rises, suffocating me as I struggle to breathe evenly.

In a blink, he's in front of me, placing my palms on his chest. "Breathe, Freckles. Breathe."

If there were a cord tethering my mind and body, it's snapped.

My nails dig into his chest as mine heaves with heavy sobs. "I could've gone my life...my whole life without..."

And then a shattered groan passes through my lips as I pound my fists into his pecs, crying out, *"Why did you do that? What did you do?"*

He lets me continue my assault until I weaken, then places my arms between us, squeezing them between my chest and his.

"I'm so sorry." His voice cracks. "But I swear he will never hurt you again."

He lowers us to the ground and cradles me in his lap like a toddler, clutching on to me.

"How much do you know?" I ask hoarsely, hating that he could have *seen* me.

"I know he stole from the company and why you left," he murmurs. "He was trying to force you to leave with him. You're so strong, Tillie. You got away. You started over in a new town with a new job, and you're strong enough to get through this. You are."

I can't tell if his words are meant to assure me, him, or both of us, but they bring me back to the last night at my dad's...

Sitting in my room, I heard footsteps echo down the hallway. No one should have been in this part of our house with every amenity needed downstairs, so I knew exactly who it was.

I hadn't seen him since I got out of rehab. It was the safest I'd felt since turning sixteen, and I tried like hell to get my dad to set me up with an apartment away from here, but he refused. He wanted me close. With the drugs purged from my system, the shame from what I'd put myself through all these years hit me like a freight train, but it was nothing compared to the disgust I felt from giving myself to him over and over and over. The second and third months in rehab were spent vomiting almost daily every time a memory of him resurfaced.

When his footsteps stopped outside my door, I got up, moving to the far wall by my open window because I'd have rather thrown myself out of it than let him touch me again. Dad had my bedroom door and bathroom locks removed, and I was sure Holden knew that. He didn't knock before twisting the knob and pushing the door open.

His brown hair was longer and combed back, and his slacks and button-up didn't fit him as snug as usual, making his weight loss obvious. The dark circles under his eyes indicated he was stressed or hadn't been sleeping well, and I hated how much I noticed about him. He looked that way because he'd lost access to me, and I despised how a minuscule part of myself felt sorry for him. My stomach lurched violently, but I remained silent, staring at him, waiting to see what he'd say or do.

"Did you have a nice vacation?" *A nasty smirk curled his lips before he leaned against the closed door.*

"Best year of my life," *I said hoarsely, finding my voice.*

His pointed chin dipped at my tone as he raked his dark eyes up and down my body. "You look good."

Disgust curdled in my stomach, but I remained silent.

"I missed you," *he breathed out, resting his head back against the door.*

Suddenly, everything became clear. The veil of my ignorance, or compliance, had lifted. Adrenaline flooded every limb in my body at the realization.

My voice trembled as I said, "We're not together, Holden. We were never together. Everything that happened before is over. I'm not doing it again."

With every step he took toward me, the floor creaked. Fear wrapped an icy palm around my throat, and I stumbled backward until my knees buckled and I fell onto the windowsill.

"If you come any closer to me, I'll scream."

His steps paused. "Did you believe I'd move on while you were gone, doll? You belong to me. Your father doesn't care about you. He didn't even want you back home. Your little fucking boyfriend abandoned you. You have no one left. I'm all you've got. I'm the only one who gives a shit about your existence," *he hissed.*

My body trembled along with my voice. "And raping me is how you show me you give a shit?"

It was the first time I'd said the word in front of him or aloud. The way his eyes blackened had my breath stuttering.

"Don't act like you didn't enjoy yourself. I still remember the way your breathing changed every time you came."

"Leave," I hissed as sternly as possible. "Just leave me the fuck alone."

He tutted, and the sound had helpless tears springing to my eyes as he took a few more measured steps toward me. "Did you forget about what I can do to your father? Where would you end up? No education. No job. Homeless on the street. Go ahead and scream, Tillie. Every contact your father has is downstairs. A perfect night to air out his dirty laundry. Don't you think?"

My breathing was shallow as I stood frozen, watching in slow motion as he took those last couple of steps toward me, so close his chest grazed mine. When I didn't scream, he sneered and dug his fingertips into my cheeks, drawing a whimper from my throat.

"I wanted to give you time to adjust, but you seem to have forgotten exactly who you belong to. Next month, we're leaving. Together. You will come with me willingly, and your father will be thrilled to be rid of you."

He brought his lips to my cheek, using them to dry the tears that had spilled down my face. "Dry your tears, doll. We've had years together. Making you my wife is the natural escalation of our relationship."

My heart began racing so fast, I was counting down the seconds until it finally exploded. Before I could say anything, his grip tightened. "No isn't an option for you. It'll be easier for you to accept it."

I didn't say anything but searched his menacing stare for any hint, even a shred, of goodness. All that stared back at me was an empty, evil man. I loved my dad. I did. But I couldn't do this. Not anymore.

A plan formed in my mind. He wouldn't out my dad if I wasn't around because he needed the information to control me. If I disappeared, what power did he have? None. If I was wrong and he did out my dad...

I'd already walked through hell for his sins.

All I knew for sure was I had to get the hell out of this house. Dad would cancel everything. He'd already threatened it. I had a bit of cash stored away. I didn't know what I'd do when I left, but anything was better than living in constant fear.

So I nodded meekly, and his hand relaxed around my jaw as he brought his lips to mine in a bruising manner.

"There's my perfect doll," he murmured. "I'll see you tomorrow at lunch. We have a lot to catch up on."

I swallowed the bile from his implication and nodded again.

When he finally left my room, I collapsed, giving myself a moment to expel the emotions his declaration caused before standing on shaky legs and getting a bag together. Turning back toward the room I grew up in one last time, I said goodbye, then closed the door and made my way downstairs.

All I needed to do was get to the door.

Holden saw me, but instead of coming toward me, he pretended like I didn't exist.

I didn't spare him a second glance, marching toward the front door and grabbing my keys.

"Where do you think you're going?" my dad asked behind me.

"I'm going to stay with a friend. I feel suffocated."

"Every friend you have is in active addiction. You're not leaving this house."

An almost desperate plea colored his words as he snatched the keys from my hand and put them back on the hook.

"Go back upstairs, and we can talk about it tomorrow," he said, looking around at the guests filling our house, and it pissed me off. His image to the people around him was always more important than me, which is ironic since he was a criminal.

"Fuck you," I hissed.

His eyes widened in surprise because, even high and out of my damn mind, I had never talked to my dad like that, but I was done.

He reached for my arm and squeezed painfully...

My eyelids grow heavy with emotional exhaustion as I finish telling Jansen about the night I left my dad's and ended up at Presley and Dane's.

"They sound like great people."

They close completely as I murmur, "They have no idea they saved my life."

Seventeen

Jansen

TILLIE FALLS ASLEEP IMMEDIATELY after her eyes close, and I gather her in my arms, lying her in bed and tucking her in. I take a few minutes in the shower, resting my head against the tiled wall. Ice-cold water runs down my shoulders as I breathe through the murderous thoughts racing through my mind, making my heart drum with a thunderous rhythm. When that doesn't work, I bite down on my fist, screaming silently. I need the gym. A place where I can expel this violent energy, but she's here, and being near her is the only remedy I'll accept tonight.

I peek around the curtain through the open door to see her form still buried under the blanket, and I make quick work of toweling off. Faint bruises have already formed on my chest from her earlier assault. My pain had barely registered when hers was so tangible it felt like every hit was her transferring a little more to me, and God...I wish I could've absorbed every bit, leaving her without a trace of it.

Stepping into my briefs, I slide them up to my hips, the cotton absorbing the few droplets on my skin. I'm about to walk to the couch when her words from earlier rush in. She wants to be seen as a normal woman. She wants me to see her without her trauma, and in some circumstances, that won't be possible in the way she wants. Her consent is crucial because I would rather jump off a bridge onto pavement than have her look at me like I'm her abuser.

But in this instance, I won't bother asking for it because the only thing I need right now is to hold her.

After texting Granddad and Nix to let them know she's staying here, I tiptoe to the bed, pull the black duvet back, and climb in beside her. Like she's freezing to death and I'm a fire, her body shifts into mine. She buries her face between my collarbone and jaw and keeps her hands tucked between her body and my chest. I don't hesitate to wrap my arm around her, caging her to me.

I've slept beside women, but I've never had the visceral reaction I'm having in this moment. The only desire I have ever had in life is to keep moving, but now the desire to protect her and care for her is outweighing the other. To prove my affection can be freely given while expecting nothing from her in return. To help her restore her confidence and faith in herself.

The warmth from her rhythmic, soft breathing on my neck pauses, and I tip my chin down to see her eyes blinking open. She doesn't pull away from me like I expect her to at first, waking up to me wrapped around her. Instead, she draws closer, placing her thigh between my legs, trying to meld our bodies together.

"Go back to sleep. I've got you," I whisper, tucking her hair behind her ear.

"Why do you run?" she whispers back.

No one has ever asked me that.

How can you possibly enjoy traveling so much as you get older?

Why don't you want to lay down roots somewhere? Isn't it time?

How do you think you'll feel in a few years when you have no one in your life to spend it with?

Those are the questions I'm asked, but Tillie clocked the reason. Whether it's because she's running or she's come to that conclusion from our conversations, I don't know. The one thing known is she's asking me the one question I've never wanted to answer...even for myself.

Because I've been running since I turned eighteen.

Her soft voice fills the space between us again.

"You can choose to keep it to yourself." She tilts her head up, and I look down at her. "But if you get to know every personal thing about me, it's only fair I get to know something about you."

I swallow before changing position to lie on my back and look up at the ceiling.

"The first time my mom left me alone, I was six."

Her hand reaches for mine, and she laces our fingers together while resting her head on my shoulder.

"I don't remember my dad much. He died in a car accident when I was little, but I never remember feeling scared or being alone. When I woke up at six years old and couldn't find her...It's my first memory of being alone. She didn't come home for hours, and I remember it also being my first time feeling scared."

Swallowing roughly, I continue, "I went to the neighbor's house later on in the day because I was hungry. I played with her son every now and then. She'd let us play in her house when the weather was bad, but she never let him come to mine."

I clear the emotion from my throat because I still vividly remember the way I felt the next few hours of that day...

Tommy's mommy opened the door, and I felt like I wasn't alone anymore.

"Hey, Jansen," she said while looking around and over to my house. "Why aren't you in school?"

"I don't know where my mommy is." Tears filled my eyes and spilled down my cheeks.

Her jaw dropped as she peered back at my house, and she took my hand. "C'mon, sweet boy."

She got me inside and sat me down at the kitchen table, where she kneeled in front of me. "How long has your mommy been gone?"

"I-I don't know." I wiped the wetness from my face.

"Have you eaten today?"

"I had crackers." I sniffed as my belly growled.

Her eyes sparkled, and she blinked a few times before standing up and whipping around.

"I'm going to make you something to eat." She sniffed. "Any special requests?"

I shook my head shyly.

"How about pancakes?"

My mommy never made pancakes. She never really cooked any food. "Yes. Please."

Once the pancakes were done and I was eating, she asked me questions while sitting beside me.

"Has your mommy ever left you alone before?"

I shook my head no.

"What kind of food does your mommy make you?"

I wrinkled my nose. "Cereal, sandwiches, and the box with the penguin."

She nodded slowly. "What kind of stuff do you and your mommy do together at home?"

I didn't know why she wanted to know so much about my mommy.

"We watch TV. She's tired all the time, but sometimes we draw."

She smiled and her forehead wrinkled, but she didn't ask any more questions.

Tommy got off the bus a few hours later. I was so excited to play with him, and then his daddy got home.

They whispered to each other while Tommy and I watched TV and ate a snack.

It was dark out before a car door slammed next door. Tommy's mommy stared at his daddy, and he went out the door while she told me to stay inside.

I was confused. Mommy had been gone all day,, and I wanted to run to her, give her a hug, and ask her where she went. I stood by their window and watched as he talked to her, and she put her face in her hands as her shoulders shook. I didn't want her to cry. It always lasted a long time, and it made her sleepy. Too sleepy to play.

He came back inside and said they had to let me go, but Tommy's mommy hugged me closely to her. My heart started to feel like when I ran really fast because I wanted to go home.

"We can't send him back, Ty. What if it happens again?"

"We can't keep him here either. She said she had an emergency and didn't mean to be gone so long. You said this has never happened before."

Her grip loosened around me as she took my hand and led me out the door and across their yard. I saw my mommy standing there and started running. She dropped to her knees with her arms out, and I crashed into them.

"Sorry, baby. I'm sorry," she whispered in my ear, kissing my cheek and forehead.

Tommy's mommy cleared her throat. "If this happens again, I'll have to call someone and let them know."

"It won't," she said in her angry voice. "Thank you for watching him, but I've got him now."

Tillie's thumb rubs small circles on my hand.

"She drilled it into me that if I ever left when she wasn't there, people would come to our house and take me away. Once she knew I was scared enough to listen, she would leave me for an hour or two here and there, but when I was eight, she disappeared for two days."

"Did Ron know what she was doing?" she whispers.

"By that time, she and my grandparents had a falling out. We moved a lot. There were two summers I spent the majority of with him and Grandma, but when I went home...I didn't have a way to call, even if I wanted to, but she instilled so much fear in me that I wouldn't have. I made sure to get up, catch the bus, and come straight home. I didn't leave the house until she was back. My teenage years before I could work were spent trying to stay gone as much as possible, but I wasn't very social, so finding friends was...difficult. I would wander around town until I needed to sleep."

"So...you don't mind moving around so much because you felt trapped when you were younger."

My sigh is heavy. "If I'm in the same place for too long, I feel like I'm being trapped. Like I'll never be able to leave."

She sits up in bed, looking around the apartment, and cool air hits the moisture gathered on my arm where her head was lying.

"You don't need to waste your tears on me, Freckles. I'm fine."

Her chuckle is light and sad. "I think you truly believe you are."

I grit my teeth from an unwanted kernel of frustration caused by her tone. "Because I am. I've built a successful business. I travel. There isn't one thing about my life for me to complain about."

She tilts her head, gaze searching mine, then bows her head before looking away, which only intensifies my frustration.

Sitting up and resting my back against the black velvet headboard, I rub my eyes with the heels of my palms. "Say what you want to say."

Her shoulders tense at my tone, but when she looks back at me, there's a challenge. "Your parents have both passed, you don't keep in good contact with your remaining family, you push everyone away because you don't want to be 'disappointed'"—she uses air quotes—"before you even give them the chance to prove you wrong. You choose to do life alone, and I think it's because you don't want to be left or forgotten again."

Who the fuck does she...

My blood simmers from how she dug through all of my shit and called me out in a matter of minutes, and before thinking through the words about to leave my mouth, I bite out, "When are you going to the police and reporting Holden?"

She yawns. Fucking. Yawns. "Report him for what? Screwing him so my father wouldn't lose everything?"

Putting a finger up for each of the bastard's crimes, I start listing off his offenses. "Statutory rape when you were sixteen. Blackmail that would also surely count as sexual assault. Mental and emotional damage. Christ, Tillie, you were addicted to drugs to get through his assaults."

Her face remains stoic, but I zero in on the color darkening her cheeks as she presses her lips together.

Her raspy reply has me seeing red. "I'll deal with him on my terms."

"The fuck you will. You can't run from him forever," I growl.

The smirk on her face is infuriatingly sexy as she leans toward me, speaking with a placating tone. "But that's what we do, right? We run. I'll be fine, Jansen."

Reaching over, I turn on the lamp by the bed so she can see how serious I am about this situation. "That's cute what you did there. Throwing my response back at me, but I'm not running from a psychopath who abused me for nine years. I'm running from my past."

She looks at my chest in horror, bringing a shaky palm to her mouth. "Did I do that?"

I don't spare the bruises a glance. "You didn't mean to. It's not a big deal."

I attempt to slide closer to her, but she leaps from the bed, and a small piece of me withers.

Her face shows her horror as she continues to look at the marks she left. "I want to go home."

I'm not sure she even notices me standing from the bed and walking closer to her.

"I texted Nix and Granddad earlier and told them you were staying here."

Her voice trembles as she begs, "N-no, please take me home."

Gathering her wrists in my hands, I bring them to my chest as she tries and fails to pull them away, while resting my lips on her forehead. "You didn't know what you were doing, Freckles." My lips move softly over her skin. "It's okay. You didn't mean to."

Her chest heaves as she shakes her head.

"I'm not taking you back to the boat. I'll sleep on the couch, but I want you here tonight. I need you here," I murmur.

"Why would you even—"

"Do you want a T-shirt to change into?"

Why would I want her to stay? Because right now, calming her and having her near is the only thing that matters. I won't give a voice to those feelings. Maybe I'm a coward, or maybe I don't want our eventual separation to be harder.

Her nod is meek, and her embarrassment is evident by her lack of fire, combined with the flush on her cheeks. Releasing her wrists, I glide my hands up her arms, shoulders, and neck until I reach her face. My thumbs glide over the smattering of freckles I'm so fucking obsessed with.

Soft pants escape through her parted lips, and my cock instantly hardens.

She's about to find out if she meant what she said earlier because, regardless of tonight's revelations, I don't want her to feel as if anything is wrong with her. I want the fire inside her to spark again. With my thumbs under her chin, I tilt her head back.

She blinks slowly, and I give her one, two, three seconds to tell me to fuck off or back away before I'm dipping my head and parting her lips with mine.

The first stroke of my tongue has her gripping my hips.

The second has her plastering her body to mine.

By the third, I'm swallowing her raspy moans.

My hands slide down to her waist, and I push her back toward the bed, lifting her onto it.

Our lips stay fused until I'm fully on top of her.

I rise onto my forearms with her head still cradled in between.

Raven hair fans out over the duvet, her gaze roams over my face, and I give her time to decide whether this is what she wants.

Just when I think this is about to end, her hands wrap around the back of my neck, pulling me down to her.

Eighteen

Tillie

AREN'T WE ALL SUPPOSED to have a certain first-time experience? The one where we awkwardly fumble around, still unsure of our bodies and the other person's expectations.

If we're lucky, the person we choose will make sure we're doing okay, and if we're unlucky, they'll use our bodies for their two-minute gratification before pushing our needs aside.

My first time was forced. It was selfish. It was painful. I hadn't experienced anything before his assault. And I spent the day after googling whether the inside of my vagina could bruise and swell.

I used to think my *real* first time, the first time I got to choose, was with Rhett. I was so out of it, I didn't have a chance of feeling self-conscious, and he wasn't the type of guy who left me hanging.

But now, with Jansen's lips on mine, the way his hand roams my body over my clothes, and the nervousness I feel, I believe this is my *real* first time. Clear-headed and completely aware of every touch, every breath, every noise.

Jansen slides his hand under my shirt, and my breath catches.

I still remember every criticism *he* made about my body.

"You should do some crunches to tighten your stomach."

"I don't mind having something to hang on to, but I can fucking squeeze a handful of your sides."

"Self-tanner can hide the stretch marks on your legs."

"You're nowhere near the hottest girl I've been with."

Then, when my addiction amped up, he celebrated my near-skeletal frame.

His words continue to assault my mind, and I don't feel Jansen's hand slip away until his thumb is brushing my bottom lip.

"No, Tillie." His voice is rough and low.

My eyes, squeezed shut, open to find him looking down at me.

"He doesn't get to take any more from you. Not your thoughts. Not your pleasure. Nothing."

My nod is jerky. Before I can manage words, he's pushing up and standing from the bed. The hurt and misplaced rejection must be written on my face. With his gaze locked on mine, he pushes his briefs down his legs and steps out of them.

Oh. My...

I thought Jansen in trunks was sexy, but him standing completely naked in front of me has my body responding in ways I never knew it could. My nipples pebble, and every inch of skin flushes. The heavy length between his legs demands my attention, and desire pools between my own.

My voice trembles. "What if...what if I can't?"

"Can you put your trust in me tonight?"

It's unnerving how comfortable he is with himself while standing in front of me completely vulnerable.

He reaches for me, and I make no move to get away from him. Instead, I'm drawn to him. Earlier, he called me a siren, and he's the only sailor I care to ensnare. Heat glides down the path his palms travel to raise my arms and lift them gently over my head. His touch never leaves my body as he traces the same path down until he reaches the hem of my tank top.

"Can I?" he whispers.

I nod.

Goosebumps appear on my skin from the sensation of his touch, soft and light, as he lifts my tank top over my head and tosses it aside. I bring my forearms to my chest and attempt to cover myself, but he takes my hands, placing them on his toned stomach instead.

"You can cover me, never yourself," he says in a raspy whisper.

His fingers find the button on my shorts, and for a moment, I forget how to breathe.

My eyes find his, and he repeats, "Can I?"

I nod again, still unable to form a sentence.

His warm palms glide down my thighs, and my breath hitches.

I've never spent money on frivolous lingerie, but in this moment, as I lie here in a plain black bra and yellow bikini underwear, I wish I had.

At this point, I'm panting, trying to inhale a full breath.

"What now?" My voice shakes as he pulls the jean shorts down my legs and tosses them aside.

His tongue glides along his bottom lip as his gaze leaves a trail of heat from my head to my toes.

"Now I hold you." He crawls onto the bed behind me and wraps an arm around my waist, pulling me against him.

"You have me half naked in your bed, and you want to...cuddle?"

A warm trail of goosebumps appears on my ear and neck where he peppers small kisses. "I need you to be comfortable with me. When I touch you, I want you to be present. So, tonight, I'll hold you. I'll kiss you. I'll play with your hair. And I'll run my hands along your skin, so when it's time, you'll know without a doubt whose hands are worshiping your body."

My chest blazes as I try to swallow down the emotions his declaration has surfaced.

Men like this don't exist.

Even my best friend didn't do this.

Did you let him?

I couldn't. I couldn't tell him.

I've made so many irreparable mistakes, yet in a world of monsters, I happened to come across my unicorn.

His thumb glides across my cheek, wiping away the tears I didn't know had fallen.

"What are you thinking, Freckles?" he murmurs with his lips against my ear.

A shiver runs down my spine at the sensation, and a giggle escapes me. When I turn my head to look at him, he has a brow quirked.

"You're a unicorn." I laugh, my chest shaking along with the sound until it turns into a sob.

His brow lowers as his gaze softens.

"I'll be your unicorn," he whispers.

His hands continue to wander over my skin while his lips pepper me with kisses from my cheek down to my shoulder, and I fall asleep with his warmth enveloping me, his fingers caressing my hair.

·····••·····

He's an oven.

The feeling of stickiness wakes me from a peaceful sleep.

Desperate for water, I slowly untangle our limbs and climb out of bed, sneaking to the refrigerator.

As I uncap the bottle and take a sip, thoughts of last night rush into my mind. Sure, I've felt comfortable with a man, with Rhett, but I've never felt seen. I've never had anyone know what I need and make me feel completely safe. Vulnerable isn't something I'm used to being, but Jansen makes it easy.

I tiptoe across the floor and climb back into bed. He reaches for me and pulls me into him, still asleep. I drape my leg over his thigh, and his hips pulse as his cock hardens.

Until last night, I wasn't worried about mistaking Jansen for that monster during sex. Even now, I don't think I would. It wasn't memories of *him* that assaulted me last night, but his *words* and how he made me feel worthless. Jansen made me feel like I could be cherished instead of picked apart.

Moonlight shining through the two sheer-curtained windows on the wall beside the bed is enough to see now that my eyes have adjusted. He could reject me, but it's a chance I'm willing to take.

My nerves have my hand trembling as I glide my palm along his warm and silky length. His hips pulse again, and I keep a slow pace. The sleepy groan he releases is the sexiest thing I've ever heard, making me feel more confident. I crane my neck to see his face, and his brows are dipped, a look of pleasure contorting his features. Knowing I put it there causes a throbbing sensation between my legs.

Feeling more brazen and needing more of him, I kiss the outline of his sharp jaw. The rough abrasion from his short stubble is enough to put me in sensory overload, and he's not even touching me.

I continue to plant kisses along his jaw, until my lips land on the spot behind his ear. Capturing his lobe between my teeth, I nip it and then glide my lips back down his neck. His hips begin to pulse a little faster, and that sexy mouth of his opens to release another groan as he twists his head to the side, giving me more access. Inching down his body, I switch between kissing and nipping his shoulders, chest, and stomach. The smattering of hair covering his chest and trailing down from his belly button to his pelvis has my body responding like a beggar.

Every part of him is toned and beautiful. I pause in my descent when his scar is at eye level. I brush the raised tissue with my finger before kissing it and settling down farther between his thighs.

One thing I was always grateful for was that Holden never cared for oral. He never gave a damn about my pleasure, but he didn't like it on himself either.

Nerves break apart in my stomach, multiplying and spreading. I have no fucking idea what I'm doing, only that I want to do it.

His cock is rock hard, thick, and long. A bead of liquid rests atop the head, and I bend down, licking the slit. His hips jerk with his sharp intake of breath.

"Tillie?" he asks in a shallow, raspy voice filled with surprise.

"I want to, but if you want me to stop, I will," I whisper.

Our eyes remain locked, his chest rising and falling. He stays silent, so I dip my head and run my tongue along the thick vein underneath. Circling my tongue around the tip has him hissing through his teeth.

Every reaction from him sets my body off.

I swirl my tongue again before taking him fully into my mouth, gliding my lips down along the silky skin. His taste, the texture, his reaction—everything about this moment and him has me on the edge of an orgasm. I moan around his length, and he shifts his leg over and between mine, propping it up so I'm straddling his thigh.

The pressure to my clit sends tiny shocks of pleasure to my core, and I rock my hips back and forth until my body tenses from embarrassment.

I continue gliding my lips up and down, swirling my tongue around the length, and hollowing my cheeks, focusing solely on him and not the throb between my legs.

Until he begins rocking his thigh.

"You don't need to be embarrassed with me, Freckles," he breathes out. "Grind your pussy on my thigh. Use me."

How is this real?

His words and the pressure building between my legs have me whimpering.

I peer up through my lashes, finding his bottom lip caught between his teeth and his eyes locked on his thigh.

"You're fucking soaked," he groans and runs his tongue along his bottom lip.

I hollow my cheeks again, and his thigh drops.

"Just like that," he hisses.

Holy fucking hot. I do my best to keep the same suction, and he winds my hair around his fist, pulling back gently.

"If you don't want my cum running down your throat, you've got to stop."

But do I? Hell no, because I want him to fall apart completely.

I hollow my cheeks even more, keeping the suction as I bob up and down. The muscles in his stomach tighten as the first spurt of liquid hits the back of my throat. And I don't release his length from my mouth until I've swallowed every last drop.

As soon as I lift my head, he's on me.

His hand fists the back of my hair again as his lips part mine.

The throbbing between my legs had ebbed a little, but now it's back and almost painful.

"I need to taste you," he begs against my lips.

Insecure thoughts race through my head, causing me to become lightheaded.

"I've never—no one's ever..." My words stumble, and I tuck my chin.

He pushes up on his forearms and nudges my jaw with his pointer finger to face him. His curious gaze searches mine. "You've never had oral sex?"

I shake my head no, my cheeks burning once again.

His brows rise in surprise. "You gave me the best blowjob I've ever had in my life, and that was your first time?"

I nod sheepishly and swallow down the irrational jealousy his words cause.

He uses the pads of his fingers to skim across my bare skin, and chills appear in their wake from my neck to my chest as he reaches the clip on the front of my bra. His eyes ask permission, and I bite the corner of my bottom lip, nodding. With one flick of his fingers, the band releases. He pushes the straps down my shoulders and exposes my breasts.

Heat floods my cheeks, but he doesn't notice as he stares in a trance. Palming them, he tweaks my nipples between his fingers, causing my breath to hitch from the shock of pleasure traveling down to my core.

In a raspy voice, he says, "There isn't one part of you that isn't just as alluring as the next."

He lays me down on the bed and sits back on his calves, his fingers inching beneath the hem of my underwear. As he slides them down my legs, I can't inhale a full breath, and the second my center is exposed to the cool air, I gasp.

Ever since I entered rehab, staying shaved or waxed has not been a priority of mine. It was freeing after being told for years how *my* anatomy needed to look. I trim and groom, but I'll never be bare again.

Trembles rack through my body, and my nails dig into my palms in anticipation of his disappointment.

Instead, he throws his head back, groaning dramatically, as he strokes himself. "Not one fucking part of you."

Heat continues to build behind my hips, and I flush at his praise, but I'm still nervous.

After settling between my thighs, he leans down and kisses me, cupping my center completely while grinding his palm against my clit. Our tongues are battling each other for dominance in the hottest, messiest kiss I've ever had.

The heat behind my hips has now rushed directly to my clit, pulsing and intense.

I jolt from the shock of it and release a moan into his mouth. He removes his hand, and I cry out in frustration because I was *right there*.

His deep chuckle fills the space as he kisses a trail from the corner of my mouth to my chest. He palms both of my breasts and kneads while flicking his tongue around one nipple. The short stubble lining his jaw and mouth scraping against my skin only adds to my sensory overload. But when he wraps his lips around the bud and sucks it into his mouth, I'm done for. I run my fingers through the top of his hair.

"Please, Jansen. I need to come," I beg, writhing against him and the sheets sticking to my sweat-coated skin.

"Are you with me?" he asks softly, looking up to search my face, and my heart cracks at the vulnerability in his voice.

I'm so on edge right now, my voice cracks. "There's only you. I'm with you. Please."

He doesn't need any more reassurance. With a bruising grip, he palms my thighs and wraps them around his neck. Not a second goes by before he places his face between my legs and licks one long, glorious stroke. The pressure he uses with his tongue as he circles my clit has a rush of liquid fire racing to my center, and I detonate, arching off the bed. My thighs clench his face until I'm trembling.

He licks me through my orgasm, bringing me down until my thighs loosen and I start to feel incredibly sensitive.

When his tongue traces a circle around my clit again, I sharply inhale. "It's too sensitive," I gasp.

Instead of pulling back, he runs a palm up my stomach, to my breast, squeezing and tweaking the sensitive bud. And his lips brush against my center as he says, "Breathe through it, Freckles. I need one more. You can handle one more."

His mouth latches onto me, and the sounds slipping past my lips are feral cries from pleasure so intense it's almost painful. The muscles in my stomach loosen as I force myself to inhale steady breaths through my nose. I release his hair, fisting the sheets instead, but every sense I have is focused between my legs as I lift my head to watch him feast. His mouth glistens with my arousal as his tongue continues to lap at the moisture gathering. Every groan that slips up his throat vibrates against my pussy as his stubble scrapes and burns deliciously against my thighs. With my every inhale, his spicy scent fills my nostrils. And when he sucks my clit into his mouth and circles his tongue, my second orgasm edges full force.

"Don't stop. Keep doing that," I cry out, running my hand through his hair and fisting it again, holding his face in place.

And he does. He keeps his tongue moving at the same pressure and rhythm until my core's clenching around nothing, and I'm crying out again in pleasure.

Intense spasms have my body trembling violently before turning to mush. My legs tingle and shake from the aftershocks of the two greatest orgasms I have ever experienced.

Once I'm back down on planet earth, I peek at him and notice my hand still has his hair in a vise and he's smirking at me.

"Shit." I let go like the strands caught fire. "I'm sorry."

He doesn't say anything but turns his face and kisses both of my thighs before climbing beside me.

"Don't ever apologize for anything that happens while we're in bed again," he murmurs. "You could punch me in the face, and I'd still get off. You're fucking intoxicating."

His hips grind against my ass, proving just how intoxicated he is. As I begin to reach for his length behind me, he grabs my hand and wraps both of our arms across my chest. "This is only going to lead to one ending, and I want you to be completely ready for it."

"I am," I breathe out. "I stayed with you, only you, the whole time."

"I was doing something you've never experienced before," he says in a gentle tone. "And when I have you for the first time, I want to be sure I'm the only man consuming your mind."

"You will be," I promise.

"I know," he whispers, entwining our bodies. "Get some sleep, beautiful."

For the second time, I fall asleep with his body wrapped around mine, but this time I'm satisfied in a way that leaves me wanting so much more.

Nineteen

Jansen

Waking up to Tillie naked and warm against me, with her perfect tits on display, felt like a sucker punch to the gut while my heart damn near beat out of my chest, and I willed my dick to behave. I'll leave, and she'll always be the one who is unforgettable but unattainable. She deserves to live some semblance of the life that was stolen from her.

Instead of going to the diner and risking her running out on me, I make her breakfast here. I've got bacon sizzling, eggs frying in the pan, and coffee percolating by the time she's stretching her arms above her head.

"Morning," I call out.

A small smile appears on her face, and I'm relieved she doesn't seem like she wants to run out.

She sits up on the bed, holding the blanket across her chest.

"What is this song?" She yawns.

"You've never listened to Sleep Token?"

"Hypnosis" plays in the background, and it's one of their harder songs but still amazing.

And fitting.

"No, but I like it. Didn't take you for a metal fan, though." She searches around the bed and the floor beside her.

"Your clothes are on my side," I say casually. "And I listen to all types of music."

So she's not uncomfortable, I gather plates from the cabinet and pile the food on, letting her collect her clothes and make it to the bathroom without an audience. After the door clicks, I amble to the bed—flashes of last night running through my mind—and set to making it.

Cleanliness and structure have always been important in my routine. I knew at an early age if I wasn't going to pick up, I'd have to settle for living in filth. I was doing laundry by age nine, the dishes every day, and picking up after myself—and my mother.

"You didn't have to make breakfast," she mumbles from behind me, pulling me from the past.

"Well, I couldn't risk you running out on me again." I smirk, walking over to her and wrapping my arms around her before kissing her forehead.

"I'm done running." Her voice is hard, but her eyes are soft when she looks up at me.

We eat in relative silence, but it's comfortable. When she's done with her coffee, she gets up and takes her dishes to the sink. My gaze tracks her every movement, like she's a magnet pulling me in. Warmth seeps slowly through my chest from seeing her so comfortable in my space as she washes her dishes. I'm not sure she even notices the way her hips move along with the rhythm of the song playing. Once she's placed them on the rack, she turns and leans against the counter.

"Do you think I could have the afternoon off?" Her lips purse as her forehead creases. "I don't want special treatment. If I can't, it's okay. I need a day after last night to...clear my head," she finishes in one breath.

I know she isn't talking about what happened between us, and her having a day off is the least I can do after destroying a piece of her world.

"I'll pick up your shift. Don't worry about it."

She captures her bottom lip between her teeth, and I can tell her mind is on…shit, on everything. "I'll run you home so you can rest, and I'll come by tonight."

"No," she blurts out. "No, I have to get errands done, and then I'll probably be in bed for the rest of the day."

Her cheeks darken a shade as she looks away from me, and my stomach drops.

"Tillie." My voice is stern as I strut toward her. "What's going on?"

"Nothing," she squeaks out. "Last night was a lot, and I need to process it."

"Including us?"

She palms my face, sliding her thumb against the stubble on my chin. "It's nothing to do with you, I swear. Last night was—" She blows out a slow breath. "It was amazing. *You* were amazing."

"I understand, so why am I feeling like there's something you aren't telling me?" I look at her skeptically.

"Because you're paranoid?" She tries to laugh it off. "C'mon. I need a shower and HBO."

The drive over to her place doesn't reassure me. She's quiet the entire way, but her fingers stay interlaced with mine. I'm not ignorant of the fact what I told her was a big deal. The last nine years of her life revolved around one man's lies and manipulations. Knowing the truth took a part of her. I saw it. Saw the confusion, betrayal, and revelation as the fog cleared.

I'm not sure where she'll go from here, but I intend to be here for as long as I can.

When I pull into the spot in front of her slip, I keep my foot on the brake. "Call me if you need anything." I bring her knuckles to my lips, kissing them.

"I will, and I'll see you tomorrow." Her lips brush against mine for a kiss that ends too soon for my liking, before she gets out and walks inside without looking back.

Mason's already at the bar when I get back, going through inventory.

I swear, I'm going to miss his work ethic after I leave.

"How'd last night go?" he asks with a raised brow when I walk up to the bar.

"It was good."

He swats the towel at my shoulder and chuckles. "I'm sure it was."

"I know I can trust you, but I don't need the whole staff talking about my personal life or Tillie."

He raises a brow at me. "Then I guess you shouldn't have kissed Tillie in front of the one woman who'd probably slip something into your drink if she had the opportunity."

"Jesus Christ." I scrub a hand over my jaw. "Is she on the schedule today?"

His wince tells me she is. "She'll be here at four."

"Send her to my office when she gets in. I'll be waiting there, but after she's gone, I'll take her shift." My sigh is audible, as I already dread her setting foot in my office. "I'll call Remi and see if he can make it in this evening. Tillie had to take the day off for personal reasons. If he can't, it should be fine. Sundays aren't too bad."

"It's about time you let her crazy ass go."

I knock on the bar once before heading to my office, but his voice follows me to the hallway.

"Is Tillie good?"

"She's fine," I call out over my shoulder.

She is. She's fine. She's going to be okay.

·•·•••·•··

The same niggling feeling I've had since this morning is still gnawing at me when a knock raps on my open door at 3:50 p.m.

Bailee clears her throat. "Mason said you wanted to see me."

She starts to close the door behind her, batting her lashes.

"Leave the door open, please."

Her mouth twists in a pout, and it only solidifies my reasoning for doing this.

"Have a seat," I say in my no-bullshit tone, causing her face to drop.

Once she's in the chair, I steeple my hands on the desk. "Once this meeting is done, I expect you to clear out your belongings."

Her jaw drops, and I internally smile but keep my face neutral.

"Why are you firing me?"

My mouth twitches in annoyance. "You've made several advances I've shut down; the staff have seen it and aren't comfortable with it. They've come to me with comments you've made about me and other members of the staff."

She scoffs, her thin eyebrows lowering and pulling together. "This is about Tillie."

"No, Bailee, this is about you and your unwillingness to take the word *no* for what it means."

She crosses her arms and sits back in the chair with a smug look. "I'm fired, but you can fuck the trash. Seems like the power dynamic around here is unbalanced."

Hearing her call Tillie trash has my vision tinting. I lean forward with a look that tells her not to fuck with me—a message she receives, judging by how her arms tighten and the smug look wipes off her pinched, undesirable face.

"If you speak of her like that again, I'll make you wish you hadn't. You want to work in this town again? Because I can make several phone calls to ensure you do not. Your continuous sexual harassment is the reason you're being let go. I'm putting together a solid team, and your attitude toward other employees is less than desirable."

She goes to speak, and I raise my hand to shut her up. "Get out of my office and collect your things. You can pick up your last paycheck on Friday."

The color tinting her cheeks and the glare she directs my way before stomping out of my office like a child, slamming the door, assure me she's not done causing problems. I'll worry about it another day.

The next few hours go by in a blur. Summertime has brought in more people to the lake, and our typical slow Sunday is busier than usual.

Remi was able to make it in at seven, so when he gets behind the bar, I take a few minutes to check my phone. I have one text from Tillie and two from Granddad.

> **Tillie:** I hope you're not having to work too hard

> **Granddad:** If you're up for dinner tonight, I'll grill us some steaks.

> **Granddad:** Tillie and Nix went out of town, so it'll only be the two of us. Maybe we can get some fishing in?

I call him, and he picks up on the second ring. "Hey, Grandson, what time are you—"

"What do you mean they're out of town?"

"Err. Tillie said she had something to take care of and they'd be back later tonight."

My heart burns like it's either about to explode or stop beating.

"And you had no reservations about two addicts going out of town together?" I hiss.

"They're adults, Jansen, and I trust Tillie." His voice is irritatingly calm.

"Yeah? Well, maybe you shouldn't." I end the call before he can respond and then dial another number.

The line continues to ring before going to an automated voicemail. "You've got an hour to call me back before I hunt your ass down, and your time starts now."

She lied to me. I *knew* she was acting odd this morning, and *I trusted her* when she told me she was taking the day off to *process* and *rest*.

Twenty

Tillie

EARLIER IN THE DAY...

WITHOUT looking back at Jansen, I race into the houseboat.

Nix is sitting on the couch with his laptop. His fingers fly across the keys, and his concentration must be solely on that because he doesn't even glance up when I walk in.

"Can you be ready to hit the road in two hours?" I ask.

He pulls his focus away from his laptop with a look of confusion. "What?"

"I'm going out of town today, and I need you to go with me."

"What's going on, Tills?" He places the laptop beside him, giving me his full attention.

"*Please*, Nix. I can't tell you why, but I *need* you to trust me and *need* you to be with me," I plead.

Jansen can't go with me. Not for what I'm about to do.

This morning, when I woke up, shame built and expanded inside me. Not only for what I found out last night, but also from what happened between Jansen and me.

When I went to the bathroom to change, I could feel it. The shame was potent, covering me in a thick grime, snuffing out any spark of passion the memories from last night lit. While I looked at myself in the small mirror, fury I've never felt burned through my limbs, the grime.

He ruined my life.

He ruined *me*.

I had the most amazing sexual experience I've ever had, and it was tainted by the feelings *he* instilled in me.

Holden will no longer take anything from me, and I will never run from that piece of shit again.

Nix rubs my shoulders, pulling me from my downward spiral to hell. "Is it Jansen? What happened?"

My deep breath in and out is audible. "This has nothing to do with Jansen," I say, resting my forehead against his chest. "You're my friend, and right now I need a friend."

I lift my head, my chin still resting on his chest. "Please?" I whisper.

His eyes search mine before he nods. "Whenever you're ready."

The drive back to Sayersville is spent listening to music. Anything to help me hold on to the rage simmering inside me because I know I'll need it for what I'm about to do.

"You're seriously not going to tell me anything about why we're going back to Sayersville?" Nix asks for the third time.

We're thirty minutes away from town, and the trembling in my hands has started, so I make sure to keep a grip on the steering wheel. He doesn't know anything about what I've been through, and that is exactly why I brought him. Jansen wouldn't have let me near him. Nix will be upset if he ever finds out the truth, and if the time comes, I'll deal with it.

"Look," I start, glancing at him, "I need to take care of something so I can start completely fresh in life."

He lifts his brows. "I'm only concerned because you're white-knuckling the steering wheel the closer we get, and you're tight-lipped about the whole situation. I want to be here for you, but I need to know how."

"You're doing everything I need you to. You're coming with me as moral support."

His sigh is audible, but he doesn't say anything more.

When I take the familiar roads to his house, my entire body enters fight-or-flight mode. The closer we get, the more rapidly my heart races. Every breath turns shallower, and adrenaline has my blood pumping, making my body feel numb.

My flight mode. I hold on to the adrenaline, but fuck everything else.

Nix reaches for my shoulder, but I focus on the memory of Jansen's voice and everything he told me last night.

"Stay here, and do *not* get out of the car, Nix. I mean it."

He looks from the colonial-style house with white siding and blue trim, then back to me. His nostrils flare at my hard tone, but he dips his chin in agreement.

From the outside, this house looks beautiful. He's decorated the inside casually. Neutral colors and a few pieces of random artwork hang here and there. It's void of life, much like he is.

This house holds my pain. It holds the memories of my muffled cries—memories of slaps and verbal abuse when I wasn't "performing" well enough for him. One particular day, I tried to leave while he took a phone call. Before I could get down the first step of the staircase, his hand wrapped around the nape of my neck, startling me and causing me to jolt forward, down half the stairs. At first, he looked panicked—almost like he might truly care—as he rushed to me and started tenderly checking my limbs. I remember thinking that maybe it wouldn't be so bad if he could show emotion. If he could show a side of his humanity, but as soon as he was sure I didn't need medical assistance, a switch flipped. I'll never forget his eyes as they stared into mine. Almost black. Dead. Haunting. He grabbed me by my hair, forcing me back up the stairs. That day taught me Holden didn't have an ounce of humanity in him. I was nineteen.

Focusing on keeping my breathing even, I follow the neat stone path along the row of perfectly symmetrical shrubs to his front door.

My balled fist trembles as I lift it to pound the wood twice.

When the click of the lock sounds, I take two giant steps backward, stumbling.

A young woman with blond hair and a yellow sundress opens the door. She has house shoes on her feet, telling me she's comfortable here. "Can I help you?"

Before I can answer, my eyes lock on her midsection, and my vision begins to haze.

He moved. He had to have moved.

"Babe. Who's at the—" His words cut off when he notices me.

The mask slips for a split second before the muscles in his face relax as he looks at the woman now leaning into his side.

"This is the new assistant who started last week. I forgot about some paperwork and told her to stop by if she was available so I could sign them. Why don't you go back inside?" The lie rolls off his tongue so easily.

She looks at my empty hands and back at him. "She doesn't have any paperwork."

I clear my throat, jerking a thumb over my shoulder toward my car. "It's in the car."

Her gaze is skeptical, and I want to scream, "*Yes. Your instincts are spot on. He's a manipulative, lying monster. Run.*"

But I can't.

When I leave here today, it *has* to be over.

"I'll be right in," he says sternly, causing her to nod.

His stare remains fixed on me as she walks through the door and closes it behind her.

He takes a step forward.

I take two back.

His feet halt, and he places his balled-up fists in his jean pockets while searching up and down his street for anyone who might witness this.

I was never allowed to drive to his house. I'd meet him at a park outside of town, where I'd leave my car, and he'd drive me back to his house, parking in the garage. No one ever knew I was here.

If word gets back to my dad about me being at his house today, questions will rise, and the thought has me chuckling internally. Not having the power in this situation must be striking a match to his fury right now.

"She's pregnant. Is it yours?"

He tips his head. "Yes," he grits out.

I clench my teeth to keep my jaw from dropping. *Poor fucking kid.*

"She seems to be around your age." My head tips to the side, and he lurches toward me.

"Watch your mouth."

I hold my trembling hand out in front of me like a shield. "Don't fucking move, or I swear to God, Holden...Everyone on this street will know I was here today."

The smirk on his face has me internally recoiling. "I knew you'd come back. I've been inside of you for years. You can try to run, but I'm a part of you now. I always will be."

Bile rises in my throat.

"Her baby changes nothing. You're only making this harder on yourself, but your dad's going to be the one who suffers in the end."

"I know you've been asking about me around town, trying to figure out where I am. I'm sure it's surprising, the town's golden junkie being able to catch wind of it. Seems like more people than you realize *do* give a shit about me after all, but I'm here to tell you it ends today." I'm lying out of my ass right now, but my spine straightens as Jansen's voice filters through my thoughts.

Holden notes the change in my posture and moves toward me again. This time, I let him. Then I take two steps toward him, standing toe to toe.

"I was so gullible. I never questioned you. Not once. Protecting the only family I had was the most important thing to me. You knew how close we were." My voice cracks, but I don't take my eyes off his. I don't want to miss one detail of his reaction. "But now I have proof that you're the one who's been embezzling money from my dad's company."

His mouth turns down for only a second before he places the smirk back into place. "Bullshit."

"If you ever ask about me again. If you ever look for me. If you ever come *near* me again, I will go to the police. I will destroy your fucking life, Holden."

He tilts his face toward mine, close enough to look intimate, and sneers, "You expect me to believe a junkie whore found proof that doesn't exist? If you ever fucking threaten me again, I'll—"

An inferno replaces the blood running through my veins. I place my cheek on his and speak in a low voice. "This junkie whore has a connection and proof of the videos and pictures you took of me. How many of those were taken before I turned eighteen? You were twenty-eight when you started *raping* me. I don't think *anyone* would disagree with me about consent."

Jansen never mentioned *those* files, but Holden doesn't know that, and I'm not ignorant enough to believe he would delete them.

His chest halts all movement, his body frozen. If the temperature around us could drop, it'd be ice cold. He pulls his face back from mine as several emotions pass over his face—surprise, fear, anger.

My smile is sweet, which only makes him angrier. "You stupid bitch. You won't say anything. You'd have to admit to being my whore for the past nine years," he sneers.

My smile stays in place despite the internal slices his words cause. "I'm no longer anything to you, Holden. It's over. Come near me again, and I'll open the can of worms, landing you in a prison cell with the other piece of shit rapists. It's where you belong."

I turn to walk away, but he grabs my arm. "You think I'm going to let you walk away?"

"Are you going to kill me? Right here in your front yard with your pregnant girlfriend in the house?" I ask incredulously, ripping my arm from his hand. "We're done. This is over. Stay the fuck out of my life, and no one will ever know."

"Tills?" Nix calls out, slamming the car door.

Holden's stare zeroes in on Nix.

"I'm coming," I call over my shoulder. "You let me go, and it's done. Don't make this harder for yourself."

But his eyes don't meet mine again. Instead, they stay focused on Nix, his eyebrows furrowed and his breathing ragged.

He doesn't say another word as I step away from him and walk toward Nix, whose eyes are locked on me.

"Are you okay?" His gaze follows me around to the driver's side.

"Get in the car," I say calmly, but the quiver in my voice is obvious.

Once we're both in, I back out of his driveway without sparing him another glance. After I'm on the main road, I pull off to the side, losing every ounce of composure I maintained standing in front of him.

Frantically rubbing the spot our cheeks touched, feeling like I have a million ants crawling over my body, I cry out, "No. No. No. *Fuuuuck*."

I held it in. I did it. I faced him without a single tear. Without fear. But now I'm being overtaken by it. My system is shutting down as it floods my body, drowning me. My fingers claw at my throat from the lack of oxygen.

"What the hell, Tillie?" Nix pulls my hands away from my throat and grips my chin in his hand. "Breathe, Tills."

And I try. I do. But I can't get a full breath in. My eyes widen in panic, and he crushes his lips against mine. Prying my mouth open with his in a move similar to Jansen's.

Maybe it's a shock factor, but my sigh into his mouth is audible as my lips move of their own accord.

This is wrong. I know it's wrong, but it also feels right because he's bringing me back down. His hand slips to my cheek, and he continues to move his lips against mine. With each movement, I'm taken further and further away from my pain and memories. Our mouths stay fused until I feel damn near suffocation and have to pull back.

He rests his forehead on mine and strokes my cheek with his thumb. "Are you okay?" he whispers.

The question has tears pouring down my cheeks because *yes*. I feel like I could finally be free, but at the same time, I know I will *never* be okay.

"I'm driving us back to Novaridge. You rest."

Exhaustion settles into my bones until my entire body feels heavy, making any movement difficult. He lifts me, placing me on his lap, before settling me into the seat beside him.

Once he has me buckled, he pulls back onto the road and toward the town that's become my haven.

Twenty-One

Jansen

It's eight o'clock by the time her car pulls into the marina. I stay exactly where I am, taking up space on her foredeck.

Nix gets out of the car first from the driver's side, and it feels like a punch to the gut. He walks over to the passenger side, opening the door and helping her out. She uses the side of his body, leaning against it to hold herself up. All at once, I'm furious, nauseous, and concerned.

As he walks along the dock, his mouth moves close to her ear, forming words I can't hear. When he finally notices me, his steps halt for a second before continuing.

"Hey, Jansie," he murmurs.

"Don't fucking 'hey' me, kid," I spit out. "Where the hell have you two been, and why can't she stand by herself?"

Tillie's sigh is audible. "If the only reason you're here is to lecture us, you can leave. I have no more energy for men who think they have control over my life," she rasps, her voice nearly gone.

"*Wow*," I breathe out. "After *everything* I told you. After you *lied* to me this morning and left town without saying anything. After I sat here for an hour, worried out of my damn mind because you couldn't bother to let me know what was going on, you don't have the energy?"

She straightens her spine as guilt blankets her features. The sun setting behind her makes her look even more ethereal than usual. Even in her leggings and the dark blue sweatshirt swallowing her body.

"Why didn't you answer your phone, Nix?" I ask while gripping his jaw lightly and tilting his head to get a good look at his pupils.

His nostrils flare as he pushes my arm away from him.

"Are you serious, man? I'm not high. I forgot my phone when we left."

Tillie steps in front of Nix, tears welling and close to spilling over. "Did you honestly believe I would let him anywhere near drugs?"

No. I know you never would.

Tipping my chin, I narrow my eyes. "You lied to me, bailed on your shift, didn't tell me where you were going, and I had no clue when you were coming back. Neither one of you answered your goddamn phones. What was I supposed to think?"

The tears she's been holding back spill over her cheeks. After wiping them away with the back of her hand, she holds her head high as she looks me in the eye. "I am *not* your mother," she says in a soft but stern voice.

I'll never forget this feeling. It's comparable to a dozen frozen arrows being shot through me all at once.

Our gazes lock, but I don't miss the small gasp that leaves Nix.

I lean down, my nose practically touching hers.

"*Fuck you*," I choke out.

"No, fuck you, Jansen. Fuck *you* for thinking so low of me, and fuck you for telling me the truth. Fu-uck y-you," she sobs, covering her mouth with a trembling hand and stepping around me to get through the sliding door.

Nix scrubs both hands over his face, sighing wearily. "I'm going to stay at Granddad's."

"No need. I'm leaving." I start to walk past him, but he stops me with a firm hand on my chest.

"You have no idea how much it's killing me to walk away from her right now, and if you give a shit about her at all, you won't. She needs you because I think you know more than I do. Whatever she did today...the guy she went and saw...it took a piece of her, Jansen. I've never seen her so upset before. She had some kind of attack when we—"

Unable to listen to him finish, I burst through her sliding doors. The bathroom light isn't on, so I head straight to the back, opening the door to her bedroom.

She's curled up in the middle of the bed with her face pressed into the comforter. Her shoulders and back shake, but her cries are silent. I kick my shoes off before scooping her into my arms, cradling her to my chest. She doesn't hesitate to wrap her arms tightly around my neck, burying her face there.

"Why, Freckles?" I ask in a pained voice. "Why would you go near him?"

"I ne-needed to t-t-tell hi-im. I'm tired."

"Shhh." Rocking her gently, I rub small circles on her back. "It should've been me with you."

Her head shakes against my neck. "You cou-couldn't."

"I know," I murmur in her ear.

What would've happened if I'd gone with her? I have no doubt I would've beaten the shit out of him. The thoughts I have about Holden and what I want to do to him are unhinged. What if I'm capable of unrestrained violence? It's a question I've been asking myself daily. I have the fucker's address. I could go anytime, but fear holds me back. We never truly know what we're capable of until we're put in a situation that permits it. Driving to Sayersville and beating him to a bloody pulp would land me in jail, away from Tillie. Away from the life I've built. She's worth it, but not at the cost of having to go the entirety of my life *without* her.

My heart picks up speed while thoughts continue to spiral through my mind.

Because one thing is clear.

Tillie Porter owns a piece of me now.

Her body goes completely lax in my arms, and I lay her down gently on the bed, settling in beside her. She rolls over, using my chest as her pillow, and I stare down at the woman who started out as an inconvenience. Weeks ago, my only goal was to get rid of her, but now I can't imagine being here without her.

Sleep doesn't come easily, but as soon as my lids close, a loud clap of thunder sounds, causing Tillie to jerk awake. The next crack of thunder lasts for a few seconds, and her body trembles against mine.

"I'm here," I whisper. "You're safe."

She nods weakly, wrapping herself around me tighter.

When I was little, storms used to scare me too. My mom would be gone, and the rumbles of thunder would feel like they shook our house. As a little boy, alone, I was terrified I'd get blown away or the house would fall on top of me. So I'd take my blanket with me under my bed and cover up completely.

We're not getting under her bed, but I do pull the comforter up over both our heads, blanketing us entirely.

"Are we hiding from the thunder?" she whispers.

"We are," I whisper back, kissing her hair.

Her finger traces circles on my side. "I was so angry when I woke up this morning because I felt so much shame, and nothing about what happened between us was shameful."

I don't have a degree in psychology, but she needs more than me saying "*It's okay, just don't feel ashamed*," and usually, finding the right words can be tough for me.

This time, they come easily. "Let me carry your shame. You don't have to hide it from me, Freckles. I'll hold you through it, talk you through it, or pleasure you through it, but let me hold some of it too."

Her hands push my shirt up, and I take the hint, pulling it over my head and tossing it aside.

Pleasure, it is.

After I've wrapped us both in the blanket, she presses her face into my chest, kissing a path to my neck. My cock instantly hardens as her small hand travels down my abdomen to the waistband of my pants.

"Not tonight," I say, my voice raspy. "Tonight is about you."

Gripping the hem of her leggings, I slide them, along with her underwear, down her legs. When I push her sweatshirt up, her breasts are on full display, her peach-colored nipples taut.

The groan working its way up my throat is feral. I've never been addicted to a person the way I am to her. I'm already addicted to her snarky-ass attitude, her affection, her taste, and her voice, and I haven't even been inside of her yet.

She pulls the sweatshirt off, tossing it aside.

"Anything I do or say that you don't like, you need to tell me. Okay?"

Her lips silently mouth "*Okay*" as she nods, her chest rising and falling at a rapid pace.

"Spread your legs," I whisper in her ear, eliciting a shiver from her and a soft moan to pass through her lips.

If her moans were the last sound I ever heard, I'd be perfectly content. Needing to hear more, I nip her jaw and kiss my way down her neck. She writhes beneath me, her breathy moans my new favorite soundtrack.

I'm not sure how I'm still able to function with every drop of blood in my body rushing straight to my dick. Once I have her pebbled nipple between my teeth, her hand grips the back of my hair as her nails dig into my scalp, and she guides my face to the other side.

"How wet do you think you are right now?" I ask, coming up for air.

Her hips lift in response, seeking relief. "Find out."

I don't hide the grin on my face. Her bossy and snarky side is sexy as fuck. When I throw the blanket back, she winces. Her self-consciousness is obvious, and I can only imagine why. Add it to the number of reasons that piece of shit doesn't deserve to breathe the same oxygen as the rest of us.

I glide my hands over her, starting at her thighs and roaming up to her neck. Cradling her nape, I lift her toward me and onto my lap. Her eyes have a hard time meeting mine, even if she is enjoying this. With my pointer finger, I push the stray hairs framing her face behind her ears, and she turns into my palm, her cheeks flushed.

A low rumble of thunder sounds again, and the rain pouring down sounds against the roof and glass. I spread her out on the bed and sit back on my calves, unable and unwilling to stop my gaze from roaming over her body.

Absolute perfection.

"Give it to me," I request, staring at her until she's brave enough to make eye contact.

Her brows furrow. "What?"

"I said I'd carry your shame, so give it to me for tonight."

Her throat works as she swallows.

"Tonight is about taking back your power. I want to be the man to give you everything I can, but you have to let me. You have to trust me."

A few seconds pass in silence before she takes a deep breath.

"He...he always commented on my weight. When I was on drugs, I lost a lot of weight, but now I'm sober, and my appetite is back. I've gained a bit."

Sliding further down the bed, I slip both of her thighs around my neck and kiss every inch of them. Her mouth parts, and her emeralds glisten, looking like true gems.

Only once every inch of her thighs has been caressed by my lips do I look up at her. "Your body is perfection, Tillie. You are the most beautiful woman I've ever met. You hypnotized me the second you walked into my office." I slide my hands farther up her thighs, stroking the sensitive creases on both sides with my thumbs. "Truthfully, every time you walk away from me, I can't help but admire your ass and curves."

She chuckles, giving my hair a playful squeeze. I rest my cheek on the inside of her thigh, waiting to see if she needs to say anything else.

"He called me his whore today. He always did, but I hadn't heard it in so long I almost forgot." Her words die off as she avoids looking at me. "And knowing what I know now—that it was...it was all for nothing—I've never felt more like it."

I'm a firm believer in everyone having the facts, but a part of me wishes I'd never told her about Holden and the embezzlement, but her dad would've found out eventually. The truth was inevitably going to come out.

I continue to remind myself that tonight is about her feelings, about giving her a piece of her power back, even if it's small. My feelings are minuscule. The only thing that matters right now is her and her pleasure.

"You are *not* a whore," I scold, placing my face between her thighs in line with her pussy. I lick one long stroke, circling her clit with my tongue.

I'm considering the possibility of her allowing me to keep my face here all night. Her scent is intoxicating; her taste has me ravenous. I've always prided myself on never falling into the pattern of addiction my mother did, but tonight proves I've inevitably repeated history. Tillie is *my* addiction.

As I continue to eat, she pulls my hair and writhes against my mouth. She's close, and I want to be face-to-face with her when she comes. I want to watch her fall apart and swallow down every moan. When I pull back, she whimpers. I settle beside her, gripping her thigh and wrapping it around my waist.

She looks at me through her lashes, and I don't waste another second before fusing my mouth to hers. Before Tillie, I've never kissed a woman with such raw abandon. Her small hand clutches my jaw, and my cock *weeps*.

She gasps into my mouth as I glide a finger through her slick seam and slowly push it inside her. The second I curl my finger, she rocks her hips, and I add a second. I part my mouth from hers to search for any sign she's uncomfortable. She's definitely not. Her eyes are heavy-lidded, and her tongue sweeps along her bottom lip, beckoning my mouth back to hers as she grips my nape, tugging me down. I keep my pace, rubbing her clit with my thumb.

Only when I feel like we might very well suffocate do I pull back slightly, breathing out against her lips, "You're not a whore. You're my siren. *Mine*, Tillie."

The delirious smile she gives me as she nods has my chest burning with fucking delight. Her hips pick up their pace, and the slick heat between her thighs continues to pool in my hand, sliding down my wrist the longer she grinds. I almost laugh at the thought of my dick being jealous of my hand, but goddamn.

"That's right, Freckles. Fuck my hand. Come all over it," I breathe out, closer to a release of my own than I'd like to admit.

She pulls my face down to hers by my jaw, crushing her lips to mine right before she cries out in the sexiest raspy voice, "Jansen, *yes*, I'm coming. I'm coming."

Her pussy pulses around my fingers.

Done for.

Groaning into her mouth, I come harder than I did when my cock was in her mouth. Our lips don't separate until we've both come down from the high.

After a few minutes of lying here and catching our breath, I get up. She notices the dark spot on my shorts.

"Did you...?" She stares at me in disbelief.

Embarrassed is something I am not. "I told you, Freckles. You're my siren. Everything about you is intoxicating and stimulating."

She bites her bottom lip to contain her smile.

"I'll be right back." After getting a warm washcloth and discarding my briefs and shorts, I return to the room.

If I could capture a moment of her to keep forever it'd be this one. Her eyes closed with her arms splayed loosely above her head. Raven hair fanned out on the boho blanket, every perfect curve on display, and one thigh hiked up, resting on the other. She's a vision of absolute fucking perfection.

Her lids flutter open to find my intense gaze glued to her, and a soft smile stretches across her lips. I stalk toward the bed, parting her thighs with my palms. She's not as hesitant this time as they fall to the side, opening herself up to me. The washcloth sliding down her seam has her biting the corner of her lip and releasing a small moan.

Once she's completely taken care of and sated, I climb into bed next to her, pulling her back to my chest, wrapping my arm around her, and palming her breasts.

The last thing I hear before she kisses my arm and drifts off to sleep is "And you're my unicorn."

Twenty-Two

Tillie

This morning, I wake before Jansen. His palm still cradles my breast, and his thigh rests between mine. If last night taught me anything, it's that walking away from this man will be hell, but I promised we'd part without a fight.

I start to move, but his hand tightens, and his lips graze the back of my neck as he nuzzles into me. My usual swarm of butterflies takes flight low in my belly at his affection. He groans when I turn my body to face him, and I rest my head on his bare, toned chest while wrapping myself around him.

"Morning, beautiful," he rasps, palming my cheek.

I place a light kiss on his chest in response. The shame isn't as intense this morning, and I'm hopeful it won't always feel this way, but there is a certain feeling hitting me full force. My craving—to numb; to forget.

It claws through my guts, shredding my insides as the butterflies disperse. The anger from Jansen's revelation of Holden's lies has dissipated, and a dangerous sort of indifference has taken its place.

But I shouldn't be.

Fury and devastation should remain front and center.

My relationship with my dad is ruined, and I'm not sure if it's worth repairing. *Maybe he would be better off never knowing.* That means I'm indefinitely sacrificing any chance of future healing because I'll never be able to sit in front of him without telling him my story. Resentment simmers in my chest, but not at Holden. This time it's reserved for my dad. He never asked questions. He never tried to understand why his straight A, respectful, and loving daughter fell so far from grace.

The craving takes on a pulse of its own in my gut, and I'm not sure I have the strength to carry on. I feel numb to the possibility of him coming for me again. I'm hopeful he'll stay away, but in a sense, he's already imprisoned me. The truest statement he made yesterday was that he would always be a part of me. It has me wanting to shed my skin, my thoughts, and my sanity.

Jansen's groggy voice filters through my thoughts as he strokes a thumb along my temple. "Can feel your mind reeling."

"I'm sorry about bringing up your mom last night. I shouldn't have done that," I say instead of voicing my thoughts.

He sighs. "I shouldn't have accused Nix of anything. I knew you would never put him in a position like that, but I was terrified at the state you were in and angry that you disappeared while lying to me."

"It did look pretty bad," I admit.

"Until I acquired the truth." He tilts my chin up while tipping his down to look at me. "I'm in awe of you, even if I'm pissed I wasn't with you."

"Promise me something?" I ask while still holding his stare.

"Anything," he answers without hesitation.

"You'll never feel responsible for me or my addiction."

His eyes narrow as he sits up, forcing me to do the same. My nipples peak, drawing his attention to them. Cursing under his breath, he grabs the pillow beside him and holds it against my breasts.

"Hold that so I don't get distracted," he commands gruffly.

My answering chuckle has his gaze bouncing back and forth between mine as his forehead creases. "Why do I feel like you're asking me to promise that for future admittance?"

Heat fills my cheeks from his very accurate assessment because I'm *tired*. Tired of carrying it all, of having to live day in and day out with the memories. Every part of me—mind, body, and spirit—has already been defiled, tainted.

His voice portrays his panic and a slight edge when he speaks next. "Look at me."

When I don't, he grips my chin lightly, tilting my face up again. My eyelids remain squeezed shut, knowing he'll take it as an admission, but not wanting him to *see* the absolute truth.

"Open your damn eyes and *look* at me."

I do, and the fire in his steely gaze has my breath catching.

"You don't get to give up. I won't let you. You're Tillie fucking Porter. The strongest woman I have *ever* met."

Shame rages in my chest like a beast rattling its cage, and I break his stare in favor of the floor while I shake my head.

"Stop. *Please* stop," he begs. "You confronted him yesterday. *You* did that. *You* are *not* a whore. *You* are *not* the abuse you suffered at his hands."

Ripping my face away from his hand, I attempt to put distance between us, but I'm on my back with him hovering over me in seconds.

"Jansen, stop."

"Make me," he says without a hint of animosity in his voice.

My heart rate picks up. "Get off me."

"No."

A second of panic seizes my limbs before I remember who the fuck is on top of me, and a hot surge of anger quickly releases them.

I shove at his chest, and he chuckles humorlessly. "That's all you got?"

I grip his jaw forcefully. "Get the fuck off of me," I demand through gritted teeth.

His amber eyes flare. "Fucking make me. Or do you like being so goddamn weak?" he sneers.

Without thought, I lash out, striking him, and his face turns with the force of it. My chest heaves as I snake my hand between us, cupping his manhood, and squeeze.

He groans and coughs before flipping us effortlessly so I'm now lying on top of him. Digging my nails into his rib cage, I push myself up until I'm straddling him. He smirks, and I lash out again, but this time he catches my wrist.

"There it is," he says as he brings it to his lips.

Still pissed off, I snatch my wrist from his grip, glaring at him. "What in the hell are you talking about?"

He palms my hips. "The fighter inside you."

At his admission, the anger slips away, and my shoulders relax.

Lifting his upper body effortlessly, he adjusts me on his lap, and I drop my forehead to his. "Seriously, Jansen? All that to make a point?"

"To show you that you're stronger than you think. To prove that you are safe with me. I'll take on whatever you need me to, Freckles."

"I'm not your responsibility," I whisper, my voice cracking.

"No, you're not. You're more than that, and this morning you woke up feeling helpless, but I am *begging* you to see that you're not."

Not having the heart to tell him I'm close to a downward spiral, I lean closer, placing a soft kiss on his lips before lying down on top of him and burying my face in his neck.

Jansen eventually leaves to get back to the bar early, and since my shift doesn't start until five, I opt to stay home. Did he call Nix before leaving and demand that he come home? Yes. Now we're both not allowed to be alone, unsupervised. After last night, Jansen needed a change of clothes, for which he did *not* provide an explanation.

"How are you liking it?" I ask Nix as his fingers fly over the keys of his laptop while sitting at the dinette table.

I've been in the same position—sprawled out with a blanket—on the couch all day. My body is growing increasingly restless, but I can't find the will to move. So far, I've spent the day binge-watching *Bridgerton*.

"Hmm?" he hums, his concentration solely on the screen in front of him.

Sitting up, I stretch my limbs out before padding to the refrigerator for some of the cut-up fruit I prepared and then head outside on the deck. The sunshine soaks into my skin, warming me up, and I feel better than I have all day as my thoughts drift.

If I do slip, that could be it. I may never come back to myself. Everything Presley and Dane have done for me would be for nothing. I'd lose the first job I enjoy. Nix would probably get discouraged about his recovery, but Jansen...Jansen would be so disappointed. It may not be something he could forgive, and parting on unforgivable terms isn't what I want for us.

The sliding door opens, and Nix struts outside, taking the seat across from mine. "Can we talk?" he asks, leaning his forearms on his knees.

Nerves take flight in my belly because I know what he's going to ask. "Sure."

"Who was the guy?"

It's right then that I notice the usual weight of my secret is much lighter.

"He works with my father. He assaulted me and felt like he had a claim over my life. I needed him to know he didn't anymore."

"You took me to the house of a man who assaulted you and didn't think to let me in on who in the hell he was?" he grits out.

Looking him in the eye, I try my best to let him see my apology. "I took you *because* you didn't know about him, and now...I want to move on, Nix. I can't keep holding on to it the way I have been. It's destroying me. It's almost like I'm decaying from the inside out."

His face softens as he reaches for my hand, and I let him. "Then we won't talk about it again unless you want to."

Wiping beneath my lashes with my free hand, I manage a small smile. "Thanks. You're my best friend."

His answering grin is small, but the pain is noticeable. Pain that I'm causing because of my mixed signals. I wish he understood how much it takes for me to call someone a friend.

"About last night..." I start.

"I did the only thing I could think of to pull you out of what was happening. I'm sorry if I crossed a line. You're with Jansen. I promise I understand, and it won't happen again."

Nudging his leg with my foot, I chuckle to ease the tension. "I'm not upset with you at all. I just don't want anything to come between us. I've never been close to someone the way I am with you. It may be hard to hear, but you feel like my family now. I've never really had that before."

A boyish grin appears on his face. "Well, you can't refer to me as your brother, but I guess second cousins could do. Kissing cousins, and all that." He winks, and I snort, laughing harder than I have in a long time as relief rushes over me.

Losing Nix would be equally as heartbreaking as losing Jansen, but for different reasons. They both own a piece of my heart now. I glance up to see him looking out over the water. His eyes no longer have bags beneath them, and I'm hoping that means sleep has been coming easier.

I stretch my legs out and rest my feet on his knees. "You seem happier. Less on edge than you were."

"I'm good." He relaxes further in the chair. "Honestly, I feel better than I have in a long time. The job is good. Space away from my dad has been freeing. For once, I'm excited about what the future holds. There's no desire to fuck up."

Blinking slowly, because I want to feel that confident in myself one day, I say, "I can't wait to see what life has in store for you."

Over the next couple of days, I do my best to stay present, but the need to suppress my emotions or feel nothing at all grows stronger by the day. It's like being dragged down into a deep hollow of misery, while I fight to stay on the surface. When I'm not recalling the remarks Holden made to me, I'm thinking about my dad. Reflecting on him has led me to think about my mom for the first time...well, ever. She'd cross my mind throughout my childhood, but there was never this betrayal I feel now. If she'd been around, if she hadn't abandoned us, maybe those things never would've happened to me. Those thoughts take me to where I might be now if they hadn't.

Would I have gone to college?

Would I be in a serious relationship or married by now?

Or would I have moved to a new city and focused on myself?

Who was Tillie Porter *supposed* to be?

It's become an obsession. I fantasize about a life that doesn't exist, but unfortunately, when the fantasy ends, I'm thrown back into my current reality.

Then there's the new revelation, continuing to play on a loop in my mind...

Holden is going to be a father. Bile rises in my throat every time I conjure the image of her swollen stomach and his admittance. If he's capable of doing what he did to me, how in the hell will an innocent child get away from him unscathed? That woman has no idea what kind of monster she's attached herself to, and my never-ending guilt continues to wrap itself tighter around my neck like a noose.

Liquid douses my hand, forcing my mind back to the here and now. "Shit," I hiss, grabbing a towel and cleaning up the mess I've made from overfilling the glass.

"Been that kind of day, darlin'?" an older gentleman in a suit sitting at the bar asks, chuckling.

Forcing a small laugh, I reply, "You could say that."

"I'm Joseph." He reaches out a hand in greeting, and I take it, shaking once before letting go and discreetly wiping my hand.

"What can I get for you, Joseph?"

"I'll have a glass of water. I'm waiting for the manager to come out for our meeting. I arrived a little early to get a feel for the place," he answers, looking around.

Before I can say anything, Jansen appears, glancing at me before turning to Joseph. "Hey, Mr. Brooks. Sorry to keep you waiting."

"No apologies necessary. I was checking the place out and chatting with your bartender, here." He gestures to me with a smile. "I didn't get to ask how you like working here?"

My eye twitches. A horde of hornets has replaced the usual swarm of butterflies, causing a stabbing pain in my stomach. He wasn't supposed to sell until late July or August.

"Tillie," Jansen says, a note of concern on his face.

"Sorry. Yes. I love working here. We stay fairly busy, and I love the entertainment offered. There's rarely a boring day," I answer easily, smiling.

Noting a few drink orders Ivy put in, I excuse myself to take care of those, and they walk back to Jansen's office.

"You've been spacey today, girl. Everything okay?" Ivy asks twenty minutes later, once there's a break between patrons.

"Our towels are soaked from the amount of alcohol we've had to wipe up." Remi, my favorite bartender other than Mason, chuckles.

"Just an off day," I say, shaking my head.

"What are you doing this weekend?" Ivy asks.

Yesterday, I called Presley and asked if they could go ahead and come down, assuring her the man who showed up on her doorstep shouldn't be a problem anymore. If he is, I know Dane will take care of it on their end.

"I have some out-of-town friends coming in. We'll probably spend some time on the water. I'm not sure if they're bringing their baby or not."

"Ugh," she groans dramatically with a pouty lip. "I love babies."

"You should come by. Presley's great. It'll be fun having everyone together," I offer, even though the thought of it has me internally panicking.

"Sounds better than spending another weekend up here on my day off."

"It's bad form to invite one friend to a get-together in front of another friend. I know you like me more," Remi pipes up, popping his hip and crossing his arms to act offended.

Of all the employees at Clovers, he brings the most life into the place when he's here. He's always easygoing and joking around.

I swat a towel at him. "Sure, Remi. You're welcome to come by."

"I have plans with the parents this weekend, but thank you *so much* for the invite."

Rolling my eyes, I laugh at his antics, only stopping when Jansen and Joseph, or Mr. Brooks, exit his office.

"I look forward to hearing from you," Mr. Brooks says as they shake hands, and he sees himself out.

"Tillie," Jansen calls out, "can I have a minute?"

Remi "*ooohs*" in a low voice and waggles his brows.

"Be right back," I murmur, walking toward the back and barely catching his teasing, "I bet."

Once I'm in his office, I remain in the doorway, leaning against it. "What's up?"

"Can you close the door, please?" he asks while looking down and signing the papers in front of him. He's wearing his usual fit. Black or grey slacks with a solid button-up. Today, he has the sleeves rolled up to his elbows, showcasing his forearms. I'm an arm girl, apparently, because my gaze remains transfixed until I shake my head, clearing my throat.

"It's getting pretty busy out there." I try to give myself an out.

Something simmers beneath his amber gaze. A hunger I recognize. But his doesn't send a shiver of *fear* down my spine. No, the look in his eyes only sends a shiver of anticipation.

"I haven't been able to get you into a room alone since I left your bed." Closing the door, I lean my back against it. "You're a busy man."

He raises a brow in challenge. "Are you going to stay by the door?"

"Depends on what you have in mind?" I muse.

He swivels his chair and rests his head against the back of it, sprawling out. Before he can get a word out of his mouth, my feet are moving toward him. Once I'm standing in front of him, he palms my waist and pulls me onto his lap sideways. After placing a light kiss on my jaw, he rests his head back again.

"Need me to carry anything, Freckles?"

"Seriously?" I choke out, embarrassed.

I thought this was going somewhere else, and he's asking me about the one thing I don't care to talk about. My feelings.

"Do you know what your nickname is around here?" He chuckles, rubbing his thumbs along my skin.

"Bar queen, yes, I'm aware," I huff.

"Because you can work circles around anyone behind the bar. Your attention to detail is unmatched. You're proactive and willing to help every employee in any position. Riley told me how many times you've gone into the kitchen to help him on busier nights when you're waitressing." His smile, full of pride, melts my insides.

"I like to stay busy. Ivy is just as amazing. Mason could run the bar by himself. Remi knows all the cool moves to put on a show—"

"I know how amazing my team is. I hired them, after all," he teases.

"And Mr. Quinn," I sigh, holding a hand to my chest with dramatic flair. "He is the *most* humble boss one could hope to have."

"Humble enough to admit I made a critical error in hiring one employee, which was handled during Sunday's shift." He smirks.

"You fired Bailee?"

"I did. Remi is more than happy to pick up her shifts."

I lean back until I can stare him down. "But you didn't fire her because of me, right? Because if you did, there was no need. I'm capable of ignoring her."

He mocks offense, scoffing. "No one gets to speak ill of the bar queen." He slices a hand through the air. "But no, while you were a part of my decision, her continued sexual harassment and unsubtle commentary couldn't be overlooked any longer."

"Can't say I'll miss her," I deadpan. "But I do need to get back out there."

Placing a quick kiss on his lips, I stand and practically race to the door. Mentally patting myself on the back for not asking about his meeting or how much time we have left together.

"And don't think I missed your little deflection," he calls out. "Next time I ask, you won't be able to."

I turn in the doorway. "Presley and Dane are coming down for the weekend, so I guess whatever you had in mind will have to wait," I say with a sweet smile.

His answering chuckle is deep. "We'll see."

Twenty-Three

Jansen

Friday couldn't come soon enough. Mason is taking on the role of manager this weekend, and luckily, we've had no call-ins. For the next two days, I plan on remaining by Tillie and Nix's sides.

"Nix, I asked you to wipe down the kitchen," she huffs as I open her sliding door.

"Aren't these your friends? I don't understand why you're spiraling right now," he replies incredulously.

"Yes, but they've allowed me to stay here, and I don't want them to think I'm trashing the place, so can you please get it done?" She's in the zone, making sure everything is tidied and in its place. I'm not sure she even heard me come in.

"Yes, ma'am!" He over flourishes with a hand salute. "I will wipe the bits of dust off the kitchen counter and table." He huffs a laugh before picking up the rag.

She reaches for the yellow throw pillow resting on the couch and launches it at his back. "Phoenix, I'm three seconds from physically attacking you and then shoving the socks you leave in the corner of this living room down your throat," she growls.

He turns, looking at her like she's sprouted a third eye, then throws his head back and laughs.

As she steps toward him, he assumes a defensive stance, holding the towel up, and I choose to make my presence known.

Chuckling at their antics, I ask, "Do you need me to do anything, Freckles?"

Her head whips around, and she looks past me with a full, beautiful smile taking over her face. I turn and note a man and woman standing behind me.

The woman, who I'm assuming is Presley, rushes past me and pulls Tillie in for a hug.

"I love what you've done with the place," she gushes.

"I haven't done much. A few things here and there."

The man, Dane, steps in and beside me, watching the girls' reunion.

"Did you guys bring Emmy?" Tillie asks, looking around Presley at Dane's empty arms.

"Dane's mom is watching her, so we're child-free this weekend." She whoops.

Turning to face Dane, I hold out a hand. "I'm Jansen."

"Ahh, the new boyfriend." He smirks, taking my hand.

"No," Tillie exclaims while I say, "Yes."

Her eyes widen at my response as a pink hue graces her cheeks. In truth, we haven't defined anything, but she's definitely not my friend, and I can't introduce her as my addiction, so girlfriend is the easiest explanation.

Her emeralds narrow on me before looking back and forth between Presley and Dane. "We're good friends without a label, but if you need one, the most accurate would be *boss*."

"Kinky." Dane laughs as Presley tries to fight her grin.

"Well..." Presley clears her throat. "I think it's great you have a *friend*." She turns, looking around, then spots Nix.

"*Oh my God*, I haven't seen you in *years*," she exclaims, marching over to him and pulling him in for a hug.

"You two know each other?" Tillie asks, confused.

"He moved to Sayersville during my junior year when he was a sophomore, but he was always in advanced classes."

"I believe I'm the reason you passed chemistry," Nix teases, chuckling.

"What have you been up to over the years?"

He palms the back of his neck and squeezes like he'd do when he was a boy and embarrassed. "I went to the University of Arkansas and only came home a few weeks each summer. I graduated a few months ago."

I glance over at Dane to see how he's faring with this reunion and find him sitting on the couch, watching the interaction without a hint of animosity.

Tillie watches them with a furrowed brow and a slight curl to her lip. In a few steps, I'm behind her. The space seems even smaller with five people piled in. I pull her against me and wrap my arms around her chest. "Not your boyfriend, huh?" I whisper into her ear.

"I never even noticed him there, but we went to school together," she murmurs absentmindedly.

Deflection wins again.

For now. Because it's obvious this new revelation is bothering her.

"You were a senior, weren't you?"

"Yes, but it further proves how out of it I was," she murmurs.

I squeeze her a little tighter and place a kiss on her jaw, delighted when she can't hide the shiver it causes.

"There wasn't much to know. Kid was a nerd."

Nix gives me a pointed look over Presley's shoulder. "I heard that, asshole."

I chuckle and tip my head toward the door. "You want to walk over to Granddad's with me for a few?"

"Are you both Ron's grandsons?" Dane pipes up.

"We are. Nix is my first cousin."

He stands from the couch. "Mind if I walk over with you? I haven't seen him since last summer."

"No problem, man."

Loosening my arms, I palm Tillie's shoulders and kiss her temple before stepping over to the sliding door.

"I'll bring the tattoo kit inside on my way back," Dane calls out, looking at Tillie.

"You're getting a tattoo?" I ask.

She bites her full bottom lip and shrugs. "Maybe."

Nix and Dane step out, but I continue to take her in for a few more seconds before I nod and walk out after them. I've had the intense pleasure of seeing her completely naked, so I know there isn't a single inch of her skin covered by permanent ink. Which makes me wonder if this is about expression or pain...

"How is she?" Dane's question interrupts my thoughts.

Nix glances at me before looking out over the water.

"She's the best employee I've got. Loved by the people in town. She seems to like it here." I keep my response brief because he may be her friend, but she hasn't divulged certain things to either of them, and I sure as hell won't share her story without her blessing.

He nods thoughtfully, but before he can say anything else, Granddad calls out from the short distance between us.

"Dane, I didn't know you were coming down. How the hell are ya?"

When we step onto his dock, they shake hands, and Granddad pulls him in for a hug.

"Been good. Emmy's growing like a weed."

"Did you bring her down with you?" he asks.

"No. We haven't had a getaway yet, so my mom offered to watch her for the weekend." Dane smiles while he pulls out his phone to show off pictures of his daughter.

While they're catching up, I walk into his houseboat, Nix following me in.

He clears his throat awkwardly. It's always been a nervous habit for him when he has something to say, so I turn toward him with a raised brow. "What's up, kid?"

Nix's gaze doesn't meet mine as he walks past me and roots around in the fridge. "I need to clear my chest about something…"

Confessions he could make filter through my thoughts, causing my heartbeat to quicken a bit.

Instead of saying anything, I lean against the counter with my arms crossed over my chest and wait.

When he finally looks at me, guilt is etched in every line of his face. "When Tillie and I went out of town, I kissed her while she was having a panic attack. She wouldn't stop scratching at her face and crying. My words weren't getting through to her, so I kissed her," he rushes out.

Our stare off lasts several tense seconds before he looks away. The feeling taking center stage is betrayal, and surprisingly, not from my cousin.

"It wasn't some hot make-out session, Jansen. She was…I don't even know what she was, but it helped pull her out of it."

Words still evade me because she didn't tell me about it.

He glances at me before rubbing a hand across his jaw. "Don't be upset with her. She didn't—" He pauses while seemingly searching for the right words. "She didn't ask for it or initiate it."

"Yeah, let's talk about that. Tillie is vulnerable. Don't ever kiss her again unless she initiates it, or you and I are going to have a problem."

Shock registers on his face, widening his eyes, before his features harden and his jaw tics. "No need to worry, Jansie. She's made it clear she chooses you."

"I know I haven't been around. I've…I've had my own shit to deal with, but I plan on making more of an effort when I eventually leave. You're important to me, and I love you. But so is she. I've never felt this way about anyone, little cousin. I've never even tried."

He crosses his arms, his lips twitching. "You're a thirty-one-year-old man and you've never been in a relationship? Yikes."

Laughing, I elbow his ribs gently. "Fuck off. Are we good?"

"We're good. If you want, I can give you *the talk* later to make up for your lack of experience." He waggles his brows playfully, and I barrel toward him, putting him in a headlock.

"You little shit." I laugh, goading him on as he tries to escape my hold.

My phone buzzes in my pocket, and I let him go to check it, seeing Gabe's name on the screen.

"Everything good?" he asks.

"I need to take this," I murmur while stalking outside and to the end of the dock before answering. "What's up?"

"I'm giving you a heads-up. All of the proof has been gathered and sent to Mr. Porter regarding the embezzlement. He'll receive it within the next forty-eight hours."

I blow out a relieved breath. My biggest hope is that Mr. Porter files charges. It doesn't seem as if Tillie plans to, but her well-being is my priority right now. If reporting him isn't something she can mentally handle, it's hard for me to push the subject, especially after the truth was revealed.

A new fear awakens, and I can't contain the thought. "Do you think he'll come after her?"

His seconds of silence heighten my fear. "I wouldn't put it past him. Be prepared for anything."

"Let me know if anything suspicious pops up?"

"Of course. Phoenix was a great hire, by the way. Not sure what I expected, but he's a great asset to my team."

Pride in my cousin has my lips twitching. "Glad it's working out. I'll talk to you soon."

After hanging up, I take a few minutes to get my head right before walking back over to Tillie's slip. When I approach, the sound of female laughter rings out, and an even more familiar voice has been added.

"She's one lucky bitch, for sure." Ivy sighs.

My steps pause.

"It's not permanent. We've mutually decided it has an end date. Once he sells the bar, he'll be leaving."

The confusion in Presley's voice is evident when she asks, "So why would he call you his girlfriend?"

Tillie groans. "Because fuck buddy sounds too brash, I guess."

Anger courses through me, igniting the blood pumping in my veins.

"He doesn't look at you like a fuck bud—"

My sudden and loud steps interrupt Presley's statement—one I appreciate because what the fuck just came out of Tillie's mouth? My *fuck buddy*.

Three sets of wide eyes stare back at me, but mine are locked on her and the deep crimson staining her cheeks.

Yeah, I heard you, Freckles.

Tearing my gaze, almost impossibly, from hers, I give my attention to the girls sitting beside her. "Would you all want to grill at my granddad's before going out on the water?"

"I'm starving," Ivy proclaims.

"I figured Dane would want to spend some time over there," Presley seconds.

"Mind if I have a few minutes with my *fuck buddy*?" I ask, noticing Tillie's downturned, guilty expression as she wrings her hands.

"Mhmm."

"Sure."

They both speak in unison while shuffling past me, but Presley pauses and looks back at Tillie. "Are you okay, or do you want me to stay?"

My anger ebbs from that statement alone because this is what Tillie needs. People who genuinely love and care for her.

She smiles softly at her friend. "I'm okay. Promise."

Only when their footsteps sound far enough away do I utter a word. "Your fuck buddy, huh?"

Even though her cheeks are still pink, she meets my tone with one of her own. "Your girlfriend, huh? Relationships don't have a set expiration date. I was only being honest."

I know she's right, but it doesn't stop the pain her words cause. The last few days, I've been going back and forth because leaving her seems like an impossible option for me. My meeting with Mr. Brooks should've been a relief, but instead, I've spent the days since trying to come up with a feasible and professional way to decline his offer.

"Nix told me about what happened between the two of you when you were out of town."

She huffs, sitting back against the chair and crossing her arms. "Of course he did."

"Why didn't you?"

Her chin tips as she purses her full lips. "Because it didn't mean anything. He reacted to my emotional breakdown, and I didn't want it to affect your relationship."

"Bullshit," I spit out. "You know it meant something to him."

She's out of the chair and standing toe to toe with me in seconds. The crease between her brows is visible, along with the sheen in her eyes. "I made it very clear to him how I felt, so don't you fucking dare accuse me of leading him on. His tongue didn't even enter my mouth. He was freaked out, and I was barely able to register fucking reality," she says in a low, raspy voice, trying her damndest to rein in her emotions.

When I attempt to palm her face, she bats my hand away. "I'm not the only one of us who's fractured or broken. Work out your insecurities, and don't get pissed off at me about something *you* agreed to. And if you ever insinuate that I'm leading Nix on again, whatever this is will end."

Her exhale is shaky before she speaks again. "You've been there for me in ways I will always be grateful for, but you don't get to lift me up while also making me feel like a whore. You're leaving, and I may be fucked up, but I hope one day I'm healed enough to live a normal life. If I'm not, then my life won't amount to much. Regardless, it won't always include you, Jansen." Her voice cracks on my name.

This time, when I palm her face, she doesn't pull away, and my eyes lock on the freckle in hers. "I've never once thought you were a whore. This is new territory for me because every time I'm reminded this is temporary, I—" My pause to find the right words is her cue to put physical distance between us as she backs away, wiping her cheeks with the heel of her palm.

"Let's go to Ron's," she murmurs as she walks past me, and I let her.

I let her without another word because, for the first time in my life, a woman has taken me over, and I don't know what in the hell to do about it.

Twenty-Four

Tillie

Anything he said would've ended up causing me more pain because I know he only wanted to reassure me somehow, but his pause only proved he couldn't. Or won't.

Before I can make it to Ron's, Ivy appears in front of me. "Why didn't you tell me there were two of them?" she whisper-shouts with her arms spread wide.

"What?" I choke out a laugh at her dramatics.

"The guy over there who resembles our boss, but much younger?" Her eyes sweep to the side without moving her head, obviously not wanting to turn to look back.

Ah. She wasn't working the day Nix arrived, and he hasn't come into the bar once since he's been here.

I purse my lips to contain my laugh. "I don't believe they look *that* much alike."

Her jaw drops. "You're joking, right? They have to be brothers. And I mean, there are differences, like one is thirty and already claimed, but the other one looks closer to my age."

"*Ouch,*" a deep voice sounds behind us. Ivy squeezes her lips together but still manages to snort.

"Thirty may seem old to you now, but you'll be thinking differently in a few years," Jansen muses as he walks past us. "And he's my cousin," he calls out over his shoulder as he continues walking.

Rejection bubbles in my gut, but I pop each one rising to the surface. I didn't give him a chance to utter a single word, so I can't be mad about watching his perfectly sculpted back in a white T-shirt and toned legs in red board shorts as he strolls away from me.

Ivy snaps her fingers, bringing my attention back to her. "Hey. You can have *all of that* later, but I need all the details before I go back over there. Mason and I are never going to happen, so moving on is my next step."

"Right. His name is Nix. He's staying with me for the summer, but he's from Sayersville. I'm not sure if he wants to go back, but it's a few hours from here. He's got a good job, and he's an extremely caring person." My expression turns serious. "You're both adults, but don't use him for a rebound and run back to Mase when he realizes he's being an idiot. Which he will. Nix deserves someone who's all in."

Suddenly, her expression turns wary, almost nervous. "You don't have feelings for him, do you?"

"He's my friend. But he's been through a lot, and he's Jansen's cousin." I won't mention any kissing because it would only open the conversation to topics I'm not discussing.

She nods, seemingly going over her decision in her head. "Well, there's no harm in introducing myself and seeing where it goes. He may not even be interested." Her dark brown eyes widen, looking at me for reassurance.

With a playful roll of my eyes, I slip my arm through hers and guide us back down the dock. "He'll be interested."

A couple of hours later, we're all sitting on the deck eating the burgers and corn Ron grilled. After Ivy's official introduction to Nix, they've been inseparable. Right now, they're sitting stretched out on the dock together, and I can't help but smile when Ivy throws her head back laughing at whatever Nix said. She's five foot one, curvy, has a beautiful tawny complexion, an infectious personality, and amazing curls currently resting atop her head. She's the whole package. Of course Nix was taken with her. Even from here, I can see the affection for her in his eyes. The way they linger, and the grin that's been a permanent fixture since she told him her name.

When I look over at Presley and Dane, she's sitting in his lap, and he has an arm wrapped possessively around her middle. Seeing them has me thinking of Rhett and the last time I saw him. I can't help but ask the question I've been wanting to know.

"How is he doing?" I ask Dane. From the corner of my eye, I notice Jansen's head swivel toward me.

Dane and Presley look at each other, having a silent conversation I'm not privy to.

"What?"

Dane finally speaks. "He's good. He went back to North Carolina a couple of weeks ago."

"So Lucy came around?" My smile and relief are genuine because he deserves to find happiness.

Dane side-eyes Presley, and it's obvious there's something they don't want to say, but I won't push it. They're still active in his life, and I never will be again.

"Whatever it is, you don't need to worry about telling me. I'm happy if he's happy." I give them an out, which Dane takes.

"If you're set on getting a tattoo, I'd spend as much time in the water as you can beforehand. You won't be able to swim until it's healed."

"There's a spot not far from here we could go," I offer, looking at Jansen to find his gaze already on me.

Something's there I haven't noticed before. His posture is rigid. The muscle in his jaw feathers, but he doesn't look angry, only more…intense. A bow that's been strung too tightly. Maybe what I said gave him more perspective, and he's ready to end this. The thought makes me physically nauseous, which clues me in on where my soon-to-be battered heart lies.

"Jansen," I mutter when he still hasn't uttered a word.

Clearing his throat, he runs a hand through his hair. "Granddad still has his canoe, so we could all make it out there together."

Presley stands. "We'll head back to the boat and get changed."

"Ivy, do you need to change?" I call out.

Her smile is wide when she faces me. "I wore mine."

"I'm going to get everything ready," Jansen grumbles.

My heart races as I step into his path and place a palm on his chest. "Are we okay?"

He wraps his hand around mine, giving it a light squeeze before pulling it away. "Yeah. We're good," he responds in a low tone before leaning down to press a quick kiss to my cheek.

My cheek.

Then he's stepping around me and away. Looking around, I busy myself by picking up trash, and only when I stride through Ron's sliding door do I let the moisture gathering slip from my lower lashes. This is what I wanted, after all. To feel this kind of heartbreak. Soft but sad laughter bubbles up my throat at the insanity of my logic from weeks ago.

"It'll work out, darlin'," Ron's deep voice sounds from behind me.

Startled, I whip around with a hand over my now rapidly beating heart. "Sorry, I didn't know you were in here."

I try to suppress the tears, and for the most part, I do. My throat burns from the effort, though, and I blink rapidly.

"Come sit." He nods toward the chair on the other side of his table. His houseboat is much larger than the one I'm staying in, so he has a full table that could seat five to six instead of two.

Wiping away the evidence of my heartache, I do, picking at my nails.

"My grandson sat outside staring at you for about fifteen minutes straight with a look I know well." His voice holds amusement, and when I glance at him, his mouth is tipped up at one corner.

"What did *the look* tell you?"

He regards me thoughtfully for a few seconds before answering, "What he feels for you is scaring the shit out of him. You're it, darlin', and he has some things to figure out."

"You sound so sure." I sniff, pretending I'm shooing an invisible bug while wiping my cheeks as discreetly as I can.

He shrugs, smirking. "I'm an old man now. I see things more clearly, and it's the way I looked at Clover when I realized she was the only woman I'd ever want."

"We both agreed this had an expiration date." I shrug. "He runs, and I...I don't even know where I belong anymore."

"You belong anywhere. Everywhere. You're stronger than you give yourself credit for." He lays his hand atop mine, and I feel only comfort from the touch.

"Every morning, I wake up and think, 'This is it. This is the day everything changes. This is the day I get myself back.'"

Ron leans back, running a hand through his salt-and-pepper hair. It's the first time I notice the resemblance to his grandsons. "I may not know the details of what you've been through, but when something happens that changes us, we have to make peace with who we become after. There's not a damn thing wrong with the woman I've come to know. She's caring. A hard worker. Makes a great dip. Knows how to keep my two knucklehead grandsons in line."

Shaking my head, I giggle at his observations and wipe my nose as he continues, "What I do know with a hundred percent certainty is that you're going to overcome it, but only if you want to."

"Doesn't *everyone* want to?" I ask sharply, feeling defensive.

"No," he sighs, shaking his head. "Some people can't see past the destruction. They never get a chance to rebuild."

Before I can say anything more, Jansen slides the door open, looking between us. "Presley and Dane are back, so we can head out if everyone's ready."

"Thank you, Ron," I murmur.

"Anytime, darlin'," he says in a low voice, patting my hand with a soft smile.

When I step outside, Jansen's gaze roams over my face in that seeing way of his, which I'm sure shows traces of my emotional state. Placing a hand on my elbow, he guides me to the corner of the deck farthest away from the dock and stands in front of me to block everyone's view.

"What's wrong?"

"It's nice to have everyone together. Ivy and Nix seem to be hitting it off?"

He answers my question with a raised brow. "Can you ever answer anything without deflecting?"

"I'm not." I cross my arms and pop my hip. "It *is* nice having everyone together, and it's made me a little emotional."

His amber eyes, almost gold in the sunlight, convey his skepticism, but he doesn't say anything else while we gather everyone and paddle to their childhood spot.

On our way over, my thoughts are stuck on what Ron said about people who can't see past the destruction to rebuild. I'm terrified to see past it. Terrified to hope or dream of a life free of my mental prison. I've only ever been the woman I am now, and yes, I daydream about the woman I could've been had Holden never staked his sick claim on me, but she feels mythical.

She is free of filth. Confident. The thought of shaking a stranger's hand doesn't quicken her heartbeat. She meets someone who cares enough to stick by her side always, because they know she *won't* disappoint them. She *couldn't* because *she's whole*.

"I'm surprised more people aren't out on the water," Presley states.

"It'll be more crowded next weekend for the Fourth," Jansen replies as he climbs out and holds the canoe steady for everyone to do the same. I take his offered hand and climb out. But when I move to walk down the bank, he grips my wrist, pulling me into his side.

Once everyone's out and far enough away, he turns to me, palming my cheeks and tilting my face up. Again, he takes on a serious expression, but he doesn't say anything. The thought of what he might say, and the warmth of his palms, has my body trembling. Instead of waiting, I plaster the side of my face against his bare chest. He took his shirt off on the way over, causing his skin to absorb the heat. I wrap my arms around him tightly, and this sudden need to crawl inside him and wear his body as my armor consumes me.

The jarring reality of it has me placing a quick kiss over his heart and backing away.

"Come on." I nod to everyone who's laying out their towels before walking their way.

An hour later, the girls and I are floating in the water, while the guys sit on the bank chatting.

"I'm not waiting for someone who doesn't value me," Ivy tells Presley after explaining the situation with her and Mason.

Presley nods thoughtfully. They hit it off like I knew they would. "Life's too short to wait for people to change their minds. Our time is valuable."

Ivy's face drops as her palms rest atop the water, pushing her hands apart and bringing them back together. "I'll be stuck in this town for the rest of my life. I'm okay with it because my mom and my siblings need me, but it's frustrating that he won't *listen* to me when I've explained the situation. He sees me at the bar occasionally, blowing off steam, and assumes I'm chasing nothing but good times."

"Why do you need to be here for your family?" I'm a little sad this is the first time we're having a deeper conversation.

She purses her lips. "My dad had a stroke a couple years ago. He was only forty, but he never regained total mobility on his right side. He gets disability, but it's not enough to cover everything. My mom works from home so she can care for him, so I help out with bills and give her a break by assisting with my brother and sister."

"Sounds...heavy," Presley remarks sadly.

"It is." Ivy sighs, sinking deeper beneath the water. "But they're my family, and I can't walk away from them."

"They're lucky to have you. I'm sorry about your dad," I add, admiring her for her selflessness as my thoughts center around the fact I've lost the only family I have.

She shrugs, her shoulders slipping above the water. "I'm lucky to have a family as close as we are. He's still our goofy dad and my mom's soulmate, just doesn't move as well anymore."

Presley wraps her arms loosely around Ivy's shoulders. "C'mon, Tillie." Her head tips back.

I wade toward them, and we wrap our arms around Ivy, hugging her tightly before we release each other, and Ivy asks about Emmy.

Spotting a familiar break in the woods on the opposite side of the bank, I swim toward it. "I'll be right back," I call out over my shoulder.

I'm not exactly sure how to get to the cliff ledge, but I assume if I follow the path, it'll lead me to it. I search the dirt trail in front of me since I'm barefoot and take in the noise around me. It's late enough to hear the chorus of crickets. Birds chirp to one another, and the sound seems to echo. Laps of water rush the bank from boats vrooming down the lake. The varying sounds of nature and life being lived should be peaceful or inspiring. And maybe it would be if my thoughts weren't being surrounded by a dense, numbing fog. When I reach a break in the trees, the ledge becomes visible, and the soles of my feet soak up heat from the rough rock.

My mind transports back to the night when I told myself I'd fall out of my window before he touched me again, but I was too weak to follow through with it—too afraid of the consequences.

With shallow breaths, I inch toward the edge until the lake and everyone below come into view. The height is enough to make my knees tremble, while my head begins to feel lightheaded.

If I fall now, I'll land in water. I should be okay.

But if you're not, if it all goes away, would it really be so terrible?

Once I'm at the very edge, I turn with my back toward the lake. At this point, I'm no longer breathing evenly. Every sound seems muffled by the whooshing of blood in my ears. I'm only vaguely aware of the sounds from below as I squeeze my lids shut, spread my arms, and allow my body to fall back.

But I never plummet.

Two strong hands wrap around my waist and yank me forward with a force that causes us to collide with the ground, his body breaking my fall. My eyelids remain sealed as warm palms cup my face. Every limb on my body shakes violently.

"I wanted to prove I could do it," I whisper.

Twenty-Five

Jansen

"Do what?" My voice shakes as I frantically search her body for any sign of injury.

I had already started wading through the water to cool the burn on my skin from the clear-skied sun beaming down. Tillie didn't notice me moving closer to them when she began paddling toward the path to the ledge, and I decided to follow her in case she went the wrong way or wanted to jump with someone.

Fear like I've never known surged through my chest and propelled me forward when I saw her on that ledge. The rise and fall of her chest and the way her body tipped backward had black dots spotting my vision. I didn't know if I wanted to scream or if my heart was going to stop. I'm almost positive it did for a few seconds.

When I'm certain there's no immediate sign of injury, I crush her to me, running my fingers through her raven strands as we lie there. Her breathing calms, and the sting from her nails digging into my skin tethers me to the here and now. The moment she registers reality, her entire body stiffens and shoots up like an electric current has traveled through it.

She brings a trembling hand to her mouth, taking in my lying form and the cuts and scrapes along my forearm and down my side. "Oh my God. I'm so sorry," she chokes out.

Sitting up, I wince from the sharp ache radiating from my side. I'm almost certain it's a bruised or cracked rib. The physical pain doesn't compare to the pain staring back at me, shining through her emeralds.

"You said you wanted to prove you could do it? Do what, Tillie?" I huff, terrified to hear her answer.

She looks everywhere but at me. "I don't...I'm not sure. I—"

"Did you try to hurt yourself?" My voice cracks from the emotions I'm having a hard time taming. Anger, confusion, and relief.

Her eyes find mine, and her throat works. Those few seconds of hesitation speak more of her truth than she realizes.

Gripping her chin between my pointer and thumb, I bring my face down to her level. "Did you try to hurt yourself?"

A wrinkle appears between her brows, and she audibly swallows. "No."

"You're lying," I choke out as memories from one of the worst nights of my life play over and over in my mind.

She forces her chin sideways, out of my grip. "I wanted to see the ledge, and then this memory...I only wanted to know how it would feel. I was falling into the water. It didn't seem dangerous."

"You have to jump a certain way. Do you have *any idea* what could've happened to you? You could've drowned. You could've injured yourself," I growl, my vision blurring.

Noting my emotions, she softens her face. "It's fine. I'm okay."

"You could've died, Tillie, and I would've had to see you." My voice gives out as my chest shakes with the effort it's taking to keep my emotions locked in.

Tillie is intuitive. Maybe only with me, or maybe with everyone, but it's as if she can *see* the memories she's conjured up. Climbing into my lap, she wraps her body around me like a shield.

"If you jump, I jump," I mumble into her neck, deeply inhaling her familiar scent.

It's enough to even out my breathing and calm my shot nervous system.

She pulls back, keeping her arms locked around my neck as she blinks slowly.

I tuck the wisps that have fallen out of her messy bun, now framing her face, behind her ear. "Your hair is always messy."

Her jaw drops, and I move in, placing a kiss on the corner of her mouth. "I love it. I love you," I murmur, feeling like I might very well have a heart attack. I didn't mean for those three words to tumble out, but like hell am I taking them back.

Before she can say anything, heavy footsteps pound the dirt, heading our way. "What the fuck, guys, are you okay?" Nix asks, panicked.

Nope. An aneurysm. I'm going to have a fucking aneurysm.

Ignoring Nix, I keep my focus solely on Tillie, who's looking at me like she can't figure out if I'm her lover or her new enemy. "I mean it."

Her sad smile puts me on edge. "Maybe...Or maybe I scared the hell out of you."

When I try to lean forward, pain shoots through my right side, and I hiss. "My emotions have been fucked since you walked into my office and spoke."

She assesses me quickly and gasps. "Your side is already bruised. Nix, help me stand him up," she commands, looking at him.

Once they've both got me up to a standing position, I wave Nix away, assuring him I'm fine, but Tillie insists—rather bossily—on remaining tucked into my side with my arm around her shoulder.

"Can you paddle the canoe to this side so he doesn't have to swim?"

"On it," Nix says. "Jansie got fucked up, so we have to take the party back to the marina," he calls out to the group, whose attention is fixed solely on us.

"I finally convince Presley and Dane that I'm okay, and this happens."

Glancing down at her, I notice her bottom lip caught between her teeth. "You *are* okay. This was an accident."

She has to be okay. If she's not, I'll continue to ensure that she *will* be okay. My emotions were heightened, but I didn't tell her I loved her because of it. No, I told her I loved her because, for a split second, I imagined her gone. The pain from the thought of never touching her, laughing with her, hearing her voice…It's more excruciating than the physical pain I'm in at the moment, making it hard to breathe.

The paddle back is hell. Everyone keeps telling me to lay down the paddle, but the guilt blanketing Tillie's face has me assuring them I'm okay. Granddad greets us on the dock, but his smile falls when he sees the state of my side.

"What the hell happened out there?" he shouts. Granddad rarely speaks over a certain octave, so when I glance over at Tillie and her breath hitches, my annoyance flares.

"Shit happens, Granddad. No need for the yelling." Putting both palms on the dock, I push up, lifting myself out of the canoe, but I'm unable to contain my painful groan.

"Get inside, and we'll get you cleaned up."

I overhear Tillie telling Dane and Presley they can head back over to their boat. She assures them she's fine and she'd never been cliff jumping before, so she wasn't fully aware of the dos and don'ts. Nix and Ivy stick around, and Ivy stays as close as possible to Tillie. It seems I'm not the only one she scared the hell out of. She truly doesn't understand the effect she has on people.

Once I'm on the couch, Granddad searches for his first aid kit.

"I think we should go to the hospital," Tillie suggests.

"I'm not going to the hospital. It's only my rib, and I doubt it's broken. If it is, they'll tell me to ice it and take it easy."

She fusses over the pillows, trying to make sure I'm comfortable. "What if you punctured a lung? You could start having trouble breathing. We need to go. You can have an X-ray done to be safe."

"I'm breathing fine, but if anything changes or I feel worse in the morning, I'll go."

"Ron, is it okay if we stay here tonight?" Tillie calls out, looking me right in the eye.

"What are you doing?" I hiss.

Ivy becomes animated, clapping her hands. "We can all have a sleep-over!"

I look to Nix for help, but his attention is solely locked on Ivy.

"You all can stay here anytime," Granddad says with a bag in hand, looking at me and smirking.

"I doubt driving is going to be very comfortable, Jansie," Nix adds in.

Traitor.

I've always liked my own space. I don't need to own it; it only needs to shelter the items I carry with me and be comfortable enough for me to land.

"She can drive my Jeep back to the bar." I nod toward Tillie, whose lips are pinched together.

"I want Presley and Dane to be able to enjoy some time alone, but I also don't want to be too far because they came down to see me. It's rude."

"The bar is ten minutes away," I deadpan.

Granddad douses my side with rubbing alcohol. "Fuck. A little warning next time," I grit out.

He grunts, carrying on.

Ivy takes the seat next to Tillie, who's tearing up while watching Granddad clean my cuts, and wraps an arm around her, rubbing her shoulder.

"I'm *fine*. There's no need for you to be upset."

"I was so stupid. I shouldn't have done that. The rest of the night is ruined." She sniffs.

Ivy responds before I can. "It *was* pretty dumb, but you didn't know. We are absolutely having a crash course on proper cliff-jumping techniques for any future rebellion."

Nix snorts while Tillie chuckles, the sound releasing some of the tension in my shoulders. "My cliff-jumping days are over."

Ivy hums, resting her temple on the top of Tillie's hair. "I think that's for the best."

"I'll text Presley and let her know we'll see them in the morning. They *do* deserve a little alone time."

"So do we," I mumble, grumpy as hell about this situation.

The glare she directs my way has my lips twitching, and I shoot her a wink.

"I'll go grab some sheets and extra blankets. Nix, you know how to get the pull-out bed ready. Jansen and Tillie can have the spare room." Granddad looks at Ivy. "I have an air mattress if you'd be more comfortable with your own space?"

Her cheeks darken. "Uhm, no, it's okay. We can make it work."

Three hours later, after being forced to watch a rom-com about a fake proposal, and everyone has rinsed the lake water off, Tillie and I head to the spare room. Nix and Ivy are still sitting up, talking and enjoying each other's company. I'll admit, it's nice they've hit it off, but I also know Mason is going to be bothered by it. It further proves that when you care about someone, you hold on for as long as you can, or you move out of the way.

"I want to take you on a date," I murmur into her hair once we're both settled into bed.

"You don't have to. Days like today are more than enough." She nestles further into my side.

"I want to. You deserve more than what I've given you. We can visit the city or take a weekend getaway. I'll take you wherever you want to go, Freckles."

"You've given me more than you realize. I know you're busy, especially now with a potential buyer. Taking me out should be the least of your priorities right now." Her voice doesn't convey a hint of sadness or snark, but her entire body tensed against mine when she mentioned the buyer. Her leg over my waist and arm around my shoulder tighten their hold.

When I attempt to turn toward her, a hiss escapes from the pain radiating up my side. With a hand on my chest, she pushes gently to keep me on my back and lifts on her forearm so we're eye to eye. Her wavy hair falls forward, framing her face. In the dark, her eyes look almost black, and her features are more stark against her pale skin—full lips, round cheekbones, dark sculpted brows, and button nose.

She's so beautiful, it steals my breath for a second, as my earlier admission makes my chest ache with longing. For as long as I'm alive, I know I'll long for this woman.

"What I said earlier *was* due to fear," I rasp.

Her gaze drops, and I run my fingers through her soft strands. "Look at me."

Once her eyes meet mine again, I continue, "It was fear of existing in a world without you. There are no words to describe how that felt. My life away from you would only be spent thinking of you and wondering where you are or who you're with. I'm not walking away from you, only to long for you the rest of my life. Please don't make me."

The rise and fall of her chest is heavy, each breath escaping through her parted lips. And when she crushes her lips to mine, I sigh my relief into her mouth before deepening the kiss. I'm not sure what the future holds. Tillie has a lot of healing she needs to get through, but I'll remain by her side through all of it.

Those three words aren't said again tonight. Instead, I pour every feeling I have for her into the kiss that eventually steals both of our breaths before we fall asleep, her body wrapped tightly around mine.

Twenty-Six

Tillie

THE PAIN ISN'T AS sharp as I expected while Dane outlines the design he helped me choose, the dull buzz of his tattoo gun filling the silence. When I told him where I wanted it placed and why, he tapped his marker against his chin, deep in thought for a few minutes, before he uncapped it and began to draw on the inside of my elbow.

At first, I wasn't sure what he was drawing, but then tears filled my eyes at the beauty of it. *A lotus flower.* With his focus still on my arm, he explained that they represent rebirth and resilience. The perfect symbolism to cover up the marks of my past.

He kept the lines fine and shading minimal. But as he's cleaning the ink off a final time, I notice a single mark hasn't been covered fully. Dane sees me eyeing the spot, and he squeezes my wrist softly, waiting for me to look up.

"We can't live in shame because of the people who stole a piece of us. If you want, I'll cover the mark, but we all have scars, and you're choosing a path of resilience despite what was stolen from you. That one scar is proof of how resilient you truly are."

Presley sniffs back tears with a look of devastation, her gaze volleying back and forth between us. When I look back at Dane, he nods once, and a deep kind of mutual understanding passes between us. I fling myself forward, wrapping my free arm around his neck, and his hands circle my back, holding me just as tightly.

"It's perfect the way it is," I choke out.

Emotion swims behind his blue eyes when he pulls back, but he grins despite it. "You'll need to keep this wrapped for a few hours. Tomorrow night, clean it with antibacterial soap. After, you'll need to clean it at a minimum of twice a day. I brought a balm for you to use to keep it moisturized. You can't pick at the skin, and make sure you keep it out of direct sunlight for long periods. Think of it like a very pretty wound."

"Thank you so much. I've already sent money to Presley."

"*Tillie*," she groans.

My pointed look has her scoffing playfully and waving me off.

"He worked on a weekend trip. It's the least I can do."

"You don't work a day if you love what you do," he says as he cleans up the work area he set up. "I'm happy I could do it for you."

Jansen knocks lightly before opening the sliding door. One of our bar taps had a malfunction, so he headed there to see if he could fix it before calling someone in. Instead of his normal working attire, he's more casual in dark green chino shorts and a grey cutoff, showcasing his arms.

Nothing more than a kiss happened between us last night because I respect Ron, and I would be *mortified* if he heard something he shouldn't. But looking at Jansen now, desire stirs to life in my core. The spark in his eye as he catches me checking him out, and the way his lips curve, tell me he knows where my thoughts have gone.

"It's done." I hold my arm up proudly.

He strolls toward the dinette where I'm sitting. When he reaches me, he bends down, pressing his lips to mine and holding them there for a few seconds before he leans back to look at my arm.

"It's beautiful." He takes in the detail, and I see the moment he, too, notices the scar left uncovered. "It's perfect." The awe shining in his amber eyes matches his hushed tone as he rubs a thumb over the clear wrap Dane used to protect it.

"I'm surprised you don't have any," I remark with a raised brow.

"My body is marked enough, but if I ever choose to get one, I'll plan a trip to Sayersville."

"Appreciate it, man," Dane says.

"It sucks you all are leaving in the morning, but I'm sure you're ready to get back to Emmy."

Presley takes the seat opposite me. "I am, but she's had a good weekend with her grandparents. His mom has been sending me updates every three hours."

Dane sits next to her, pulling her into his side. "Yeah, she's sent *you* updates. I haven't gotten a single one."

"She knows I'm not used to being without her."

"When she's old enough, she's going to the shop with Daddy."

She scoffs. "You are not taking our daughter to work with you."

He looks down at her with a devilish glint in his eye. "By that time, you'll be busy with the babies I've yet to put inside you."

Jansen and I choke out a laugh as Presley's jaw drops. Laughing, she elbows his side. "Behave."

His answering wink and kiss to her jaw assure me I made the right call by letting them have their own space last night.

"I need to wash the sheets, don't I?" I groan and wrinkle my nose.

Dane smiles cheekily as he locks his sight on Presley, who's biting her lip to stop from smiling. "Nope."

·········

Cheers erupt from the patrons crowding the bar and tables, while a handful "boo" at the screens playing some big basketball game. We haven't stopped moving in two hours, but the excitement surrounding us has me buzzing with energy.

"Can you get the drink orders for table seven?" Mase shouts at me over the noise as he continues placing his completed orders on the bar.

"Already done. *Claire*," I call out as she zooms past, halting her steps. "Can you take these to table seven?"

She holds up a dainty finger. "One minute." Her voice is full of apology, her wavy blond hair falling out of her ponytail and her face flushed.

"I've got it," I reassure her, smiling.

"*Thank you*," she mouths, turning sideways to avoid a patron while speed walking to another table.

It's rare that both part-time waitresses are working the same shift, especially on busier nights, so her frazzled state makes perfect sense.

Once I've delivered the drinks and am back at the bar, Mason's gruff laugh reaches my ears before he sings, "*You are the baaar queen,*" in the melody of "Dancing Queen."

I nudge his shoulder with mine and stick my tongue out. My chest squeezes with giddiness as laughter bubbles up my throat, but I notice someone new at the bar, so I swallow it down.

"What can I get you?" I ask the guy waiting, quickly wiping the sweat from my brow with my shoulder, and work on autopilot while I mix one of the three Jameson Whiskey Sours a patron just ordered from Mase.

"I'll have a Guinness."

"Bottle or draft?"

"Draft, please."

"Here's one," I call over to Mase, sliding the glass down the bar.

I am the queen, after all.

He winks and places the glasses on a tray.

While filling the glass with Guinness, I glance up to observe the bar. The game is almost over, but we're a couple of hours from closing, and the place hasn't dwindled in bodies. Luckily, the drink orders *are* dwindling.

"Enjoy." I smile, setting the glass down on a cardboard coaster in front of the patron, and attempt to start on my next task.

"Are you new in town?" he calls out.

Inwardly groaning, I turn back and start wiping the bar to keep myself busy. "I am."

"When did you move up here?" He sips his Guinness, but his eerie stare remains on me. Mid-thirties, I'd guess, military-style fade, and a clean-shaven jaw. He doesn't look very imposing, but it's always the ones who appear so innocent that end up being the worst.

His use of the word *up* has me pausing. Mainly because Novaridge is north of Sayersville.

People can use that phrase without any real knowledge of direction, but he's also a man. Aren't men supposed to be good with directions?

"How long have you lived in Novaridge?" I ask without answering him.

"I asked you first." He smirks.

I do my best to hide how uncomfortable he's making me as I continue to busy myself. "I've been here a while."

"What's your name?"

"Anne," I say automatically, not wanting to give him my real name because my skin is crawling.

"Well, *Anne*," he emphasizes, "hopefully I'll see you around." He winks, attempting to give off flirty vibes, but he's missed the mark because faint warning bells sound off in my head. After throwing a twenty down on the bar, he leaves.

"Dude needs to learn how to flirt. That was painful to watch," Mason jokes as he leans on the bar beside me.

My gut tightens, but I attempt to laugh the worry away. "Some men only give creep."

"Seems like people are attempting to sober up. If you want to take a breather, go on ahead." He nods toward the back, and as soon as the words leave his mouth, my bladder begs for relief.

After scurrying to the bathroom, I lock myself in a stall and pull my phone out. Presley sent a video of Emmy "crawling," except it looks more like a one-legged booty scoot.

> **Presley:** Can you imagine seeing this at night? It's creepy as hell.

I laugh out loud at the text she sent along with the video. The sound of people filters in as the bathroom door opens and closes quickly, muffling the noise again.

> **Me:** Agreed. I'd have a mini heart attack. Lmao.

Putting my phone away, I open the stall door, and my hair feels like it's being ripped from my scalp as someone drags me sideways. They fling me to the cold tile with force, causing my head to ricochet off the floor. My vision blurs, and my ears ring while a weight covers my body.

No, no, no.

Blood whooshes in my ears as I release a scream that vibrates my vocal cords, yet somehow sounds muffled.

The slam of the door echoes, and the weight disappears. I'm suffocating while trying to suck in a full breath. My lids are squeezed shut as hands wrap around my arms, but I flail, shuffling backward until I'm resting against a hard surface with nowhere to go.

"No, please. No," I beg, but it's soundless. I'm taken back through time when *he* dragged me up the stairs by my hair. When he'd wrap his hand around my throat, squeezing.

A voice filters in, pulling me from my mental torment. "I fucking warned you, Bailee. Call the damn cops," it growls, and a whimper escapes me from the instant relief it offers me.

"Open your eyes, Freckles. It's me," the gruff voice begs, and the nickname has my shoulders dropping as the tension leaves my body.

Jansen appears through my hazy vision, and I lurch forward, clinging to him. All my senses return, and my eyes open again to find Mason and Claire in the bathroom with us as he inspects her knuckles.

Mortification over what happened and my response to it has my chest heaving while I place my trembling hands over my face. "I'm so sorry," I exclaim, shaking my head.

"You have *nothing* to apologize for." Jansen's tone is low and angrier than I've ever heard from him.

"How many people heard? How am I supposed to show my face in here again?" My frantic voice cracks.

"You shouldn't give a damn what anyone thinks. You were fucking attacked," he growls.

Releasing a harsh breath, I stand slowly and take in my surroundings. I focus on everything in the bathroom to stop my mind from pulling back in time—droplets on the sink, a chip in the paint by the mirror, the soap dispenser that looks low. A bout of nausea slams into me and has me taking deep breaths in through my nose. An inkling of pain registers a little above my ear on the side of my head. Reaching up with shaky fingers, I discover a small bump. But when I pull my fingers back, they're thankfully dry.

He's wrong. My response to her assault is humiliating. I should've been able to do *something* to protect myself. Instead, my mind turned against me. It brought me back to the past.

The other waitress, Marlee, steps into the bathroom doorway. "The officer is here."

Jansen takes my hand to lead me out, but my feet remain rooted.

"Tillie," he grits out. "You need to be with me to make a statement."

Pulling my hand from his, I back up. "What would you like me to say? Hello, Officer, she pulled my hair, and I freaked the hell out, so I curled up into a worthless ball because my mind took me back, and I wasn't here. I was there. I was there with him," I rush out, digging my nails into my arms that are crossed tight around my waist.

"*Yes*," he hisses, "I would *love* for you to say just that so more questions could be asked, and you'd *finally* file a report against the piece of shit."

Mason clears his throat. "We're going to get back out there. What would you like me to tell the officer?"

My gaze follows his voice to see him and Claire standing awkwardly with their eyes on the floor.

"Please don't repeat anything I said."

"We promise," Claire says with conviction as she takes a single step toward me. "But Bailee can't get away with this."

"She will because what she did wasn't a big deal. My reaction to it was."

"Look down," Claire murmurs.

When I do, I spot a clump of dark hair on the floor.

Heat races through my veins at the sight of my dark strands forcibly ripped from my head and discarded on the dirty floor.

"I pulled her off you. What she did *is* a big deal. Your reaction to it doesn't change that."

"Can you..." My voice cracks, and I inhale a deep breath, clearing my throat. "Can you please tell the officer to come back here?"

They both nod solemnly and head back out to the floor. Jansen and I don't speak again. An EMT strolls into the bathroom with the police officer. She shines a bright light in my eyes, causing me to wince.

"Your pupils are nice and responsive," she assures me.

Her fingers press against a tender spot on my head, and I jolt, hissing.

"I'm advising you to go to the hospital to have this checked out. There's a sizable knot."

I refuse despite Jansen's insistence.

"You're going. With them or me. Pick one."

My aggravation at his smarmy tone has me snapping at him. "And how many times did I ask you to go to the hospital over your ribs? I'm fine. Leave it."

His nostrils flare, but he shoves his hands in his pockets and stays silent while I make the report to the officer.

Bailee is arrested and won't be allowed back into the bar. Jansen urged me to file a temporary restraining order, to which I refused.

Though I won't deny feeling a sliver of satisfaction at seeing Bailee placed in handcuffs with a swollen lip.

"You're staying with me tonight," Jansen tells me as he leads me from his office, where I stayed the remaining hour of my shift.

There's no point in arguing. The EMT told him if I started feeling nauseous or dizzy, he'd need to take me to a hospital. As soon as those words left her mouth, I knew he wouldn't be letting me out of his sight.

He's barely said ten words since we left the bathroom, but the tension in his face and body is obvious. Guilt from the injuries he's still dealing with, along with what happened tonight, settles in. Trauma is a word I despise because it's typically used as a cause for any negative event people go through. When my therapist tried to figure out the root of my addiction, she would explain how possible it is to heal from the trauma we experience, but healing has never felt possible for me. If healing isn't possible, is it really trauma, or is it more? How am I supposed to willingly attach myself to people I could end up hurting? How can I attach myself to someone like Jansen, who's already been through hell?

It feels like I've taken tiny steps forward, only to be knocked back on my ass.

When we reach the apartment, I breathe in the comforting aroma of him and his space, while my feet carry me straight to the couch.

I glance at him in the kitchen and note the rigid muscles in his back as he roots through cabinets before slamming them closed. His chest heaves as he grips the counter until his knuckles are white, then pounds a fist against it once.

"*Fuck*," he calls out, hanging his head between his shoulders while taking deep breaths.

"This needs to end," I state in a low, lifeless voice.

He turns his head to look over his shoulder, and his dark brows draw together. "I'm sorry. I shouldn't be slamming shit." He runs both hands through his hair and squeezes the back of his neck.

"No, I mean us. We need to end." His shoulders go rigid, causing his biceps to flex before his chest rises and falls with his deep exhale.

I hate that even while I'm distressed, my body still reacts to his like it's starving.

Exhaustion weighs him down, etching across his face and slumping his shoulders as he drops his hands to his side. "No."

"Tell me about when your mom died."

Clenching his fists, he crosses his arms over his chest. "Don't want to talk about it."

"You found her?" I push.

When he doesn't say anything, I continue, "You found her, and that's why you got so scared when you thought I was trying to hurt myself."

Silence...Although his eyes plead for me to stop.

"How much did you have to care for her over those years?"

Silence.

"How many times did you have to pick up the pieces from her decisions?"

More. Fucking. Silence.

"How many times did you have to put *yourself* back together when she inevitably crushed you *again*?"

He nods slowly, his gaze never leaving mine. With slow, measured steps, he saunters toward me. I'm not sure if I'm pissed off at his response—or lack thereof—or relieved that he hasn't agreed yet and insists I leave. However, it's better to break my own heart than leave him with the task of doing it.

I'm starting to believe he never willingly could.

Twenty-Seven

Jansen

It's comical how she believes bringing up my childhood and dead mother will have me throwing her out on her ass. The comparisons she's attempting to shove down my throat aren't parallel.

My mother chose to remain on the dark, barren path she was on, traveling further and further down until she couldn't find her way back. Tillie's already chosen the path that's led her back to light and love; she only has to keep going.

When I've reached the couch, I plop down beside her and pull her into my side.

"I'm serious, Jansen," she squeaks as she attempts to pull away from me, but my hold remains.

"I'm taking you on our first date in the morning."

She pulls away again, and I let her. "You deserve more. In one week, I've injured you and made a scene at your bar. How many good days have we truly had? How many more bad things need to happen before you're finally convinced I'm not worth the trouble?"

Her question stings a bit, but I'm even more determined to change that. "What happened with Bailee tonight was my fault. I should've fired her the second time she came onto me, and I shouldn't have goaded her by kissing you. I made you a target. *Me.* Tonight is on *me*, and I'm so sorry."

She melts back into my side. "It's no one's fault but hers," she whispers.

"You know how I feel, Tillie. You're worth everything to me."

Her small laugh has my throat closing, because her reaction to what I say next is going to go one of two ways. "I signed the paperwork today to accept the offer on the bar."

She sits up, putting a bit of space between us while attempting to clear the emotion from her throat. "That's good news."

"I'm staying."

Those two words gain her full attention. "What do you mean?"

"I'll still travel for work when I need to, but I'm not leaving anytime soon. I'm staying for as long as I can."

The sheen in her eyes brightens the usual emerald, but she quickly shakes her head, closing them. "No, you can't put your life on pause for me."

Gripping her chin lightly, I turn her face up to meet mine. She'll never accept words, so I bring my lips down to hers. At first, she remains still, until I part her lips with mine, and then the dam breaks. She throws her leg over and straddles me. I'm only momentarily aware of my ribs before my desire for her overrides the pain.

That lust triples when her fingertips find my belt buckle, but I grab her wrist, placing her hand on my chest instead. "You have a knot on your head," I murmur against her lips.

She huffs her frustration, and my answering chuckle has the little tease rolling her hips with a smirk. A groan works its way up my throat as my blood rushes south, and my head falls back. I palm her waist and squeeze to still her movement as I try to remember how to form a sentence.

"Will you let me take you out tomorrow?"

"So I *do* get a choice?" she muses.

"No, but I'd love to hear you say yes."

She runs her small fingers through my hair affectionately before leaning down and nipping my ear. "Yes," she whispers, sending a shiver down my spine and straight to my dick.

Once the answer is spoken, I jump up like I've been electrocuted. "Bedtime," I announce as I walk to the bathroom to take an ice-cold shower.

Her laughter sounds behind the door, and hearing it has a smile stretching across my face.

·····•··•·····

"Where are we going?" she asks for the fifth time as we drive farther out.

"You'll see." I grin as I kiss the back of her hand and steer the Jeep into the parking lot.

I told her to wear something she could easily move in, and that was the worst and best suggestion I could've made as she sits beside me in a dark blue spandex set of shorts and a fitted crop tank top with a flannel tied around her waist. Her dark hair is slicked back in a low bun, and her face is bare of any makeup.

The strength it took me to keep my hands to myself last night should earn me a gold medal in the Olympic sport of "keeping your dick in your pants when the woman you're obsessed with is lying next to you." After getting out of the shower, I put together some ice for her head. This morning, the knot had gone down significantly, and she promised the pain level was nonexistent. So I moved forward with my initial plan. We'll still take it easy today, though.

The old metal building looks a little rundown, but it's kept me sane while I'm in Arkansas.

She squints, trying to read the sign on the entrance, then turns her skeptical gaze on me. "You brought me on a date to a gym? I'm not sure if I should be insulted by this or not."

Rolling my eyes, I get out and stalk to her door, opening it. "You know damn well I worship your body. This isn't about working out. Trust me." I offer my hand and release a breath when she takes it.

Getting her to come in was the easy part. Getting her to participate in what I have planned may take more persuasion. Her hand clings to mine as we stroll through the door. The smell of rubber and musk has me taking a deep, calming breath. The center of the giant space has a large boxing ring, while the remaining four corners have mats with different equipment set up. Jonathan, the owner of the gym, struts over to greet us.

"Hey, man." He claps my back before acknowledging the extremely nervous woman beside me.

"You must be Tillie. I'm Jonathan. It's nice to meet you," he says with a genuine smile that has some, but not all, of her tension releasing.

"You too. What, uh...what are we doing today?"

He knows I didn't plan on telling her until we were here. Less of a chance of her backing out or making it something more than it is.

"Jansen here signed you up for a few self-defense classes. I usually teach it and work one-on-one with students, but he assured me you'd be more comfortable with him."

Her posture is rigid, almost defensive, and I can tell she's too in her head about this.

"Can we have a minute?" I ask, and he tells us to find him when we're ready.

"What the hell," she hisses.

"You need this," I deadpan.

She bites her bottom lip and side-eyes the ring in the center.

"This isn't about weakness or what happened yesterday. This is about your confidence and being able to defend yourself."

Both of her hands rest atop her head, and she puffs her cheeks, only to release the breath slowly. "Fine," she says, while marching toward the center. "But you should consider looking up what a date is."

"This is a perfect date. I'll get to have my hands on you the entire time." I wink.

The devilish gleam in her eyes as she smiles tells me I may regret that statement later on.

"We're going to focus on three holds to get out of today. The bear-hug escape, wrist-grab escape, and headlock escape," Jonathan informs us. "We'll start with the bear hug. Jansen is going to stand behind you and wrap his arms around you. From there, I'll give you instructions."

I stand behind her, palming her waist first. I place a soft, quick kiss on her cheek before wrapping both hands around her waist and arms, encasing her.

"Without thinking about it, what's your first instinct to do to get out of his hold?" Jonathan asks.

Immediately, she uses her strength to barrel forward, and I lift her off the ground.

"Good. That's usually the first instinct someone has. They panic and want to get away from the person as fast as possible, but it won't do anything for you."

Jonathan steps into the middle of the ring. "This time, when he wraps his arms around you, I want you to reach up and grab whatever part of his arms you can so he can't move them up. Then I want you to lean back, widen your stance, and drop your weight."

This time, she does exactly that. She's able to wrap her small hands around my wrists. When she leans into me and drops her weight, her body slides down mine, and I bite back a groan.

"Good." Jonathan nods. "Now, with both of you in this position, what part of your body could you use to strike him?"

"Uhm, I could kick his knees from behind or throw my head back."

"Yes, a heel strike. Good. Anything else?"

"I could..." She releases one of her hands, keeping the other one over mine, and reaches behind her to cup my groin, squeezing slightly, and there's no doubt she feels how hard I am.

My arms squeeze a little tighter. "He said tell, not show," I grunt.

"Sorry, I got into it there for a second," she murmurs, looking back to Jonathan to see amusement in his gaze. "I could also elbow his sides."

"The most important action you can take with this hold is to keep your hands placed on his arms until they release. If he's able to slide his arms to put you in a chokehold, your chances of getting away have now lowered."

"Makes sense. Don't move my hands. Got it." She nods, and I relax my arms around her waist but keep them wrapped around her as we listen to Jonathan explain how to get out of the other two holds, which require a little more...skill.

"Today is about showing you how to escape, but also to show you what type of strikes we'll be working on in the upcoming sessions."

She follows his directions with the wrist grab, stepping to the side and maintaining a strong stance, then wrenches her arm forward with force and practices a palm-heel strike.

When I grab her right wrist with my right hand, she steps to the left, drops down, rises up, and strikes my arm away with force.

Every time she breaks free, her face lights up more and more.

The headlock has her feeling more nervous, though. She paces in small steps, shaking her wrists out. She may trust me, but trust won't make this hold any easier for her, and I want to try to keep her panic to a minimum.

I kiss her temple before leaning down. "I'm going to keep my elbow loose. If you start to panic, lift your hands or say stop," I whisper in her ear.

Her nod is jerky, but her body relaxes into me as she takes a deep breath in and lets it out, preparing for my arm. Like I promised, my elbow is loose, but her chest rises and falls rapidly despite it.

"If you have room, drop your chin to create more breathing space, then find the opposite elbow and push up with as much force as you can while twisting."

She doesn't wait for him to finish his directions before she uses every bit of strength she can muster to push up on my elbow as she twists and shoves me back.

I grunt from the force, but the prideful smile taking over my face has her chin tipping up and her lips twitching.

"Well done," Jonathan praises, clapping.

"Damn, Rocky. Where'd that strength come from?"

Her neck and face flush as she shrugs a shoulder.

"Now Jansen is going to put on some protective equipment so you can use a little more force with what you've learned."

Shit.

Once I've got padding on, I walk back onto the mat. "Go easy on me, Freckles," I joke, and a fire of challenge blazes in her eyes.

I'm a little nervous, but I'm also damn proud of how seriously she's taking this. By the end of the class, she's managed to kick my ass through the padding, and God help any man's balls she comes into deadly contact with.

Jonathan hands us each a water bottle. "So...how'd you like it?"

She beams at him. "I loved it. Thank you so much, and thank you for letting Jansen lead it."

"Jansen is probably more of an expert than I am. He has a few more years of practice," he jokes.

She blinks up at me. "Do you box?"

"I've been involved with MMA and boxing since I took the free classes at my old community center in middle school." I shrug. "It's no big deal. It helps me blow off steam, and when I was younger, it kept me from getting my ass kicked. Kids aren't too friendly if you're dirt poor and have to use the school's locker room to shower because the water at home has been shut off for weeks."

Her mouth sets in a hard line. "Little bastards."

Chuckling, I sling an arm over her shoulder and pull her into my side. "Some of the little bastards got what they had coming," I jest.

"I'll see you guys next week. We'll work on the strikes more," Jonathan informs us before we head out.

"You did amazing in there." My voice reveals my pride in her.

When I get to her door to open it, she presses her body into mine until my back is against the Jeep. With my shirt fisted in her hands, she stands on her tiptoes and fuses her lips to mine.

I love it when she takes control like this; paired with the strength and confidence she showed in the gym, my already thin line of patience has snapped.

"Are you ready?" I breathe into her mouth.

She pulls back, blinking.

"Will you be certain in knowing who's going to be buried inside you?" I murmur, palming her cheeks. "Are you with me?"

"Always."

Twenty-Eight

Tillie

The drive back to his place is filled with silent but deliciously tense anticipation. My confidence that I'll know exactly who I'm with is unwavering, and it speaks to the kind of person he is that he wanted to wait until I knew without a doubt.

"Your ribs?" I rasp, my voice hoarse.

He reaches for my thigh, squeezing lightly. Heat rushes and builds between my legs.

"My ribs are fine."

At the gym, I took extra care to ensure I aimed my jabs at his left side. With light force, I swat his right side, causing him to wince.

"You *liar*. They're still sore," I exclaim.

"If you're not ready for this, we can find something to do. I don't want you to say yes if you aren't, but my ribs are the last thing on my mind at the moment."

I interlace our fingers with a silent chuckle. "I don't want you injuring yourself."

He scoffs playfully. "I'll be just fine, Freckles."

To keep my mind from spinning and my nerves under control, I focus on it being the Fourth of July and how, hours from now, the bar will be packed if the traffic is any indication. Our usual order for alcohol and food was tripled in preparation. Jansen said the campground on the other side of the lake wouldn't have a reservation available from now until Sunday.

By the time we pull into the parking lot, I'm ready to climb into his lap, but I notice a single car is parked in front of the bar.

"The hours are marked clearly on the damn door." The scowl on his face and the impatience in his voice have laughter bubbling out of me. It's nice to be so desired by another person.

We get out, walking hand in hand to the bar entrance without sparing the vehicle another glance. Before he can get the door unlocked, the car door opens, and we both turn.

Jansen releases a small huff of annoyance before plastering on a grin. "We're closed right now, sir. We open at one."

My body goes rigid as I stare at the man walking over to us with slow steps. His eyes, the same color as mine, never leave me. Jansen notes our reactions, glancing back and forth between us, before stepping in front of me as a shield.

"Can I help you?" he bites out.

"I'm here for my daughter," he gruffs, though his voice cracks on the last word, and something in me physically cracks upon hearing it.

Sidestepping Jansen, I fix my stare on the window beside my dad. "How'd you find me?"

"Hired someone. He had a picture of you, so he knew as soon as he saw you who you were, but when he asked your name, you told him Anne. Tillie Anne. I drove straight here and decided I'd wait until you showed up."

His voice is rough and low, the emotion and exhaustion evident. Jansen's hand, still wrapped around mine, pulses, letting me know he's here. And I know if I asked him to make my dad leave, he would.

Slowly, my gaze wanders to the man who represents everything I've lost, and I swallow around the ache in my throat his appearance causes.

He looks disheveled in a wrinkled button-up and jeans. His eyes have dark bags beneath them, and his greying hair is messy, as if he's run his fingers through it a hundred times. It's jarring to see him in this state. The last time I saw him so unkempt was the night of my overdose.

"Wh-why are you here, Dad?" I stammer as my throat closes.

When moisture gathers and falls over his lower lashes, he lets out a pained cry, and I collapse.

Before he can get to me, Jansen already has me in his arms. "I've got her," he tells him, his voice thick with emotion.

Once Jansen has the door unlocked and he's stepped through, he nods, motioning for my dad to follow, then locks up behind him. With the space empty, Jansen sits me at a table and goes behind the bar to grab some water. My gaze follows his every move as I use him as a focal point to keep me tethered to the here and now until we're all seated. None of us seem to want to speak first.

Unable to look at him, I pick at the skin on my thumb. "How'd you find out?"

Those four words have another pained mewl leaving his lips before he answers in a gruff voice, "I received information about an employee embezzling funds. When I found out it was..." He pauses, not wanting to speak his name. "When I found out who it was, I called him in and confronted him about it. Son of a bitch knew how to work several schemes. If I hadn't gotten the evidence, it never would've been on my radar."

My hands tremble as he pauses again. "I figured he'd beg forgiveness or at least show remorse, but he was a smug bastard about it. With that information, I had enough proof to remove him as a partner, and I threatened legal action. Then he told me..." His shoulders quake with his next shuddery exhale.

I've never heard my father sob, but with his face in his hands, the something in me that cracked earlier shatters. I don't say anything to ease his pain, because I'm still so fucking angry. Angry he didn't *see*. He didn't *ask*. I spent years believing I was protecting him when I *needed* him to protect *me*.

As I sit here and watch the emotional havoc he's experiencing, I don't shed a single tear despite the turmoil clawing through me. My voice is low but devoid of emotion when I ask, "What did he tell you?"

He cradles his head in his palms when he speaks. "He told me he had…pictures…and videos of you two that he would release if I pressed charges. He made sure I understood it could ruin you."

I scoff. "Little late for that."

He ignores my statement. "When…" He pauses, his throat working. "When did he rape you the first time?"

His very direct question is jarring, and for a moment, I stare at him. "Sixteen. The first time you sent him to the house with dinner during the blackout. He said you were the one embezzling money, and he had proof."

"Did he show you proof?"

The question feels like a slap I physically flinch away from.

Jansen's deep voice chimes in, snapping, "She was a kid who was scared her only parent would end up in jail."

He doesn't spare Jansen a glance, and for some reason, it irks me. "None of this is your fault, Sweets. I only asked to see how far he'd taken his monstrous lie." When he reaches across the table for my hand, I pull it back.

"You couldn't have known what was happening, but you had to know *something* was off, Dad, and you never asked." Once the dam that has held my words behind it cracks, the fissure widens, and they rush through. "I was a straight-A fucking student. I was more comfortable being at home than going out. We had inside jokes and watched our favorite shows together, and you never once thought it was odd when all of that changed overnight?"

He sniffs as the muscle in his jaw feathers. "I didn't know what to make of it. You were getting older. I thought it might have something to do with your mother being absent or the crowd you were hanging out with. Rhett was a horrible influence, and you were spending more and more time with him."

"He was the only person I could depend on, and you ruined his fucking reputation," I shout. "God, Dad, he was sober. He'd *been* sober for over a year."

"You overdosed at his house." His statement is spoken with skepticism, and still, after discovering the truth...He *still* doubts my word.

"Holden and I met up twice a week. That was the deal. That had always been the deal, but he wanted more, and I felt trapped. I told Rhett you'd kicked me out and I had nowhere to go so he'd let me stay with him. We...we got into an argument, and he asked me to leave. I used *what I already had on me* while he was in his bedroom."

He rubs his temples. "Holden convinced me you'd gotten it from Rhett."

"Because Rhett was the only person I had, and he wanted to isolate me from him too."

We both sit there silently stewing over the past, over the what-ifs, over all the secrets coming to light.

"I want you to come back to Sayersville to file a report."

My jaw drops as I stare into green eyes identical to mine. "I can't. No. I don't ever want to set foot into Sayersville again."

Each pain-filled word cuts through him. His heartbreak is evident in the droop of his shoulders. The sheen in his eyes. "He can't get away with this."

"Dad, I'm sorry about the money—"

"I don't give a damn about the money, Tillie Anne. He *used* you as a get-out-of-jail-free card. His embezzlement started that year, and he manipulated you into believing me a crook so when this day came, he had something to hold over my head. My daughter. *My little girl*," he exclaims while pounding a fist against his chest.

"Dad." My voice cracks. "I just want to move on." As I run my hands down my face, the bone-deep exhaustion from this nightmare has me saying, "Call his bluff and file charges for the embezzlement. I'm twenty-five. If pictures or videos of me get out, it's not the end of my world. I've been through worse."

Jansen's arm wraps around my shoulder, pulling me into him, and he kisses my temple, his lips moving against it. "Gabe can have the pictures and videos wiped from his computer. He didn't want to before in case you needed evidence one day."

I snap my neck sideways so fast I could potentially have a case of whiplash. "Did you see them?"

"No. I didn't see anything," he assures me, shaking his head.

Every muscle in my face hardens as his betrayal trickles in. "But your friend did?"

"He only saw enough to know what he was looking at."

Embarrassment and anger weave together, making me dizzy as I stand, knocking the chair back. "Dad, I don't live far from here. Can you take me home?"

"Don't do this." Whatever Jansen sees on my face has him pressing his lips together in a line while his jaw tightens. A hint of panic sparks behind his eyes. "I'll take you home."

Ignoring him, I storm toward the door, but he steps in front of me, blocking my path.

"I don't want to be near you right now. You lied to me. You could've told me the whole truth."

"You're embarrassed and upset right now. I understand."

My dad steps beside me, putting a hand on Jansen's chest to back him up.

He bats his arm away and sneers, "Don't fucking touch me."

Dad stands to his full height, nose to nose with Jansen. "She wants to go home, so we're both walking out of that damn door, son."

He tips his chin, his nostrils flaring, so I place my palm firmly on his chest. "No."

That one word deflates him, even as his chest heaves.

"I'll be back for my shift, but I *need* space right now."

Palming my cheeks, he presses his lips to my forehead before slinking past us to the back hallway without another glance.

Dad and I are silent on the drive, other than me calling out directions. When he pulls into the marina and parks, he relaxes into his seat. "So this is where you've been?"

"Home sweet home. It's nice, and I like the town."

He nods thoughtfully. "We used to come here when you were still a toddler. Your mother loved the lake."

"Why don't you ever talk about her?" There will always be a type of biological pain from being abandoned by the woman who birthed me, but I've never once asked how he felt about when she left him too.

He shrugs dejectedly. "Never saw a point. She chose to leave us, and when she did, I promised I'd always try to fill that gap. I failed, and I don't see how I'll ever be able to make up for it."

Right now, I don't have the mental or emotional capacity to coddle him. "I'll text your phone my new number. I meant what I said, though. Call his bluff."

He nods, clearing his throat and looking out the windshield at the lake. "Do you have cameras?"

"No. He doesn't know where I am."

"If I found you, he can too." His words send a shiver down my spine.

"I'll get cameras as soon as I can," I promise.

"And keep the fellow around." He looks at me pointedly.

Mention of Jansen has a lump forming in my throat, but I manage a nod.

"I love you, Sweets," he croaks out.

"I love you too."

We don't hug, and the awkwardness of our goodbye as I unbuckle to step out of the car leaves me feeling numb. Instead of the truth bringing us closer, it's like the rift between us has only widened further. As he pulls out of the marina, my chest heaves with sobs I refuse to let out. Suffering doesn't end with the truth. Rather than relief, a different form of misery arises, clawing at my psyche. Because the whole truth can bring clarity.

Holden was the puppet master, and I, his willing puppet. I knew about the photographs and videos. Those could have been evidence if I had sought help. In the beginning, I could blame my lack of action on manipulation and naivety. As I got older, my lack of sobriety and clear thinking could be used in my defense. Or...did I become too comfortable in his pattern of abuse? Did being resigned equate to my consent?

Pausing on the walk up my dock, I bend over with my hands on my knees, taking deep breaths to curb the onslaught of nausea. Once my breathing evens out, I continue inside.

Ivy and Nix are curled up on the couch. But as soon as he sees my face, he's up and next to me with a gentle touch on my arm. "What's going on?"

"Stomach bug. I'm going to lie down. You guys have fun tonight." The only facial expression I'm capable of right now is a grimace as I pass them and lock myself in my bedroom.

As I undress and curl up under my comforter, the only word running on a loop in my head is...*why, why, why.*

··········

After a couple hours of fitful rest, I pull myself from bed and drag my feet to the bathroom, hoping a shower will help. Glancing into the living room, I see they've already headed out, but something on the small counter catches my eye, causing my body to heat and my chest to cave all at once. Desire to forget, to slip into the black, overrides all rational thought. My steps are heavy-laden as I trudge to the bottle, clutching it in my hand.

Twenty-Nine

Jansen

"You can't leave, man. We're busy as hell, and without Tillie, I need someone else with me behind the bar."

"This isn't like her. You know that." A note of panic laces my voice. A plea. My nervous system is shot.

"I'll call Ivy."

"It's July Fourth, Mason. Ivy's three sheets to the damn wind right now."

"Remi?"

"Tried him. He's not picking up."

"Could your granddad check on her?"

"He's apparently out of cell range, and Nix won't answer his damn phone."

"Shit," Mason hisses in frustration. "Okay. I'll take cocktails off the menu. Bottles or drafts for tonight only. We can cut the price to make up for it, but I'm going to need to put in another liquor order."

Squeezing his arm in thanks, I take my first full breath since Tillie no-showed her shift, and run out the door. She lives ten minutes from the bar, but I make it there in seven. My heart rate spikes as I cup my hands on the glass to peek inside, then stops beating at the sight before me.

If this door isn't unlocked, Dane's going to be pissed.

Thankfully, it is, and I throw it open and rush inside. She's half naked, face down on the floor, half of her body in the bathroom and the other half in the hallway. Her color is ashen, and for a moment, I'm not a thirty-one-year-old businessman in love with a trauma-ridden woman. I'm seventeen again, getting home from my shift at the local pizza place to find my mother lying on her back on the living room floor, dead from aspirating her vomit.

With a trembling hand, I brush her hair off the side of her face, causing a small groan to slip past her lips. My sigh of relief is heavy until my nose picks up the smell of alcohol on her breath. I don't realize how hard I'm grinding my molars until my temples begin to throb.

"Up and at 'em," I grunt, lifting her in my arms and placing her in the shower. Her head lolls to the side like a ragdoll, and the sight makes what I'm about to do a little more satisfying.

It only takes a few seconds before the ice-cold water has her gasping for breath. When she tries to crawl out of the shower, I block her attempts.

Goosebumps cover her body, and her lips quiver as her teeth gnash together, chattering.

"Sobered up yet?"

She looks up at me through her lashes as she jerks a nod. I grab the towel off the hook and reach into the shower to turn the knob. Her body violently trembles as I wrap the towel around her and pick her up, cradling her against my chest.

"I'm so damn angry with you," I mutter, kicking her bedroom door open.

She's still in a bra and underwear, so I root through her drawers under the bed to find her a dry pair, along with a T-shirt to throw on. As quickly as possible, she's dressed and under her comforter. Her calm breathing assures me she's warm. After grabbing a bottle of water from the fridge, I help her sit up to hydrate before she passes out again.

When I stand from the bed to move to the living room couch, her raspy voice calls out, "Stay."

"I'll be on the couch."

"Stay with me," she slurs.

Rubbing a hand across my jaw, I sigh. "I can't tonight."

"Please." Her soft voice drifts off. "Hate me tomorrow."

"Damn it, woman," I whisper-growl, kicking my shoes off and lying beside her on top of the comforter. "I'll never hate you." I reach out, tucking her damp hair behind her ear.

She slowly blinks her eyes open before they close again, and her face screws up. "I fucked up," she mewls, burying her face in the pillow.

Turning on my side so I can face her, I continue to rake my fingers through her hair. "You did...What happened?"

Another stuttered breath passes through her lips before she tries to talk, her words coming out sloppy. "His puppet, willingly, for too long."

My vision blurs from her admission. From the way she's being crushed into tiny pieces, trying to interpret his vile actions, all while blaming herself. In her mind, it's probably easier. Placing the blame on herself keeps her comfortable in remaining silent. It also gives her a reason. "Your willingness wasn't eagerness, nor was it ever your consent, Freckles. You got away when you could."

Her mouth turns down into a grimace as she nuzzles her face against the pillow and whimpers, "It hurts."

"What hurts?" I whisper.

She blindly reaches for my hand, currently still in her hair, and places it on her chest over her heart. "Just want it to stop hurting," she mutters, and seconds later, her breathing evens out as she crashes.

Tillie Anne Porter has awakened something visceral inside me. I've never wanted to consume another person's pain the way I do hers. Every nightmare, every soul-sucking memory, every bout of physical or emotional pain she feels because of her memories. I'd wear it all like a cloak, tied around my neck for the world to see and judge, if it meant she could live the rest of her life in peace. Her suffering is mine. Her weaknesses are mine. Her happiness is mine. *She* is mine.

And it's about time she truly figures that out.

Nix comes home at two in the morning. When I open her bedroom door, he's standing in front of the refrigerator, chugging orange juice. He looks over at me, smiling sheepishly. "Hey, man," he whispers. "Sorry if I woke you up."

"How did Tillie get her hands on a pint of tequila?"

His brows furrow in confusion. "What?"

I nod toward the empty bottle I spotted on the counter earlier. "She got so drunk she passed out in the hallway."

Crossing my arms, I tuck them to keep myself from wringing his neck prematurely. He at least appears to be completely sober.

"Shit. Is she okay?"

"She's passed out in bed. Do you know where she got the alcohol or not? It wasn't the bar, and she didn't have her car."

He rubs the back of his neck nervously. "Ivy must have left her bottle here. She was taking a shot before we went to her cousin's party."

"It better not fucking happen again," I spit out.

He raises a brow, giving me a pointed look. "She works at a bar, Jansen. If she wanted to have a drink, she was going to have one with or without Ivy leaving a damn bottle lying around, and you know it."

I grumble my annoyance at the probability of him being right. I have no serious idea about her mental state because she's used to keeping it locked down, and while I'm aware she's shared more with me than anyone, tonight has made it obvious that she still believes this fucked-up situation is hers to carry alone. She could've called me, told me she was struggling, and I think that's what hurts most.

Not being given the chance to be here in the capacity she needed.

"There's always a chance of her slipping up in one way or another, but you love her." It's not a question but a statement he's making.

Curious, I can't help but ask, "Do you?"

He matches my stance, leaning against the counter. "It's kind of hard not to."

Blowing out a breath, I let my head fall back against the wall, looking at the ceiling. "I swore I'd never live the way I did with my mom ever again."

"How was that?" he asks softly.

"Living with the fear of never knowing how each day would go. Never being able to depend on her. She'd leave, and I'd feel this pit"—I splay a hand across my stomach, feeling the ghost of pain, or maybe a new pain caused by the woman tucked soundly into bed—"because every single time, I always thought, *this is it. This is the time she won't come back.*"

I'm pulled from the past when Nix wraps his arms around me. He doesn't say anything, and after a few seconds, he leans back and rests his palms on my shoulders while looking me in the eye.

"Tills deserves someone who can fight *beside* her. You can't erase her past, but you sure as shit can give her hope for the future. Her life's been bleak, man, and she had a minor slip, but she is strong as hell. You *know* that. So in a few hours when she wakes up hating herself, because she will, try not to let the past with your mom affect how you handle it."

His hands drop from my shoulders, and even though his little speech was mature and accurate, I can't help but chuckle. "I'm supposed to be the one giving your young-ass advice."

"Middle-aged bachelors need advice from time to time." He smirks, shrugging.

"Fuck off," I laugh, punching his shoulder.

"Well, I'm gonna hit the sack. I've got to be up in four hours. I'll head to Granddad's in the morning to work so you two can...hash things out." He winks.

Shaking my head, I tell him goodnight and return to Tillie's room. Stripping down to my boxers, I toss my slacks aside and climb into bed beside her. As soon as the mattress dips, her body searches for mine, and I pull her back into me, wrapping my arm around her waist.

······

Sunlight streams into her bedroom, forcing my heavy lids to blink open, but she isn't beside me. Instead, she's sitting cross-legged at the end of the bed, wearing only a T-shirt and underwear. Her hair is down and messy, but she looks sexy—and nervous, judging by the way she's chewing her lip.

"I poured you coffee. It should still be warm." She nods to the table beside me. "Or I can get you some orange juice?"

My lips twist as I try to fight a smile. "Coffee's good."

"On a scale from one to ten—"

"Ten," I huff, sitting up and reaching for the coffee to take a sip.

She tuts. "You didn't let me finish."

The sheets fall to my waist as I scoot up to lean against the headboard, interlacing my fingers before resting them on my stomach. Her gaze roams over my upper body.

Clearing my throat, I raise a brow when her eyes meet mine again. "You were saying?"

"Right." She shakes her head. "How mad are you? Because I know I fucked up, and I'm sure finding me in that state yesterday was..." She tilts her head from side to side, searching for the appropriate words.

"Traumatic. Terrifying. Perhaps add a hint of betrayal," I list off, helping her out. "Why couldn't you have picked up the phone? I would've been here."

She swallows and stares down at her hands. "My thoughts spiraled, and from there, it felt like I was moving on autopilot."

"What thoughts?" I may be in love with her, but this can only work if she's able to demonstrate the same vulnerability and trust it's taking me to remain by her side.

After a few tense seconds of silence, she glances at the ceiling, keeping her tears at bay. "Knowing I could've done something—anything, really—to stop it and realizing I didn't because I'd...grown used to it. He tried forcing me to marry him, for fuck's sake. Who marries a *victim*? Unless he truly believed I was...willing."

Understanding of where her head was at yesterday makes my chest ache as anger sears through me, along with the relief seeping into my bones from her choosing to let me in. If Tillie has taught me anything about myself, it's that I'm not as emotionally stunted as I've always believed.

"Or you were caught up in a pattern of abuse with a manipulative monster and felt helpless to find a way out of it."

Her small, noncommittal shrug has my jaw tensing. "So, if someone experiences domestic violence at the hands of their partner but stays out of fear, you believe they stayed, or remained silent about it, because they were *willing participants* and didn't want help?"

Her nose wrinkles. "Of course not," she spits out.

Shrugging, I scrape a hand across my jaw. "Seems like you do."

"Seems like you're trying to be a dick," she volleys back, venom laced in her tone.

"Seems like you don't want to accept the truth because you don't want to heal. You'd rather have your version to fall back on to excuse any future behavior or mistakes, because accepting blame keeps you weighted down. You don't have to allow yourself to hope for the future or work toward the best version of yourself. You can use it as justification to remain exactly where you are. It's weak, and you're not fucking weak, Tillie."

She tips her chin in defiance, a storm brewing behind her emeralds, darkening them to a forest green. I ready myself for whatever defense she's preparing in that complicated, infuriatingly beautiful head of hers. Nix was right. I have to fight beside her, and fighting beside her means reminding her of her strength, even if it's a brutal assessment.

"You're a therapist now?"

"No, but we should probably find you one," I deadpan. "Come here." I lean forward, reaching for her.

Surprisingly, she doesn't hesitate. She climbs onto my lap, straddling me. "Is this real?" she asks, her gaze peering into mine. Searching.

"It's been real since the day you pushed me into the lake."

Using my fingertips, I trace a path up her thighs, her sides, and her back. Goosebumps appear on her skin, and I reach under her oversized shirt to unhook the clasp on her bra. She doesn't hesitate to strip the shirt over her head, letting it and her bra fall between us. The shaky breath she releases grazes my cheek, and I look up to see her pupils dilated. Her nipples pebble as I roll them between my thumb and pointer finger, and I watch, mesmerized, as her teeth sink into her bottom lip while she grinds her hips.

"Clean bill of health. Got checked four months ago, and I haven't been with anyone since."

"I was tested in rehab. All good," she breathes out. "I have the implant in my arm."

I keep her body melded to mine as I reach over and blindly feel around for my pants, find them, and dig through the pockets to find my wallet and a condom.

The foil square pinched between my fingers causes my cock to leak and my vision to haze. I stand up and move to the end of her bed. Pushing my briefs down and tossing them aside, I smirk as she rubs her thighs together to find relief. Those emeralds in her face are drawn to my cock, and I grasp it, circling my thumb around the bead of cum resting on the tip. The rise and fall of her chest set my rhythm for every stroke.

"Spread your legs."

Her creamy thighs part, falling to the side, and evidence of her desire soaks through the grey lace underwear I put on her last night. There's no stopping my groan at seeing her lying there, dark hair fanned around her, her peaked nipples begging for attention, and the visual evidence of her desire makes my mouth water.

With sexy confidence, she presses her thighs together and hooks her thumbs in the sides of her panties, pushing them down to her ankles, where she kicks them aside and spreads her thighs again, leaving her pussy bare and my heart pounding.

I physically can't wait another second to taste her. My knees barely settle into the mattress before I palm her waist and lift her as I fall back. Her look of confusion is adorable. "You're going to sit on my face."

"No, I'll suffocate you," she hisses.

"I'd die a happy man. Now, sit on my fucking face so I can eat."

Thirty

Tillie

HOLY FUCKING LUST. It pumps urgently through my veins, drowning out every monster I've ever known. The second my thighs slide against his face, he palms my ass and forces my weight down at the same time his mouth latches onto me.

I palm my mouth and bite the skin resting against my lips.

"He's not here, Freckles, and I want to hear you," he says against my center, reaching up and ripping my wrist away from my face before he spears his tongue as deep inside of me as he can.

Shocks of pleasure ignite within my body and send violent tremors through my limbs. Every whimper, moan, and cry that slips past my lips collides and echoes against the shackles I'm finally breaking free from. My mind can only focus on the intense pulsing in my clit and the need to chase that euphoric feeling. And each masculine moan that vibrates against my pussy from him tasting me has me feeling like a goddess. I place my palms flat on the wall in front of me as I throw my head back and rock my hips wildly, riding his tongue.

Seconds later, my orgasm crashes through me. As I cry out, trying to lift my hips, he palms my waist, holding me down on his face while he sucks and circles my clit with his tongue in tandem until my continued cries have calmed. He's priming me for another orgasm, but right before my core tightens, he lifts me by my waist and positions me above his already condom-sheathed cock.

He's giving me control, I realize, as I take in the sated look on his gorgeous face from tasting me. I've yet to lay a hand on him, but he looks like he's the one who came so hard he saw stars.

I don't look away from him as I sink inch by inch until I'm fully seated. His lips part, and I bend down, licking their outline before brushing my tongue against his to taste myself. It's erotic as hell, and I could cry from how comfortable I feel with this man.

"Fuck. Fuck, hold still," he begs.

My core pulses around him, and his deep groan sounds tortured. "Fuck it, it feels too good. Ride my dick like you rode my face," he pleads while propping himself up on an arm and lapping at my breasts.

His lips find my nipple, and he bites down before circling his tongue around it and sucking. The pain mixed with pleasure drives up the intensity, but I need more.

"Jansen." My voice is breathless but sultry. It's foreign to my ears, heating my cheeks. "I need you..."

"What do you need, Tillie?" he asks, placing kisses along my neck and jawline.

"I need you to fuck me."

He stills, but his grip on my waist tightens. He leans back slightly to catch my eye, and I run my hands through his hair, nipping his bottom lip with my teeth and pulling before releasing it. "I know what you're doing, but right now the only thing I want to feel is your cock—"

Before I can finish speaking, he's got me underneath him. Staying on his knees, he bends my legs, holding them at his side while he enters me in one thrust. At first, my cry sounds pained, and his hips freeze, but I reach around, digging my nails into his ass as I pull him forward.

His thrusts start again, shallower, until I've fully accommodated his size.

"More," I beg.

That one word crashes through the wall of his self-restraint, and he pounds into me with reckless abandon. "*Yes*," I gasp, fisting the sheets with one hand and clawing his thigh with the other. My body feels like it's being ripped apart in the absolute best way possible. It's almost too much. I *need* to come, and the intensity fills my eyes with tears.

A raspy cry breaks free from my throat, and his face twists with worry.

"Don't fucking stop," I cry out, my voice cracking.

"What do you need, Freckles?" he breathes out.

He slows his thrusts but never stops hitting the foreign spot inside me. "I've never felt this before. It's too intense," I gasp. "Your magical unicorn dick is going to kill me."

A look of understanding dawns on his face—about what, I'm not sure. I didn't know my body *could* feel like this. Leaning over, he grabs a pillow and lifts my hips, shoving it under them. And when he bends down again, the angle is just right while he claims my mouth in the most erotic kiss we've shared, slowly mapping every inch of my mouth with his tongue.

"Lock your ankles around my hips," he commands.

His thrusts quicken in pace, and he uses the pads of two slick fingers to circle my clit with exactly the right amount of pressure while his other hand pushes on my lower stomach. My core tightens almost painfully before I detonate, pulsing and clenching around his cock. He throws his head back, releasing the sexiest groan I've ever heard before bending down to silence my shrill cries with his mouth.

When we've both come down from our orgasmic highs, he lies beside me, whispering his praise into my ear, but I don't catch most of it.

If a hormone high is a thing, I'm experiencing it. Sweat has started to dry and cool on my skin. My limbs feel boneless, my head feels lighter than it's been in months, and I physically can't stop myself from becoming a sobbing mess.

"Did I hurt you?" He grips my chin, tilting my face up.

As soon as the question is out of his mouth, my emotional sobbing turns into hysterical laughter, starting small and then bubbling over. I try to turn my face, but his grip on my chin tightens, and his mouth curves into an achingly beautiful smile. When Jansen smiles, really smiles, his entire face radiates warmth.

"If you don't tell me what's so funny, my *magical unicorn dick* and I are going to be very offended. We both felt you come."

"It was...it was so...good," I manage to get out between the incessant giggle fit. "I don't...I don't know why I'm...laughing."

He lets me lie here, having some form of emotional breakdown or breakthrough, until my laughter ebbs, and I turn my body fully to face him. With my pointer finger, I trace the shape of his face, over his dark brows, down the straight bridge of his nose, and around his lips. He nips my finger playfully, smiling, and I continue my path, tracing over the two dimples below his mouth on each side that stand out when he's smiling the way he is now.

"Soooo...On a scale of one to ten, how mad are you now?" I tease.

He hums. "About a six."

"Anything else I can do to bring that number down?"

He pulls me into him, clinging to me, and I'm beginning to understand there's so much more to this man than maybe even he knows. "Keep letting me in," he whispers.

"I promise."

·•••••••••··

We stay wrapped up in each other the rest of the weekend when we're not working. We haven't had sex again, though every moment of intimacy, sexual or not, with him is something I relish. On Saturday, Ivy, Nix, Jansen, and I ordered pizza and watched the fireworks from our kayaks on the water. It's hard to explain with words how much these little moments mean to me. I never could've imagined my life the way it is right now, surrounded by people I love and trust. It may seem insignificant for me to be as happy as I am, but I've been below rock bottom, my lungs filling slowly with rubble and deceit. Maybe life is supposed to be as simple and humble as this.

Or this is the calm before the storm, and I'll ride the waves, fighting to break through the surface, until I drown.

On Monday morning, I look at the schedule and see I'm only on for two shifts, with the weekend off. Odd, since I haven't had an entire weekend off since working here, and disappointing because that's when I make the most in tips.

Setting my bag in the back, I take out my phone to check my notifications before walking out onto the floor. *Dad* pops up with one unread text, and my hands tremble as I swipe the screen to open it.

> **Dad:** I've left the information with a detective who is taking the case. He's confident he'll be able to make an arrest soon. I've made sure he understands I need to stay informed about the case's development. I'll keep you updated, but I'd feel better knowing you have cameras set up or you're staying with that fellow. I love you, Sweets.

He's going to be arrested. Holy shit. I could finally be free.

A stuttered breath of relief passes through my lips as I type out a response.

> **Me:** Thanks for letting me know, Dad. I'll have cameras set up this weekend.

With a little more pep in my step, I prance out to the bar and find Jansen sitting there talking to Mason. Bits and pieces of their conversation filter in before I'm close enough to hear it all.

"You think you can handle it completely alone?" Jansen asks.

Mason scoffs. "I've got it, Boss. You don't need to worry about anything. Enjoy your time away."

"You feel good about the interview you had? Will he be able to start this week?"

"Dilynn is a woman, but yes. She assured me she could start whenever. I'll give her a call and see if she can come in on Wednesday."

Jansen nods before I catch Mason's smirk as he throws a black hand towel over his shoulder. "I'm surprised Tillie wants to cut back on hours."

What? We *never* talked about cutting my hours. As I start to march over, both men look my way, and my face must give away that I've heard the details of their conversation.

Jansen's head falls between his shoulders as Mason chuckles, shaking his head before busying himself on the opposite end of the bar.

"What the hell?" I hiss once I'm in front of him. "I didn't ask for my hours to be cut. I need the money." My anger quickly gives way to pleading. "I know I've had to take a couple days off and no-showed, but I'll stay late. I'll clean. I'll even come in and do inventory without pay." I know I shouldn't be shown any special treatment, and honestly, not calling in is grounds for being written up or fired, but I never thought he'd punish me for it. I suppose I can't blame him, but this isn't a big town. Finding another part-time job will be next to impossible unless I look farther out, and the Corolla is on its last leg.

"Let's go to my office," he responds calmly while standing up.

"I don't want to go to your office. I want an explanation now," I snap.

He raises a brow, leaning into my space. "My office. *Now*."

This is why you don't have sex with your boss. Immediately, I feel guilty for snapping at him because *he is* my boss, and *I did* no-show. But he could've talked to me about the possibility of my being penalized for it over the weekend or during the last shift I worked. To blindside me like this with no warning seems a little cruel.

Once we're in his office, he closes the door and leans against it. I turn to face him, crossing my arms, and we stay in a silent stare off. His hands, which he shoved in his pockets, are balled up and visibly flexing. He doesn't look angry, but nervous as his tongue wets his lips.

"I did cut your hours," he finally says.

"Why?"

"I told you I'm sticking around, and I meant it. If you want to bartend for the rest of your life, great, but I want you to have time, free of financial worry, to figure out what you want in life."

His implication has my lips parting as a small gasp slips through. "You can't do that, Jansen."

He tilts his head. "Why can't I?"

"Because..." I splutter, "Because I'm not your responsibility. Because eventually, *you will* have to leave again for work. Because I *need* to be able to take care of myself."

"You deserve to live a bit of your life without stress, free to figure it out. If you want to do solo traveling, I'll make it happen. If you want to go to college, it's done. If you want—"

"Stop." A quick bolt of shock travels through my limbs. "I'm not your wife or even your girlfriend. I've never once asked for you to take care of me in that way."

The sheer intensity in his eyes has heat rushing throughout my body, burning me from the inside out. I've never felt like prey in Jansen's presence. Ever. But the way he stalks toward me now, slow and measured with his jaw tense, makes him seem predatory. My breathing slows, not in fear of his movements, but in fear and anticipation of what he'll say next.

Once he's standing so close our bodies are flush, I crane my neck to look up at him. His gaze is hard, but his hand around my waist and the other around the back of my neck have a loose hold.

"I'm getting very fucking tired of hearing you imply that you're not mine every time you're scared," he grumbles, brushing a thumb over the rapid pulse in my neck. "I don't need a label to know you're it for me. And I've already told you, I'm not going to spend my life wondering how you're doing or what you're doing when I can be beside you."

Words. A lot of words are tumbling around in my head but aren't pulling together enough for me to form a sentence. Before I can string any together, his deep, gravelly voice fills the space again. "I'm not going to break your heart, Tillie. I can't. Even if you want me to. So if you want to walk away from us, you'll have to be okay with breaking mine."

Raw vulnerability forms a deep rasp in his voice and intensity within his amber eyes, proving how serious he is about what he's said. What he doesn't know is how incapable I am of intentionally breaking his heart. I could never willingly hurt him, but a painful fear of him eventually walking away from me has me wanting to run far, far away. He'll realize one day how damaged I truly am. He'll grow tired of taking care of me when I'm at my lowest and wonder how he ever allowed himself to fall in love with a woman as broken down as me. I won't voice those fears because, in this moment, he believes he loves me. Instead, I wrap my arms around his waist, resting my head on his chest, and cling to him while inhaling his spicy scent. He cradles my head and holds me just as tightly.

Right now, wrapped in his arms, those fears dissolve, distant and foreign.

"You weren't put on the schedule this weekend because I plan on taking you somewhere." The deep timbre of his voice vibrates against my cheek as he speaks.

"Where?" I ask, settling further into him.

"Anywhere you'd like to go outside of Arkansas. We'll leave on Thursday and return on Sunday."

Leaning back to peer at him, I ask, "Why outside of Arkansas?"

"Because you deserve to experience something brand new, and I want to watch you blossom as you do."

My chest warms, and I bite the corner of my lip to keep my excited smile subdued. "Fine, but my only request is that you decide our destination."

Because I've never imagined leaving Arkansas, so I haven't got a clue where I'd want to go.

He bends down to kiss me, and as soon as his tongue brushes against mine, a familiar aching need pulses through my core. The moan I release into his mouth has him picking me up by my thighs. My legs wrap around his waist as my hips move of their own accord, demanding friction. Before laying me out on his desk, the flutter of papers and clatter of objects hitting linoleum sounds out.

He stands over me with his fingers poised on the button of my shorts and a gleam in his eyes, waiting for my approval. When I eagerly nod, he unbuttons my shorts and slides them down my legs.

"I've imagined this a hundred times. You spread out over my desk like this." His nostrils flare and he groans when he realizes I'm bare beneath the shorts.

A win for forgetting to do laundry.

Shrugging sheepishly, I bend my knees, placing my feet on the desk, and let my thighs fall apart. His lips part as the rise and fall of his chest become visible. The reaction he has from my body every time he sees it is slowly healing the wounded, ridiculed girl inside me. There's never a desire to hide from him anymore; in fact, it's quite the opposite. The amount of time I spend daydreaming about his tongue, his fingers, and being filled by him feels borderline obsessive.

I'd always thought a sex drive was impossible for me. Now, with Jansen, I fear I'm switching over to the other side. It's all I think about some days. Some mornings, I wake up from dreams that had me on the precipice of what could've been a delicious orgasm. My shame is minimal when he's the one bringing forth my pleasure, but it's significant when it's *my* mind or body trying to wring it out. I've made one move on him of my volition, but I've been afraid of the endless void I could succumb to by taking what I know he'll offer.

So I wait.

I wait for him to make the move.

I wait for him to come to me.

I wait for him to take control.

Thankfully, he doesn't make me wait long.

His finger gliding through my slit brings me back to the present as my back arches, and I focus on him and him alone. When he sinks to his knees, his mouth latching onto me, I swallow my gasp and lose myself in every sensation.

Thirty-One

Jansen

"Don't be afraid to use all of your force, Tillie," Jonathan reminds her at our second self-defense session on Wednesday afternoon.

I throw my hands out to the side with wide eyes. "Are you *wanting* to see me get my ass kicked? She's using enough force for sparring."

I've been unable to hold a strong stance, feeling every one of her hits and kicks through the padding I'm wearing. Not to mention the bulge I've been sporting from watching her dominate every move.

Jonathan crosses his arms and grins. *The bastard.*

"It's okay," she pants, bending over and grabbing her water bottle. "Jansie can't handle anything more today."

I raise a brow at her placating tone and use of my "reserved for two" nickname. "Okay, Freckles. Let's see what you've got."

Before she can respond, I rush her, grabbing her wrist, which she maneuvers out of before kicking me in the stomach. Thank God for the padding because I'd be on the ground right now, gasping for air. Our eyes soak each other in, studying the other's movements. I rush her again, and she kicks out like I expected her to. A spark of fire brightens her emeralds, and her nostrils flare. Before she can make another move, I wrap my hand around her calf, pulling her body into mine.

The sheen of sweat covering her flushed face and chest glistens under the fluorescent lighting above the mat. And the slight hitch in her breathing when I palm her hip with my other hand and squeeze has arousal pumping through my veins. But she wastes no time using my thigh as a stepping stool for her free leg and gets her arm around my neck. She has no padding on, so when I push up with force on her arm and it releases, I wait until her feet drop to the mat before sweeping them out from under her.

A hiss slips through her teeth as she lands on her back, and a thud sounds from her tiny fists slamming the mat in frustration. I cough to cover my laugh and reach a hand out to help pull her up. The second her mouth tips in one corner, I know I'm fucked, and her leg sweeps out at lightning speed as I lose my footing, tumbling sideways.

"Bad sportsmanship, Freckles," I breathe out.

Her answering laugh is more joyous and carefree than I've ever heard from her. The effect the sound has on me is noticeable. My smile can't be contained as I turn my head to look at her, placing a palm on my racing heart.

We lie there, catching our breath, until Jonathan gets a call.

"I can be there in thirty minutes," he rushes out, sounding panicked.

When he hangs up, he walks over to me. "My mom had a bad fall, and my dad is freaking out. If I leave you the keys, can you lock up for me?"

"No worries, man. I'll drop them off in the morning."

"Thanks. Nice work today, Tillie," he tells her before jogging for the door, but before it closes behind him, he adds, "Feel free to use the locker room."

"I hope she's okay." She winces while standing.

"We can hit the showers before leaving. You look a little sore," I muse.

Her answering glare makes me chuckle as she swats my arm.

I show her to the ladies' locker room before I head to the men's. In some ways, I'm still lost on what is appropriate with her and what isn't. I could spend every day inside her, but the thought of her believing I care more about sex than simply being in her presence twists my guts.

High-pressure water pelts down on me as I step into the shower to wash away the evidence of our workout. But the memories of her dominating another class are seared into my memory. And that, paired with my excitement for tomorrow, takes me from half-mast to painfully hard. Resting my forehead against the cool tile, I fist my cock and groan. The last time I had her beneath me was Monday on my desk, and while I threw all caution to the damn wind about tasting her, there wasn't enough time for much else. I don't need to fire another person for uttering a single unsavory word about her—especially not before this deal goes through.

The white nylon curtain is pushed aside, and she appears beside me like I summoned her, completely naked, with her hair down. My gaze greedily roams over every inch of her body as my hand continues to pump.

She steps into the shower, closing the curtain, and I turn to face her. Her body is tense, like a tightly bound coil. A beautiful red flushes her cheeks as her eyes travel down my chest to my hand. Then she's springing forward. My back hits the tile as her lips glide across my chest to my neck. Nipping, licking, sucking. Her small hand travels down my stomach and covers mine. I'm about fucking done for. I wrap her soft strands around my fist and tug gently. She tilts her head, looking at me through her lashes, her emeralds half-lidded with dilated pupils. Reaching down, I lift her by her thighs, and she locks her legs around my waist. She immediately rocks her hips, my cock gliding through her soaked slit.

"I don't have a condom on me, but I sure as fuck will not be leaving this shower until you've etched my name in the walls," I growl, so turned on, the only thing I can envision is rutting inside her, but I'll never put her at risk.

Her moans reverberate off the tile, surrounding us in an endless loop of my new favorite acoustic. I lean down, taking a pebbled nipple into my mouth, swirling my tongue around the bud, then bite down. When her hips pick up their pace, my balls tighten, and I'm thrusting, imagining her pussy pulsing around my cock.

"Come with me, Jansen." She mewls while pressing her mouth to mine, licking the seam until I open for her. This kiss is different. It's not rushed or sloppy. It's slow and thorough.

She pulls back first, resting her forehead against mine as her hips pick up their pace. Ecstasy-fueled cries slip past her lips before her muscles tense, and as soon as my name rolls off her tongue, ropes of my cum land on her lower stomach. Her legs are still draped around me when she palms my face and peppers kisses on my cheeks and lips. My chuckle has her clinging to me, burying her face in my neck.

"Can I know where we're going now?" she asks.

"Not a chance, but I thoroughly enjoyed your efforts," I murmur, squeezing the round globes of her ass before turning and placing us both under the spray of water.

···•••·•••··

I paid a small fortune Monday night to book us plane tickets for Thursday. Tillie's dad called the bar, leaving me a message about Holden and an arrest being made in the next few days. My only thought was getting her out of Arkansas before shit hit the fan.

The illuminated clock on the dash ticks over to four thirty in the morning as I park the Jeep in the airport parking lot. We're both exhausted from the night before and running on five hours of sleep. Excitement swims through my veins, though, boosting my energy as the engines of a plane roar overhead and I envision an entire weekend alone with my girl. But that excitement dims when I look over to see Tillie worrying her lip between her teeth.

"What's wrong?" I ask, reaching over and running my thumb along her lower lip, releasing it from her teeth.

"I've never been on a plane." A note of panic or fear, maybe both, colors her voice.

"Your first time flying is always a little unsettling, but the flight isn't long, and you might love it."

She nods and opens her door to climb out. After grabbing our suitcases from the back, we hustle through the busy airport. This is why I prefer driving, but it would've eaten away at our time together, and I want as much time alone with her, away from work and responsibilities, as I can get.

We check in, drop our luggage off, and dash to the security gate. She keeps her hand wrapped around my bicep as we weave through people gathered or milling around.

I release a heavy sigh of relief through my nose once we're standing in line as I drape my arm around her shoulder, pulling her into my side. The beep and buzz of security wands and hum of belts fill the space, along with constant chatter. When I glance down, I note she's picking the skin around her nails.

"Still nervous?"

"This is going to sound crazy," she whispers, "but I'm terrified they'll find drugs or something on me."

"Did you bring any drugs with you?" I muse.

She scoffs. "Obviously not, but clearly I'm paranoid."

"You're anxious. We'll make it through security, and then we'll grab some coffee while we wait."

The line moves slower than molasses, all while Tillie's nerves continue to climb. But eventually, we make it to the front, hand over our boarding passes, and endure the metal detector. Once she makes it through without her imaginary drugs being found, her shoulders relax, and her excitement takes center stage.

"What made you decide on Colorado?" she asks as we sit in the lounge.

Yes, lounge. I may have spent more money this week on pleasure than I have in my entire adult life, but she's worth it.

"It's a beautiful state with a lot to do and great food."

She starts to pull her phone out of her pocket.

"I thought we could turn our phones off for the weekend, until we get back to Arkansas," I suggest.

"What if something happens to the houseboat, and Nix can't get a hold of us?"

"Granddad knows more about boats than we do, and he has Dane's number."

"What if something happens at the bar?"

"I trust Mason to handle it on his own."

"What if—"

"*Tillie.*" I pull her over onto my lap. "I want to spend this weekend entirely focused on you and being with you."

She wraps her arms loosely around my neck and rubs her nose against mine. "Deal."

Forty minutes later, we're boarding. "This is fancy," she murmurs.

"I wanted you to have the best experience, so we're flying first class."

She stiffens as her gaze roams over the space, then her shoulders round as she sinks further into her seat. "You didn't need to. I can't even imagine how expensive this was."

"Your comfort is worth it." Interlacing our fingers, I bring her hand to my lips before settling them both in her lap.

Takeoff has her pressing her face into my shoulder and clinging to my hand so hard it's almost numb, but once we're in the air, she relaxes. Her lids drift closed a few times before her limbs jerk and she sits up.

"Why don't you take a nap? We've got a couple hours before we land."

"I'd feel bad sleeping through a flight you paid so much for," she responds groggily.

Right then, the flight attendant walks past, and I grab her attention. "Can you get her a blanket, please?"

"Of course, sir."

"I'm not going to sleep," Tillie gripes.

I shrug. "That's fine."

Ten minutes later, she is *sound* asleep, cuddled up in the reclined seat with her mouth open and her hands tucked under her chin. As I sit in this seat thousands of feet in the air, I'm buried beneath the weight of my emotions for her. They're nearly suffocating, because I no longer possess even a sliver of control over my feelings. She has no idea how much I love her. How badly I want to take care of her. I'd do anything to protect her. She's strong and resilient, but I want to be her shield, her first line of defense, so she can let her guard down and begin to heal. To dream. To *live*.

While my gaze roams over her features, one word sounds off continuously in my mind, loud and cliché but accurate.

Mine. Mine, mine, mine.

The plane jostles as we dip beneath the clouds and sink lower in the sky, nearing the landing strip, and I run my thumb along her cheek. "It's time to wake up, Freckles," I whisper in her ear.

A shiver has her shoulders shimmying as she slowly blinks. Once she's more alert, her eyes widen comically before she sits up and wipes the drool off the side of her face.

"Your spit doesn't disgust me," I muse while lifting a brow.

I barely catch her eye roll before she's looking out the window, but the hitch in her breathing is audible. "*Oh my God*," she exclaims, her forehead practically touching the glass.

"It's beautiful, isn't it?"

"No, it's...more," she sighs.

The landing has her small hand wrapped around my forearm with the grip of a pro wrestler. We make our way to baggage claim, then out into the open air. The Tundra I rented is waiting for us outside, and I lead her to it. Once we're in and buckled, I set the GPS directions to the cabin rental we'll be staying in.

She's been pretty quiet since we got off the plane, and now she's staring blankly out the window, like her body is here but her mind elsewhere.

Placing my palm on her thigh, I squeeze lightly, and she shakes her head a little, turning to smile at me.

"Talk to me," I plead. Our trip has only begun. There's no way I've fucked it up this badly already.

Clearing her throat, she straightens her shoulders, adjusting herself in the seat. "Are you...rich...or something?"

My boisterous laugh has her features turning down.

"You should see your face right now. Would you prefer if I had nothing?"

"No, you ass," she clips, trying to pry my fingers from her thigh. "But I'm very aware you spent a lot of money on this trip, and I feel like...like I have nothing to offer you in the grand scheme of things."

It physically pains me—an invisible but sharp slash to my insides—to know how she feels. Since she was sixteen years old, she's viewed herself as a transaction. She doesn't see herself the way I do. The way Granddad, Presley, Dane, Ivy, and Nix see her.

"Every laugh I get to hear. Every smile I get to soak in. Every look of awe on your face. Every word you'll speak. Every touch you'll share with me. All of those things are what you have to offer, Tillie."

Her fingers that were trying to pry my hand from her thigh are now squeezing tightly as she swallows and keeps her gaze on the front windshield.

She's quiet the rest of the way to our destination, but her fingers stay interlaced with mine. Her quiet gasps as we travel through the mountains are the highlight of the drive. The GPS directs us up a winding road. Seclusion was something I searched for, and this little cabin miles away from neighbors provides it.

Her face may as well be plastered to the passenger window as we drive up to the cabin and park. "Holy *shit*, Jansen. This is...incredible," she chokes out.

"You deserve it, Freckles." I step out, inhaling the fresh mountain air with the sweet scent of pine, and round to the passenger side.

Before I can make it to her door, she's out of the pickup and spinning to take in the sights. We're about twenty miles out of Denver, and the view here is incredible. Trees are scattered around the property, but not enough to block the view of the mountain range in the distance. Tillie spins, clenching and unclenching her fists, then shaking out her hands. I've never seen her express this level of excitement or wonder, so much so, she's trying to contain it.

While the view is incredible, I couldn't look away from her if I tried, and when she finally turns to face me, my heart skips a beat at the radiant smile on her face. A smile that lights up her eyes and shows the hint of a small dimple I've never noticed in her right cheek. She is *always* beautiful, but right now she's fucking radiant.

I'm still lost in her when she runs toward me and leaps into my arms. Her legs wrap around my waist while her arms fling around my neck.

"*Thank you, thank you, thank you,*" she squeals.

The moment has a sheen building behind my eyes as I bury my face in her hair, inhaling the familiar citrusy scent. We've never talked about the future. I've only declared my sticking around, but here in the mountains of Colorado, I know without a doubt that I'm clinging to the woman who will be my forever.

Thirty-Two

Tillie

I'M NO STRANGER TO financial security. So I know Jansen spent an absurd amount of money on this trip. Last-minute tickets, last-minute lodging, and tack on the groceries stocked in the refrigerator upon arrival. This log cabin alone had to cost a fortune. It's an A-frame with a wraparound porch, which has rocking chairs with a "welcome to the mountains" doormat in front of the dark wooden front door.

As soon as we walk inside, I breathe in a slight woody aroma. The interior is what you'd expect with log walls, but windows are framed into every exterior wall, providing the perfect views. The ceilings are tall, and the space is relatively open. The kitchen has stainless-steel amenities, a beautiful grey stone island top with a complete log dining table on the opposite side. The living room provides a flat-screen TV mounted above a fireplace, with a large forest-green L-shaped couch.

It has two bedrooms and one bathroom, but the master bedroom has the best view. It's the only room upstairs, a loft essentially, with square windows covering the entire wall and triangles at the top. I've never been so excited to go to sleep, if only so I can wake up to the view.

I'm still standing here in awe when warm arms envelop me from behind. Jansen skims his lips along my neck, breathing deeply, before resting his cheek against mine. Goosebumps rise on my body, while arousal burns like an inferno in my core, but I do my best to douse the flames. I made my move in the gym, and as I initially believed, a need—or craving—has arisen.

So instead, I stand perfectly still, waiting for him to claim me. Waiting for his hands to glide along my skin, or eager lips to press against my own. After a couple of minutes, it's clear he has no intention of doing any form of claiming.

Stepping forward, I spin around to face him, taking his hands in mine while putting distance between us. "How about I make us some sandwiches or something? I'm starving."

His gaze roams my face for only a second before he grins. "Whatever you want."

We've spent today planning the next two and exploring the property. Hours later, we're sitting on the back deck, watching the sun go down. Golden rays of light reach skyward toward the clouds from behind the mountains. It's breathtaking.

Jansen sits beside me in one of the four red Adirondack chairs circling a small standing fire pit. His hand wraps around my wrist, pulling my attention away from the sky that makes me feel small but whole. The same sky that stretches infinitely, that lightning streaks through as thunder booms, releasing sheets of rain, and that powerful winds are sent down from. It's the same sky that rages, only to calm again. The same sky that darkens, only to light again. There is so much beauty, symbolism, and hope in that.

Tugging me to stand, he guides me over to sit on his lap, tucking my hair behind my ear. My entire body is an exposed nerve, quivering from the arousal pulsing through me from his touch alone.

"Need me to carry anything, Freckles?" he asks while using a curled finger to turn my face toward him.

"I'm good," I breathe out, losing myself in his amber gaze.

His brow quirks. "Your entire body went board-straight when I sat you down in my lap."

When I don't say anything, he continues, "I want you to know...I don't expect anything from you for this trip. At all."

A mix between a huff, a groan, and a growl passes through my lips before I push up from his lap and stomp inside. Childish? Maybe, but I'm so over the kiddy gloves he uses around me involving sex. He's been touching me in teasing ways all day, and yes, I may be having some confusing feelings around shame, but I don't want to *ask* for what he so obviously wants to give. I saw the subtle spark of darkness in his eyes when I begged him to fuck me harder. He loves control, and the only thing I want is for him to stop handling me like glass. I don't want to have to *ask* to be fucked. He's giving me all the control when all I want is to be lost to his.

Before I can get to the stairs, he grabs my wrist and spins me around.

His gaze is steely as he grits his teeth, causing heat—no, flames—to fill my core. "You don't get to act like a brat because I'm trying to be a good guy."

Tugging my wrist from his grip, I throw my arms out wide. "Clearly, you're a good guy, Jansen."

My arms fall, slapping against my outer thighs as I turn on my heel to walk upstairs.

"Stop fucking walking away from me." His voice is low, but his tone is hard, commanding.

Frustration mounts within me, reaching its peak as I spin around and step into his space, our bodies a hair's breadth apart. "I have asked you not to treat me like I'm made of glass, but you insist on it, dancing around your own needs and desires."

"What in the hell are you talking about?" he grits out. "Are you talking about me taking care to assure you're comfortable? Are you talking about me letting you lead? Because you've jumped down my fucking throat before, making it clear you don't like any insinuation of you being a whore. I don't want you to think you owe me or that I expect anything because I planned all of this."

His words lash out at my skin, creating tiny cuts.

"Interesting, I thought I made it clear your insinuation of me leading Nix on when he wanted to fuck me, according to you, was what made me feel like a whore," I deadpan.

Maybe it wasn't the exact implication, but right now, I don't care.

The muscle in his jaw pops as his stance turns rigid, but before he can say another word, my palms are on his chest, lightly pushing him away from me.

"I've never once asked you to be someone you're not, or to relinquish the control you crave. I've been waiting for you to fucking wield it, but if that makes me a whore..." My voice cracks on the last word as the rest of what I wanted to say dies off, along with the anger.

That, maybe, is my deepest shame. To crave his dominance, his possession, when I should be sickened by it.

My gaze moves from his balled fists that continue to clench, up to his corded arms showing off his veins even more prominently, to the swift rise and fall of his chest and shoulders. I don't dare glance at his face. I don't want to see the confusion or pity in his eyes when he understands what I'm asking for, what *I crave*.

"I need space," I rasp before taking the stairs two at a time.

But when I reach the top, my feet are lifted off the ground as he moves us farther into the room.

"You don't get any more space," he growls in my ear. He sets me back on my feet and spins me around, his grip on my waist tightening. "I have one hard limit. I'll never call you a whore in bed or anything related."

I shake my head quickly, soaked from his rough grip and raw aggressive essence bleeding through. Jansen is an amazing man, but he's also a force to be reckoned with. He's shown me in simple ways since we met, but this. This is the force of his I want to shatter beneath.

"If you have any, I need to know now because I'm not asking again," he grits out, his voice tight.

My mouth is dry, my entire body sparking like a live wire, but somehow, I choke out, "I trust you to take care of me."

And with those eight words, his control snaps.

His lips pry mine apart before his tongue delves inside to explore. Once he's ravished my mouth, leaving me breathless, he strips me bare of clothing.

The floor creaks with every step he takes to the dresser where he put his clothes away earlier, and he pulls out a red bandana. He doesn't ask for permission as he moves behind me, secures it over my eyes, and leads me to the bed. My heart pounds at a violent rhythm, leaving me lightheaded from nerves and anticipation.

"Get on the bed. Ass up and face down," he commands.

I do as I'm told, crawling onto the bed before settling on all fours and resting my cheek against the cool sheets, my hands stretched out in front of me.

The ghost of his touch glides across my thigh, and I jolt forward. The loud slap that comes next rips a gasp from deep in my chest; the pulse of the sting travels from my ass down to my clit. He kneads the spot before showing the other cheek the same treatment. My desire is slick between my thighs, and I bite my lip to stifle the moan.

"When you're with me, you don't silence your voice. I want to hear it," he says while smacking the same cheek again.

This time, I let out a whimper, rubbing my thighs together, and desire smears between them. His warm hands pry them apart before he cups my center.

"And you don't get any relief until I give it to you," he rasps.

Spreading my thighs farther apart, I rock against his hand, moaning from the slight reprieve.

"So fucking greedy," he groans, pushing a finger inside me and curling it to hit the spot he found, causing me to cry out. When he adds another one, he gets exactly what he wanted before. My voice, loud and desperate as I buck against his hand.

My core pulses while liquid heat rushes through my veins. But the moment every pulse begins to blur together and my pussy clenches, he pulls his fingers out, leaving me empty.

"I'm a little upset with you, Tillie." His hands slide up my back. One hand wraps around my neck, pulling me against his hard chest, while the other kneads my breast, pinching my nipple between his fingers. I push back against him, and his hard cock slides between my slick heat, coating it in my desire. All too quickly, he pulls his hips away.

Reaching behind me, I grip the nape of his neck and cant my face, searching for his mouth. His tongue slides against mine as my hand inches down to my swollen clit. I stifle my moan against his mouth as I work myself, but it's not the same. A stuttered breath ricochets from my lungs as he grips my wrist, stopping the circular motion, and takes my lobe between his teeth.

"I'm attuned to every fucking breath you take. I admire your effort, though," he murmurs in my ear, causing my body to quiver from the warmth of his breath. My flesh is nothing but an exposed nerve. My thighs are sticky, and he's denying me an orgasm.

Turning on my knees to face him, I trace a path up his chest with my palm until I find his jaw. I grip it forcefully, tugging him toward me as we both fall back.

His lips curve against my mouth.

"Stop smiling and make me come," I snap.

"*Good fucking girl,*" he growls.

His weight disappears, and I'm about to rip the blindfold off when his mouth latches onto my center, sucking and swirling his tongue around the sensitive bud. A jolt racks my body as I grip his hair, forcing his head to stay *right there*. Spice and cedar fill my nostrils, and every swipe or swirl of his tongue through my folds reaches my ears. I can't see him, but I can hear him, smell him, and my imagination kicks in as I try to picture what he looks like right now. The throbbing in my clit could be a second heartbeat as it pulses deliciously against his tongue, and my core begins to clench around nothing. I cry out, squeezing my thighs against his smooth face because if he stops, I might kill him. He licks me through my orgasm until I'm so sensitive, I'm now pulling his head away.

The blindfold is ripped from my head, and while my eyes are adjusting to the light, he thrusts deep inside me. He grips the headboard behind me and drives into me with enough force the crown of my head meets the hard surface.

Oh my fuck.

My cries are shrill as I meet every thrust with my own. The way his hips roll into mine, his corded arms flexing above me, and the feral, masculine groans he's releasing have another orgasm barreling through me, and this time when I come, my pussy clenches hungrily around his cock. He drops down, cradling my head between his arms, and doesn't look away from me as he continues to thrust with reckless abandon, chasing his own release. He doesn't ask if I'm okay. He doesn't look at me with worry. He gives me what we *both* need.

Finally.

A bead of sweat rolls down the side of his face to his neck, and the taste of salt touches my tongue as I lick the path it rolled down. He releases another sexy groan before his lips caress my neck, and he bites down, soothing the sting with his tongue. His hand wraps around my throat, lightly squeezing.

"I said you'd have to break my heart." He rolls his hips, deep and slow, as his forehead rests against mine. "But I will chase you down to the ends of the fucking earth if *you ever* walk away from me."

Maybe warning bells should be ringing in my ears, but they don't because it's him—*my* Jansen.

Locking my legs around his waist, I palm his cheeks and tilt his face. When his soft gaze meets mine, my eyes fill with the weight of what I'm about to say because I've never felt so complete, so full of warmth in my entire life, and his never stray from mine as he waits, continuing his deep, slow thrusts.

"I love you," I breathe out.

Wide amber eyes bounce back and forth between mine before his lips skim a path along my jaw while his hips pick up the pace.

"Say it again," he chokes out, his scattered breathing tickling my ear.

"I love you."

He moans. "Again."

"I love you, Jansen," I cry out, and his muscles lock as he holds himself deep inside me, pulsing with his release.

He doesn't pull away; he stays rooted, lying on top of me. Every breath he takes warms the side of my neck, and I wrap myself around his sweat-coated body while running my fingers through his hair, scratching his scalp. The thought of this, being in his arms every single night, fills my stomach and chest with a warm, thick sensation. With a quick kiss to my neck, he lifts his hips, leaving me empty.

After we've showered, we lie back down, my body wrapped around his as I trace the raised skin on his stomach with my index finger.

"What happened?" I whisper, hoping he'll open up, but preparing for him to shut down.

His hand covers mine, squeezing, while my face rises and falls with his chest.

"I was eight. My mom had come home after being gone for two days straight. She went straight to the couch and passed out, so I wanted to make sure she ate when she got up. I'd been eating peanut butter sandwiches and whatever else I could find while she was gone." He takes another deep breath, squeezing my hand a little harder. "I wanted to try making macaroni, so I filled the pot and let the water boil. I had to stand on this old stool we had to stir, and when I went to take the pot to the sink, I fell back."

Anger simmers inside me, along with helplessness for the little boy I never knew.

Jansen's chuckle is hollow and sad. "My screams didn't even wake her up. I had to shake her awake, and the entire way to the hospital, she was drilling the story we'd tell into my brain. She let me mix the macaroni, and while she went to the bathroom, I tried to finish making it by myself. She told me if I told the truth, they'd take me away, and I'd never get to see her again."

Nothing I say right now could ease the pain he's feeling. Instead, I move down his body, kissing his scar before settling into him again. He turns sideways, cradling my face against his chest.

"I found her," he rasps. "When I was seventeen, I came home, and she was dead on the floor. She'd choked on her vomit. I always knew she had a problem, but she hid the evidence well enough. We had alcohol in the house, but she never brought anything else in. She never brought people over. I guess I didn't truly understand how bad it was until the toxicology report came in. She had a pharmacy of drugs in her system. We'd have good days, though. Days when she would talk to me, cook, and ask about my life as if we didn't live in the same house. Then she'd disappear again."

My lips purse, the words I'm about to say souring my stomach, but knowing, or feeling, the truth in them. "Maybe it was her way of protecting you. Disappearing. I know she abandoned and manipulated you, but perhaps in her mind, leaving was a way to keep you safe. To keep you away from that part of her world."

His voice causes a soothing vibration against my cheek. "Never thought of it like that."

"It's not an excuse, but maybe a reason."

He doesn't say anything else but adjusts his body so his head is resting on my chest as he tangles his limbs with mine. My chest pinches, knowing how much I've brought up and put him through with my actions. A small voice whispers, telling me he's been through enough in life, and I'll only cause him more pain.

Squeezing my eyes shut, I force the wallowing whisper away.

Thirty-Three

Jansen

It's about an hour's drive to the first place we want to visit. After making breakfast at the cabin, we head out early to beat the high temperature.

Last night, a weight was lifted. A weight I wasn't aware of until Tillie. I've never shared stories of my childhood with anyone. You can't change who you come from or the circumstances of your life when you aren't old enough to have control, but I did. I had to take control. Government assistance only covers so much, and Mom's odd jobs never lasted. I started working as soon as I could. *I* bought my first car. *I* figured out how to pay the bills and manage the money. *I* made sure to keep everyone at arm's length to protect our secrets.

Now I'm thirty-one and tired. Bone-deep tired of being alone. I've been living in survival mode, protecting myself, my entire life. When Tillie told me she loved me, it was the most vulnerable I've ever felt because, while I can control my love for her, I'll never be able to control her love for me. Be it fleeting or lasting. So when she asked about my scar, I found myself *wanting* to tell her. I want to hand over all the dark, raw, broken parts of myself that now feel too heavy to carry alone for as long as she'll let me.

Her voice, soft and sure, fills the cab as she sings along with "The

Night" by Morgan Wade. Her hair is braided back in two French braids, and she decided on black spandex shorts and an oversized white T-shirt.

"Your voice is beautiful," I tell her once the song ends.

"I'll tell my showerhead and steering wheel you said so."

"You never sang in front of anyone when you were younger?"

She adjusts in the seat, interlacing her fingers through mine resting on her thigh. "I was in a couple of musicals before..."

I squeeze her thigh, letting her know we don't have to talk about it. For the rest of the drive, she sings, and I'm happy to listen, soaking up these moments with her.

The sky is blue and clear, other than a few scattered clouds.

We've already hiked a trail to see the balancing rock, which was a little mind-blowing.

Tillie's lips were pursed as she watched people climb it or sit on a ledge of the rock for pictures. "Sooner than it's meant to, this won't exist because people don't respect it."

Her awe quickly shone through after. "How crazy is it that this has remained balanced through thunderstorms, wind, and snow?"

"It's a miraculous sight," I responded, folding my arms around her from behind. She lifted her arms to wrap her fingers around my forearms, relaxing into me further before whispering, "Yeah. It is."

Now we're walking the central trail in the Garden of the Gods, our necks craning to see the top of the jagged sandstone formations, but my gaze quickly returns to her. Nature can be healing, providing us with a perspective on our lives no other human being can. It's why I brought her here. To be surrounded by open spaces and beauty that has continually taken her breath away. To give her hope.

"I wish I could live in this moment every day." She sighs.

"What do you mean?" I pull her into my side as we make the trek back to the parking lot.

"There's never been a time when I've felt the way I do right now, with you, being surrounded by all of this. Simply saying I'm happy minimizes what I'm feeling."

Her words provoke a thought, or an idea, and I hold on to it with an iron grip, determined to make it our reality.

Suddenly, she stops walking and steps in front of me, fisting my shirt. "I want to apologize for last weekend. After everything you shared with me last night, I can't imagine the painful memories I've brought up for you."

She's right. She can't imagine, in the same way I can't imagine the pain from the memories she carries. "You had a little slip. Next time, I'd like it if you opened up to me before you reach that point."

Her eyes dim as she looks down. "I haven't really had a chance to think about how I derailed my sobriety. I cut the anklet I had made in rehab off that night. I've been taking life one day at a time since I got out, and I'm so pissed at myself for giving in." She looks up, her gaze tracing a path over the landscape before us. "Now it feels like such a petty waste. Giving in so easily."

Palming her cheeks, I tilt her face up. "You found out some hard truths these past few weeks on top of everything you've already been through. Give yourself some grace, yeah? You didn't fall completely off the wagon."

"Guess so. You said next time, and I really don't want there to be a next time."

"Then there won't be," I respond with every bit of conviction I feel. "You have me now. Always, Freckles. So when you're feeling crushed beneath the weight of your past, allow yourself to lean on me. I'll pull you from the rubble."

"I don't deserve you. You know that, right?" she croaks.

"It's not about what you deserve or what I deserve. It's about what I'm willing to accept and give. And I want to give you the fucking world."

She swallows, blinking slowly. Her hands slip around the back of my neck as she lifts on her toes and fuses her lips to mine. Citrus and musk invade my nostrils as her taste glides across my tongue. The pads of her fingers dig into my nape, and in seconds, every part of her body is leaning into mine. My cock swells painfully, public be damned. A series of whistles reach our ears, and we break apart, laughing silently as I rest my forehead against hers. Her stomach chooses this moment to grumble with the force of fucking thunder.

"Let's get you fed, Freckles. You're going to need the sustenance for later."

We decide to grab dinner at a quaint Italian bistro. We split a small margherita pizza and chicken saltimbocca. Her love for food is another reason I chose Colorado, and I plan on taking her to dine in Denver before we leave.

After we pay, she insists on walking downtown to see the shops. "I need to work off some of those carbs," she jokes.

A red haze clouds my vision, but I still notice how her eyes light up as we walk down the sidewalk, looking through the shop windows. Her steps slow next to a bookstore at the same time another store across the street catches my eye.

"Why don't you go look around, and I'll meet you in there?" I nod toward the door, opening it for her to walk inside.

Tillie crosses her arms, raising a brow with one corner of her mouth tilting up.

"Get your sassy ass in there, and I'll be right back."

She rolls her eyes and snorts but shuffles inside.

A bell chimes as I step through the door of the bookstore twenty minutes later. I inhale the scent of leather and parchment as I stroll down the aisles and find her in the thriller section between two shelves. Five paperbacks rest in her arms. Her bottom lip is pinched between her thumb and pointer as she scans the titles, and I saunter over to her and slip the books from her while she finishes looking at the titles.

"Thank you," she groans dramatically, rubbing her arms.

"I didn't know you liked to read."

She shrugs, pulling a book from the shelf and turning it over to read the blurb. "I used to read a lot."

Used to. I'm living for the day when I never have to hear those words slip past her lips again. When I've given her so many new memories, she's able to embrace the woman she is now, and "before" doesn't cross her mind.

I shuffle the books around, reading through the titles she got, and smile when I notice four out of the five are romance; the fifth looks like a horror.

"Quite a selection." I chuckle, watching a natural rouge fill her cheeks.

She decides on two more thrillers before we head to the front.

"We're doing a buy one, get one half-off sale," the young girl at the counter says, smiling while she rings us up. "Your total is $101.94."

I pull out my wallet, but Tillie bats my hand away.

"You're not paying for this. I have my own money. Remember, *Bossman*?" She waggles her brows playfully.

Smirking, I pull my card out and tut. "If you take her card, I'll have to leave a review that your books have mites."

The cashier's eyes widen, looking between me and Tillie, who elbows me in the ribs. "I'm so sorry. He will *not*." She glares at me while holding her card out.

"I won't." I grin, shrugging. "Maybe."

"Sorry, girl, but I just started this job," the cashier whispers, charging my card, but her pursed lips reveal her amusement as she stifles her laugh.

Tillie scoffs playfully, tapping my chest with her palm. "Careful. We don't want your puffed-out chest ripping through your shirt, big boy."

Nodding toward the cashier, who's holding back laughter with a cherry-red face, I wink and take hold of the bag in one hand and Tillie's in the other. "Thank you."

Later that night, she brings a blanket out on the back deck, which provides a scenic lookout over a mountain and trees during the day. Since we're at a higher elevation, the night air is cooler. Her nipples peek through her silk pajama top, and goosebumps cover her arms.

"C'mere," I whisper, pulling her into me and wrapping as much of my heat around her as I can while we stargaze.

Her contented sigh has my body and mind relaxing even further. "Need me to carry anything, Freckles?"

"Nope. Happy to be alive, Jansie."

That damn nickname.

Reaching around, I pinch her ass, causing her to yelp and giggle.

"Have you thought any more about what I said on Monday?" I hold my breath, waiting for her to pull away and claim her independence. She doesn't understand yet that her independence is what I'm trying to give her. I only want to ensure the journey there is easier.

But...she doesn't pull away. She relaxes into me further, every curve of her body fitting perfectly against mine.

"I want to do something that matters. I'm not sure what yet, but I *need* to help people. To make up for all of my wrongs," she whispers into the night.

Before I can speak, she places a finger over my lips. "I'm talking about the people I've hurt along the way. My dad, friends, Rhett, and Blaine." Her voice cracks. "I wish I had done more for him. Instead, I tuned out everyone around me. Nothing existed or mattered to me if it wasn't helping me forget or numb."

"You can't focus on what you can't change, Freckles. Sooner or later, you're going to have to make peace with your past, knowing you were hurting as much, if not more, than the people around you. What did you say about my mom the other night? It wasn't an excuse, but a reason, and you had more of a reason to tune it all out than most."

She doesn't say anything else. Her cheek glides against my chest with her nod. Now, I feel, is a good time to give her the gift I got earlier. Sitting up, I reach into my pocket and pull out the small black box.

She lies there, looking between me and my hand. "What is it?"

"My promise to you."

Opening it, I take out the white-gold anklet with tiny pearls spaced apart and a crescent moon in the center. My hands tremble as my heart rate spikes. I've never bought a woman jewelry before, and I'm aware of how much I want her to like it. This is new territory for me, but when I risk a glance at her face, her bottom lip is caught between her teeth as her emeralds shine. I palm her calf and glide my hand down the smooth skin to her ankle, placing it in my lap.

"You'll never have to go through life alone again. I love you. Scars and all, Tillie. I didn't know it was possible to feel this way about another person, but it feels like my heart has always beat for you, and it's finally found a steady rhythm since finding you. It's found where it belongs."

She sits up, running her finger across the anklet I clasped on while attempting to explain my raw feelings for her. Then she throws her leg over my lap, straddling me while peppering my cheeks, lips, and jaw with kisses.

I fucking love when she does this.

With her palms on my chest, she gently pushes until I'm on my back. And for the next thirty minutes, she takes complete control on the spacious deck under the Colorado stars.

Thirty-Four

Tillie

"I'm not sure I can do this," I admit, freaking the hell out a little while looking up at the inside of this massive multicolored balloon.

Jansen's laugh rumbles through his chest, against my back. "You're the one who *wanted* to do this."

"I know, but...now we're standing here, and I'm...I'm pretty sure my knees are about to give out."

This idea seemed so fun and whimsical, but pure terror has my knees shaking, my breathing choppy, and my palms clammy. Beads of sweat dot my forehead and chest. When the pilot, Liam, squeezes the lever attached to the burner, fire roars upward into the balloon, making me flinch.

The basket lifts, and I turn, clinging to Jansen and pressing my face into his chest. He immediately places one hand in my hair while using the other to rub soothing strokes down my back. I focus on my breathing, inhaling his familiar scent.

"She doing okay?" Liam calls out.

"I'm fine," I call back, my voice muffled.

"The weather conditions today are close to perfect with six-miles-per-hour winds. We're ascending to a thousand feet, which is the minimum. I'll let you know when we get to that point. You're not gonna want to miss it," Liam explains.

Slowly, I turn in Jansen's arms until I'm facing Liam. A slightly crooked smile takes over his face. "There she is."

Jansen wraps an arm around my middle as he splays a hand possessively on my stomach. At least, that's what it feels like. Especially when he drops his cheek to mine, the stubble on his face scraping deliciously against my skin, and places a kiss on my neck. He doesn't say anything, doesn't claim me with his words, but by his actions. And that alone causes a shiver to run down my spine as every nerve in my body sparks under my skin.

"So, I brought something today," Jansen murmurs in my ear.

Taming the urge to wrap my legs around his waist, I ask, "Oh, yeah?"

He reaches into his back pocket, pulling out my phone. "It's on Do Not Disturb, but I thought you'd want pictures. I'm sorry, I didn't think about it yesterday."

I haven't thought about my camera once. I've enjoyed being in the moment with him, leaving the noise of the world and our problems back in Arkansas. I'm starting to understand his need to run from it. This is the first time I've felt as if I can breathe and exist without a dark shadow at my heels.

"We don't need it. I can promise you I'll never forget," I assure him.

"How about one?"

The plea in his voice has the corners of my lips tipping up. "Liam, could you take a quick picture of us?"

"Absolutely."

Jansen winds both arms across my middle, leaning down to rest his cheek against mine. He wiggles his fingers, tickling my sides, causing me to laugh.

"Got it." Liam smiles, looking between us as he hands the phone back. "How long have you two been together?"

It seems as if I've known Jansen much longer than I have. Our feelings for each other aren't measured in time, but in true, soul-deep connection. "Not long, but when you know, you know." Tip-toeing, I kiss his cheek.

"We're up as far as we'll be going. Whenever you're ready." Liam nods.

Jansen palms my shoulders with a gentle squeeze. "You ready?"

Taking a deep breath in through my nose and releasing it slowly through my mouth, I nod and turn. I thought the view from the plane was majestic, but nothing compares to this. Bright and deep, rich green trees surround the mountains as far as the eye can see.

"I've never seen anything so beautiful," I whisper in awe.

"I have. Every fucking day." His hand slides up my stomach, over my chest. "The hitch in your breathing. The way your heart started beating a little faster. The need to soak in the beauty of it...That's how I feel every time I lay eyes on you."

"All right, calm down, Shakespeare." My laugh is shaky and breathless, but the organ beneath his hand beats faster.

"I'll never be able to feel this way about anyone else. You're it for me." The seriousness in his tone sends a rush of warmth behind my hips.

·····•·····

I'm putting the finishing touches on my hair and makeup when he knocks on the bathroom door. I haven't dressed up like this in years. My dress is a cornflower blue, hugging my waist and has thick straps. The V-neck reveals more cleavage than I'm usually comfortable with, and two pieces of fabric hang down the back, which will tie into a bow. The bottom of the dress flows and hits my ankles. Instead of my typical Converse, I'm wearing a pair of tan wedges. I've curled and finger-combed my hair. The makeup, I've kept light. A skin tint with a little blush, shimmery peach eyeshadow, mascara, and a mauve lip.

"Come in," I call out, clearing the nerves from my throat.

"Are you about—" His eyes widen, drinking me in from head to toe, like he's been in the desert for days, and I'm the first cool glass of water he sees. He rubs a hand along his freshly shaven jaw before running it through his hair. I've never seen a man blush, but his cheeks darken.

"You are...I don't have words, Tillie. You're gorgeous."

Twisting my lips to stop from biting them, I walk into his chest, resting my hands on his sides. He's wearing fitted dark-wash jeans and a maroon button-up, showcasing his solid arms and chest perfectly.

"Can you tie these?" I ask, turning around.

He grasps the fabric, and his fingers glide across my back, causing a shiver to run down my spine and goosebumps to cover my skin. I'm not sure if my body will always react to his touch this way, but I hope it does. I hope it never becomes so familiar it stops triggering chills and rushes of heat afterward.

"We leave tomorrow," I state, turning around to face him again.

"I know. I wish we could stay longer."

"So how about we make it a quick dinner?" I suggest, peering up at him through my lashes.

That earns me a blinding grin. The one showing off the dimples in his smile line.

A few hours later, we're lying in bed, sated.

Teasing him through dinner proved to create the perfect storm. As soon as we got through the door, his hands were already pulling the fabric apart at my back while he wrapped my hair in his hand, kissing a path along my neck. We didn't make it to the bedroom. He stripped my dress from my body, and I sank to my knees, taking him in my mouth before he fucked me on top of the kitchen table.

My sniff has his abs tensing as he turns, placing a finger under my chin to tip it back. His eyes bounce back and forth between mine, which are currently full of unshed tears.

"I'm being a baby. I'm fine, really," I explain.

Moisture lines my cheeks from the few that escaped, and he dips down, soaking it up with his lips. "You're not. Let me carry it, Freckles."

Blowing out a rough breath, I try to gather my thoughts.

"Uhm—" My voice cracks. "I guess I'm scared to go back. I feel free here."

"I ran from everything for years, convincing myself if I was far enough away, my past couldn't reach me. It took knowing you to understand that I'd never outrun it but carried it with me."

"What do you mean?"

He turns sideways, placing his leg between mine, and runs a hand up and down my outer thigh. "I fell in love with you in a place I've spent my life running from. I'll take you far away from Arkansas if that's what you want. You'll feel relief, but the pain will still be there, lurking in the shadows, until you deal with it."

I nuzzle my body into his further, the echo of his heartbeat filling my ear. "Have you dealt with yours?"

"I think I'll always carry a bit with me, but it's...less now. You've shown me not everything is as it seems."

············

The plane ride back didn't cause as much panic for me as the first, but I can't say I'll ever *love* it. The closer we get to Arkansas, the more apprehensive I become.

After turning my phone back on, I find a few text messages from Ivy, one from Presley, and one from my dad.

> **Ivy:** We need to have another movie night soon!

> **Ivy:** Nix and I called it off after we ended up at the bar and Mason showed his ass. He wasn't supposed to be working, but he picked up a shift. We were dancing, and Nix went to the bathroom. Another guy got super handsy, and Mase punched him before dragging him out of the bar. Nix saw

> him comforting me and shut down.
>
> **Ivy:** You must not have your phone on, or I know you would've texted back by now. Idk what to do.
>
> **Presley:** You deserve a vacation. Send pictures!
>
> **Dad:** He was arrested. We won't know about bail until Monday.

A shaky breath passes through my lips. Relief and dread tangle together, tightening inside my chest, but I refuse to let it overcome me. For now, he's locked away. For now, I can breathe a little more freely and worry about the aftermath on Monday.

I sent Presley the one picture we took together, explaining that we turned our phones off, before texting Ivy and Dad back.

> **Me:** We'll get together once I'm back. I'm sorry you couldn't reach me, Ivy. I'm glad Mase kicked that guy's ass, though.
>
> **Me:** Fingers crossed.

I glance at Jansen and notice he's white-knuckling the steering wheel as he takes deep breaths.

"What's going on?" I ask, reaching over to palm the back of his neck while rubbing soothing strokes with my thumb.

"A window was broken at Clovers, and Mason decided to beat the shit out of a customer," he grits out.

I don't bring up the texts. He seems to be upset enough, and we're still thirty minutes from town. I was impressed he was able to walk away completely while still technically in charge. Jansen likes to have control over his life, so I can only imagine how he's feeling right now, knowing he left the reins to another person and it went awry.

My chest warms, and excitement courses through my veins as we pass the familiar sites of my haven before pulling into Clovers' lot. Nix is waiting, posted up against the brick. I didn't realize how much I missed him until right now. I open the door, running over to him and wrapping my arms around his back. He chuckles, squeezing me in a hug that lifts my feet from the ground.

"Did you have a good time?" he asks, setting me down and putting space between us.

"I did." I beam. "It was beautiful. What'd you get up to?"

He blows out a breath, rubbing the back of his neck. "I went home last night and binged TV until you got here. Figured you'd be sick of him by this point, so I wanted to give you a ride home." He points a thumb over his shoulder. "And I heard about the window, so I knew Jansie would have a lot on his mind."

"Did the window get broken the night of the fight?"

"No, it happened when it was closed."

I cross my arms, taking in the damage behind him. The window to the right of the door has a giant hole, now covered by plywood. "Why would someone do that?"

"Probably some shithead kids," Jansen answers, sidling up to me. "Apparently, someone broke in. Mase didn't realize it until he was doing inventory. He's watching the feed now. Some high-end liquor was stolen, so I need to stay here, and I know you two probably want to catch up. Do you mind if he takes you home?"

"Are you sure you don't need me to stay and help with anything? I don't mind."

Jansen leans down, kissing my temple. "I've got it. Go home and relax."

Biting my lip, I push down my unease. I'm sure it has everything to do with the fact that the bar was broken into.

"I love you," I murmur.

He palms my face with both hands, tilting it, and seals his lips to mine. "I love you too."

Thirty-Five

Jansen

"What do you have?" I ask Mason, who's sitting at my desk in front of my laptop, his chin resting in his steepled hands.

"Who the fuck wears a mask to steal alcohol? Aren't petty criminals supposed to be dumb? This guy wore a mask, gloves, and a hat."

"Are you sure it's a guy?" I walk behind him, leaning down to get a look at the screen. The thought of Bailee's toxic ass being responsible for this runs through my mind.

"Positive. I considered Bailee, but she's been MIA since her dad left her in jail until she saw the judge. Word from one of the patrons is he's tired of her shit. Anyway, *he* reaches in to unlock the door, roots through the liquor, doesn't attempt to open any registers, but then walks back here. Probably to take a piss because he appears a few minutes later, and nothing looked out of place in your office. Your apartment was still locked."

"So it probably *was* a dumbass youngin'." I rub a hand over my jaw. "I guess it's good he didn't trash the place."

He closes down the feed and leans back in the chair with a heavy sigh.

"What happened with the patron?"

"Some prick was getting handsy with Ivy after she'd already shut him down. When I confronted him and told him to leave, the asshole made a disgusting remark about her. I saw red."

"I'd say you handled it appropriately." I squeeze his shoulder. "Have you already made a report to the police?"

"You really have nothing else to say about it?"

"Yeah. No charges were filed, so that's good for you, and I hope the fucker felt like shit in the morning."

He shakes his head, huffing a laugh. "I made a report, cataloged what was missing, took pictures of the damage, and reported to insurance."

"Seems like you've got it all under control. I'm going to stick around for a few hours, make sure nothing else is amiss, and catch up on paperwork. Mr. Brooks wants to keep the team we have in place, but I suggested you take over as the general manager."

"Thanks, man. Means a lot. It's going to be different without you here."

"I'm sure I'll be back to visit." That statement alone surprises me as I say it aloud because I know it's the truth. Being here is still painful, but it's duller now. Memories with my cousin, Granddad, the people I've worked with, and Tillie have piled up, burying the more unfavorable ones.

It's around ten when I shut my laptop and rub my eyes. Exhaustion from traveling and the day's events weigh me down. I should go upstairs and crash, but I've gotten used to sleeping next to my siren. Pulling out my phone, I send her a text.

> **Me:** I've gotten used to sleeping beside you. I'm about to leave work and head over.

I knead the muscles in my neck and stand to stretch, noticing the filing cabinet slightly ajar.

When I pull it open, nothing seems wrong until I find Tillie's file out of alphabetical order. My guts twist as I pull it out, flipping the manila folder. My lungs seize before it drops from my hands as I scramble for my phone.

Grabbing my keys, I press dial, praying she answers.

She doesn't.

I try Nix next.

No answer.

I'm running to my Jeep, bypassing Mason's shouts.

My last call is to Granddad. I'm already on the road, driving as fast as I can. When he doesn't answer, I leave a rushed voicemail, begging him to go to Tillie's, and my fist connects with the steering wheel.

"*Fuck*." My heart pumps at a pace that has every breath leaving my lungs spasmodically. I focus on centering myself. I have no idea what I'm about to walk into, but pure dread seeps from my pores. Intuition is a powerful force.

What should've been a ten-minute drive takes five, but every second is inestimable.

As I turn sharply into the marina, I'm dialing 911.

Before the dispatcher can finish their sentence, I'm giving instructions. "There's been an assault at Novaridge Marina, slip sixty-three. I need an ambulance and the police. I'll leave the line open. Hurry."

Taking half a second to breathe, to center myself, I leave the door open as I rush down her dock with the lightest steps I can manage. As soon as my boot lands on the boat's bow, a manic male voice sounds from inside. I twist my neck to look inside without being seen and spot Tillie lying on top of Nix, shielding him while Holden points a gun down at them.

I'm ripping the door open before another thought can enter my mind. Right now, I'm not Nix's cousin or the man who loves Tillie beyond reason. I'm Holden's worst fucking nightmare. Inhuman and expendable.

He startles and turns, firing a shot. A sharp crack echoes as I charge him, my shoulder connecting with his chest, and send us both to the ground. The clang and scrape of metal hitting linoleum assures me the gun has slipped from his hand. He grapples for purchase underneath me, his fist connecting with my jaw, but I don't register the pain as I deliver a blow of my own, stunning him enough that I'm able to deliver another. And another. And another. He's not a person right now. Nothing but flesh and bone.

His hand reaches for my face, pushing and squeezing with little force. Male grunts and gurgles reach my ears, but something has been unleashed.

A darkness lives inside all of us, ready to slither out from the crevices in our psyche. When an opportune moment reveals itself, splitting the fissure wider, the question of how far we'd go for the people we love is answered.

In this moment, as my knuckles split and grind against the exposed bone in his face, my darkness surrounds and shadows my soul. As my hands pause in their assault to wrap around his throat, I take in the physical damage I've caused, but it still doesn't feel like enough for the damage he inflicted *inside of her*, so I squeeze harder, determined to seal his lungs. To make him feel the suffocation she must have felt every single day.

His thready pulse assures me I'm almost there when an elbow locks around my neck, pulling me backward into a hard mass. Muffled shouting sounds through the high-pitched ringing in my ears.

"Stop, Grandson." Gruff words from my granddad's mouth break through. Clear and strong.

My body relaxes further into his hold as I turn my head. I propel from his arms to the ground next to theirs. Her entire body is atop Nix, her arms caged limply around his head. With trembling fingers, I check her pulse, pushing her hair back. Relief rushes through me from the faint beats, but my stomach curdles from the sight of her swollen and bruised face and the blood sticking to the hand I used in her hair.

"Granddad, help," I rasp. He crawls closer, shock evident in his features, as we gently roll Tillie on her back. Not a twitch of her eyelids or sound passes through her lips.

Nix's pulse is stronger, beating against my fingers as he groans.

"An ambulance is on the way, Nix. Hold on. We're here."

A small amount of blood pools beneath his head. Granddad takes over with Nix, tears running down his face as I hover over Tillie, rechecking her pulse. It's still faint but there. Sirens wail from a distance. Her white tank top has been cut down the middle, and on the inside of her elbow, a streak of blood has dried.

My consciousness starts to come back fully as my chest wrenches from the guttural sob I release. Placing my temple against hers, I palm her cheeks with shaky hands, carefully rubbing my thumbs along the bruised skin, while whispering hoarsely in her ear.

"I know you want to give up, but I'm *begging* you not to. I'm *begging* you to *fight* because *I need you*. I'll take you far away, wherever you want to go. I'll stand beside you while you figure out your dreams and make plans. I swear to God I'll do anything to heal you, but I *can't* live in a world where you don't exist. If you jump, I jump. Remember, Freckles?"

"Oh my God," a woman's voice breathes out so quietly I nearly miss it, but her voice firms when she speaks again. "Sir, I need you to move back so we can do our jobs."

Squeezing my lids shut, I soak in the feel of her for one more second. "*Please*, Freckles. Hold on. *Fight*," I whisper before tearing myself from her side, bringing my trembling hand to my chest and the other to my mouth.

"I think he drugged her," I croak, informing the medics.

She does her assessment, releasing Narcan into each of her nostrils, and calls out to her partner, "We need to load her and go."

I glance over to see Holden still unconscious while a man works on him. The look on my face and tightening of my fists have an officer stepping closer to me.

"I'm Officer Jenkins. Can you step outside with me and tell me what happened? I have first aid training, so we can get a look at those knuckles."

"Can I go with her?" I rasp, feeling like my eyes are about to roll out of their sockets from moving constantly over the space, trying to keep Tillie, Nix, and Holden in my view.

Tillie gasps, the sound painful and beautiful all at once. I interlace my fingers behind my head, my chest heaving as I walk outside.

Officer Jenkins follows me despite the scene; his face remains stoic. "You can't. I need to get the details, and I'll give you a ride to the hospital after."

"Tillie and I got back from Colorado today."

"Tillie is the injured female? I'm going to need as much detail as possible, sir."

"Her name is Tillie Anne Porter. The man with the head wound is my cousin, Pheonix Cade Pierce. The other man with the beaten face is Holden Warren. He's from Sayersville, Arkansas. Holden works for Tillie's father, Daniel Porter, but he was caught embezzling money. An arrest was supposed to be made. I was at the bar cleaning up after a break-in."

When Tillie is taken out of the houseboat, I start to step toward her, but the officer blocks my path with his hands on my shoulders. "I can tell you've walked into and been through hell, but I really need you to focus on me and let them do their jobs."

I push on my eyes—burning from contained emotion—with the heels of my palms, before pushing my hair back and taking a deep breath.

Officer Jenkins continues when he's sure I'm not moving. "I saw the report on that break-in earlier today. A window was broken and a couple liquor bottles were stolen."

"I thought that's all it was too, but when I was about to leave for the night, I noticed my file cabinet had been messed with, and the document with her personal information was missing. I drove straight here and walked in on him standing over Tillie and Nix. She was lying on top of Nix. When I slid the door open, it surprised him, and he let off one shot before I took him to the ground. We fought until he was unconscious."

"What time did you leave the bar?"

"A little after ten."

"What time did you and Tillie arrive back in town?"

I fist my hair, trying to remember the exact time. "Around six, I think. We had a later flight and the drive back."

"Do you believe Holden is the one who broke into the bar?"

"I'm positive he is, but my camera footage shows a man fully covered up. The station should have it. My manager took care of the report."

"What time did you and Tillie part ways?"

"Nix was waiting for us at Clovers when we got there, and they left together to come back here about ten minutes after we pulled in."

"They went kayaking," Granddad's gruff voice chimes in from behind the officer. "I'm Nix's grandfather. Tillie and Nix went kayaking around 6:45 for about an hour. I grilled some burgers when they got back. I can't remember exactly what time they left. Maybe a few past nine."

"And you're positive Nix had nothing to do—"

"Nix wouldn't hurt a hair on her fucking head," I spit out. "Holden is solely responsible for this. It's revenge for her dad going to the police and turning him in."

"I have to get all of the facts, and that means asking every question. Leaving no stone unturned."

Granddad puts a hand on my shoulder, squeezing as I release a harsh breath while shaking my head.

"I've got all I need for now, until they're all recovered enough to talk. Let's get your hands looked at. It looks like you may have been cut on your shoulder." He nods to the blood pooling under my left sleeve.

"I think the bullet grazed my arm when he fired," I inform him.

"Jesus Christ," Granddad murmurs, running his hands over his face.

"Let's clean you up and get you both to the hospital."

Thirty-Six

Jansen

Two days.

Two days of nonstop fluids.

Two days of machines incessantly beeping.

Two days of doctors and nurses using the word *patience*.

Over and *fucking* over.

Two days of pure continuous agony.

And she still hasn't woken up.

It feels like I'm outside of my body, watching the chaos but doing everything I can to keep it together. I got in touch with her dad yesterday, and he's been on a rampage ever since. I'm not allowed to see anything in her medical files because I'm not her family, and her dad is being tight-lipped despite my insistence and temper.

Holden was arrested on Friday, but because of a personal connection with a judge, he was released Saturday afternoon—off the books until Monday. Mr. Porter never got a notification. Several phone calls have been made to his lawyer and the district judge about the judicial misconduct used in this case.

Aunt Lin and Uncle Tony arrived early Monday morning after the accident. Nix woke up that afternoon with a hell of a headache and thankfully no brain damage, but I can see the hollowness under and in his eyes. He's barely spoken a word to anyone unless it's to ask if Tillie is awake yet.

I'm at the visitor waiting center, pouring coffee, when Aunt Lin sidles up next to me. "I sent Nix to stay with you and Granddad, so how did my boy end up in a situation like this with some woman who—"

"Some woman..." I chuckle hollowly, slamming the cup I've poured on the counter. Hot liquid sloshes over the rim onto my hand, but the fire spreading through my veins masks the burn. "That woman's name is Tillie, and she has done more for Nix in the past few weeks than anyone. I walked into that hellscape to find the woman I fucking love shielding his body with her own. So when *that woman* wakes up, be sure to fucking thank her."

Her eyes are wide with a sheen as she stares at me, unable to find words, it would seem. She reaches for my arm. "Jansen, I'm sorry."

Shaking her off, I grunt my acknowledgment before trudging back to Tillie's room, but I pause at the door. Mr. Porter has a book open next to her on the bed, while he holds her other hand and reads. He chokes up on a few words, but I stay back, giving him this moment. Instead, my gaze lands on her. The doctor said the bruising on her face would get worse before it got better. The fair skin on the left side is swollen, covered in deep shades of purple and yellow, with abrasions. Luckily, no serious damage was done to her jaw. Her throat has bruising in the shape of a handprint, and I'll admit to being afraid of knowing of any others. Every time I look at her, a rush of dread and panic kicks up my heart rate.

When he closes the book, I walk into the room, handing him the other cup of coffee. Neither of us has been able to stomach much food since being here.

He accepts the cup with thanks and leans back in his chair, clutching the book in his lap. "She used to love this book when she was little."

I pull a chair beside her bed on the other side, sitting down and wrapping my hand around hers, squeezing little pulses and praying she'll squeeze back. "I wouldn't be surprised if it was some sort of silly romance book or if she somehow turned it into one," I murmur, a small grin forming from thinking about a young Tillie.

He chuckles. "Yeah, she was always a hopeless romantic in her younger years. Always choosing rom-coms or sappy romance movies when it was her turn to pick."

His expression morphs from nostalgic to pained. "I truly don't understand how I failed this miserably. How I didn't notice the small details and changes in her. A man's most important job in life is to protect his family. She is all I have, and still, I failed."

Sitting up, I clear my throat. "Maybe she didn't want you to see her pain, so she hid it in any and every way she could. You were her only family, and she thought she was protecting you. It's not an excuse for everything you missed, but maybe her reason."

His gaze remains locked on her while tears fall from his lower lids. "It should've been me, but damn it, son, I'm glad she found you. Someone who didn't hesitate to protect her, no matter the cost."

"She's carved out a piece of my soul, sir. There isn't a single thing I wouldn't do to make sure she's happy and thriving and loved."

He nods, handing me the book, a worn vintage copy of *Peter Pan*. "I'm going to give you two some privacy and stretch my legs."

I find the page her dad marked and continue reading to her. After ten minutes, I slam the book closed and focus on what I'm sure I just felt. Gently squeezing her hand, I wait...

Seconds later, her hand weakly grips mine back.

"Tillie?" I gruff through the tears clogging my throat. My hand hovers over her face that I'm afraid to touch, so I settle for her hair. "Open your eyes, Freckles. I haven't seen my favorite pair of emeralds in days."

Her face turns down while one corner of her mouth turns up, as if smiling pains her. The remote with a red call button is lying on her other side, and I reach over to press it and let the nurses know she's finally awake. "Nix?" she whimpers with her eyes closed.

I lean over and kiss the back of her hand. "He's doing good. He's ready for you to wake up."

Her chest starts to rise and fall faster, the numbers on the machine rising. "I can't...my eye..."

"Shh, it's okay." I rest my forehead against her temple with feather-like pressure while caressing her hair. Every word is sandpaper scraping a path up my throat as I say, "Your eye is still a little swollen, Freckles, so take your time."

"Holden?" Her voice cracks, ripe with fear.

"I don't know if he's alive or dead. He was taken to a different hospital, and from there he'll be arrested and charged."

I lower my voice to a whisper only she can hear. "If he lives, he's never getting out, and if he does, I'll finish what I started. I swear to you he will *never* lay a finger on you again."

Minutes later, the room holds her dad, me, a nurse who checks her vitals, and the doctor who came in on her heels. "I'm Dr. Damani. Your scans have all come back clear. Because you were unconscious, we needed to place a catheter to release your bladder. We'll get it removed as soon as you're able to walk around."

Tillie's eyelids can only part slightly, but she nods along with the doctor's assessment.

"Before we discuss anything else, would you like to speak privately, or is it okay for these two gentlemen to remain in the room?"

Her tongue swipes her dry lips before her face turns up to the ceiling. "Privately," she rasps.

Before I can object, Dr. Damani gives me a sharp look, letting me know she won't accept any pushback, and her dad eats the short distance between them, kissing her forehead. His lips move beside her ear in a hushed tone, and I don't catch the words, but note the way her shoulders relax slightly as she rests her temple against his cheek.

"You should go home and change, grab us some food from Nelly's, maybe?" Tillie suggests, softening the blow.

"I'm coming right back," I promise as I lean over her to kiss the top of her head. Touching any part of her frequently is the only reassurance keeping my fear at bay.

"Take your time. I'm not going anywhere," she tries to joke.

"I love you."

Her bottom lip wobbles, but she forces a grin, nodding.

"I'll walk out with you." Mr. Porter walks up beside me, placing a hand on my shoulder.

Our steps scuff against the linoleum floor as we amble down the hallway, but a surge of relief travels through my limbs, and my knees buckle. Mr. Porter holds one side of my frame up, but then Granddad is right beside me, holding the other. He mistakes my reaction for something else, and his grip on my arm tightens.

"Is she okay? What's happened?" Panic causes every word he speaks to shake.

"She's awake. She's finally awake," I breathe out in short pants as my vision hazes, and I collapse into his side.

I barely notice the grip on my other arm disappearing as I cling to Granddad and fist his shirt.

"Nothing in this lifetime can hold that girl down. She's a survivor," he gruffs reassuringly, and my hold on him tightens as the relief I felt earlier crashes into my terror of the unknown.

We stand this way for minutes, until my fists loosen their hold on his shirt, and I'm able to stand solid on my own two feet again.

It's almost impossible to unwind the tightly coiled fear that rattles in my chest and stomach as I leave the hospital. At this moment, I haven't completely lost her, but I'm terrified of how many more pieces that son of a bitch has ripped from her.

I did not take my time before rushing back to her. An hour and thirty-two minutes later—yes, I kept track—I'm walking to her room and spot her lying on her side, with Nix sitting beside her on the very edge of the hospital bed. Their voices drift through the door, and I pause, leaning my back against the wall beside it out of view.

"The pain outweighs the craving right now. I'm hoping it stays that way." Tillie's broken voice filters through.

"You didn't want to relapse, Tills, you were forced. That reason alone is why you'll get through this," Nix says with conviction.

"What if I'm not strong enough to stay clean anymore? What if it's all too much now?" She sniffs, and the sound has me rubbing the ache in my chest with the heel of my palm.

Nix is quiet for a few seconds, and I'm pushing up to stand, to go to her and tell her how strong she is, when his voice sounds out again. "I love you, Tills. Ivy loves you. Granddad loves you. Presley and Dane. Hell, even my mom, after coming in and talking to you for ten minutes, probably loves you. But Jansie...He loves you beyond reason or doubt. *All of us* will hold you up when you feel like falling, but Jansie...He'll never put you down."

"You're...my...best friend," she hiccups.

I collapse back to the floor as tears glide down my cheeks. My little cousin is right; I'll never let her fall. From the moment she walked into my life, I was done for. It made no fucking sense, and in the beginning, I hated the way I thought about her. But after knowing her, imagining a life without her in it is a kind of indescribable ache. If she relapses, we'll deal with it. If she takes weeks or months or years to overcome this, I'll be beside her. For the rest of her life, if there is air in my lungs, she will *never* face anything alone again.

It takes me a bit to compose myself enough to stand and walk into the room.

When I finally do, she's asleep again, her hands curled under her face, and he stares at the wall in front of him without blinking.

"How's she doing?" I whisper.

"Traumatized," he says hollowly. "They were able to remove her catheter but said she'd need to stay here another night or two for observation."

"How are you doing?"

"I couldn't protect her." He swallows thickly. "It all happened so fast. He'd broken in and was waiting for us. I remember a sharp pain in my head and her scream before everything went black."

After placing the bags of food on the small counter, I sit next to him, palming his knee. "Look at me."

His lids squeeze shut before he turns his head as a bead of liquid rolls from the corner of his eye.

"None of this is your fault. You had no idea what you were walking into. There's only one person to blame."

"She's saved my life twice now"—his voice cracks—"and I couldn't protect her just once."

"You don't believe you've saved her life? You've given her a best friend. Every day you've been here has put missing pieces back into place for her. Given her joy that was stolen from her for so long. She loves you, Nix."

His solemn hazel gaze falls, and he nods, sniffing back his emotion. "A cop came to take our statements. Tillie asked for an update on Holden. He's alive." His throat works. "I wish you'd killed him."

So do I, and it weighs heavily on my conscience now that the adrenaline is gone, because if I had, I don't believe I would've felt anything from it other than relief.

I nod without voicing my thoughts. "He's going to prison. They'll take good care of him there."

"How's your hand?"

Careful not to overextend my fingers, I hold it up. "It's doing good. The years of boxing came through. I needed a couple knuckles stitched up." Luckily, I was right, and the bullet only grazed my arm. After a bandage, I was set.

"Ivy wants to come up here, but I've told her not to. Not until Tillie is ready to see people."

"You're allowed to have someone here for you, Nix. You went through hell. Let Ivy come up here for *you*."

"Yeah. Maybe I will." He bites the inside of his cheek and squeezes the back of his neck. "I'm going to head back to my room. I'm supposed to be discharged tomorrow, and then I don't know if I'm going home or back to Granddad's."

"Let me know, yeah?"

Tillie stirs as he maneuvers out of the bed and stands. Before he can walk past me, I pull him into me, wrapping my arms tightly around him.

"Love you, Jansie," he croaks.

"Love you too, man."

Tillie's eyelids twitch as she tries to open them fully.

"I got you some soup and mashed potatoes. A weird combination, but I thought it'd be better on your stomach."

"Thank you," she chokes out with a rasp.

"Can I hold you?" There's an urgency to my words. A plea in my voice.

She nods and sniffs, her chest shaking. "Please."

Climbing in beside her, I'm careful not to touch the IVs attached to her, prepared for any timidness she may show after being almost murdered.

But she doesn't. Her arm wraps around my middle as she lays her face gingerly on my chest. Those actions alone crash through the wall I've built up, sending every emotion I've been suppressing rushing to the surface.

The side of her face jerks from the movement of my chest as I try my fucking damndest to redirect the flow. My throat aches and my eyes burn, so I close them, hoping that for only a second, I can be a man holding the woman he loves. Not a man who almost killed another. Not a man who watched the woman he loves almost die after being brutally assaulted, while he pleaded with her to stay.

I squeeze my eyes tighter together, and then her cool palm cups my cheek. "It's okay, Jansen. Let it out."

Shaking my head, I lay my hand atop hers, biting the inside of my cheek until the taste of copper fills my mouth to distract myself. To give my mind another form of pain to focus on.

"I heard you, and I fought as hard as I could to stay with you," she whispers.

A broken whimper I've never heard before escapes me. Refusing to take a chance on hurting her further, I curl my fingers around her hand as soft as possible to guide it away from my face, but she pushes back. "No. You don't get to hurt in silence or feel ashamed. I held on, Jansen. I held on so I could spend the rest of the time I have left in this world with *you*. All of you. Please don't push me away when we need each other the most."

"I need to be strong for you right now," I croak.

Her thumb glides across my cheekbone in featherlike strokes. "We *both* need to heal, Jansie. Neither one of us can do that if we're not honest about our feelings. If we try to lock what happened into a hush box to store away. It doesn't work. You know it doesn't."

"I'm terrified to know what happened to you." I swallow the lump in my throat.

Her body goes rigid against mine. "You don't have to know," she whispers.

"I do, because you're not allowed to carry everything alone anymore. So let me carry it, Freckles."

She blows out a breath, and I force myself to listen to her assault with little reaction. She breaks down once, and I soothe her until she's able to speak again. By the time she's finished, every fiber of my being regrets not finishing what I started.

Thirty-Seven

Tillie

September 5th, 2024

I rub my clammy palms down my thighs, taking deep breaths like my lawyer told me to after I'd informed her I'd testify. There's a deep-rooted fear tucked inside my psyche now. The fear of death and darkness. Every night before I go to sleep, I turn on a light with a glow soft enough it won't wake Jansen but bright enough to see my immediate surroundings. That's the last bit of fear I'll allow him to cause me. I didn't move forward with pressing charges against him from the past. My attorney seemed to understand and figured out a way to involve a piece of it in this trial, where I could say what he did to me out loud in court.

"Ms. Porter, can you tell me about the night of June 24th, 2015?"

"Objection, Your Honor. That date, including any testimony, is irrelevant to this case and hearsay."

Milena, my attorney, opposes Holden's attorney's objection. "This date is important to prove that Holden Warren had a history of abuse against my client. Evidence was submitted in discovery."

"Overruled. You may answer the question, Ms. Porter," the judge rules.

Instinctively, my gaze latches onto Holden. My hands tremble, my mouth dries, and blood whooshes through my ears. Milena steps into my direct line of sight, blocking my view of him. She made it clear that taking back my power doesn't mean I need to look at him with my testimony; it means speaking out and sharing my story.

I release a shaky breath and clear my throat before answering the question. "It was the first time he recorded himself raping me."

"*Objection*," his attorney calls out in outrage.

"Your Honor, my next question will offer clarity."

"Overruled," the judge decides. "Proceed with the question."

"How old were you at the time?"

"Sixteen."

"Do you remember how old Mr. Warren was?"

"He was twenty-eight, I believe."

Low murmurs spread throughout the courtroom.

"Order." The judge slams his gavel, and my body jerks at the sound.

"I want you to walk me through the night of July 14th, 2024, when you're ready."

"My friend Nix and I walked over to the houseboat we were living in after eating dinner with his grandfather. It was around nine o'clock, I believe. The lights were off when we walked in..."

July 14th, 2024

Nix laughs at my impression of Dorothy from *The Wizard of Oz* as I click my heels three times and quote the famous line.

The entire houseboat is shadowed in darkness as my fingers slide against the wall in search of the switch. Light illuminates the space, and my gaze lands on a grin stretched across Nix's mouth. In seconds, a sickening crack reaches my ears and tightens every muscle in his face. The scream I release bounces off the walls as his knees buckle. Holden becomes visible, still holding the gun in an upward position as Nix's body hits the floor with a thud.

"I told you not to fuck with me," Holden snarls, grabbing my throat and squeezing, the skin beneath his palm glacial.

The gun in his other hand points down by his side. Quickly taking advantage of that, I lift my arm between us and use force with the outside of my forearm to bat his away as I wrench my head back. My heel comes into contact with his stomach as I kick out, causing him to double over with a huff.

I turn to open the door, but an unmistakable clicking sounds. It rings in my ears, louder than it should be, looping through my mind, the nail in my coffin—the end.

"You walk out the fucking door, and I'll kill him."

His voice is calm. Empty. I squeeze my eyes shut, swallowing down the terror chilling my veins.

Turning on trembling legs, I face him and think...

What if I had just gone with him?

Would it have changed him?

Would it have been enough to tame this more sinister version of him?

Or was it always destined to end like this?

"What do you want?" I choke out.

"What I've always wanted. Your obedience, dollface. And you haven't given me that since your dad ruined you with rehab."

The glacial chill inside me starts to burn, reminding me that, for right now, I'm still alive, though I accept I probably won't be for long. So I cling to the pain and allow it to build up, to overcome me.

My gaze sweeps over Nix. All of Holden's attention needs to remain on me, so I step around Nix and walk into the kitchen, putting as much distance between us as Holden turns from him to face me.

I cock my head, crossing my arms and digging my nails into the skin. "What did you think was going to happen by tracking me down? Did you believe I'd come with you voluntarily? The truth's out, Holden. You're a fraud. You have no leverage. But you could've gone through with the charges of embezzlement and possibly gotten no time."

He chuckles darkly, prowling toward me with slow, measured steps.

"You don't get to walk away from me. I'm ingrained in you. Your mind. Your body. There is no escape from me, but I'm sure you were relieved hearing I'd been arrested, weren't you?" he asks with a raised brow and wide grin. His finger traces the side of my face.

"So, instead of taking your chance of no jail time, you come here to assault me in hopes of...what?"

"You know," he sighs dramatically, the stench of alcohol rolling off his breath. "I really, really hate when you use those ugly words."

I inch away from him until my lower back hits the edge of the dinette table. There is no reasoning with him, because he can't seem to grasp it. If he did, he never would've come here. He would've let it die. But he's pathologically sick, and my entire being is weary. If I'm going to die tonight, I'm going down with a fight. Keeping his rage aimed at me is my only hope for Nix making it out alive.

Straightening my spine, I force every fiber of agony over the trauma suffered at his hands, by his words, to the surface. "You are nothing but a man I allowed to take advantage of me for too long. You are nothing but wasted potential with a sadistic, twisted soul. But most of all, you're weak. So fucking weak, Holden. So don't believe for a second that I've been spending these blissful months out of your reach miserable or broken down."

He points the gun at his side blindly behind him, without a glance back. "Because of him?"

Terror floods my senses, but I force myself to laugh. "No. He's my roommate, not the man I've been fucking. Willingly."

His eyes darken before he charges toward me. His hand wraps around my throat before he slams me back on the table. The odd angle causes me to yelp. "Don't act all high and mighty now. You're nothing but a used-up whore. You're washed up, a failure, and for you to believe anyone could love you is not only laughable but pitiful."

My throat shakes under his palm as I struggle for a breath. His hand releases slightly, allowing oxygen to rush into my lungs before I can speak again. "He doesn't need to love me to have me screaming his name."

His fist connects with my face, striking more than once. I welcome the pain, embracing the likelihood that my end is here, but I won't show weakness. So I keep forcing myself to laugh as tears streak my face.

"There always was one thing that made you compliant. Let's see if it works again, shall we?"

Every inch of my skin feels like it's being pricked with sharp needles from the intent in his words, and for the first time since setting foot inside, I beg. "I'll do whatever you want," I rasp. "Please don't."

"If you don't lie still and quit fighting me, I will fucking shoot him," he growls.

He leans over me, using his forearm to pin my chest down, as his hips weigh down on top of me.

"I said I'd do what you wanted," I cry out, my chest heaving as I shake my head back and forth while his other hand rustles around his pocket.

"Please," I sob. "Please don't."

"This is what I want," he bites out, his tone hollow as he ties something around my arm and pulls it as tight as he can. "Don't scream again."

He'll kill me. It's been so long, and he knows nothing. He'll use too much, but I press my lips together to keep from telling him that. When the sharp prick of a needle sinks into my skin, I silently scream, my body trembling as beads of sweat and tears absorb each other, rolling down my temples. Seconds later, I'm being swaddled in warmth, a deep breath filling my lungs and slipping heavily through my lips as a rush of dark euphoria dances fluidly beneath my skin.

His hand slips roughly beneath my tank top, gliding down until he cups my center. His heavy body weighs me down, trapping my limbs, but I reject the part of my brain that wants to ease into compliant submission. With strength I never knew I possessed, I place my hands on his chest and push with as much force as I can muster. When his weight disappears, I lift my legs and kick out.

"I fucking warned you," he growls.

When his words register, I lift my head, and my eyes connect with his back as he steps away from me, moving closer to Nix.

"No," I breathe out. Fear like I've never felt breaks through the dark haze, and adrenaline pumps headily within me. I claw for it, grasping it, and will it to get me across the space as my flesh feels like it's being pricked a thousand times over by pins and needles. On trembling legs, I throw myself toward Nix, landing on top of him. Hair rips from my scalp as I thrash and cling to him, digging my nails into his skin, anchoring myself to him while covering as much of his body as I can with mine.

Nix mutters weakly, and my chest floods with relief and aches from hopelessness all at once.

Holden's voice is muffled, sounding farther and farther away.

"Fucking kill m-me...'n' go," I slur.

There's a clang of glass and a crash before everything begins to fade, but before it does, I *feel* Jansen's presence. Only when his familiar, gruff voice whispers in my ear does my entire being exhale because I know I'm finally safe.

Present day

When I'm finished telling the jury the details of that night, I look directly at him. He's scrawnier, with shaved-down hair, hollow eyes, and a blank expression. My gaze seeks out the bench in the front row, roaming over Dane, Presley, Ivy, Nix, Mason, Dad, Ron, and Jansen. He mouths "*I love you*," filling me with warmth and strength.

Looking directly into Holden's dead stare, I say, "I hope for the rest of your miserable life you remember me on this stand today. Forever out of your reach. I wish I could rip every memory of me from your mind, but when you *do* think of me...I want you to know that I am *living*, seeing the world, and I'm *loved* beyond reason. You didn't break me, Holden."

His nostrils flare, the only reaction to my words.

"Has the jury agreed on a verdict?" the judge asks, and I hold my breath, clinging to Jansen's hand.

"We have, Your Honor," a male juror states, handing their verdict to the bailiff.

I'm not sure of every single offense he was charged with, but there were many. First-degree home invasion, aggravated assault and battery, and drug distribution. He was charged for the first time he recorded my rape because it was the only visual evidence I could stomach Gabe finding and handing over.

But I don't care about the number of charges or what they are. I care about the number of *years* he'll spend in a six-by-eight prison cell.

With every charge being called out, the bailiff responds with guilty, and every breath taken in and exhaled feels lighter. He's given the maximum sentence on all charges, including the embezzlement charges in my dad's case. Tallying up the years, I muffle my cries with my palm. Eighty-two years without the possibility of parole.

"It's over, Freckles," Jansen murmurs in my ear.

I nod against his chest, feeling a sort of infinite relief...because I made it. I survived.

An hour later, we're all at Clovers laughing and celebrating our win. I never did go back to work. Jansen insisted I take time to heal in every way before figuring out what I want to do next, and I didn't fight him on it. We both needed each other to lean on while we dealt with the trauma of that night, and Nix needed both of us.

Ron has been chatting with Mr. Brooks since we arrived. This is the first time he's come into the bar since Jansen flipped it, and the pride filling his eyes as he continuously looks around has a grin permanently etched on Jansen's face.

My heart.

"How's it going with Mr. Brooks?" I ask Mason, reaching for a mozzarella stick.

"It's pretty much the same. We miss you two, but everything has been a smooth transition."

Ivy smirks. "Mase fell in love with the man when he found out he had an ancient comic book collection."

Mason rolls his eyes, tossing a napkin at her. "He has the first series of *The Invincible Iron Man* from 1968. It's a four-thousand-dollar comic book. I feel honored that he even let me touch it."

"If it's not a vintage bag, Ivy doesn't care," Nix jokes and laughs with his arm around her. They've been inseparable since August, and I couldn't be happier. I sat down with her and explained the beginning of our friendship, and it gave Ivy a bit of clarity on why Nix reacted the way he did seeing Mason and Ivy that day. Because if there's one thing I've learned about Ivy, her self-respect is sky high. As it should be. And the chance she's giving Nix will be his last.

Fingers crossed for no fuckups.

Mason hasn't made any big declarations of love or gotten in the way. Sometimes when he looks at her, I notice it. A subtle sadness in his gaze. He's always quick to clear it and smile as if nothing bothers him. But sometimes it really is too late. Not everyone gets the happy ending with the person they want, and I know it's somehow more painful for him because he could have.

Dad finalized his sale of the firm last week and decided on early retirement. I never asked him why because I knew. It was no longer his refuge, but a prison.

"We should plan a vacation in the next year," Dad suggests. "It'd be nice to get away."

"Sounds good, Dad." I smile, hugging him before he leaves for Sayersville. "Text me some ideas."

He guffaws. "You're the young one, Sweets. You let me know where you'd like to visit."

Our relationship will take a lot of time to rebuild, but it's been better in the last couple of months than it has been in years. I grew into a person he didn't care to know, and I villainized him for years based on lies. We're essentially strangers, but hopefully one day we'll share the bond we once had, or a different one altogether.

"We should head back too. Emmy's had a tough week with her teeth, and Grandma's to the point of asking to dab some whiskey on her gums," Presley explains.

"We're proud of you, Tillie," Dane tells me, placing a hand on my shoulder and squeezing. "What you did today was badass."

I shake off the compliment. "It was…tough, but I'm happy I was able to tell my story without breaking down."

"I'm talking specifically about you looking the piece of shit in the eye and telling him that while his life is over, yours is really beginning."

"Yeah, I suppose it *was* pretty badass," I muse.

When everyone has cleared out, I start to walk toward the apartment. Mr. Brooks let us stay until we figure out what's next for us.

Jansen reaches for my hand, pulling me into him. "Actually, I have a surprise for you. While you were preparing for court yesterday, I was putting some things in motion."

My brows dip. "And what *things* are we talking about?"

"Follow me."

We walk outside, but when I look for the Jeep, it's nowhere in sight. Jansen pulls a fob from his pocket and hits a button, causing the headlights on a black Tundra to flash as he guides me over to it.

"You got a new truck?" I ask, confused.

"*We* did."

He insists that what is his is also mine. I wouldn't say it bothers me because I don't take advantage, but being a woman with no job or clear idea of her future career can leave me feeling a little helpless some days.

"That's great, Jansie. She's a beaut," I joke, tapping the side.

"I'll admit, this isn't the big surprise, but it'll take us to it."

"Now I'm dying to know."

He pulls a bandana from his pocket, causing my cheeks to flush because it is *our* bandana, and holds it out with a grin.

"Humor me?"

Rolling my eyes playfully, I turn, letting him tie it. The drive to wherever we're going isn't too long, but my nerves are shot from the anticipation. After guiding me out of the truck, he walks me forward, and gravel crunches beneath my shoes.

"Ready?" he asks.

I nod as he pulls the bandana down. "It's...a camper?"

Jansen stands in front of me, gripping my chin to tilt my face up. "I told you I'd do whatever to make you happy. We haven't figured out what's next, I know, but this"—he stretches an arm out wide, gesturing to the trailer—"is what can give us the freedom and mobility to do or go wherever we want."

"Wait, so...you bought this for us to live in together?"

He runs a hand through his hair. "I did, but if you don't want—"

I squeal, jumping up as he grips my thighs, and wrap my legs around his waist. I pepper kisses over his face, and he chuckles, holding me tighter.

"Can we go inside now?" I ask, bouncing in his arms while trying to temper my excitement.

The inside is more spacious than I thought it would be. He lets me walk around and look at everything. A dinette and a sofa sit next to each other. A fake fireplace takes up the opposite wall, next to what looks to be a hallway. The colors are neutral, with white walls and countertops to brighten the space. When I see a stove with an oven, I almost shed a tear.

Peeking my head into the bathroom, I sigh. "The bathroom is still tiny, but I think the shower is bigger than the houseboat's, so I'll take the win," I call out before sliding a cream panel over, leading to a bedroom with a fairly large bed and a TV mounted on the wall.

I rush back to the living room area and freeze with wide eyes, spotting him down on one knee, holding a black box in his hand.

My jaw drops. "You *cannot* buy a truck, a place for us to live, and a ring to propose all at once."

He raises a brow, smirking. "Why not?"

"Because I can't...I don't have..." I stammer, my words forgotten as he stands and walks toward me.

Pushing his fingers through my hair, he asks, "Need me to carry anything, Freckles?"

"I'm scared," I whisper.

"Why?"

"Because I've never been this excited over anything in my entire life, but the thought of spending my life with you, just like this, feels a little like a dream." I shake my hands at my side to ebb the excited jitters forcing their way through my body.

"A dream come true," he assures me, pulling a silver band with a teardrop diamond from the box and placing it on my ring finger.

This time, when my lips meet his, it's slow and more sensual. Pushing his shirt up, I place my palm on his warm, toned skin.

"Three times in one day. Damn, I'm lucky." His lips move against mine as he lifts me and walks us to the bedroom.

We ended up having a serious talk about my guilt involving sex. I thought I'd had it under control until after the attack. When my body was healed, I found myself constantly wanting it, and it made me feel ashamed, broken somehow. If I were normal, maybe I would've needed a longer break. Maybe I wouldn't need it as much. He assured me he had absolutely *zero issue* with my sexual appetite, but we could develop a code of sorts for when I was feeling too in my head about it. I place my palm under his shirt, and he knows it's go time.

As soon as my back hits the mattress, he's on top of me, and I push his chest. "Wait. You didn't even ask me."

He looks confused for a second before he bats my hands away and leans down again, cradling my head with his forearms and rubbing the tip of his nose along mine. "Tillie Anne Porter. Will you marry me?"

"I don't know, it's all happening so fast," I feign dramatically, grasping the back of his neck with both of my hands as I roll my hips against his.

He rolls us sideways, swatting my ass. "Believe me. Not fast enough."

"Yes," I whisper against his mouth, smiling.

I used to believe a happily ever after wasn't meant for me. I was too broken, too tainted, and too chagrined. Until I found a man with a soul who could mend the fractures in mine, and we collided.

Thirty-Eight

Jansen

One year later...August 2025...

"Were you able to get any recording done today?" I ask my gorgeous *wife*. After going back and forth, she finally told me she didn't want a big wedding. She wanted it to be the two of us, alone. So I found the nearest little chapel and wifed her up hours after her admission. It wasn't fancy. There were no dresses, tuxes, or a flashy show, but it was honest and intimate. A day I'll never forget.

"I did. I was able to film a few days' worth of videos. How was the store?"

Six months ago, Tillie told me she wanted to talk about her experiences on social media. To give people a space where they can talk openly and freely about the trauma they've endured. It took a couple of months, but her rawness and vulnerability grew a large audience, and she was able to monetize off that. When she told me she wanted to donate half of her proceeds to advocacy groups for addiction and survivors of sexual abuse, I fell in love with her even more. It's been therapeutic for her to talk so openly about something she hid for years. At seven o'clock every night, she spends an hour reading through her messages, making sure to respond to everyone she can, and many people reach out.

She was asked to attend a local high school assembly next week to share her story and signs of behavioral changes to look out for in those around you who might be suffering from addiction or abuse. As soon as she ended the call, she laughed and had a complete meltdown about how "she was nobody" and "they should bring in a professional, not a silly social media creator."

I remember the day vividly because we ended up having the best sex to date. Sometimes she still struggles with serious self-deprecation, and I love nothing more than to spank it out of her. While we lay in bed afterward, I told her she was the perfect guest speaker for the assembly because she had firsthand experience. She recognized all the ways her trauma had changed and shaped her. Not to mention, she was currently working on her associate's degree in psychology and was determined to work with youth someday.

I sit down next to her, pulling her onto my lap. "It's finally starting to turn enough profit to dig it out of the hole it was in. I'd say we have another three to four months, and then we'll be moving on."

We ended up in Arizona after leaving Arkansas. It's been unexpected how much I miss Novaridge and the people we left behind, but we're planning a trip back at the end of the year.

"Amelia told me she and Lainey could join us this weekend," I inform her. Before I met Tillie, I never would've considered forming genuine friendships with people when I travel. It seemed pointless, but I'm working on opening up more instead of holding everyone at arm's length.

Amelia is the current manager of the small corner shop in town. Usually, I come in, take over, and sell once the store is ready, and when it is, I'll be selling directly to her and her wife. Amelia's great-grandmother opened the store, and it was sold out from under the family four years ago, so I was happy to agree to sell it back to the people it belonged to.

"I'll have to make Lainey another big bag of trail mix, and I went ahead and ordered our next book to read. You can pick those up from the post office tomorrow," she cheers.

Lainey and Tillie hit it off right away and have since started their own two-person book club. "I love how it's your birthday weekend and you're giving gifts." I laugh. "Is it another romance?"

She leans down, placing a soft kiss on my lips, hers moving against mine when she says, "It's a true crime about two women who hired professional hitmen to off their husbands so they could be together."

"I told you I'd chase you to the ends of the earth, even in death. I'd wrap my spirit around your pussy like a chastity belt."

Her hand barely moves beneath my shirt before the mood shifts, and she sits up straight in my lap, clearing her throat. "Speaking of chastity belts..."

My brows draw together at her sudden nervousness.

"The implant birth control I have is about to expire. I need to decide if I want another five-year implant or something that I'll be able to stop taking if we ever..."

Now I'm sitting up straight. I'll admit, I never imagined having kids until Dane and Presley brought Emmy down, and I watched Tillie interact and cuddle with her. But even then, I knew if it weren't something Tillie wanted, I'd be content with her alone. "What do *you* want to do?"

She groans in frustration. "This isn't something you leave up to me completely without a say because you want to make me happy. This is about another tiny human being brought into our lives. We've never talked about kids."

"Okay." I shift in the seat. "Well, I never planned on having any kids after the childhood I had—"

"Of course, yeah, I understand. I'm sorry I even brought it up—"

"Tillie."

"And I don't want you to think I'm not happy with our life, because I am. I don't need a—"

"*Freckles*," I say more firmly to end her rant.

She presses her lips together, meeting my eyes.

"If you had let me finish, I would've been able to say that I never imagined a lot of things until I met you. Seeing you with Emmy was the first time I imagined what it'd be like."

Once Tillie was physically healed, Presley and Dane brought Emmy down for a few days. She attached herself to Tillie's side. Only "My Tiwwie" could lift a finger for her. When I woke up one morning, they were cuddled up on the couch, Emmy's tiny hand wrapped around Tillie's, and it was the first time the thought of having a child ever crossed my mind.

Her eyes soften as she relaxes further into me.

"But I didn't bring it up because this was still new, and ultimately, it's your body that will go through changes and your mental health that could be affected. So if you're asking me if I'd ever want to put a baby in you, my answer is yes. But if it's not something you want, then I promise I won't feel like I'm missing out on anything. I'm perfectly happy with you and you alone."

Her emeralds glisten as she brings her lips to mine and slides her warm palm beneath my shirt. "For now, how about we get some practice in?"

·····•·••····

A week later, I'm sitting off to the side of the bleachers in the high school gym, watching Tillie speak to hundreds of students. She nervously runs a palm down her navy-blue slacks, adjusting the collar of her white silk sleeveless blouse. Her raven hair has grown longer in the past year and now rests a few inches below her collarbone in waves. Every day, I still find myself staring at her in awe.

"Hi." She smiles, clearing her throat. "My name is Tillie Quinn. I'm a victim and survivor of sexual assault and a recovering addict. Both of those, for me, were mutually exclusive. My abuse led to my addiction, which started at sixteen. I hid it as well as I could, until eventually, it swallowed me whole."

She takes a steadying breath before continuing, "I'm going to share a little bit of my story today. Why I started using drugs, and how an adult man manipulated me into my sexual abuse as a teenager. Then we're going to talk about the signs to look out for in the people around you so that you can help someone who may feel as though they're drowning without a way to break through to the surface."

I watch her tell her story, and as my eyes roam over the students in the gym, I could hear a pin drop. Their attention is completely rapt on her. And when she finishes, every student in the gym stands and claps for the woman who found her way back to herself. She performs a cute little curtsy, wiping the moisture away from beneath her eyes.

When her eyes find mine, I bring my palm to my chest, mouthing, "*I love you.*"

I'm graced with one of her radiant smiles, lighting up her face as she puts the microphone in front of her mouth again. "I love you too, Jansie."

Epilogue
Tillie

Three years later...October 2028...

"We can leave whenever you're ready. Say the word," Jansen assures me for the hundredth time since we decided to come.

I haven't been back to Sayersville since the day I confronted Holden at his house with Nix. My dad visits us, or we plan vacations elsewhere, but today is Emmy's fifth birthday. I didn't want the past to hold any more power over me. So we decided to stay in my childhood home with my dad while we're in town. It was weird, walking inside after four years, but I found myself reminiscing on the good memories I had here over the years as my dad pulled out photo albums like an excited mother showing pictures of her newborn. My heart melted at the sight.

"I handled going back home pretty well. I'm not going to chicken out now just because Rhett and Lucy are here. It's been years, and we're all adults. It's not like we ended on horrible terms."

"If I believe you're stressed in the slightest, I'm carrying you out of there." He rests his palm on my swollen stomach, which decided to pop out last week at five months.

"Okay, Mr. Overprotective, can we go inside now?"

He huffs something unintelligible before getting out and opening my door to help me down. Because apparently, I can't step down without his hand anymore.

Presley opens the door, running toward me and wrapping her arms around my neck before leaning back again. "Oh my gosh, you really have filled out," she gushes, placing a hand on my stomach.

"She's growing, all right." Jansen beams.

"Well, let's get inside. The food's done, and Emmy is excited to see you and your belly."

"Has your postpartum been better?" I ask her. I've spent plenty of nights and early mornings on the phone with her after the birth of their son, Elliot, giving her an ear when she was buckling beneath the weight of it.

"I'm finally starting to feel like myself again. Some days are still tough, but the medicine I started has helped a lot." She smiles, and it looks genuine.

Warmth wraps around me as we step inside; there are plenty of faces I've never seen before, but one I have. He's holding a little boy with brown curls, talking to Dane.

"Where's Mommy?" the little boy asks.

"She's in the kitchen, I think. Do you want to go check?" Rhett's deep voice spears me in the chest. I didn't realize how much I missed him until now. He looks the same but different all at once.

The little boy nods, and he sets him on his feet. When he stands at his full height again, he turns our way, and our eyes meet. Different emotions pass over his face, and I believe that's why I was so nervous to see him today. He knows the truth about my past now. A past with moments he was so involved in.

Dane nudges Rhett's shoulder with his own as they walk over to us.

"Hi." I smile.

"Hi." He smiles back.

"This is my husband, Jansen." I introduce them, lacing my fingers through Jansen's.

"It's nice to meet you. I'm Everett—or Rhett." He puts his hand out to shake, and Jansen accepts.

"I've heard a lot about you," Jansen responds cordially.

He wasn't thrilled about meeting him because of the few details I'd shared previously, but I assured him they would get along great if he could move past it. It'd be hard not to get along with Rhett.

"Let's go to the kitchen so you all can grab a plate," Presley suggests, and we all follow her.

Standing in the kitchen is a beautiful woman with long, wavy hair, a few shades lighter than the little boy's she's holding. The same little boy Rhett put down.

"Luce," Rhett calls out to her. "This is Tillie and her husband, Jansen."

He walks over to her, pulling her into his side. "This is my wife, Lucy, and our son, Linden."

"Hi," I say nervously, rubbing my stomach for comfort. While Jansen wasn't excited to meet Rhett, I was nervous to meet Lucy. I know I played a part in her husband's pain. Some women wouldn't want to look past that, but apparently Lucy has.

"It's so nice to meet you finally," she boasts while walking over to me and pulling me in for a hug.

I must not hide my confusion very well because Rhett clears his throat nervously. "We've followed your story on social media. Lucy is a bit of a fan." He chuckles.

Lucy's cheeks pinken when she pulls back. "I love everything you've done to help advocacy groups, and your content about living in a camper and traveling is pretty captivating."

"She is very captivating," Jansen agrees, leaning down to kiss my cheek.

"*Tillie*," Emmy squeals, running toward me and jumping, but Jansen catches her as soon as her little feet leave the ground.

"We have to be careful with Tillie's belly until after the baby is here," Jansen tells her gently.

When her bottom lip starts to wobble, Jansen's eyes widen in panic. "Don't cry, you didn't do anything wrong."

"I'm sorry." She sniffs, sucking her tears back in.

"You made her cry," Linden's small voice accuses Jansen as he narrows his tiny eyes, identical to his father's.

"It's okay, Linden, I almost did something bad." She sniffs again.

Jansen groans, hugging her. "You're killing me here, kid."

"You'll definitely have to handle all of the discipline." Presley laughs, looking pointedly at me.

"Only men with daughters can understand their power." Dane shrugs, laughing.

"Can you put her down so I can hug her?" Linden asks Jansen.

A squeak of laughter slips through my lips before I can stop it, so I turn, hiding my face.

"Uh, sure," Jansen murmurs, setting Emmy back on her feet.

Linden, who is younger but the same height, pulls her in for a hug. "It's okay, Emmy. You're not bad."

"I think you've made an enemy," I whisper to Jansen, leaning into him.

He scoffs and shakes his head, grinning. I'm pretty sure every adult in the room melted from Linden's care for his friend. Another trait I have no doubt he inherited from his daddy.

Emmy whispers in Linden's ear, and his little head nods before he turns to me. "Can we touch your belly, Tillie?"

"Sure." I smile. "You guys don't need to ask."

Four little hands cover my stomach, and she kicks. Their eyes widen before they start giggling.

Rhett strolls over to me with a grin on his face. "All right, guys, let's give Tillie's belly a break."

Both kids huff and reluctantly step away.

"Can we talk?" he asks, his eyes bouncing back and forth between mine.

I look to Jansen, not for permission, but to reassure him that I'll be fine as I nod. "Lead the way."

I follow him outside to the front porch as my heart thuds in my ears. The cool air outside is a relief as it rushes across my warm skin.

Once we're seated on the concrete steps, a tense silence takes over. A lot of words, explanations and apologies, race through my mind, but his deep, gravelly voice fills the air between us before I can say anything.

"I'm sorry I never noticed." His gaze is downcast on his hands, which he's rubbing together nervously.

"You did." I bump his shoulder with mine. "You always tried to get me to talk about myself and the cause of my emotional spirals. But there was only so much you could do when I wasn't ready to tell the truth."

"I was so mad at you for so long. And you went through all of that alone, without—"

"We were kids, and I wasn't completely alone. Even if I couldn't be what you needed, I did have you. Regardless of how it seemed, I did and still do care about you."

He shakes his head as he looks up with a pained expression blanketing his features. "I turned you away when you needed me, and I'm not sure how to forgive myself for that."

"Always the hero," I mumble, snorting when his eyes widen.

I reach for his hand and squeeze once before letting go. "I'm glad you turned me away, because you were taking care of yourself. Yes, I went through something extremely traumatic, and it may even seem like I had a good excuse to treat you the way I did, but it didn't mean you had to accept it. And if you had, we could've missed out on the lives we were meant to have."

His shoulders drop a little more as if some of the weight he's been carrying has suddenly lifted. At the same time, my stomach decides to growl.

He stands, chuckling, and offers me his hand to do the same. "Let's get you some food."

"There's no more damn room in there for food," I groan and grip his calloused hand in mine as I pull myself up.

I'm pulled lightly into his chest as his warmth wraps around me, but it feels different. Final. Not that I'll never see him again. I'm sure I will.

But it's the final bit of closure we both needed.

A couple hours later, I'm sitting at the table with Lucy and Presley. Everyone has gone home, leaving the six of us. Jansen warmed up to Rhett faster than I expected when they started talking about their businesses. Rhett has grown his in North Carolina, becoming one of the most sought-after carpenters.

Jansen wanted to be less hands-on, so he started a business-consulting firm to give him more time with us. Instead of going in, they share whatever aspect they're struggling with, and he sends an immaculately detailed report on how to fix it. It opened up the doors to more businesses that aren't necessarily at risk or want to sell but want to improve performance. We still plan on traveling for now. We love the lifestyle and seeing new things. When it's time for the little one to start school, we'll either buy a house and settle down, or I'll homeschool. We've talked about what that would look like a lot. Socialization is important, and that's been our major concern. We've also talked a lot about fostering in the future, but we still have a few years to figure it all out.

"You look happier than I've ever seen you," Presley remarks, dragging me out of my thoughts.

"I am. I'm very lucky to have gained everything I have."

"You worked hard for it," Lucy says. "Your videos are a testament to that. Not everyone could do what you do. Put themselves out there the way you have."

"Speaking of." I sit up, stretching my back. "I hope you don't mind...Presley has shared a few details about what you've been through. If you're interested, I wanted to make a sit-down video with you where you can talk about your late husband. We could donate a hundred percent of the proceeds to any suicide prevention advocacy group of your choice."

Tears gather on her lower lashes.

"I'm so sorry, I don't mean to overstep. It's completely okay if you want to tell me to fuck off," I rush out.

"No." She laughs, wiping under her lashes with her sleeve. "I've never really thought about sharing my story. I ran from it for a long time, until I met Everett. Even then, it still sometimes felt like I'd failed Gavin, my late husband," she explains. "If it could help someone feel less alone, I think I'd like to do it."

Reaching for her hand on the table, I squeeze once lightly. "I'm happy you found each other. I'll create a list of questions if that would be easier, and you can approve the ones you want, and we'll toss the ones you don't."

"That sounds great."

A knock sounds at the front door, and Presley smiles like the Cheshire Cat and jumps up to answer it.

"Sorry we're late. She had a shift run over, and traffic was rough," a familiar voice explains, and I jump up, rushing to the door.

"*Nix*," I squeal, practically jumping on him and wrapping my arms around his neck. Another familiar voice clears her throat. "*Ahem.* Am I invisible?"

My smile is wide as I wrap my arms around Ivy. "I've missed you guys so much."

"That's why you need to come settle down in Novaridge when you're done traveling the US. And be quick about it," she bosses with a raised brow. "I don't intend to miss every moment of my goddaughter's life."

She says this often, and every time she does, it seems more and more enticing.

"Let's go out back. Jansen is going to be so surprised to see you. We had no idea you'd be here," I tell Nix, leading the way to the back door.

"I asked Presley to keep it under wraps."

As soon as Jansen notices Nix, he's strutting toward him and pulling him in for a hug, clapping his back. "We were going to come see you before leaving, little cousin."

"I know, but we wanted a little more time with you guys. We've had to skip a lot of our weekly video calls." Nix tries to shrug his feelings away, but I still know my best friend well.

"Well, I'm glad to have both my little lost boys together again." I bump my shoulder into Nix's, and he places his hand on my belly.

"Ivy's right, ya know. Novaridge is waiting for you all to come home."

My gaze locks on Jansen's, and I know he feels it too. The pull to settle. To be surrounded by the people we love more often.

"Soon," Jansen promises him, leaning down to place a soft kiss on my lips.

Another hour or so later, we're all sitting around the firepit, sharing details about our lives that the others have missed and vice versa. As I look at the people surrounding me, laughing and talking, giggling, tiny humans running around, my heart is so full it could burst.

Who would've thought that my grumpy-ass, judgmental boss would end up giving me the best gift of all? He's given me so much more than encouragement, confidence, strength, love, and a way to see the world... He's given me family.

The End

Curious about Rhett and Lucy?
You can read their second-chance romance now,
w/KindleUnlimited or in paperback.

Stay up-to-date on new releases, giveaways, and more!
Visit **bnkruseauthor.com** to sign-up for my newsletter.

You can join the journey with me on:
Instagram: @bnkruseauthor
Tiktok: @bnkruse94
Facebook: B.N. Kruse

Acknowledgements

The first to thank are always the readers! If you've made it this far, THANK YOU. This story, though fictional, carried very personal themes for me. I did my best to be as sensitive as possible but also pour in a little of the feelings I've been plagued with over the years. If you related to Tillie or Jansen at all, I hope you're glowing now. Full of life and love.

Thank you to my wonderful mom and stepmom for always being the first to read my work. I'm so thankful to have both of you! Mom, you didn't get a grandchild named Jansen, but I hope the book character makes up for it. I feel like he'd fit right in with our bunch. Lol.

To my beta readers, Marissa, Kelsey, and Alana. Thank you all for your continued support and honesty. It means more than you know.

To my editor, Brooklyn from Brazen Hearts, you were the BOMB. You helped me take this book to the next level. Editing is always a little daunting, but you made it exciting and fun with your commentary and skill. Thank you for every thorough explanation and kind word of encouragement throughout the process. I so look forward to working with you again!

To my sister, Alana, for the cover design... This cover means so much because you were involved in the process. I can't wait to start on cover number three. Love you!

Last, but not least...James. Thank you for being a real one and reading my books. Your support means everything to me. Thank you for the tough love when I spiral through the process, along with the encouragement to keep going, to keep writing. I love you most.

www.ingramcontent.com/pod-product-compliance
Lightning Source LLC
LaVergne TN
LVHW041656060526
838201LV00043B/455